SUPER SAD TRUE LOVE STORY

SUPER SAD TRUE LOVE STORY

A Novel **GARY SHTEYNGART**

RANDOM HOUSE  NEW YORK

Super Sad True Love Story is a work of fiction. Names, characters, places, and incidents either are the product of the author's imagination or are used fictitiously. Any resemblance to actual persons, living or dead, events, or locales is entirely coincidental.

Published in the United States by Random House, an imprint of The Random House Publishing Group, a division of Random House, Inc., New York.

RANDOM HOUSE and colophon are registered trademarks of Random House, Inc.

LIBRARY OF CONGRESS CATALOGING-IN-PUBLICATION DATA
Shteyngart, Gary.
Super sad true love story : a novel / Gary Shteyngart.
p. cm.
ISBN 978-1-4000-6640-7
eBook ISBN 978-0-679-60359-7
I. Title.
PS3619.H79S87 2010
813'.6—dc22   2009037971

Printed in the United States of America on acid-free paper

www.atrandom.com

2 4 6 8 9 7 5 3 1

FIRST EDITION

Book design by Simon M. Sullivan

SUPER SAD TRUE LOVE STORY

DO NOT GO GENTLE

FROM THE DIARIES OF LENNY ABRAMOV

JUNE 1

Rome–New York

Dearest Diary,

Today I've made a major decision: *I am never going to die.*

Others will die around me. They will be nullified. Nothing of their personality will remain. The light switch will be turned off. Their lives, their entirety, will be marked by glossy marble head-stones bearing false summations ("her star shone brightly," "never to be forgotten," "he liked jazz"), and then these too will be lost in a coastal flood or get hacked to pieces by some genetically modified future-turkey.

Don't let them tell you life's a journey. A journey is when you end up *some*where. When I take the number 6 train to see my social worker, that's a journey. When I beg the pilot of this rickety United-ContinentalDeltamerican plane currently trembling its way across the Atlantic to turn around and head straight back to Rome and into Eunice Park's fickle arms, *that's* a journey.

But wait. There's more, isn't there? There's our legacy. We don't die because our progeny lives on! The ritual passing of the DNA, Mama's corkscrew curls, his granddaddy's lower lip, *ah buh-lieve thuh chil'ren ah our future.* I'm quoting here from "The Greatest Love of All," by 1980s pop diva Whitney Houston, track nine of her eponymous first LP.

Utter nonsense. The children are our future only in the most narrow, transitive sense. They are our future until they too perish. The song's next line, "Teach them well and let them lead the way," encourages an adult's relinquishing of selfhood in favor of future generations. The phrase "I live for my kids," for example, is tantamount to admitting that one will be dead shortly and that one's life, for all practical purposes, is already over. "I'm gradually dying for my kids" would be more accurate.

But what *ah* our *chil'ren*? Lovely and fresh in their youth; blind to mortality; rolling around, Eunice Park–like, in the tall grass with their alabaster legs; fawns, sweet fawns, all of them, gleaming in their dreamy plasticity, at one with the outwardly simple nature of their world.

And then, a brief almost-century later: drooling on some poor Mexican nursemaid in an Arizona hospice.

Nullified. Did you know that each peaceful, natural death at age eighty-one is a tragedy without compare? Every day people, individuals—*Americans,* if that makes it more urgent for you—fall facedown on the battlefield, never to get up again. Never to exist again. These are complex personalities, their cerebral cortexes shimmering with floating worlds, universes that would have floored our sheepherding, fig-eating, analog ancestors. These folks are minor deities, vessels of love, life-givers, unsung geniuses, gods of the forge getting up at six-fifteen in the morning to fire up the coffeemaker, mouthing silent prayers that they will live to see the next day and the one after that and then Sarah's graduation and then . . .

Nullified.

But not me, dear diary. Lucky diary. Undeserving diary. From this day forward you will travel on the greatest adventure yet undertaken by a nervous, average man sixty-nine inches in height, 160 pounds in heft, with a slightly dangerous body mass index of 23.9. Why "from this day forward"? Because yesterday I met Eunice Park, and she will sustain me through forever. Take a long look at me, diary. What do you see? A slight man with a gray, sunken battleship of a face, curious wet eyes, a giant gleaming forehead on which a dozen cavemen could have painted something nice, a sickle of a nose perched atop a tiny puckered mouth, and from the back, a growing bald spot whose shape perfectly replicates the great state of Ohio, with its capital city, Columbus, marked by a deep-brown mole. *Slight.* Slightness is my curse in every sense. A so-so body in a world where only an incredible one will do. A body at the chronological age of thirty-nine already racked with too much LDL cholesterol, too much ACTH hormone, too much of everything that dooms the heart, sunders the liver, explodes all hope. A week ago, before Eunice gave me reason to live, you wouldn't have noticed me, diary. A week ago, I did not exist. A week ago, at a restaurant in Turin, I approached a potential client, a classically attractive High Net Worth Individual. He looked up from his wintry *bollito misto,* looked right past me, looked back down at the boiled lovemaking of his seven meats and seven vegetable sauces, looked back up, looked right past me *again*—it is clear that for a member of upper society to even remotely notice me I must first fire a flaming arrow into a dancing moose or be kicked in the testicles by a head of state.

And yet Lenny Abramov, your humble diarist, your small nonentity, will live forever. The technology is almost here. As the Life Lovers Outreach Coordinator (Grade G) of the Post-Human Services division of the Staatling-Wapachung Corporation, I will be the first to partake of it. I just have to be good and I have to believe in myself. I just have to stay off the trans fats and the hooch. I just have to drink plenty of green tea and alkalinized water and submit my genome to the right people. I will need to re-grow my melting liver, replace the entire circulatory system with "smart blood," and find someplace safe and warm (but not too warm) to while away the angry seasons and the holocausts. And when the earth expires, as it surely must, I will leave it for a new earth, greener still but with fewer allergens; and in the flowering of my own intelligence some 10^{32} years hence, when our universe decides to fold in on itself, my personality will jump through a black hole and surf into a dimension of unthinkable wonders, where the things that sustained me on Earth 1.0—*tortelli lucchese,* pistachio ice cream, the early works of the Velvet Underground, smooth, tanned skin pulled over the soft

Baroque architecture of twentysomething buttocks—will seem as laughable and infantile as building blocks, baby formula, a game of "Simon says *do this*."

That's right: I am never going to die, *caro diario*. Never, never, never, never. And you can go to hell for doubting me.

Yesterday was my last day in Rome. Got up around eleven, caffè macchiato at the bar that has the best honey brioche, the neighbor's ten-year-old anti-American kid screaming at me from his window, "No global! No way!," warm cotton towel of guilt around my neck for not getting any last-minute work done, my äppärät buzzing with contacts, data, pictures, projections, maps, incomes, sound, fury. Yet another day of early-summer wandering, the streets in charge of my destiny, holding me in their oven-warm eternal embrace.

Ended up where I always end up. By the single most beautiful building in Europe. The Pantheon. The rotunda's ideal proportions; the weight of the dome lifted above one's shoulders, suspended in air by icy mathematic precision; the oculus letting in the rain and the searing Roman sunlight; the coolness and shade that nonetheless prevail. Nothing can diminish the Pantheon! Not the gaudy religious makeover (it is officially a church). Not the inflated, down-to-their-last-euro Americans seeking fat shelter beneath the portico. Not the modern-day Italians fighting and cajoling outside, boys trying to stick it inside girls, mopeds humming beneath hairy legs, multi-generational families bursting with pimply life. No, this is the most glorious grave marker to a race of men ever built. When I outlive the earth and depart from its familiar womb, I will take the memory of this building with me. I will encode it with zeros and ones and broadcast it across the universe. See what primitive man has wrought! Witness his first hankerings for immortality, his discipline, his selflessness.

My last Roman day. I had my macchiato. I bought some expensive deodorant, perhaps anticipating love. I took a three-hour, slightly masturbatory nap in the ridiculous glow of my sun-strangled apartment. And then, at a party thrown by my friend Fabrizia, I met Eunice—

Wait, no. That's not exactly true. This chronology isn't right. I'm lying to you, diary. It's only page seven and I'm already a liar. Something terrible happened before Fabrizia's party. So terrible I don't want to write about it, because I want you to be a *positive* diary.

I went to the U.S. Embassy.

It wasn't my idea to go. A friend of mine, Sandi, told me that if you spend over 250 days abroad and don't register for Welcome Back, Pa'dner, the official United States Citizen Re-Entry Program, they can bust you for sedition right at JFK, send you to a "secure screening facility" Upstate, whatever that is.

Now, Sandi knows *everything*—he works in fashion—so I decided to take his vividly expressed, highly caffeinated advice and headed for Via Veneto, where our nation's creamy palazzo of an embassy luxuriates behind a recently built moat. Not for much longer, I should say. According to Sandi, the strapped State Department just sold the whole thing to StatoilHydro, the Norwegian state oil company, and by the time I got to Via Veneto the enormous compound's trees and shrubbery were already being coaxed into tall, agnostic shapes to please their new owners. Armored moving vans ringed the perimeter, and the sound of massive document-shredding could be divined from within.

The consular line for the visa section was nearly empty. Only a few of the saddest, most destitute Albanians still wanted to emigrate to the States, and that lonely number was further discouraged by a poster showing a plucky little otter in a sombrero trying to jump onto a crammed dinghy under the tagline "The Boat Is Full, Amigo."

Inside an improvised security cage, an older man behind Plexiglas shouted at me incomprehensibly while I waved my passport at him. A competent Filipina, indispensable in these parts, finally materialized and waved me down a cluttered hallway to a mock-up of a faded public-high-school classroom decked out in the Welcome Back, Pa'dner, motif. The Mexican otter from the "Boat Is Full" campaign was here Americanized (sombrero replaced by red-white-

and-blue bandana worn around his hirsute little neck), then perched upon a goofy-looking horse, the two of them galloping toward a fiercely rising and presumably Asian sun.

A half-dozen of my fellow citizens were seated behind their chewed-up desks, mumbling lowly into their äppäräti. There was an earplug lying slug-dead on an empty chair, and a sign reading IN-SERT EARPLUG IN EAR, PLACE YOUR ÄPPÄRÄT ON DESK, AND DIS-ABLE ALL SECURITY SETTINGS. I did as I was told. An electronic version of John Cougar Mellencamp's "Pink Houses" ("Ain't that America, somethin' to see, baby!") twanged in my ear, and then a pixelated version of the plucky otter shuffled onto my äppärät screen, carrying on his back the letters ARA, which dissolved into the shimmering legend: American Restoration Authority.

The otter stood up on his hind legs, and made a show of dusting himself off. "Hi there, pa'dner!" he said, his electronic voice dripping with adorable carnivalesque. "My name is Jeffrey Otter and I *bet* we're going to be friends!"

Feelings of loss and aloneness overwhelmed me. "Hi," I said. "Hi, Jeffrey."

"Hi there, yourself!" the otter said. "Now I'm going to ask you some friendly questions for statistical purposes only. If you don't want to answer a question, just say, 'I don't want to answer this question.' Remember, *I'm* here to help *you*! Okay, then. Let's start simple. What's your name and Social Security Number?"

I looked around. People were urgently whispering things to their otters. "Leonard or Lenny Abramov," I murmured, followed by my Social Security.

"Hi, Leonard or Lenny Abramov, 205-32-8714. On behalf of the American Restoration Authority, I would love to welcome you back to the *new* United States of America. Look out, world! There's no stoppin' us now!" A bar from the McFadden and Whitehead disco hit "Ain't No Stoppin' Us Now" played loudly in my ear. "Now tell me, Lenny. What made you leave our country? Work or pleasure?"

"Work," I said.

"And what do you *do*, Leonard or Lenny Abramov?"

"Um, Indefinite Life Extension."

"You said 'effeminate life invention.' Is that right?"

"*Indefinite* Life *Extension,*" I said.

"What's your Credit ranking, Leonard or Lenny, out of a total score of sixteen hundred?"

"Fifteen hundred twenty."

"That's pretty neat. You must really know how to pinch those pennies. You have money in the bank, you work in 'effeminate life invention.' Now I just *have* to ask, are you a member of the Bipartisan Party? And if so, would you like to receive our new weekly äppärät stream, 'Ain't No Stoppin' Us Now!'? It's got all sorts of great tips on readjusting to life in these United States and getting the most bang for your buck."

"I'm not a Bipartisan, but, yes, I would like to get your stream," I said, trying to be conciliatory.

"Okey-dokey! You're on our list. Say, Leonard or Lenny, did you meet any nice *foreign* people during your stay abroad?"

"Yes," I said.

"What kind of people?"

"Some Italians."

"You said 'Somalians.'"

"Some Italians," I said.

"You said 'Somalians,'" the otter insisted. "You know Americans get lonely abroad. Happens all the time! That's why I never leave the brook where I was born. What's the point? Tell me, for statistical purposes, did you have any intimate physical relationships with any *non*-Americans during your stay?"

I stared hard at the otter, my hands shaking beneath the desk. Did everyone get this question? I didn't want to end up in an Upstate "secure screening facility" simply because I had crawled on top of Fabrizia and tried to submerge my feelings of loneliness and inferiority inside her. "Yes," I said. "Just one girl. A couple of times we did it."

"And what was this *non*-American's full name? Last name first, please."

I could hear one fellow sitting several desks in front of me, his square Anglo face hidden partially by a thick mane, breathing Italian names into his äppärät.

"I'm still waiting for that name, Leonard or Lenny," said the otter.

"DeSalva, Fabrizia," I whispered.

"You said 'DeSalva—' " But just then the otter froze in mid-name, and my äppärät began to produce its "heavy thinking" noises, a wheel desperately spinning inside its hard plastic shell, its ancient circuitry completely overtaxed by the otter and his antics. The words ERROR CODE IT/FC-GS/FLAG appeared on the screen. I got up and went back to the security cage out front. "Excuse me," I said, leaning into the mouth hole. "My äppärät froze. The otter stopped speaking to me. Could you send over that nice Filipina woman?"

The old creature manning this post crackled at me incomprehensibly, the lapels of his shirt trembling with stars and stripes. I made out the words "wait" and "service representative."

An hour passed in bureaucratic metronome. Movers carried out a man-sized golden statue of our nation's E Pluribus Unum eagle and a dining table missing three legs. Eventually an older white woman in enormous orthopedic shoes clacked her way down the hall. She had a magnificent tripartite nose, more Roman than any proboscis ever grown along the banks of the Tiber, and the kind of pinkish oversized glasses I associate with kindness and progressive mental health. Thin lips quivered from daily contact with life, and her earlobes bore silver loops a size too large.

In appearance and mien she reminded me of Nettie Fine, a woman whom I hadn't seen since high-school graduation. She was the first person to greet my parents at the airport after they had winged their way from Moscow to the United States four decades ago in search of dollars and God. She was their young American mama, their latkes-bearing synagogue volunteer, arranger of English lessons, bequeather of spare furniture. In fact, Nettie's husband had worked in D.C. at the State Department. In further fact, before I left for Rome my mother had told me he was stationed in a certain European capital. . . .

"Mrs. Fine?" I said. "Are you Nettie Fine, ma'am?"

Ma'am? I had been raised to worship her, but I was scared of Nettie Fine. She had seen my family at its most exposed, at its poorest and weakest (my folks literally immigrated to the States with one pair of underwear between them). But this temperate bird of a woman had shown me nothing but unconditional love, the kind of love that rushed me in waves and left me feeling weak and depleted, battling an undertow whose source I couldn't place. Her arms were soon around me as she yelled at me for not coming to visit her sooner, and why was I so old-looking all of a sudden ("But I'm almost forty, Mrs. Fine," "Oh, where does the time go, Leonard?"), along with other examples of happy Jewish hysteria.

It turned out that she was working as a contractor for the State Department, helping out with the Welcome Back, Pa'dner program.

"But don't get me wrong," she said, "I'm just doing customer service. Answering questions, not asking them. That's all American Restoration Authority." And then, leaning toward me, in a lowered voice, her artichoke breath gently strumming my face: "Oh, what has *happened* to us, Lenny? I get reports on my desk, they make me cry. The Chinese and Europeans are going to decouple from us. I'm not sure what that means, but how good can it be? And we're going to deport all our immigrants with weak Credit. And our poor boys are being *massacred* in Venezuela. This time I'm afraid we're not going to pull out of it!"

"No, it'll be okay, Mrs. Fine," I said. "There's still only one America."

"And that shifty Rubenstein. Can you believe he's one of *us?*"

"One of us?"

Barely sonic whisper: "A *Jew.*"

"My parents actually love Rubenstein," I said, in reference to our imperious but star-crossed Defense Secretary. "All they do is sit at home and watch FoxLiberty-Prime and FoxLiberty-Ultra."

Mrs. Fine made a distasteful face. She had helped drag my parents into the American continuum, had taught them to gargle and wash out sweat stains, but their inbred Soviet Jewish conservatism had ultimately repulsed her.

She had known me since I was born, back when the Abramov *mishpocheh* lived in Queens in a cramped garden apartment that now elicits nothing but nostalgia, but which must have been a mean and sorrowful place all the same. My father had a janitorial job out at a Long Island government laboratory, a job that kept us in Spam for the first ten years of my life. My mother celebrated my birth by being promoted from clerk/typist to secretary at the credit union where she bravely labored minus English-language skills, and all of a sudden we were really on our way to becoming lower-middle-class. In those days, my parents used to drive me around in their rusted Chevrolet Malibu Classic to neighborhoods poorer than our own, so that we could both laugh at the funny ragtag brown people scurrying about in their sandals and pick up important lessons about what failure could mean in America. It was after my parents told Mrs. Fine about our little slumming forays into Corona and the safer parts of Bed-Stuy that the rupture between her and my family truly began. I remember my parents looking up "cruel" in the English-Russian dictionary, shocked that our American mama could possibly think that of us.

"Tell me everything!" Nettie Fine said. "What have you been doing in Rome?"

"I work in the creative economy," I said proudly. "Indefinite Life Extension. We're going to help people live forever. I'm looking for European HNWIs—that's High Net Worth Individuals—and they're going to be our clients. We call them 'Life Lovers.' "

"Oh my!" Mrs. Fine said. She clearly didn't know what the hell I was talking about, but this woman with her three courteous UPenn-graduated boys could only smile and encourage, smile and encourage. "That certainly sounds like—something!"

"It really is," I said. "But I think I'm in a bit of trouble here." I explained to her the problem I had just experienced with Welcome Back, Pa'dner. "Maybe the otter thinks I hang out with Somalians. What I said was 'Some Italians.' "

"Show me your äppärät," she commanded. She raised her eyeglasses to reveal the soft early-sixties wrinkles that had made her face exactly how it was meant to look since the day she was born— a comfort to all. "ERROR CODE IT/FC-GS/FLAG," she sighed. "Oh boy, buster. You've been flagged."

"But why?" I shouted. "What did I do?"

"Shhh," she said. "Let me reset your äppärät. Let's try Welcome Back, Pa'dner again."

Several attempts were made, but the same frozen otter appeared along with the error message. "When did this happen?" she asked. "What was that *thing* asking you?"

I hesitated, feeling even more naked in front of my family's native-born savior. "He asked me the name of the Italian woman I had relations with," I said.

"Let's backtrack," Nettie said, ever the troubleshooter. "When the otter asked you to subscribe to the 'Ain't No Stoppin' Us Now!' thing, did you do it?"

"I did."

"Good. And what's your Credit ranking?" I told her. "Fine. I wouldn't worry. If you get stopped at JFK, just give them my contact info and tell them to get in touch with me *right away.*" She plugged her coordinates into my äppärät. When she hugged me she could feel my knees knocking together in fear. "Aw, sweetie," she said, a warm tribal tear spilling from her face onto mine. "Don't worry. You'll be okay. A man like you. Creative economy. I just hope your parents' Credit ranking is strong. They came all the way to America, and for what? *For what?*"

But I did worry. How could I not? Flagged by some fucking otter! Jesus Christ. I instructed myself to relax, to enjoy the last twenty hours of my year-long European idyll, and possibly to get very drunk off some sour red Montepulciano.

My last Roman evening started out per the usual, diary. Another halfhearted orgy at Fabrizia's, the woman I have had relations with. I'm only mildly tired of these orgies. Like all New Yorkers, I'm a real-estate whore, and I adore these late-nineteenth-century

Turinese-built apartments on the huge, palm-studded Piazza Vittorio, with sunny views of the green-tinged Alban Hills in the distance. On my last night at Fabrizia's, the expected bunch of forty-year-olds showed up, the rich children of Cinecittà film directors who are now occasional screenwriters for the failing Rai (once Italy's main television concern), but mostly indulgers of their parents' fading fortunes. That's what I admire about youngish Italians, the slow diminution of ambition, the recognition that the best is far behind them. (An Italian Whitney Houston might have sung, "I believe the *parents* are our future.") We Americans can learn a lot from their graceful decline.

I've always been shy around Fabrizia. I know she only likes me because I'm "diverting" and "funny" (read: Semitic), and because her bed hasn't been warmed by a local man in some time. But now that I had sold her out to the American Restoration Authority otter, I worried that there might be repercussions for her down the line. Italy's government is the last one left in Western Europe that still smooches our ass.

In any case, Fabrizia was all over me at the party. First she and some fat British filmmaker took turns kissing me on the eyelids. Then, as she was having one of those very angry Italian äppärät chats on the couch, she spread her legs to flash me her neon panties, her thick Mediterranean pubic hairs clearly visible. She took time out of her sexy screaming and furious typing to say to me in English: "You've become a lot more decadent since I've met you, Lenny."

"I'm trying," I stuttered.

"Try harder," she said. She snapped her legs shut, which nearly killed me, and then went back to her äppärät assault. I wanted to feel those elegant forty-year-old breasts one more time. I made a few slow gyrating motions toward her and batted my eyelashes (that is to say, blinked a lot), trying, with a dose of East Coast irony, to resemble some hot Cinecittà leading lady of the 1960s. Fabrizia blinked back and stuck one hand down her panties. A few minutes later, we opened the door to her bedroom to discover her three-year-old boy hiding beneath a pillow, a cloud of smoke from the main rooms draping him twice-fold. "Fuck," Fabrizia said, watching the small, asthmatic child crawling toward her on the bed.

"*Mama,*" the child whispered. "*Aiuto me.*"

"Katia!" she screamed. "*Puttana!* She supposed to watch him. Stay here, Lenny." She went off looking for her Ukrainian nanny, her little boy stumbling through the Hollywood-grade smoke behind her.

I went into the corridor, which seemed like the arrivals lounge at Fiumicino Airport, with couples meeting, coming together, disappearing into rooms, coming out of rooms, fixing their blouses, tightening their belts, coming apart. I took out my dated äppärät, with its retro walnut finish and its dusty screen blinking with slow data, trying to get a read on whether there were any High Net Worth Individuals in the room—last chance to find some new clients for my boss, Joshie, after having found a grand total of *one* client during the whole year—but no one's face was famous enough to register on my display. A sort-of well-known Mediastud, a Bolognese visual artist, sullen and shy in person, watched his girlfriend flirting ridiculously with a less accomplished man. "I work a little, play a little," someone was saying in accented English, followed by cute, hollow female laughter. A recently arrived American girl, a yoga teacher to the stars, was being reduced to tears by a much older local woman, who kept stabbing her in the heart with one long, painted fingernail and accusing her, personally, of the U.S. invasion of Venezuela. A domestic came carrying a large plate of marinated anchovies. The bald man known as "Cancer Boy" followed dejectedly on the heels of the Afghani princess to whom he had given his heart. A slightly famous Rai actor started telling me about how he had impregnated a girl of good standing in Chile and then fled back to Rome before Chilean law could hold him accountable. When a fellow Neapolitan showed up, he said to me: "Excuse us, Lenny, we have to speak in dialect."

I continued to wait for my Fabrizia while nibbling on an anchovy, feeling like the horniest thirty-nine-year-old man in Rome—a very serious distinction. Perhaps my occasional lover had fallen into an-

other's arms during our brief separation. I did not have a girl waiting for me in New York, I wasn't sure I even had a *job* waiting for
me in New York after my failures in Europe, so I really wanted to
screw Fabrizia. She was the softest woman I had ever touched, the
muscles stirring somewhere deep beneath her skin like phantom
gears, and her breath, like her son's, was shallow and hard, so that
when she "made the love" (her words), it sounded like she was in
danger of expiring.

I caught sight of a Roman fixture, an old American sculptor of
small stature and dying teeth who wore his hair in a Beatlesque mop
and liked to mention his friendship with the iconic Tribeca actor
"Bobby D." Several times I have pushed his drunken rotundity into
a taxi, telling the cabbies his prestigious address on the Gianicolo
Hill, and handing them twenty of my own precious euros.

I had almost failed to notice the young woman in front of him, a
small Korean (I've dated two previously, both delightfully insane),
with her hair up in a provocative bun so that she resembled vaguely
a very young Asian Audrey Hepburn. She had full shiny lips and a
lovely if incongruous splash of freckles across her nose, and could
not have weighed more than eighty pounds, a compactness which
made me tremble with bad thoughts. I wondered, for example, if her
mother, probably a tiny, immaculate woman humming with immigrant anxiety and bad religion, knew that her little girl was no
longer a virgin.

"Oh, it's Lenny," the American sculptor said when I came around
to shake his hand. He was a High Net Worth Individual, if barely,
and I had tried to court him on several occasions. The young Korean
woman glanced at me with what I took to be serious lack of interest
(her default position seemed to be a scowl), her hands clenched
tightly before her. I thought I had blundered onto a new couple and
was about to make my apologies, but the American was already
starting to introduce us. "The lovely Eunice Kim from Fort Lee,
New Jersey, via Elderbird College, Mass.," he said in the brawling
Brooklyn accent he thought was charmingly authentic. "Euny's an
art-history student."

"Eunice *Park,*" she corrected him. "I don't really study art history. I'm not even a college student anymore."

I was pleased by her humility, acquiring a steady, throbbing erection.

"This is Lenny Abraham. He helps old stockbrokers live a little longer."

"It's Abramov," I said, with a subservient bow to the young lady. I noticed the glass of inky Sicilian red in my hand and drank it in one go. All of a sudden I was sweating all over my freshly laundered shirt and ugly loafers. I took out my äppärät, flicked it open in a gesture that was *au courant* maybe a decade ago, held it stupidly in front of me, put it back in my shirt pocket, then reached for a nearby bottle and refilled my glass. It was incumbent upon me to say something impressive about myself. "I do nanotechnology and stuff."

"Like a scientist?" Eunice Park asked.

"More like a salesman," the American sculptor rumbled. He was notoriously competitive over women. At the last party, he had championed over a young Milanese animator to get a blow job from Fabrizia's nineteen-year-old cousin. In Rome this passed for breaking news.

The sculptor made a half-turn toward Eunice, partly obscuring me with one thick shoulder. I took that as my sign to leave, but whenever I began to do so, she would glance my way, casually tossing me a lifeline. Maybe she was scared of the sculptor herself, worried she would end up on her knees in a dimly lit room.

I drank heavily, eyeing the sculptor's broad attempts to impress the thoroughly unimpressible Eunice Park. "So I says to her, '*Contessa,* you can stay in my beach house in Puglia until you get back on your feet.' I don't have time for the beach anyway. They want me to take up a commission in Shanghai. Six million yuan for two pieces. That's what—fifty million dollars? I says to her, 'Don't cry, *contessa,* you sly old bird. I've been down to nothing myself. Not a *centavo* to my name. Practically grew up in the Brooklyn Navy Yard. First thing I remember was a sock to the face. Bam!' "

I felt sad for the sculptor, and not just because I doubted his chances with Eunice Park, but because I realized he would soon be dead. From an ex-lover of his I had learned that his advanced diabetes had almost cost him two toes, and the heavy cocaine use was maxing out his aging circulatory system. In the business we called him an ITP, Impossible to Preserve, the vital signs too far gone for current interventions, the psychological indicators showing an "extreme willingness/desire to perish." Even more despairing was his financial status. I'm quoting directly from my report to boss man Joshie: "Income yearly $2.24 million, pegged to the yuan; obligations, including alimony and child support, $3.12 million; investible assets (excluding real estate)—northern euro 22,000,000; real estate $5.4 million, pegged to the yuan; total debts outstanding $12.9 million, unpegged." A mess, in other words.

Why was he doing this to himself? Why not keep off the drugs and the demanding young women, spend a decade in Corfu or Chiang Mai, douse his body with alkalines and smart technology, clamp down on the free radicals, keep the mind focused on the work, beef up the stock portfolio, take the tire off the belly, let us fix that aging bulldog's mug? What kept the sculptor here, in a city useful only as a reference to the past, preying on the young, gorging on thick-haired pussy and platefuls of carbs, swimming with the prevailing current toward his own nullification? Beyond that ugly body, those rotting teeth, that curdled breath, was a visionary and a creator, whose heavy-handed work I sometimes admired.

As I buried the sculptor, marching behind the pallbearers, comforting his beautiful ex-wife and cherubic twin sons, my eyes watched Eunice Park, young, stoic, and flat, nodding along to the sculptor's self-serving remarks. I wanted to reach over and touch her empty chest, feel the tough little nipples that I imagined proclaimed her love. I noticed that her sharp nose and little arms were lightly coated with moisture and that she was matching me in the drinking department, plucking off wineglasses from passing trays, her tightly wound mouth turning purple. She wore fancy jeans, a gray cashmere sweater, and a string of pearls which lent her at least ten years of age. The only youthful part of her was a sleek white pendant—a

pebble almost—which looked like some kind of miniaturized new
äppärät. In certain wealthy precincts of trans-Atlantic society, the
differences between young and old were steadily eroding, and in
other precincts the young were mostly going naked, but what was
Eunice Park's story? Was she trying to be older or richer or whiter?
Why do attractive people have to be anything but themselves?

When I next looked up, the sculptor had placed his heavy paw on
her negligible shoulder and was squeezing hard. "Chinese women
are so delicate," he said.

"I'm not that delicate."

"Yes, you are!"

"I'm not Chinese."

"Anyway, Bobby D. and Dick Gere were fighting at a party. Dick
came to me and said, 'Why does Bobby hate me so much?' Wait.
What was I saying? Do you need another drink? Oh! You made the
right choice coming to Rome, kitten. New York is finished these
days. America is history. And with those fuckers in charge now, I'm
never going back. Fucking Rubenstein. Fucking Bipartisan Party. It's
1984, baby. Not that you would get the reference. Maybe our book-
ish friend Lenny here could enlighten us. You're so lucky to be here
with me, Euny. Do you want to kiss me?"

"No," Eunice Park said. "No, thank you."

No, thank you. A nice Korean girl, graduate of Elderbird College,
Mass. How I longed to kiss those full lips myself and cradle the
slightness of the rest of her.

"Why not?" the sculptor shouted. And then, because he had long
lost the ability to gauge short-term consequences, he shook her by
the shoulder, a drunken shake, but one that her tiny body looked ill-
equipped to handle. Eunice looked up, and in her eyes I saw the familiar anger of an adult suddenly dragged back into childhood. She
pressed one hand to her stomach, as if she had been punched, and
looked down. Red wine had spilled on her expensive sweater. She
turned to me, and I saw embarrassment, not for the sculptor, but for
herself.

"Let's take it easy," I said, putting my hand on the sculptor's taut, moist neck. "Let's maybe sit down on the couch and have some water." Eunice was rubbing her shoulder and backing away from us. She looked as if she was expertly holding back the tears.

"Fuck off, Lenny," the sculptor said, giving me a little shove. His hands were undeniably strong. "Go peddle your fountain of youth."

"Find a couch and chillax," I instructed the sculptor. I moved over to Eunice and put my arm within the vicinity of her, but not directly upon her. "I'm sorry," I muttered. "He gets drunk."

"Yeah, I *gets* drunk!" the sculptor shouted. "And I may even be a little bit tipsy right now. But in the morning I'll be making art. And what are you going to be doing, *Leonard*? Pushing green tea and cloned livers to geezer Bipartisans? Typing in a diary? Let me guess. 'My uncle abused me. I was addicted to heroin for three seconds.' Forget the fountain of youth, pal of mine. You can live to be a thousand, and it won't matter. Mediocrities like you *deserve* immortality. Don't trust this guy, Eunice. He's not like us. He's a real American. A real sharpie. He's the reason we're in Venezuela right now. He's why people are afraid to say 'boo' in the States. He's no better than Rubenstein. Look at those dark, lying Ashkenazi eyes. Kissinger the Second."

A crowd had started to gather around us. Watching the famous sculptor "act out" was a great source of entertainment for the Romans, and the words "Venezuela" and "Rubenstein," spoken with slow, accusatory relish, could arouse even a coma-bound European. I could hear Fabrizia's voice announcing itself from the living room. As gently as possible, I prodded the Korean toward the kitchen, which led to the servants' quarters, which enjoyed a separate entrance to the apartment.

In the half-light of a bare bulb, I saw the Ukrainian nanny petting the sweet, dark head of Fabrizia's boy, as she maneuvered an inhaler into his mouth. The child registered our intrusion with little surprise, the nanny began to say "*Che cosa?,*" but we trooped right past her and the small tidy stash of clothes and cheap mementos (a cooking apron depicting Michelangelo's David astride the Coliseum) that made up her immediate possessions. As Eunice and I clambered down the noisy marble stairs, we heard Fabrizia and others give chase, summoning the wire-mesh enclosure of the elevator to their high floor, eager to catch up with us and hear what had happened, how the sculptor's considerable drunken anger had been stirred. "Lenny, come back," Fabrizia was shouting. "*Dobbiamo scopare ancora una volta.* We have to fuck still. One last time."

Fabrizia. The softest woman I had ever touched. But maybe I no longer *needed* softness. Fabrizia. Her body conquered by small armies of hair, her curves fixed by carbohydrates, nothing but the Old World and its dying nonelectronic corporeality. And in front of me, Eunice Park. A nano-sized woman who had likely never known the tickle of her own pubic hair, who lacked both breast and scent, who existed as easily on an äppärät screen as on the street before me.

Outside, the southern moon, pregnant and satisfied, roosted atop the outreached palm trees of Piazza Vittorio. The usual immigrant gaggle were sleeping off a long day of manual labor or tucking in their mistresses' children. The only pedestrians were stylish Italians staggering back from dinner, the only sounds the hum of their bitter conversations and the hissing electric rattle of the old tramcar that surveyed the piazza's northeastern side.

Eunice Park and I marched ahead. She marched, I hopped, unable to cover up the joy of having escaped the party with her by my side. I wanted Eunice to thank me for saving her from the sculptor and his stench of death. I wanted her to get to know me and then to repudiate all the terrible things he had said about my person, my supposed greed, my boundless ambition, my lack of talent, my fictive membership in the Bipartisan Party, and my designs on Caracas. I wanted to tell her that I myself was in danger, that the American Restoration Authority otter had singled me out for sedition, and all because I had slept with one middle-aged Italian woman.

I eyed Eunice's ruined sweater and the obscenely fresh body that lived and sweated and, I hoped, yearned beneath it. "I know of a good dry cleaner that can fix red-wine stains," I said. "There's this Nigerian up the block." I stressed "Nigerian" to underline my open-mindedness. Lenny Abramov, friend to all.

"I volunteer at a refugee shelter near the train station," Eunice said, apropos of something.

"You do? That's so *fantastic*!"

"You're such a nerd." She laughed cruelly at me.

"What?" I said. "I'm sorry." I laughed too, just in case it was a joke, but right away I felt hurt.

"LPT," she said. "TIMATOV. ROFLAARP. PRGV. Totally PRGV."

The youth and their abbreviations. I pretended like I knew what she was talking about. "Right," I said. "IMF. PLO. ESL."

She looked at me like I was insane. "JBF," she said.

"Who's that?" I pictured a tall Protestant man.

"It means I'm 'just butt-fucking' with you. Just kidding, you know."

"Duh," I said. "I knew that. Seriously. What makes me a nerd in your estimation?"

" 'In your estimation,' " she mimicked. "Who says things like that? And who wears those shoes? You look like a bookkeeper."

"I'm sensing a bit of anger here," I said. What had happened to that sweet, hurt Korean girl of three minutes ago? For some reason I puffed out my chest and stood up on my toes, even though I had a good half a foot on her.

She touched the cuff of my shirt, and then looked at it more carefully. "This isn't buttoned right," she said. And before I could say anything, she rebuttoned my cuff and pulled on the shirtsleeve to make it less bunched up around the shoulder and upper arm. "There," she said. "You look a little better now."

I didn't know what to say or do. When dealing with people my own age, I know precisely who I am. Not physically attractive, but at least well educated, decently paid, working at the frontiers of science and technology (even though I have the same finesse with my äppärät as my aged immigrant parents). On Planet Eunice Park, these attributes clearly did not matter. I was some kind of ancient dork. "Thanks," I said. "Don't know what I'd do without you."

She smiled at me, and I noticed that she had the kind of dimples that not merely puncture the face but easily fill it with warmth and personality (and, in the case of Eunice, take away some of her anger). "I'm hungry," she said.

I must have looked like the befuddled Rubenstein at his press conference after our troops got routed at Ciudad Bolívar. "What?" I said. "Hungry? Isn't it a little too late?"

"Um, no, Gramps," Eunice Park said.

I took that in stride. "I know of this place on Via del Governo Vecchio. It's called da Tonino. Excellent *cacio e pepe.*"

"So it says in my *Time Out* guide," the impudent girl said to me. She lifted up her äppärät-like pendant, and in shockingly perfect Italian ordered a taxi to pick us up. I hadn't felt so frightened since high school. Even death, my slender, indefatigable nemesis, seemed lackluster when compared with the all-powerful Eunice Park.

In the taxi, I sat apart from her, engaging in very idle chatter indeed ("So I hear the dollar's going to be devaluated again . . ."). The city of Rome appeared around us, casually splendid, eternally assured of itself, happy to take our money and pose for a picture, but in the end needing nothing and no one. Eventually I realized that the driver had decided to cheat me, but I didn't protest his extended route, especially as we swung around the purple-lit carapace of the Coliseum, and I told myself, *Remember this, Lenny; develop a sense of nostalgia for something, or you'll never figure out what's important.*

But by the end of the night I remembered very little. Let's just say that I drank. Drank out of fear (she was so cruel). Drank out of happiness (she was so beautiful). Drank until my whole mouth and teeth had turned a dark ruby red and the pungency of my breath and perspiration betrayed my passing years. And she drank too. One *mezzo litro* of the local swill became a full *litro,* and then two *litri,* and then a bottle of something possibly Sardinian but, in any case, thicker than bull's blood.

Enormous plates of food were needed to mop up this overindulgence. We thoughtfully chewed on the pig jowls of the *bucatini all'amatriciana,* slurped up a plate of spaghetti with spicy eggplant, and picked apart a rabbit practically drowning in olive oil. I knew I would miss all this when I got back to New York, even the horrible fluorescent lighting that brought out my age—the wrinkles around my eyes, the single long highway and the three county roads that ran across my forehead, testaments to many sleepless nights spent worrying about unredeemed pleasures and my carefully hoarded income, but mostly about death. This particular restaurant was favored by theater actors, and as I stabbed with my fork at the thick hollows of pasta and the glistening aubergines, I tried to remember forever their loud, attention-seeking voices and the vibrant Italian hand gestures that in my mind are synonymous with the living animal, and hence with life itself.

I focused on the living animal in front of me and tried to make her love me. I spoke extravagantly and, I hope, sincerely. Here's what I remember.

I told her I didn't want to leave Rome now that I had met her.

She again told me I was a nerd, but a nerd who made her laugh.

I told her I wanted to do more than make her laugh.

She told me I should be thankful for what I had.

I told her she should move to New York with me.

She told me she was probably a lesbian.

I told her my work was my life, but I still had room for love.

She told me love was *out of the question.*

I told her my parents were Russian immigrants who lived in New York.

She told me hers were Korean immigrants who lived in Fort Lee, New Jersey.

I told her my father was a retired janitor who liked to go fishing.

She told me her father was a podiatrist who liked to punch his wife and two daughters in the face.

"Oh," I said. Eunice Park shrugged and excused herself. On my plate, the rabbit's little dead heart hung from within his rib cage. I put my head in my hands and wondered if I should just throw some euros down on the table and walk out and leave.

But soon enough I was walking down ivy-draped Via Giulia, my arm around Eunice Park's fragrant, boyish frame. She was seemingly in good spirits, both loving and goading: promising me a kiss, then chastising my poor Italian. She was shyness and giggles, freckles in the moonlight and drunken, immature cries of "Shut *up,* Lenny!" and "You're such an idiot!" I noticed she had released her hair from the bun's captivity and that it was dark and endless and as thick as twine. She was twenty-four years old.

My apartment could accommodate no more than a cheap twin-sized mattress and a fully opened suitcase, brimming with books ("My text-major friends at Elderbird used to call those things 'doorstops,' " she told me). We kissed, lazily, like it was nothing, then roughly, like we meant it. There were some problems. Eunice Park wouldn't take off her bra ("I have absolutely no chest"), and I was too drunk and scared to develop an erection. But I didn't want intercourse anyway. I talked her out of her pants, cupped the twin, tiny globes of her ass with my palms, and pushed my lips right inside her soft, vital pussy. "Oh, Lenny," she said, a little sadly, for she must have sensed just how much her youth and freshness meant to me, a man who lived in death's anteroom and could barely stand the light and heat of his brief sojourn on earth. I licked and licked, breathing in the slight odor of something authentic and human, and eventually must have fallen asleep with my face between her legs. The next morning, she was kind enough to help me repack my suitcase, which refused to close without her help. "That's not how you do it," she said, when she saw me brushing my teeth. She made me stick out my tongue and roughly scraped its purple surface with the toothbrush. "There," she said. "Better."

During the taxi ride to the airport, I felt the triple pangs of being happy and lonely and needy all at once. She had made me wash my lips and chin thoroughly to obliterate all traces of her, but Eunice Park's alkaline tang still remained on the tip of my nose. I made great sniffing motions in the air, trying to capture her essence, thinking already of how I would bait her to New York, make her my wife, make her my life, my life eternal. I touched my expertly brushed teeth and petted the flurry of gray hairs sticking out from beneath my shirt collar, which she had thoroughly examined in the morning's weak early light. "Cute," she had said. And then, with a child's sense of wonder: "You're old, Len."

Oh, dear diary. My youth has passed, but the wisdom of age hardly beckons. Why is it so hard to be a grown-up man in this world?

SOMETIMES LIFE IS SUCK

FROM THE GLOBALTEENS ACCOUNT OF EUNICE PARK

JUNE 1

Format: Long-Form Standard English Text
GLOBALTEENS SUPER HINT: *Switch to Images today! Less words = more fun!!!*

EUNI-TARD ABROAD *TO* GRILLBITCH:

Hi, Precious Pony!

What's up, twat? Missing your 'tard? Wanna dump a little sugar on me? JBF. I am so sick of making out with girls. BTW, I saw the pictures on the Elderbird alum board with your tongue in Bryana's, um, ear. I hope you're not trying to get Gopher jealous? He's had way too many three-somes. Respect yourself, hoo-kah! So—guess what? I met the cutest guy in Rome. He is exactly my type, tall, kind of German-looking, very prep-pie, but not an asshole. Giovanna set me up with him he's in Rome work-ing for LandO'LakesGMFordCredit! So I go to meet him in the Piazza Navona (remember Image Class? Navona the one with all the tritons) and he's sitting there having a cappuccino and streaming Chronicles of Narnia! Remember we streamed that at Catholic? So adorable. He kind of looked a little like Gopher but much thinner (ha ha ha). His name is Ben, which is pretty gay, but he was SO NICE and so smart. He took me to look at some Caravaggios and then he kind of like touched my butt a little and then we went to one of Giovanna's parties and made out. There were all these Ital-ian girls in Onionskin jeans staring at us, like I was stealing one of their white guys or something. I fucking hate that. If they mention my "almond eyes" one more time, I swear. Anyway, I NEED YOUR ADVICE because he called yesterday and asked if I wanted to go up to Lucca with him next week and I was playing hard to get and said no. But I'm going to call him and say yes tomorrow! WHAT SHOULD I DO? HELP!!!

P.S. I met this old, gross guy at a party yesterday and we got really drunk and I sort of let him go down on me. There was another even older guy, this sculptor, trying to get in my pants, so I figured, you know, the lesser evil. Ugh, I'm turning into you!!!!! He was nice, kind of dorky, although he thinks he's so Media cause he works in biotech or something. And he had the grossest feet, bunions and this gigantic heel spur that sticks out like he's got a thumb glued to his foot. I know, I'm thinking like my dad. Anyway, he brushes his teeth all wrong, so I had to SHOW A GROWN MAN HOW TO USE A TOOTHBRUSH!!!!! What is wrong with my life, precious pony?

GRILLBITCH *TO* EUNI-TARD ABROAD:

Hey, Precious Panda!

OK, let me just say this: Ass Hoo-kah, you are majorly sick? How old was this guy? Why did you touch his feet? Are you a secret toe muncher? I am sending you a cleaning bill because I am completely VOMITING as I write this. OK, forget the wheelchair geezer. This Ben guy sounds really Media, and he works in Credit, so he must be FILTHY FUCKING RICH. Wish Gopher could get a job with LandO'LakesGMFord. Now for Grillbitch's patent advice: Go with him to Lucca, where is that exactly?, treat him like shit during the first day, let him fuck you HARD the first night, then leave him completely confused the rest of the time. He'll fall for you pronto, especially after you let him plunder your MAGIC PUSSY!!! And on the way back to Rome be all nice, so that he's left with a good impression but still not sure of himself.

So here's what's up here. This Filipino guy had a party in Redondo. Pat Alvarez, do you remember him from Catholic? And Wendy Snatch showed up in Onionskin jeans and a nippleless Saaami bra and then she starts grinding on Gopher's lap. He was like trying to push her off but she said maybe you want me and your girlfriend to thresh each other and all the time she is practically POKING his eye out with her nipple, which is one of those big fat pink DISGUSTING white girls nips. So Gopher's looking at me with this expression, like, yeah, you can thresh each other if you want too or not that's totally cool just don't make a scene. And anyway all these Flip girls who just graduated from UC Irvine are threshing the shit out of each other in the living room trying to impress some white guy (not Gopher) so I teened her like I DON'T THINK SO, WENDY SNATCH. Only I didn't say it in CAPS, it was more like no thank you and that's my BOYFRIEND'S crotch you're humping. And she actually came up to me PHYSICALLY and VERBALLED me like "Oh, I thought you were a lez cause you went to Elderbird, I didn't know you were a feminazi too" and I was like "Yeah, but even if I was the biggest lez in America I wouldn't thresh you with a fucking combine" and then guess where she ended up by the end of the party? In the bathtub getting ass-reamed and face-pissed by Pat Alvarez and three of his friends who taped everything and then put it on GlobalTeens the next day. GUESS how high her ratings went up? Personality 764 and Fuckability 800+. What is WRONG with people?

JUNE 2

CHUNG.WON.PARK *TO* EUNI-TARD ABROAD:

Eunhee,

Yesterday your LSAT come. Sally try to hide anvelope from me. You score 158. Very low. Even for rutgers law you do not get in. I dissapoint that you have same score as last time. It mean you not student enough for that. I now sometimes life is suck, but you are twenty-four. Big girl. I cannot push you any long. You must study and when you study you must not do anything! Dating nice boy extra. But all the time you must to be careful with him because you are woman. Do not give away mystery. Are there any korea boy in rome? Please forgive I have terrible english.

I Love you,

Mommy

P.S. Daddy says I shouldn't say I Love you, because I spoil you and korea parent don't say Love you to children, but I do Love you from deep in my heart so I say it!

EUNI-TARD ABROAD *TO* CHUNG.WON.PARK:

Mom, please put ten thousand yuan-pegged dollars into my Allied-WasteCVSCitigroupCredit account. I'll take the LSAT again when I get back. Ethel Kim got 154 on her LSAT and she took three test-prep classes, so whatever. I'm doing fine. It's hard to work here because you need a *permesso soggiorno,* which is a kind of green card, and they hate Americans. Otherwise I would have to work as an au pair or something. I'm already volunteering three hours a week at the refugee shelter. Did you tell that to Daddy? No, there are no Korean boys in Rome. Rome is in Italy. Look at a map.

JUNE 3

CHUNG.WON.PARK *TO* EUNI-TARD ABROAD:

Eunhee,

How do you think you have Mommy for? Any way you have trouble you write to me, not only for when you need money. When you work lawyer Mommy proud of you and you do not ask her for money. You will be proud also because you help Mommy and family. Family is most important, otherwise why GOD put us on earth? I very worry for you and Sally. Daddy not feeling good. Maybe all is my fault. I pray in church extra for you. Reverend Cho say all young people have special path. Do you know what it is your special path? Please tell me if you know, other wise we look together. And keep Jesu in your heart. It is important! Also there are korean boys everywhere. Go to korean church and you will find date. Maybe you do not understand my bad english.

I Love you,

Mommy

EUNI-TARD ABROAD *TO* CHUNG.WON.PARK:

What do you mean Daddy's not feeling good? If anything bad is happening you and Sally have to go to Eunhyun's house. Mom! Forget freaking Jesu for a second. THIS IS IMPORTANT. You're making me very scared. Did he do anything to you or Sally? I tried to call the house eight times yesterday but all I got is the voice mail. Verbal me on my Global-Teens account when you get this!

CHUNG.WON.PARK *TO* EUNI-TARD ABROAD:

Eunhee,

Do not make uncomfortable yourself. Daddy drink a little much and he get mad because I make soon-dubu with spoilt tofu. I told Sally to go for walk but she sleep in guess room and I sleep in basement. So all okay! Did you get transfer fund to AlliedWaste? Check make sure. It a lot of money so don't make me dissapoint. Enjoy rome, you make good student at Elderbird, you deserve. But now your life just begin. Do not make any-more mistake! Stay away from meeguk boy. They all have bad intent, even christian ones. I pray to Jesu every day that you find kind happiness I never have, because maybe I make sin against GOD. I have so much ashame. Write Sally more. She miss you. You have big responsibility be-cause you big sister. I am very sorry you not get LSAT score you wanted. You sad, Mommy sad. When you hurt, Mommy hurt more.

EUNI-TARD ABROAD: Sally! What is going on with mom and dad?

SALLYSTAR: Nothing. He got upset because of the soon-dubu. What do you care?

EUNI-TARD ABROAD: Why are you angry at ME?

SALLYSTAR: I'm not angry. Leave me alone. Do they have Saaami summer bras in Rome?

EUNI-TARD ABROAD: Yes, but they're eighty euros.

SALLYSTAR: How much is that?

EUNI-TARD ABROAD: Way too much. You can get it much cheaper at the Saaami store on Elizabeth Street or just order on TeenyBopper. Why do you want to wear a bra that lets everyone see your nipples? And I thought you didn't care about fashion.

SALLYSTAR: Everyone's wearing them. Even in Fort Lee.

EUNI-TARD ABROAD: Who in Fort Lee?

SALLYSTAR: Grace Lee's sister.

EUNI-TARD ABROAD: Bona? She's an idiot.

EUNI-TARD ABROAD: Sally, did dad hit you?

SALLYSTAR: He says he misses California. The office was empty all week. All the Koreans in NJ already have podiatrists. Mom's acting like a space cadet.

EUNI-TARD ABROAD: Fine, don't answer my question. Thanks for hiding my LSAT.

SALLYSTAR: Mom found it anyway. What's up?

EUNI-TARD ABROAD: I met a cute white guy here. He works for Land-O'LakesGMFord.

SALLYSTAR: It's easier to date a Korean guy. For the families and every-thing.

EUNI-TARD ABROAD: Thanks, Mom.

SALLYSTAR: I'm just saying.

EUNI-TARD ABROAD: Yeah, maybe I'll date a Korean guy like dad. That's called "a pattern."

SALLYSTAR: Whatever. You take his money. I have to go to a meeting at 1.

EUNI-TARD ABROAD: What meeting?

SALLYSTAR: Columbia-Tsinghua protest against the ARA. We're going to DC in a week.

EUNI-TARD ABROAD: What's ARA?

SALLYSTAR: American Restoration Authority. The Bipartisans. Don't you ever stream the news?

EUNI-TARD ABROAD: You ARE angry at me.

EUNI-TARD ABROAD: Sally, you don't have to live with mom and dad. You can go live at the Barnard dorm. You can get a paid internship or a job in a store. I don't want you getting Political. Let's just try to enjoy our lives.

EUNI-TARD ABROAD: Sally? Hello? Do you want me to come home? I'll fly back tomorrow if you want me to. I'll take care of mom.

EUNI-TARD ABROAD: Sally, please don't be angry at me. I'm sorry I'm not there when you and mommy need me. I'm such a fuck-up.

EUNI-TARD ABROAD: Sally? Hello? You've probably left. It's one o'clock your time.

EUNI-TARD ABROAD: Sally, I love you.

JUNE 4

LEONARDO DABRAMOVINCI *TO* EUNI-TARD ABROAD:

Oh, hi there. It's Lenny Abramov. You might remember me from our little time in Rome. Thanks for brushing my teeth! Hee hee. So, anyway, just got back to the US of A. I've been practicing my abbreviations. I think you said ROFLAARP in Rome. Does that mean "Rolling On Floor Looking At Addictive Rodent Pornography"? See, I'm not that old! Anyway, been thinking about you. Coming to NYC anytime soon? You've got a place to stay here. I've got a nice place all set up, 740 square feet, balcony, view of downtown. Can't compete with da tonino, but I make a pretty mean roasted eggplant. I can even sleep on the couch if you want me to. Call or write anytime. It was really, really, REALLY great to meet you. I'm committing the constellation of your freckles to memory as I write this (hope that doesn't make you uncomfortable).

Love,

Leonard

THE OTTER STRIKES BACK
FROM THE DIARIES OF LENNY ABRAMOV

JUNE 4
New York City

Dearest Diary,

I saw the fat man at the first-class lounge at Fiumicino. There's a special terminal for flights to the United States and SecurityState Israel, the most dilapidated terminal at the Roman airport, where everyone who is not a passenger is basically carrying a gun or pointing some sort of scanning gizmo at you. There aren't even seats for the economy-class passengers by the gates, because they can scan you better standing up, get between your folds of flesh and light you up like a six-hundred-watt bulb. Anyway, life's a lot better in the first-class lounge, and that's where I went to see if I could find some last-minute High Net Worth Individuals, some potential Life Lovers who might be interested in our Product. I could see myself strolling into boss man Joshie's office and saying, "Look at this! Even when he's traveling, your Lenny's looking for prospects. I'm like a doctor. Always on call!"

First-class lounges aren't what they used to be. Most Asian HNWIs fly private planes these days, but my äppärät picked up on some scan-able faces, an old-time porno star and a slick guy from Mumbai just starting out on his first worldwide Retail empire. They all had some money on them, if not the twenty million northern euros in investable income that I'm looking for, but there was this one guy who registered *nothing*. I mean he wasn't there. He didn't have an äppärät, or it wasn't set on "social" mode, or maybe he had paid some young Russian kid to have the outbound transmission blocked. And he looked like a nothing. The way people don't really look anymore. Not just imperfect, but awful. A fat man with deeply recessed eyes, a collapsed chin, limp and dusty hair, a T-shirt that all but exposed his large breasts, and a gross tent of air atop where one imagined his genital would be. No one would look at him except me (and then only for a minute), because he was at the margins of society, because he was without rank, because he was ITP or Impossible to Preserve, because he had no business being mixed up with real HNWIs in a first-class lounge. Now, in hindsight, I want to imbue him with some heroism; I want to place a thick book in his hands and perch even thicker bifocals on his nose. I want him to look like Benjamin Franklin. But, then, I promised you the truth, dear diary. And the truth is that from the moment I saw him *I was scared.*

With his hands clasped at his crotch, the Impossible to Preserve fat man stared out the window, his head moving forward and backward contentedly, as if he were a half-submerged alligator enjoying a sunny day. Ignoring the rest of us, he watched, with an enthusiast's abandon, the sleek new dolphin-nosed China Southern Airlines planes taxiing past our peeling UnitedContinentalDeltamerican 737s and some equally crappy El Als.

When we finally boarded after a three-hour technical delay, a young man dressed in business casual walked down the aisle videotaping all of us, focusing repeatedly on the fat man, who blushed and tried to turn away. The filmmaker tapped me on the shoulder and bade me, in slow Southern English, to look *directly* into his boxy, antiquated camera. "Why?" I asked. But that little bit of sedition was apparently all he needed from me, and he moved on.

By the time we were in the air, I tried to erase the videographer and the otter and the fat man from my mind. On my way back from the bathroom, I registered Fatty only as a pastel-colored blob in the corner, its form tickled by high-altitude sunlight. I took out a battered volume of Chekhov's stories from my carry-on (wish I could read it in Russian like my parents can) and turned to the novella

Three Years, the story of the unattractive but decent Laptev, the son of a wealthy Moscow merchant, who is in love with the beautiful and much younger Julia. I was hoping to find some tips on how to further seduce Eunice and to overcome the beauty gap between us. At one point in the novella, Laptev asks for Julia's hand in marriage, and she initially turns him down, then changes her mind. I found this particular passage most helpful:

> [Attractive Julia] was distressed and dispirited, and told herself now that to refuse an honorable, good man who loved her, simply because *he was not attractive* [emphasis mine], especially when marrying him would make it possible for her to change her mode of life, her cheerless, monotonous, idle life in which *youth was passing with no prospect of anything better in the future* [emphasis mine]—to refuse him under such circumstances was madness, caprice and folly, and that God might even punish her for it.

From this single passage I developed a three-point conclusion.

Point One: I knew that Eunice didn't believe in God and deplored her Catholic education, so it would be useless to invoke that deity and his endless punishments to make her fall for me, *but,* much like Laptev, I truly was that "honorable, good man who loved her."

Point Two: Eunice's life in Rome, despite the sensuousness and beauty of the city, also seemed to me "cheerless, monotonous," and certainly *"idle"* (I knew she volunteered for a couple of hours a week with some Algerians, which is incredibly sweet but not really work). Now, I do not come from a wealthy family like Chekhov's Laptev, but my annual spending power of about two hundred thousand yuan would give Eunice some considerations in the Retail department and possibly "change her mode of life."

Point Three: Nonetheless, it would take more than mere monetary consideration to prompt Eunice to love me. Her "youth was passing with no prospect of anything better in the future," as Chekhov said of his Julia. How could I take advantage of that fact re: Eunice? How could I trick her into aligning her youth with my decrepitude? In nineteenth-century Russia, it was apparently a much simpler task.

I noticed that some of the first-class people were staring me down for having an open book. "Duder, that thing smells like wet socks," said the young jock next to me, a senior Credit ape at LandO'Lakes-GMFord. I quickly sealed the Chekhov in my carry-on, stowing it far in the overhead bin. As the passengers returned to their flickering displays, I took out my äppärät and began to thump it loudly with my finger to show how much I loved all things digital, while sneaking nervous glances at the throbbing cavern around me, the wine-dulled business travelers lost to their own electronic lives. By this point the young man in business-casual attire had returned with his video camera and just stood there at the front of the aisle recording the fat man with a trace of dull, angry pleasure hanging off his mouth (his quarry had buried his head in a pillow, either sleeping or pretending to be).

I was looking for clues on Eunice Park. My beloved was a shy girl by comparison with others of her generation, so her digital footprint wasn't big. I had to go at her laterally, through her sister, Sally, and her father, Sam Park, M.D., the violent podiatrist. Working my lusty, overheated äppärät, I pointed an Indian satellite at southern California, her original home. I zoomed in on a series of crimson-tiled haciendas to the south of Los Angeles, rows and rows of three-thousand-square-foot rectangles, their only aerial features the tiny silver squiggles that denoted rooftop central air conditioning. These units all bowed to the semicircle of a turquoise pool guarded by the gray halos of two down-on-their-luck palm trees, the development's only flora. Inside one of these homes Eunice Park learned to walk and talk, to seduce and sneer; here her arms grew strong and her mane thick; here her household Korean was supplanted by the veneer of California English; here she planned her impossible escape to East Coast Elderbird College, to the piazzas of Rome, to the horny middle-aged festas of Piazza Vittorio, and, I hoped, into my arms.

I then looked up Dr. and Mrs. Park's new home, a square Dutch Colonial with one gaping chimney, deposited at an awkward forty-

five-degree angle into a bowl of Mid-Atlantic snow. The California
house they left was worth 2.4 million dollars, unpegged to the yuan,
and the second, much smaller New Jersey one at 1.41 million. I
sensed the diminution of her father's income and I wanted to learn
more.

My retro äppärät churned slowly with data, which told me that
the father's business was failing. A chart appeared, giving the income for the last eighteen months; the yuan amounts were in steady
decline since they had mistakenly left California for New Jersey—
July's income after expenses was eight thousand yuan, about half of
my own, and I did not have a family of four to support.

The mother did not have any data, she belonged solely to the
home, but Sally, as the youngest of the Parks, was awash in it. From
her profile I learned that she was a heavier girl than Eunice, the
weight plunged into her round cheeks and the slow curvature of her
arms and breasts. Still, her LDL cholesterol was way beneath the,
norm, while the HDL surged ahead to form an unheard-of ratio.
Even with her weight, she could live to be 120 if she maintained her
present diet and did her morning stretches. After checking her
health, I examined her purchases and felt Eunice's as well. The Park
sisters favored extra-small shirts in strict business patterns, austere
gray sweaters distinguished only by their provenance and price,
pearly earrings, one-hundred-dollar children's socks (their feet were
that small), panties shaped like gift bows, bars of Swiss chocolate at
random delis, footwear, footwear, footwear. I watched their Allied-
WasteCVSCitigroup account rise and fall like the chest of a living,
breathing animal. I noticed the links to something called AssLuxury
and several L.A. and New York boutiques on one side, and to their
parents' AlliedWaste account on the other, and I saw that their precious immigrant nest egg was declining steadily and ominously. I beheld the numerical totality of the Park family and I wanted to save
them from themselves, from the idiotic consumer culture that was
bleeding them softly. I wanted to give them counsel and to prove to
them that—as the son of immigrants myself—I could be trusted.

Next, I did the social sites. The photos flashed before me. Mostly they were of Sally and her friends. Asian kids getting furtively drunk off Mexican beer, attractive boys and girls in decent cotton sweatshirts flashing V-signs at the äppärät lens in front of doily-covered pianos and gilt-edged pastoral paintings of Jesus in blissed-out freefall. Boys roughhousing on their parents' wide bed, denim jeans upon denim jeans upon denim jeans. Girls huddled together, all eyes on a busy äppärät, serious attempts at laughter and spontaneity and light feminine "clowning around." Sister Sally, hurt kindness radiating from her face, her arms draped over an equally heavy girl in a Catholic-school uniform who has snuck her hand behind Sally to make a pair of childhood horns, and there, at the end of a chorus line of ten desperately grinning recent college grads, was my Eunice, her eyes coolly surveying an asphalted patch of California backyard and a flimsy dog-proof gate, her cheeks rising with difficulty to produce the requisite glossy three-quarters of a smile.

I closed my eyes and let the image slide into my mind's burgeoning Eunice archive. But then I looked again. It wasn't Eunice's brilliantly fake smile that had struck me. There was something else. She had turned away from the äppärät lens, while one hand was forever stuck in midair trying to quickly apply a pair of sunglasses. I magnified the image by 800 percent and focused on the eye farthest from the camera. Beneath it and to one side, I saw what looked like the leathery black trace of burst capillaries. I zoomed in and out, trying to decipher the blemish on a face that would tolerate no blemishes, and eventually distinguished the imprint of two fingers, no, three fingers—index, middle, thumb—striking her across the face.

Okay, stop. Enough detective work. Enough obsessiveness. Enough trying to position yourself as the savior of a beaten girl. Let's see if I can write three pages without mentioning Eunice Park even once. Let's see if I can write about something other than my heart.

Because, when the plane's wheels finally licked the tarmac in New York, I almost failed to notice the tanks and armored personnel carriers squatting amidst the islands of sunburned grass between the runways. I nearly failed to heed the soldiers in their muddy boots running alongside our airplane as we shuddered to a premature stop, the pilot's anxious voice over the PA system drowned out by a jagged electronic hiss.

Our plane had been surrounded by what passed for the United States Army. Soon we heard the knocking against the plane's door, the stewardesses scrambling to open it to the urgent military cries outside. "What the fuck?" I asked the young jock next to me, the one who had complained about the smell of my book, but he only pressed one finger to his lips and looked away from me, as if I too radiated the stench of a short-story collection.

They were inside the first-class cabin. About nine guys wearing grimy camouflage fatigues, in their thirties mostly (too old to serve in Venezuela, I'd guess), sweat stains underneath their arms, water bottles haphazardly stapled to their bulletproof vests, M-16s cradled against their torsos, no smiles, no words. They scanned us with their large brown ghetto äppäräti for three interminable minutes, during which the American contingent remained petulantly silent while the Italians aboard began to speak in angry, assertive tones. And then it began.

They grabbed him by both arms and tried to drag him to his feet, his vast bulk passively protesting. The American passengers instantly turned away, but the Italians were already hollering: "*Que barbarico!*" and "*A cosa serve?*"

The fat ugly man's fear washed over the cabin in putrefying waves. We felt it before we even heard the sound of his voice, which, like the rest of him, did not conform to the standards of our time: was weak, helpless, despicable. "What did I do?" he was stammering. "Look at my wallet. I'm Bipartisan. Look in my wallet. I have a first-class ticket. I told the beaver everything he wanted."

I snuck a glance at the fat man's tormentors, standing evenly around him, fingers on their triggers. Their uniforms were adorned with hasty insignia, a sword superimposed over Lady Liberty's crown, which I believe denotes the New York Army National Guard. And yet I sensed these exurban white guys were from nowhere *near* New York. They were slow and unwieldy, tired-looking, as if someone had poked them in their pupils and then circled their eyes. "Your äppärät," one of them said to the fat man.

"I left it at home," the man whispered loudly, and we all knew he had lied. As the soldiers finally pulled him to his feet, the cabin filled with the sound of a grown-up's out-of-practice whimpering. I looked back to see his baggy, ill-fitting pants, too big for his oddly tiny legs. And that's all I saw or heard of the criminal passenger on United-ContinentalDeltamerican Flight 023 to New York, because somehow the soldiers had made his crying stop, and all we could hear was the slap of his loafers among the steady thump of their man-boots.

It wasn't over yet. While the Italians had begun their angry crowing about the state of our troubled nation, murmuring the name of "*il macellaio*" or "the butcher" Rubenstein, whose blood-smeared, cleaver-wielding visage could be seen in poster form on every Roman street corner, a second group of soldiers had returned to our cabin. "U.S. citizens, raise your hands," we were told.

My Ohio-shaped bald spot felt cold against the headrest of the seat. What had I done? Should I have kept my mouth shut when the otter had asked for Fabrizia's name? Should I have said, "I don't want to answer this question," as he had told me was my right? Had I been *too* compliant? Was there time to reach into my äppärät for Nettie Fine's info, so that I could present it to the Guardsmen? Would they drag me off the plane too? My parents were born in what used to be the Soviet Union, and my grandmother had survived the last years of Stalin, although barely, but I lack the genetic instinct to deal with unbridled authority. Before a greater force, I crumble. And so, as my hand began the long journey from my lap into the fear-saturated cabin air, I wanted my parents near me. I wanted my mother's hand on the back of my neck, the cool touch that always calmed me down as a child. I wanted to hear my parents' Russian spoken aloud, because I always thought of it as the language of cunning acquiescence. I wanted us to face this together, because what if they shot me as a traitor and my parents would have to hear the news from a neighbor, from a police report, from a potato-faced anchor on their favorite FoxLiberty-Ultra? "I love you," I whispered in the direction of Long Island, where my parents live. Deploying the satellite powers of my mind, I zoomed in on the undulating green roof of their humble Cape Cod house, the tiny yuan valuation floating over the equally minuscule green blot of their working-class backyard.

And then I wanted Eunice next to me, sharing these last moments. I wanted to feel her young powerlessness, my hand on her bony knees stroking the fear out of her, letting her know I was the only one who could keep her safe.

Nine of us had raised our hands. The Americans. "Take out your äppäräti." We did as we were told. No questions asked. I held out my device in a particularly supplicating gesture, like a shamed young cub showing the mess he had made in his cage. My äppärät data were sampled and scanned to a military äppärät by a young man who seemed to be missing a face beneath his cap's long green visor. All I could make out were his arms, ropy with lawnmower strength. He cocked his head at me, sighed, then looked at his watch. "All right, people, let's go!" he shouted.

The first-class cabin disembarked with great haste. We ran down the stairs and onto the cracked JFK runway, which shuddered beneath the armadas of armored personnel carriers and roving packs of luggage carts. The summer heat stroked my wet back and made me feel as if a fire had just been put out all over my body. I took out my U.S. passport and held it in my hand, fingering its embossed golden eagle, still hoping it meant something. I remember how my parents would talk about the *luck* of their having left the Soviet Union for America. Oh God, I thought, let there still be such luck in this new world.

"Please wait underneath the 'security shed,' " one of the stewardesses sobbed to us. We walked toward a strange outcropping, amidst a landscape of forlorn, aging terminals heaped atop one another like the vista of some gray Lagos slum. We surveyed the tired buildings of a prematurely old country; in the far distance, away from the tanks and armored personnel carriers, construction cranes loomed over the half-built futuristic complex of the China Southern Airlines Cargo Terminal. A tank rolled over to us, and the nine first-class Americans instinctively raised our hands. The tank stopped short; a single soldier in T-shirt and shorts popped out of the hatch and planted a highway sign next to it, black letters against an orange background:

IT IS FORBIDDEN TO ACKNOWLEDGE THE EXISTENCE OF THIS VEHICLE ("THE OBJECT") UNTIL YOU ARE .5 MILES FROM THE SECURITY PERIMETER OF JOHN F. KENNEDY INTERNATIONAL AIRPORT. BY READING THIS SIGN YOU HAVE DENIED EXISTENCE OF THE OBJECT AND IMPLIED CONSENT.
— AMERICAN RESTORATION AUTHORITY,
SECURITY DIRECTIVE IX-2.11
"TOGETHER WE'LL SURPRISE THE WORLD!"

The Italians, convinced that the worst was behind them, had already started talking about the last ten minutes as if they had been through a thrilling geopolitical adventure; the women among them were already discussing handbag shops in Nolita where they could take particular advantage of the ailing dollar. And then I realized the fat man's smell of fear had never left my nostrils, had become embedded in my trunk-like nasal hairs, the ones Eunice had gingerly pulled upon in my Roman bed while whispering, "Ugh, *so* grodacious." And then, before I knew exactly what had happened, I was sitting on the floor of the security shed, my legs sprawled out beneath me, useless, my arms prodding the new American air, as if I were a sleepwalker or an athlete doing his stretches. My passport had fallen out of my hands. The Italians were saying something sympathetic in my direction. They were quite alert to illness, those gentle ancient people. The sounds Eunice called "verballing" were escaping from my mouth, but even if you cupped my mouth with your ear you would not be able to understand a thing I was saying.

THE ONLY MAN FOR ME
FROM THE GLOBALTEENS ACCOUNT OF EUNICE PARK

JUNE 5

Format: Long-Form Standard English Text
GLOBALTEENS SUPER HINT: *Harvard Fashion School studies show excessive typing makes wrists large and unattractive. Be a GlobalTeen forever—switch to Images today!*

EUNI-TARD ABROAD *TO* GRILLBITCH:
Dear Precious Pony,
Sup, slut? I really wish you were here right now. I need someone to verbal with and Teens just ain't cutting it. I'm so confused. I went up to Lucca with Ben (the Credit guy) and he was so super nice, paid for all my meals and this gorgeous hotel room, took me for a walk around the city walls and to this insanely good osteria where everyone there knew him and we had a 200 euro wine. I kept thinking about how he would be the perfect boyfriend and I sweated his hot skinny bod. But all of a sudden I would tell him like for no reason that his feet smelled or that he was cross-eyed or his hair was receding (which was a total LIE), and he would get all intro on me, turn down the community access on his äppärät so that I wouldn't know where the fuck his mind was, and then just stare off into space. It's not like we didn't do it. We did. And it was all right. But right afterwards I started having this major bawling panic attack and he tried to comfort me, told me I looked slutty and that my Fuckability was 800+ (which it's so NOT, because I can't find anyone in Rome who can do Asian hair) but he couldn't. I feel so much shame. I feel so undeserving of being with someone like Ben and whenever we walked down the street together or some-

thing I just kept picturing him with some beautiful supermodel or some really smart but sexy Mediawhore. Someone he really deserved instead of this fucked-up girl like me.

I got another GlobalTeens from my mom saying basically my dad was at it again. Sally had to sleep in the guest room upstairs and mom had to sleep in the basement, because when he gets really drunk he can't really handle stairs, or at least you have a lot of warning when he does.

I tried to get Sally to tell me what's going on but she only said something weak, like Mom spoiled the tofu and dad's practice has been empty, so it's mom's fault, or it's his patients' fault, or anyone's fault but his. Anyway, I've been looking at cheap air tickets, because as much as I love spending that bastard's money here, I know I'm responsible for what happens to Sally and mom.

I think a part of me is falling in love with Ben, but I know it can't happen, because another, sick part of me thinks that my dad is always going to be the only man for me. Whenever something wonderful happens with Ben I suddenly start to think of all the good things my DAD did and I start to MISS him. You know like he always helped out poor Mexicans when he had his practice in California and if they didn't have insurance, which was basically always, he would just do their feet for free. I mean what if I'm the bad daughter for leaving him and going all the way to Europe? God, I'm sorry for all this verbal diarrhea. Hey, remember when we lived in Long Beach and you would sleep over? Remember my mom would wake us up at like seven in the morning the next day yelling "Iiiireo-na! Iiiireo-na! Early bird gets worm!" I miss you so much, Precious Pony.

GRILLBITCH *TO* EUNI-TARD ABROAD:

Dear Precious Panda,

Sup, betch? I got your message just as I was getting out of the car at the JuicyPussy in Topanga and I was way sad the whole time. One of the salesladies even verballed me if I were okay and I told her I was "thinking" and she was like "why?"

I don't know what to tell you. I guess parents can be really disappointing but their the only parents we have. I mean we kind of have to respect them no matter what and if they do hurtful things we should try to get out of their way and be even ten times more loving. I wish you had an older brother like I do because he takes the brunt of everything in our family. It must suck to be the older sister in a family with no mails.

Anyway, as for Ben, I think you are definately doing things just right! He doesn't know it's all because of your inner turmoil, he thinks you're just a real tough slut and that he has to work super extra hard to get you. Does his dick kinda curve down and to the side a little? Gopher's does (he's gotten his PhD—his Pretty Huge Dick!) and I was wondering if that was the case with all white boys, the curving. See what a virgin I am? Ha ha.

You know you can verbal me anytime day or night. I feel like I don't know what I'm doing half the time anyways, but I'm so glad that we can confide in each other, because the world sometimes feels so, like, I can't even describe it. It's like I'm floating around and the moment anyone gets near me or I get near anyone there's just this STATIC. Sometimes people verbal me and I just look at their mouth and it's like WHAT? What are you saying to me? How am I supposed to even verbal back and does it even matter what comes out? I mean, at least you got up and left home and went to ROME! Who does that? BTW, do they sell this brand of pop-off sheer panties called TotalSurrender in Italy? I think they're from Milan but I can't even find them on TeenyBoppers or AssLuxury. If they have navy blue I'll pay you back, I swear. You know my size, slut. I miss you so much too, Precious Panda. Come back to sunny Cali! I think I get crotch itch when I'm on the pill. What is UP with that?

JUNE 7

CHUNG.WON.PARK *TO* EUNI-TARD ABROAD:

Eunhee,

How are you today. I hope you do not worry yourself. It is nice you write to Sally. Little sister always look up to big sister. Me and Daddy went ⌐urch and we talk together to Reverend Cho. I make sorry to Daddy ⌐ime am unconsiderate of how hard he work and that he ⌐, just perfect, specially soon-dubu which is his favorite! ☺ ⌐ that if he not feel well FIRST we pray together to GOD for guide us THEN he hit. Then Reverend Cho read to us Scripture which say woman is second to man. He say man is head and woman is leg or arm. Also we pray together and specially I unclude you and Sally because you and sister are all Daddy and me have. Otherwise we never leave Korea which is now richer country than America and also not have so much political problem, but how we were to know that when we leave? Now even in Fort Lee we see tank on Center Avenue. Very scary for me, like in Korea in the 1980 long time ago when there was Kwangju trouble and many people die. I hope nothing happen in Manhattan to Sally.

So because we leave for you everything behind, you now have big responsibility to Daddy and Mommy and Sister. ☺

I just learn how to make happy sign. Do you like it? Haha. Make me pride of you and expect of you like before.

I love you always.

Mommy

EUNI-TARD ABROAD *TO* CHUNG.WON.PARK:

Mom, why don't you and Sally come here to Rome? She can take summer classes next year. We'll get a bigger apartment and I'll show you around. You deserve a break from Daddy. There's a Christian (not Catholic) church here that has services in Korean and we'll eat delicious food and just have a good time. Maybe it'll help make me more focused because I know you're safe and then I'll be able to score better on my LSAT.

Love,

Eunice

EUNI-TARD ABROAD: Sally, do you want TotalSurrender panties? They're those sheer pop-offs that Polish porn star wears on AssDoctor.

SALLYSTAR: The one with the fake hips?

EUNI-TARD ABROAD: I think so. I can't get AssDoctor on my äppärät for some reason. Nothing works in Italy.

SALLYSTAR: They're sheer so you can wear them with Onionskins.

EUNI-TARD ABROAD: Why not just wear them with regular jeans. That way you can "protect the mystery" as Mom says.

SALLYSTAR: Hahaha. Kwan says some of the FOB Korean girls in LA don't even use condoms because they want their dates to think they're virgins. And they're like 28! Christmas Cake already.

EUNI-TARD ABROAD: SICK. But I don't really get it. You sound like you're better. Everything okay?

SALLYSTAR: Dad's feeling better, I guess. He came in to sing with me in the shower.

EUNI-TARD ABROAD: IN THE SHOWER?

SALLYSTAR: No, the curtain was there. Duh.

EUNI-TARD ABROAD: But it's a plastic curtain.

SALLYSTAR: Can you get the TotalSurrenders cheaper in Italy? You know my size. Actually I'm one size fatter. Gross.

EUNI-TARD ABROAD: Stop eating so much! And don't let Daddy in the shower.

SALLYSTAR: He's not IN the shower. It's nice to sing with him. We did "Sister Christian" and the theme song from "Oral Surgeon Lee Dang Hee." Remember how angry Daddy used to get at that show? What's that noraebang we'd go to?

EUNI-TARD ABROAD: Something-something on Olympic. You should come to Rome for the summer.

SALLYSTAR: Can't. Classes. And we're going to DC next week and there's going to be more protests all thru the summer.

EUNI-TARD ABROAD: Mommy says she saw a tank in Ft. Lee. Seriously, Sally. Don't get Political. Come to Rome! There's this huge outlet mall just twenty minutes away and they have the Saaami fall collection and Juicy-Pussy's summer line and everything at least 80 percent off.

SALLYSTAR: I thought the dollar wasn't worth anything.

EUNI-TARD ABROAD: You still save. Hello, 80 percent off. Do the math, nerd!

SALLYSTAR: I can't come. I got to look out for Mommy.

EUNI-TARD ABROAD: Bring her with you!

SALLYSTAR: Eunice, how do you think you can just pull things together and make everything change and everyone happy? It doesn't work like that.

EUNI-TARD ABROAD: What should I do? Pray to Jesu that he "changes Daddy's heart"?

SALLYSTAR: You know I don't like Reverend Cho but the one lesson I learned in church is humility. This is how it is. This is who my parents are. And I should just accept my limitations and do the best I can with what God gave me. If you don't think that you'll just make yourself miserable.

EUNI-TARD ABROAD: In other words, just give up on everything and let Jesu light the way. BTW, I already AM miserable.

SALLYSTAR: I haven't given up on anything. I'm going to be a cardiologist and I'm going to make enough money so that Daddy can retire and not have to worry about smelly white feet anymore. And then we'll all feel a little better as a family maybe.

EUNI-TARD ABROAD: Yeah, I'm sure that'll solve everything.

SALLYSTAR: Thanks for approving my dreams. You're so much like Dad and you don't even know it. Stay in Rome. I don't need two of you here.

EUNI-TARD ABROAD: I didn't mean it.

SALLYSTAR: Whatever.

EUNI-TARD ABROAD: I'm very proud of you.

EUNI-TARD ABROAD: I'm the fuck up, okay?

EUNI-TARD ABROAD: Are you still there? I'll get you those TotalSurrender panties, but you're on your own with the nippleless bra.

EUNI-TARD ABROAD: Sally! You know when you just cut me off like that you really make me sad.

EUNI-TARD ABROAD: You know I would do anything to make you and Mommy happy. Maybe I really WILL go to law school and I'll work in High End Retail and we can buy Mommy her own apartment in Manhattan so that she can be safe.

EUNI-TARD ABROAD: I'm coming home, Sally. Hello? As soon as I find a cheap ticket, I'm coming home.

JUNE 6

Dear Diary,

Here's a message from Joshie that popped up on my äppärät right after my ordeal at JFK:

> DEAR RHESUS MONKEY, U BACK YET? LOTS OF POSITIVE CHANGES **AND CUTBACKS** HERE; FEEL FREE TO REMAIN ROME AS YOU FEEL NEED; FUTURE SALARY & EMPLOYMENT = LET'S DISCUSS.

What the hell was this? Was Joshie Goldmann, employer and ersatz papa, about to fire me? Had he sent me to Europe just to get me out of the way?

I still have an old Mead Five Star notebook from when I was a child, which I've been dying to put to good use. So I ripped out an actual sheet of paper from it, put it on my coffee table, and started writing this out by hand.

STRATEGY FOR SHORT-TERM SURVIVAL AND
THEN IMMORTALITY FOLLOWING RETURN TO
NEW YORK AFTER EUROPEAN FIASCO
By Lenny Abramov, B.A., M.B.A.

1) Work Hard for Joshie—Show you matter at the workplace; show you're not just a teacher's pet, but a creative thinker and

Content Provider; make excuses for poor performance in Europe; get raise; lower spending; save money for initial dechronification treatments; double own lifespan in twenty years and then just keep going at it exponentially until you gain the momentum to achieve Indefinite Life Extension.

2) Make Joshie Protect You—Evoke father-like bond in response to political situation. Talk about what happened on the plane; evoke Jewish feelings of terror and injustice.

3) Love Eunice—Even if she's far away, try to think of her as a potential partner; meditate on her freckles and make yourself feel loved by her to lower stress levels and feel less alone. Let the potential of her sweetness enhance your happiness!!! Then beg her to come to New York and let her become, in short order, reluctant lover, cautious companion, pretty young wife.

4) Care for Your Friends—Meet up with them right after you see Joshie and try to re-create a sense of community with BFFs Noah and Vishnu.

5) Be Nice to Parents (Within Limits)—They may be mean to you but they represent your past and who you are. 5a) Seek Similarities with Parents—they grew up in a dictatorship and one day you might be living in one too!!!

6) Celebrate What You Have—You're not as bad off as some people. Think of that poor fat man on the plane (where is he now? what are they doing to him?) and feel happy by comparison.

I folded the paper up and put it into my wallet for easy reference. "Now," I said to myself, "go make it happen!"

First, I Celebrated What I Have (Point No. 6). I began with the 740 square feet that form my share of Manhattan Island. I live in the last middle-class stronghold in the city, high atop a red-brick ziggurat that a Jewish garment workers' union had erected on the banks of the East River back in the days when Jews sewed clothes for a living. Say what you will, these ugly co-ops are full of authentic old people who have real stories to tell (although these stories are often meandering and hard to follow; e.g., who on earth was this guy "Dillinger"?).

Then I celebrated my Wall of Books. I counted the volumes on my twenty-foot-long modernist bookshelf to make sure none had been misplaced or used as kindling by my subtenant. "You're my sacred ones," I told the books. "No one but me still cares about you. But I'm going to keep you with me forever. And one day I'll make you important again." I thought about that terrible calumny of the new generation: that books *smell*. And yet, in preparation for the eventual arrival of Eunice Park, I decided to be safe and sprayed some Pine-Sol Wild Flower Blast in the vicinity of my tomes, fanning the atomized juices with my hands in the direction of their spines. Then I celebrated my other possessions, the modular-design furniture and sleek electronica and the mid-1950s Corbusier-inspired dresser stuffed with mementos of past relationships, some pretty racy and scented with nether regions, others doused in the kind of sadness that I should really learn to let go. I celebrated the difficult-to-assemble balcony table (one leg still too short) and had a pretty awful non-Roman coffee *al fresco,* looking out on the busy downtown skyline some twenty blocks away from me, military and civilian choppers streaming past the overblown spire of the "Freedom" Tower and all that other glittering downtown hoo-hah. I celebrated the low-rise housing projects crowding my immediate view, the so-called Vladeck Houses, which stand in red-brick solidarity with my own co-ops, not exactly proud of themselves, but feeling resigned and necessary, their thousands of residents primed for summer warmth, and, if I may speculate, summer love. Even from a distance of a hundred feet, I can sometimes hear the pained love-cries their residents make behind their tattered Puerto Rican flags, and sometimes their violent screams.

With love in mind, I decided to celebrate the season. For me the transition from May to June is marked by the radical switch from knee to ankle socks. I slapped on white linen pants, a speckled Penguin shirt, and comfy Malaysian sneakers, so that I easily resembled many of the nonagenarians in my building. My co-ops are part of a

NORC—a Naturally Occurring Retirement Community—a kind of instant Florida for those too frail or poor to relocate to Boca in time for their deaths. Down by the elevator, surrounded by withered NORCers in motorized wheelchairs and their Jamaican caregivers, I counted the daily carnage of the Death Board by the elevators. Five residents of the NORC had passed in the last two days alone. The woman who had lived above me, eightysomething Naomi Margolis in E-707, was gone, and her son David Margolis was inviting her eclectic neighbors—the young Media and Credit professionals, the old widowed socialist seamstresses, and the ever-multiplying Orthodox Jews—to "celebrate her memory" at his house in Teaneck, New Jersey. I admired Mrs. Margolis for living as long as she did, but once you give in to the idea that a memory is somehow a substitute for a human being, you may as well give up on Indefinite Life Extension. I guess you can say that, while admiring Mrs. Margolis, I also *hated* Mrs. Margolis. Hated her for giving up on life, for letting the waves come and recede, her withered body in tow. Maybe I hated all the old people in my building, and wished them to disappear already so that I could focus on my own struggle with mortality.

In my trendy old-man's getup, I ambled with easy grace down Grand Street toward the East River Park, stepping on each curb with the profound "oy" that is the call-and-response of my neighborhood. I sat on my favorite bench, next to the stocky, splay-footed realism of the Williamsburg Bridge's anchorage, noticing how part of the structure looked like a bunch of stacked milk crates. I celebrated the teenaged mothers from the Vladeck Houses tending to their children's boo-boos ("A bee touched me, Mommy!"). I relished hearing language actually being *spoken* by children. Overblown verbs, explosive nouns, beautifully bungled prepositions. Language, not data. How long would it be before these kids retreated into the dense clickety-clack äppärät world of their absorbed mothers and missing fathers?

Then I caught sight of a healthy-looking old Chinese woman ripe for celebration and, at the speed of half a furlong an hour, tailed her down Grand Street and then East Broadway, watching her feel up exotic tubers and slap around some silvery fish. She was shopping with suburban abandon, buying everything that came within her grasp and then, after each purchase, running over to stand next to one of the wooden telegraph poles that now lined the streets.

My fashion friend Sandi in Rome had told me about the Credit Poles, yapping on about their cool retro design, the way the wood was intentionally gnarled in places and how the utility wire was replaced by strings of colored lights. The old-fashioned appearance of the Poles was obviously meant to evoke a sturdier time in our nation's history, except for the little LED counters at eye level that registered your Credit ranking as you walked by. Atop the Poles, American Restoration Authority signs billowed in several languages. In the Chinatown parts of East Broadway, the signs read in English and Chinese—"America Celebrates Its Spenders!"—with a cartoon of a miserly ant happily running toward a mountain of wrapped Christmas presents. In the Latino sections on Madison Street, they read in English and Spanish—"Save It for a Rainy Day, Huevón"—with a frowning grasshopper in a zoot suit showing us his empty pockets. Alternate signs read in all three languages:

> The Boat Is Full
> Avoid Deportation
> Latinos Save
> Chinese Spend
> ALWAYS Keep Your Credit Ranking Within Limits
> AMERICAN RESTORATION AUTHORITY
> "TOGETHER WE'LL SURPRISE THE WORLD!"

I felt the perfunctory liberal chill at seeing entire races of human beings so summarily reduced and stereotyped, but was also voyeuristically interested in seeing people's Credit rankings. The old Chinese woman had a decent 1400, but others, the young Latina mothers, even a profligate teenaged Hasid puffing down the street, were showing blinking red scores below 900, and I worried for them. I walked past one of the Poles, letting it zap the data off my äppärät, and saw my own score, an impressive 1520. But there was a blinking red asterisk next to the score.

Was the otter still flagging me?

I sent a GlobalTeens message to Nettie Fine, but got a chilling "RECIPIENT DELETED" in response. What could that mean? No one *ever* gets deleted from GlobalTeens. I tried to GlobalTrace her but got an even more frightening "RECIPIENT UNTRACEABLE/INACTIVE." What kind of person couldn't be found on this earth?

Back in Rome, I used to meet Sandi for lunch at da Tonino and we'd talk about what we missed the most about Manhattan. For me it was fried pork-and-scallion dumplings on Eldridge Street, for him bossy older black women at the gas company or the unemployment office who called him "honey" and "sugar" and sometimes "baby." He said it wasn't a gay thing, but, rather, that these black women made him feel calm and at ease, as if he had momentarily won the love and mothering of a complete stranger.

I guess that's what I wanted right now, with Nettie Fine "INACTIVE," with Eunice six time zones away, with the Credit Poles reducing everyone to a simple three-digit numeral, with an innocent fat man dragged off a plane, with Joshie telling me "future salary & employment = let's discuss": a little love and mothering.

I stalked up and down the eastern part of Grand Street, trying to get my bearings, trying to re-establish my hold on the place. But it wasn't just the Credit Poles. The neighborhood had changed since I left for Rome a year ago. All the meager businesses I remember were still there, decayed linoleum places with names like the A-OK Pizza Shack, frequented by poor patrons who pawed at the keyboard of an old computer terminal while smearing their faces with pizza oils, a moldy 1988 ten-volume edition of *The New Book of Popular Science* stacked in the corner, awaiting customers who could read. But there was an added aimlessness to the population, the unemployed men staggering down the chicken-bone-littered street as if drunk off a pint of grain alcohol and not just a bevy of Negra Modelos, their face blunted beneath the kind of depressive affect that I usually associate with my father. An angelic seven-year-old girl in braids was shouting into her äppärät: "Nex' time I see her ass I'm gonna punch that nigga in the stomach!" An old Jewish woman from my co-ops had fallen on the sun-baked asphalt, and her friends had made a protective scrim around her as she spun around like a turtle. By the razor-wired fence delineating a failed luxury-condo development, a drunk in a frilly guayabera shirt pulled down his pants and began to evacuate. I've seen this particular gent publicly crapping before, but the pained expression on his face, the way he rubbed his naked haunches while he shat, as if the June heat wasn't enough to keep them warm, the staggering grunts he spat at the direction of our city's cloud-streaked harbor skies, made me feel as if my native street was slipping away from me, falling into the East River, falling into a new time wrinkle where we would all drop our pants and dump furiously on the motherland.

An armored personnel carrier bearing the insignia of the New York Army National Guard was parked astride a man-sized pothole at the busy intersection of Essex and Delancey, a roof-mounted .50-caliber Browning machine gun rotating 180 degrees, back and forth, like a retarded metronome along the busy but peaceable Lower East Side streetscape. Traffic was frozen all across Delancey Street. Silent traffic, for no one dared to use a horn against the military vehicle. The street corner emptied around me until I stood alone, staring down the barrel of a gun like an idiot. I lifted up my hands in panic and directed my feet to scram.

My celebrations were turning sour. I took out the list I had written by hand and decided to make immediate use of Point No. 2 (Make Joshie Protect You). By a recently shuttered Bowery scones-and-libations establishment called Povertea, I found a cab and directed it to the Upper East Side lair of my second father.

The Post-Human Services division of the Staatling-Wapachung Corporation is housed in a former Moorish-style synagogue near Fifth Avenue, a tired-looking building dripping with arabesques, kooky buttresses, and other crap that brings to mind a lesser Gaudí. Joshie bought it at auction for a mere eighty thousand dollars when the congregation folded after being bamboozled by some kind of Jewish pyramid scheme years ago.

The first thing I noticed upon my return was the familiar smell. Heavy use of a special hypoallergenic organic air freshener is encouraged at Post-Human Services, because the scent of immortality is complex. The supplements, the diet, the constant shedding of blood and skin for various physical tests, the fear of the metallic components found in most deodorants, create a curious array of post-mortal odors, of which "sardine breath" is the most benign.

With one or two exceptions, I haven't made any work-time buddies at Post-Human Services since I turned thirty. It's not easy being friends with some twenty-two-year-old who cries over his fasting blood-glucose level or sends out a GroupTeen with his adrenal-stress index and a smiley face. When the graffito in the bathroom reads "Lenny Abramov's insulin levels are whack," there is a certain undeniable element of one-upmanship, which, in turn, raises the cortisol levels associated with stress and encourages cellular breakdown.

Still, when I walked through the door I expected to recognize *someone*. The synagogue's gilded main sanctuary was filled by young men and women dressed with angry post-college disregard, but projecting from somewhere between the eyes the message that they were the personification of that old Whitney Houston number I've mentioned before, that they, the children, were *de facto* the future. We had enough employees at Post-Human Services to repopulate the original Twelve Tribes of Israel, which were handily represented by the stained-glass windows of the sanctuary. How dull we looked in their ocean-blue glare.

The ark where the Torahs are customarily stashed had been taken out, and in its place hung five gigantic Solari schedule boards Joshie had rescued from various Italian train stations. Instead of the *arrivi* and *partenze* times of trains pulling in and out of Florence or Milan, the flip board displayed the names of Post-Human Services employees, along with the results of our latest physicals, our methylation and homocysteine levels, our testosterone and estrogen, our fasting insulin and triglycerides, and, most important, our "mood + stress indicators," which were always supposed to read "positive/playful/ready to contribute" but which, with enough input from competitive co-workers, could be changed to "one moody betch today" or "not a team playa this month." On this particular day, the black-and-white flaps were turning madly, the letters and numbers mutating—a droning ticka-ticka-ticka-ticka—to form new words and figures, as one unfortunate Aiden M. was lowered from "overcoming loss of loved one" to "letting personal life interfere with job" to "doesn't play well with others." Disturbingly enough, several of my former colleagues, including my fellow Russian, the brilliantly manic-depressive Vasily Greenbaum, were marked by the dreaded legend TRAIN CANCELED.

As for me, I wasn't even listed.

I positioned myself in the middle of the sanctuary to a spot beneath The Boards, trying to make myself a part of the soft jabber around me. "Hi," I said. And with a splash of the arms: "Lenny Abramov!" But my words disappeared into the new soundproofed wood paneling while various configurations of young people, some arm in arm, as if on a casual date, swooped through the sanctuary, headed for the Soy Kitchen or the Eternity Lounge, leaving me to hear the words "Soft Policy" and "Harm Reduction," "ROFLAARP," "PRGV," "TIMATOV," and "butt-plugging Rubenstein," and, attendant with female laughter, "Rhesus Monkey." My nickname! Someone had recognized my special relationship to Joshie, the fact that I used to be important around here.

It was Kelly Nardl. My darling Kelly Nardl. A supple, low-slung girl my age whom I would be terminally attracted to if I could stand to spend my life within three meters of her nondeodorized animal scent. She welcomed me with a kiss on both cheeks, as if she were the one just returned from Europe, and took me by the hand toward her bright, clean wedge of a desk in what used to be the cantor's office. "I'm going to make you a plate of cruciferous vegetables,

baby," she said, and that sentence alone halved my fears. They don't
fire you after they feed you flowering cabbage at Post-Human Services. Vegetables are a sign of respect. Then again, Kelly was an exception to the hard-edged types around here, Louisiana-bred for
kindness and gentility, a younger, less hysterical Nettie Fine (may
she be alive and well, wherever she is).

I stood behind her as she dotted golden cress along steppes of Sibe-
rian kale. I rested my hands on her solid shoulders, breathed in her
sour vitality. She leaned her hot cheek against one of my wrists, a motion so familiar it seemed to me we had been related even before this
lifetime. Her pale, blooming thighs spread beyond a modest pair of
khaki shorts, and I remembered again to *celebrate,* in this case, every
inch of Kelly's imperfection. "Hey," I said, "Vasily Greenbaum's train
got canceled? He played the guitar and could speak a little Arabic. He
was *so* 'ready to contribute' when he wasn't totally depressed."

"He turned forty last month," Kelly sighed. "Didn't make quo-
tas."

"I'm almost forty too," I said. "And why isn't my name up on
The Boards?"

Kelly didn't say anything. She was parsing cauliflower with a dull
safety knife, moisture beading her white forehead. Kelly and I had
once shared an entire bottle of wine—or "resveratrol," as we Post-
Humans like to call it—at a tapas bar in Brooklyn, and after walking her to her violent Bushwick tenement I wondered if I could one
day fall in love with a woman so unobtrusively, compulsively decent
(answer: no).

"So who's still around from the old gang?" I asked, voice atrem-
ble. "I didn't see Jami Pilsner's name. Or Irene Po. Are they just
going to fire all of us?"

"Howard Shu's doing fine," Kelly told me. "Got promoted."

"Great," I said. Of all the people still employed, it had to be that
sleek 124-pound bastard Shu, my classmate at NYU who had bested
me for the last dozen years in all of life's gruesome contests. If you
ask me, there's a little something sad about the employees of Post-
Human Services, and to me brash, highly functional Howard Shu is

the personification of that sadness. The truth is, we may think of ourselves as the future, but we are not. We are servants and apprentices, not immortal clients. We hoard our yuan, we take our nutritionals, we prick ourselves and bleed and measure that dark-purple liquid a thousand different ways, we do everything but pray, but in the end we are still marked for death. I could commit my genome and proteome to heart, I could wage nutritional war against my faulty apo E4 allele until I turn myself into a walking cruciferous vegetable, but nothing will cure my main genetic defect:

My father is a janitor from a poor country.

Howard Shu's dad hawks miniature turtles in Chinatown. Kelly Nardl is rich, but hardly rich enough. The scale of wealth we grew up with no longer applies.

Kelly's äppärät lit up the air around her, and she was plunged into the needs of a hundred clients. After the daily decadence of Rome, our offices looked spare. Everything bathed in soft colors and the healthy glow of natural wood, office equipment covered in Chernobyl-style sarcophagi when not in use, alpha-wave stimulators hidden behind Japanese screens, stroking our overactive brains with calming rays. Little framed humorous hints scattered throughout. "Just Say No to Starch." "Cheer Up! Pessimism Kills." "Telomere-Extended Cells Do It Better." "NATURE HAS A LOT TO LEARN FROM US." And, fluttering in the wind above Kelly Nardl's desk, a wanted poster showing a cartoon hippie being whacked over the head with a stalk of broccoli:

WANTED
For electron stealing
DNA killing
Malicious cellular damage

ABBIE "FREE RADICAL" HOFFMAN
WARNING: Subject may be armed and dangerous
Do not attempt to apprehend
Call authorities immediately and increase intake
of the coenzyme Q10

"Maybe I'll go to my desk," I said to Kelly.

"Honey," she said, her long fingers around my own. You could drown a kitten in her blue eyes.

"Oh God," I said. "Don't tell me."

"You don't have a desk. I mean, someone's taken it. This new kid from Brown-Yonsei. *Darryl*, I think."

"Where's Joshie?" I said automatically.

"Flying back from D.C." She checked her äppärät. "His jet broke down, so he's going commercial. He'll be back around lunchtime."

"What do I do?" I whispered.

"It would help," she said, "if you looked a little younger. Take care of yourself. Go to the Eternity Lounge. Put some Lexin-DC concentrate under your eyes."

The Eternity Lounge was crammed full of smelly young people checking their äppäräti or leaning back on couches with their faces up to the ceiling, de-stressing, breathing right. The even, nutty aroma of brewing green tea snuck a morsel of nostalgia into my general climate of fear. I was there when we first put in the Eternity Lounge, five years ago, in what used to be the synagogue's banqueting hall. It had taken Howard Shu and me three years just to get the brisket smell out.

"Hi," I said to anyone who would listen. I looked at the couches, but there was hardly a place to squeeze in. I took out my äppärät, but noticed that the new kids all had the new pebble-like model around their necks, the kind Eunice had worn. At least three of the young women in the room were gorgeous in a way that transcended their physicality and made their smooth, ethnically indeterminate skin and sad brown eyes stretch back to earliest Mesopotamia.

I went to the mini-bar where the unsweetened green tea was dispensed, along with the alkalinized water and 231 daily nutritionals. As I was about to hit the fish oils and cucrumins that keep inflammation at bay, somebody laughed at me, a feminine laughter and thus all the more damning. Casually scattered atop the luxuriant couches, my co-workers looked like the characters from a comedy show about young people in Manhattan I remembered watching compulsively when I was growing up. "Just got back from a year in Roma," I said, trying to pump the bravado into my voice. "All carbs over there. Need to stock up on the essentials like a *cuh*-razy person. Good to be back, guys!"

Silence. But as I turned back to the supplements, someone said, "What's shaking, Rhesus Monkey?"

It was a kid with a small outbreak of mustache and a gray body-suit with the words SUK DIK stenciled across the breast, some kind of red bandana strung around his neck. Probably Darryl from Brown, the one who had taken my desk. He couldn't have been more than twenty-five. I smiled at him, looked at my äppärät, sighed as if I had too much work ahead of me, and then began to casually leave the Eternity Lounge.

"Where you going, Rhesus?" he asked, blocking my exit with his scraggly, tight-butted body, shoving his äppärät in my face, the rich organic smell of him clouding my nostrils. "Don't you want to do some blood work for us, buddy? I'm seeing triglycerides clocking in at 135. That's *before* you ran away to Europe like a little bitch." There was more hooting in the background, the women clearly enjoying this toxic banter.

I backed away, mumbling, "One thirty-five is still within the range." What was that acronym Eunice had used? "JBF," I said. "I'm just butt-fucking." There was more laughter, a flash of pewter chin in the background, the shine of hairless hands bearing sleek technological pendants full of right data. Momentarily, I saw Chekhov's prose before my eyes, his description of the Moscow merchant's son Laptev, who "knew that he was ugly, and now he felt as though he was conscious of his ugliness all over his body."

And still the cornered animal in me fought back. "Duder," I said, remembering what the rude young man on the airplane had called me when he complained about the smell of my book. "Duder, I can *feel* your anger. I'll take a blood test, no prob, but while we're at it, okay, let's just measure your cortisol and epinephrine levels. I'm going to put your stress levels up on The Boards. You're not playing well with others."

But no one heard my righteous words. The sweat glistening off my caveman forehead spelled it all out for them. An open invitation. Let the young eat the old. The SUK DIK guy actually pushed me until I felt the cold of the Eternity Lounge wall against the sparseness of my hair. He shoved his äppärät into my face. It was flashing my open-sourced blood work from a year ago.

"How dare you just waltz back here like that with that body mass index of yours?" he said. "You think you're just going to take one of our desks? After doing fuck-all in Italy for a year? We know all about you, Monkey. I'm going to shove a carb-filled macaroon up your ass unless you skedaddle *right now.*"

A gigantic sitcom cheer rose up behind him—a huge *wooooo* of happy anger and joyous consternation, the assertion of the tribe over its weakest member.

Two and a half heartbeats later, the hooting abruptly ceased.

I heard the murmur of His Name and the clip-clop of his approach. The boisterous crowd was parting, the SUK DIK warriors slinking away, those Darryls and Heaths.

And there he was. Younger than before. The initial dechronification treatments—the beta treatments, as we called them—already coursing through him. His face unlined and harmoniously still, except for that thick nose, which twitched uncontrollably at times, some muscle group gone haywire. His ears stood beside his shorn head like two sentinels.

Joshie Goldmann never revealed his age, but I surmised he was in his late sixties: a sixtysomething man with a mustache as black as eternity. In restaurants he had sometimes been mistaken for my handsomer brother. We shared the same unappreciated jumble of meaty lips and thick eyebrows and chests that barreled forward like a terrier's, but that's where it ended. Because when Joshie looked at you, when he lowered his gaze at you, the heat would rise in your cheeks and you would find yourself oddly, irrevocably, present.

"Oh, Leonard," he said, sighing and shaking his head. "Those guys giving you a hard time? Poor Rhesus. Come on. Let's talk." I shyly followed him as he walked upstairs (no elevators, *never*) to his office. Hobbled, I should say. There is a problem with Joshie's skeleton which he has never discussed, which makes him balance uncertainly from foot to foot, walk in segments and fits and starts, as if a Philip Glass piece were playing commandingly behind him.

His office was packed with a dozen young staffers I hadn't seen before, all chatting at once. "Homies," he said to his acolytes, "can I get a minute here? We'll get right back into it. Just one moment." Collective sigh. They trooped past me, surprised, agitated, bemused, their äppäräti already projecting data about me, perhaps telling them how little I meant, my thirty-nine-year-old obsolescence.

He ran his hand through the fullness of hair at my nape and turned my head around. "So much gray," he said.

I almost stepped away from his touch. What had Eunice told me in one of our last moments together? *You're old, Len.* But instead I allowed him to examine me closely, even as I scrutinized the sharp, eagle profile of his chest, the muscular presence of his Nettie Fine–caliber nose, the uneasy balance he held over the earth beneath him. His hand was deep into my scalp, and his fingers felt uncharacteristically cold. "So much gray," he said again.

"It's the pasta carbs," I stammered. "And the stressors of Italian life. Believe it or not, it's not easy over there when you're living on an American's salary. The dollar—"

"What's your pH level?" Joshie interrupted.

"Oh boy," I said. The branch shadows of a superb oak tree were creeping up to the window, gracing Joshie's shaven dome with a pair of antlers. The windows of this part of the former synagogue were designed to form the outline of the Ten Commandments. Joshie's office was on the top floor, the words "You Shall Have No Other Gods Before Me" still stenciled into the window in English and Hebrew. "Eight point nine," I said.

"You need to detoxify, Len."

I could hear a clamor outside his door. Eager voices pushing one another aside for his attention, the day's business spread out like the endless corridors of data sweeping around Manhattan. On Joshie's desk, a smooth piece of glass, a sleek digital frame, showed us a slide show of his life—young Joshie dressed up like a maharajah during his short-lived one-man Off Broadway show, happy Buddhists at the Laotian temple his funds had rebuilt from scratch beseeching the camera on their knees, Joshie in a conical straw hat smiling irresistibly during his brief tenure as a soy farmer.

"I'm going to drink fifteen cups of alkalized water a day," I said.

"Your male pattern baldness worries me."

I laughed. I actually said "ha ha." "It worries me too, Grizzly Bear," I said.

"I'm not talking aesthetics here. All that Russian Jewish testosterone is being turned right into dihydrotestosterone. That's killer stuff. Prostate cancer down the road. You'll need at least eight hundred milligrams of saw palmetto a day. What's wrong, Rhesus? You look like you're going to cry."

But I just wanted to listen to him take care of me some more. I wanted him to pay close attention to my dihydrotestosterone and to rescue me from the beautiful bullies in the Eternity Lounge. Joshie has always told Post-Human Services staff to keep a diary, to remember who we *were*, because every moment our brains and synapses are being rebuilt and rewired with maddening disregard for our personalities, so that each year, each month, each day we transform into a different person, an utterly unfaithful iteration of our original selves, of the drooling kid in the sandbox. But not me. I am still a facsimile of my early childhood. I am still looking for a loving dad to lift me up and brush the sand off my ass and to hear English, calm and hurtless, fall off his lips. My parents had been raised by Nettie Fine, why couldn't I be raised by Joshie? "I think I'm in love with this girl," I sputtered.

"Talk to me."

"She's super-young. Super-healthy. Asian. Life expectancy—very high."

"You know how I feel about love," Joshie said. The clamoring voices outside were switching from impatience to a deep, teenaged unhappiness.

"You don't think I should get romantically involved?" I asked. "Because I could stop."

"I'm kidding, Lenny," he said, punching my shoulder, painfully—underestimating his new youthful strength. "Jeez, unwind a little. Love is great for pH, ACTH, LDL, whatever ails you. As long as it's a good, *positive* love, without suspicion or hostility. Now, what you got to do is make this healthy Asian girl need *you* the way you need *me*."

"Don't let me die, Joshie," I said. "I need the dechronification treatments. Why isn't my name up on The Boards?"

"Things are about to change, Monkey," Joshie said. "If you followed CrisisNet hourly in Rome like you were supposed to, you'd know exactly what I'm talking about."

"The dollar?" I said hesitantly.

"Forget the dollar. It's just a symptom. This country makes nothing. Our assets are worthless. The northern Europeans are figuring out how to decouple from our economy, and once the Asians turn off the cash spigot we're through. And, you know what? This is all going to be great for Post-Human Services! Fear of the Dark Ages, that *totally* raises our profile. Maybe the Chinese or the Singaporeans will buy us outright. Howard Shu speaks some Mandarin. Maybe you should take some Mandarin classes. *Ni hao* and all that jazz."

"I'm sorry if I let you down by going to Rome for so long," I near-whispered. "I thought maybe I could understand my parents better if I lived in Europe. Spend some time thinking about immortality in a really old place. Read some books. Get some thoughts down."

Joshie turned away from me. From this angle, I could see another side to him, the slight gray stubble protruding from his perfect egg of a chin—the slight intimations that not *all* of him could be reverse-engineered into immortality. Yet.

"Those thoughts, these books, they *are* the problem, Rhesus," he said. "You have to stop thinking and start selling. That's why all those young whizzes in the Eternity Lounge want to shove a carb-filled macaroon up your ass. Yes, I overheard that. I have a new beta eardrum.

And who can blame them, Lenny? You remind them of death. You remind them of a different, earlier version of our species. Don't get pissed at me, now. Remember, I started out just like you. Acting. The humanities. It's the Fallacy of Merely Existing. FME. There'll be plenty of time to ponder and write and act out later. Right now you've got to *sell to live.*"

The floodwater was rising. The bill had come due. I was unworthy, always unworthy. "I'm so selfish, Grizzly Bear. I wish I could have found some more HNWIs for you in Europe. Jesus Christ. Do I still have a job?"

"Let's get you readjusted here," Joshie said. He touched my shoulder briefly as he headed for the door. "I can't get you a desk right away, but I can assign you to Intakes in the Welcome Center." A demotion from my previous position, but tolerable, as long as the salary stayed the same. "We need to get you a new äppärät," he said. "You're going to have to learn to surf the data streams better. Learn to rank people quicker."

I remembered Point No. 2: *Evoke father-like bond in response to political situation. Talk about what happened on the plane; evoke Jewish feelings of terror and injustice.* "Joshie," I said. "You should always have your äppärät on you. This poor fat man on the plane—"

But he was already out the door, throwing me a brief look that commanded me to follow. The hordes of Brown-Yonsei and Reed-Fudan graduates were upon him, each trying to outdo the others in informality ("Joshster! Budnik!" "*Papi chulo!*"), each holding in his or her hands the solution to all the problems of our world. He gave them tiny bits of himself. He tousled hair. "G'wan, you!" he said to a Jamaican-seeming guy who, when you cut right down to it, was not Jamaican. I realized we were heading downstairs, over to the untamed oasis of Human Resources, straight to Howard Shu's desk.

Shu, a goddamn relentless immigrant in the mode of my janitor father but with English and good board scores on his side, was dealing with three äppäräti at once, his callused fingertips and spitfire Chinatown diction abuzz with data and the strong, dull hope that he was squarely in control. He reminded me of the time I went to a conference on longevity in some provincial Chinese city. I landed at a just-built airport as beautiful as a coral reef and no less complex, took one look at the scurrying masses, the gleaming insanity in their eyes, at least three men by the taxi ranks trying to sell me a sophisticated new nose-hair trimmer (was this what New York had been like at the start of the twentieth century?), and thought, "Gentlemen, the world is yours."

To make matters worse, Shu was not unhandsome, and when he and Joshie high-fived each other, I felt the pureness of envy, an emotion that numbed my feet and shorted my breath. "Take care of Len here," Joshie said to Howard Shu, with just a thimble of conviction. "Remember, he's an OG." I hoped he meant Original Gangster and not Old Guy. And then, before I could laugh at his youthful demeanor, at his easy ways, Joshie was gone, headed back into the open arms that would receive him wherever, whenever he felt the need of their embrace.

I sat down across from Howard Shu and tried to radiate indifference. From behind the helmet of his lustrous black hair, Shu did the same. "Leonard," he said, his button nose aglow, "I'm pulling up your file."

"Please do."

"You're being docked 239,000 yuan-pegged dollars," Shu said.

"What?"

"Your expenses in Europe. You flew first-class everywhere. Thirteen thousand northern euros' worth of resveratrol?"

"It was no more than two glasses a day. Red wine only."

"That's twenty euros a glass. And what the hell is a bidet?"

"I was just trying to do my job, Howard. You can't possibly—"

"Please," he said. "You did nothing. You fucked around. Where are the clients? What happened to that sculptor who was 'in the bag'?"

"I don't appreciate your tone."

"And I don't appreciate your inability to do your job."

"I tried to sell the Product, but the Europeans weren't interested.

They're totally skeptical about our technology. And some of them actually *want* to die."

The immigrant eyes glared at me. "No free pass, Leonard. No hiding behind Joshie's goodwill. You get your act together or we'll be conducting exit interviews. You can keep your previous salary level, we'll put you in Intakes, and you're paying for every last meatball you ate in Rome."

I looked behind me. "Don't look behind you," Shu said. "Your papa's gone. And what the *fuck* is this?" A red code was flashing amidst the steady chrome äppärät data. "American Restoration Authority says you were flagged at the embassy in Rome. Now you got the ARA on your tail? What the hell did you do?"

The world took another spin and then a tumble. "Nothing!" I cried. "Nothing! I didn't try to help the fat man. And I don't know any Somalians. I slept with Fabrizia only a few times. The otter got it all wrong. It's all a scam. The guy videotaped me on the plane and I said 'Why?' And now I can't contact Nettie Fine. Do you know what they've done to her? Her GlobalTeens address is deleted. I can't GlobalTrace her either."

"Otter? Nettie *what*? It says here 'malicious provision of incomplete data.' Fuck it, another mess for me to clean up. Let me see your äppärät. Good fucking Christ. What is this, an iPhone?" He spoke into the cuff of his shirt: "Kelly, bring me a new äppärät for Abramov. Bill it to Intakes."

"I knew it," I said. "It's my äppärät's fault. I just told Joshie that he should always have his on him. Fucking Restoration Authority."

"Joshie doesn't need an äppärät," Shu said. "Joshie doesn't need a *damn* thing." He stared at me with what could have been unimaginable pity or unimaginable hatred, but in either case involved perfect animal stillness. Kelly Nardl came huffing up the stairs with a new äppärät box that was itself a rainbow of blinking data and noise, a nasal Mid-Atlantic voice somehow embedded in the cardboard promising me "Duh berry ladest in RateMe tech-nah-luh-gee."

"Thanks," Shu said, and waved Kelly away. Seven years ago, be-

fore the mighty Staatling-Wapachung Corporation bought Joshie
out for a grotesque sum of money, Kelly, Howard, and I used to oc-
cupy the same rung of what was then called a "flat organization,"
one without titles or hierarchies. I tried to catch Kelly's eye, to get
her on my side against this monster who couldn't even pronounce
the word "bidet" properly, but she fled Howard's desk with nary
a shake of her friendly backside. "Learn how to use this thing *immediately*," Shu told me. "Especially the RateMe part. Learn to rate
everyone around you. Get your data in order. Switch on CrisisNet
and follow all the latest. An ill-informed salesman is dead in the
water these days. Get your mind in the right place. Then we'll see
about putting your name back on The Boards. That's all, Leonard."

It was still the lunch hour by my calculations. I went over to the
East River with the äppärät package continuously hollering under
my arm. I watched unmarked boats bristling with armaments form
a gray naval chain from the Triborough down to the Williamsburg
Bridge. According to Media, the Chinese Central Banker was coming to take the lay of our indebted land in about two weeks, and security all over Manhattan would be profound for his visit. I sat
down on a hard, wiry chair and stared at the impressive all-glass
beta skyline of Queens, built way before our last dollar devaluation.
I opened the box and took out the smooth pebble of the new äppärät, felt it already warm in my hand. An Asian woman of Eunice's
caliber projected herself at eye level. "Hello," she said. "Welcome to
äppärät 7.5 with RateMe Plus. Would you like to get started? Would
you like to get started? Would you like to get started? Just say 'yes'
and we can get started."

I owed Howard Shu 239,000 yuan-pegged dollars. My first stab
at dechronification—gone. My hair would continue to gray, and
then one day it would fall out entirely, and then, on a day meaninglessly close to the present one, meaninglessly *like* the present
one, I would disappear from the earth. And all these emotions, all
these yearnings, all these *data,* if that helps to clinch the enormity
of what I'm talking about, would be gone. And that's what immortality means to me, Joshie. It means selfishness. My generation's be-

lief that each one of us matters more than you or anyone else would think.

There was a commotion on the water, a needed distraction. With a burble of warm white spray behind it, a northbound seaplane took off so gracefully, so seemingly free of mechanics and despair, that for a moment I imagined all our lives would just go on forever.

THE NEXT PLANE HOME
FROM THE GLOBALTEENS ACCOUNT OF EUNICE PARK

JUNE 9

CHUNG.WON.PARK *TO* EUNI-TARD ABROAD:

Eunhee,

Today I wake up sad. But no problem! It will be OK! Only your father is very mad at you. He say you bohemia. What is this? He say you go to rome and you do not protect the mystery. He call you bad word in korean. He say you probably with black man. So shocking! He say only bohemia people go to Europe and bohemia people is bad people. He say maybe he stop being podiatrist and become painter which is always what he want but he grew up oldest son so he has responsibility to his parent and brothers. You are oldest sister. So you have responsibility. I say this already. We are not like American, don't forget! Which is why now Korea very rich country and America owe everything to China people. Daddy say you should come home and take LSAT again but this time study, but maybe Daddy a little wrong because now there is army in the street and it is dangerous. Reverend Cho tell Daddy he is sinner and he must throw away of himself, to be empty inside, so his heart will be fill only with Jesu. Also he say he should see Special Doctor to talk to and maybe take medicine so that he don't hit. But Daddy say it is shameful to take drug. Eunhee! Prepare yourself for LSAT to make Daddy happy and we can be good family again. Please forgive me because I am bad mother and bad wife.

Love,

Mommy

EUNI-TARD ABROAD: Sally, I'm taking the next plane home.

SALLYSTAR: It's not so bad. Don't listen to Mommy. She's trying to guilt you. I'm staying over at Eunhyun's this whole week. I'm so busy studying for chem I don't even have time to deal.

EUNI-TARD ABROAD: If you can't deal, then who's taking care of mom? If we're both out of the house he'll start blaming her for EVERY LITTLE THING. He'll say she drove us away and turned us both against him. She's completely un-protected. You know she'll never call the police or even Cousin Harold if he hits her.

SALLYSTAR: Don't use that kind of language, please.

EUNI-TARD ABROAD: What kind of language? That he HITS her.

SALLYSTAR: Stop it. Anyway, I still have dinner there every night so I know what's going on. He hasn't done anything major.

EUNI-TARD ABROAD: Not to her, you mean. What about you?

SALLYSTAR: I'm okay. Chem is killing me.

EUNI-TARD ABROAD: I know you're lying to me, Sally. I'll be on the next plane back and I'll see what he's done.

SALLYSTAR: Stay in Rome, Eunice! You deserve to have a good time after college. One of us should be happy. Anyway, next week I'm going to DC for that thing so I won't even see him. Don't worry about Mommy. Cousin Angela is staying over while I'm gone. She has job interviews in the city.

EUNI-TARD ABROAD: What thing in DC? The march against the ARA?

SALLYSTAR: Yes. But don't call it that. Some of the profs at school say we shouldn't mention it on GlobalTeens because they monitor everything.

EUNI-TARD ABROAD: Did Daddy call me a ghee jee beh?

SALLYSTAR: He had this crazy night where he thought you were sleeping with a black man. He said he had a dream about it. It's like he can't tell the difference between dreams and reality anymore.

EUNI-TARD ABROAD: Did you tell Daddy I help out at the shelter in Rome? Don't tell him it's for trafficked Albanian women. Just say it's for immigrants, okay?

SALLYSTAR: Why?

EUNI-TARD ABROAD: I want him to know I'm doing something good.

SALLYSTAR: I thought you didn't care what he thinks. Anyway I've got to go scan texts for Euro Classics. Don't worry, Eunice. Life only happens once. Enjoy it while you can! I'll keep Mom safe. I'm praying for all of us.

SALLYSTAR: BTW, that pewter Cullo bathing suit is on sale at Padma. The one with the chest guards that you wanted.

EUNI-TARD ABROAD: I'm already bidding on it on AssLuxury. I'll tell you if it goes over 100 yuan-pegged, and then you can buy it at Padma if it's still on sale.

JUNE 11

EUNI-TARD ABROAD *TO* GRILLBITCH:

Hi, Precious Pony.

I know you're in Tahoe so I don't want to bother you, but things have gotten really bad with my dad and I think I'm coming home. It's like the further away I am from him, the more he thinks he can get away with. Going to Rome was SUCH a mistake. I don't know if I can handle Fort Lee, but I was thinking of crashing in New York and going over there on weekends. Remember that girl you were friends with, the one with the really old-school perm, Joy Lee or something? Does she have a place for me to crash? I don't really know anyone in NY, everyone's in LA or abroad. I think I might have to stay over at that old guy Lenny's house. He keeps sending me these long teens about how much he loves my freckles and how he's going to cook me an eggplant.

I broke up with Ben. It was too much. He is so beautiful physically, so smart and such a rising star in Credit that I am completely intimidated by him. I can never reveal who I really am to him because he would just vomit. I know a part of him must be disgusted by my fat, fat body. And sometimes he just stares off into space when I treat him badly like "I think I've had enough of this crazy bitch." It's so sad. I've been crying for days now. Crying over my family and crying over Ben. God, I'm sorry, Precious Pony. I'm such a downer.

The weird thing is I've been thinking about Lenny, the old guy. I know he's gross physically, but there's something sweet about him, and honestly I need to be taken care of too. I feel safe with him because he is so not my ideal and I feel like I can be myself because I'm not in love with him. Maybe that's how Ben feels with me. I had this fantasy that I was having sex with Lenny and I tried to block out the grossness and just enjoy his very serious love for me. Have you ever done that, Pony? Am I selling myself short? When we were walking down this pretty street in Rome I noticed Lenny's shirt was buttoned all wrong, and I just reached over and rebuttoned it. I just wanted to help him be less of a dork. Isn't that a form of love too? And when he was talking to me at dinner, usually I listen to everything a guy says and try to prepare a response or at least to act a certain way, but with him I just stopped listening after a while and looked at the way his lips moved, the foam on his lips and on his dorky stubble, because he was so EARNEST in the way he needed to tell me things. And I thought, wow, you're kind of beautiful, Lenny. You're like what Prof Margaux in Assertiveness Class used to call "a real human being." I don't know. I keep going back and forth on him. Sometimes I'm like no way, it's never going to work, I'm just not attracted to him. But then I think of him going down on me until he could barely breathe, the poor thing, and the way I could just close my eyes and pretend we were both other people. Oh God, listen to me. Anyway, I miss you so much, Pony. I really do. Come to New York please! I need all the love I can get these days.

RateMe Plus
FROM THE DIARIES OF LENNY ABRAMOV

JUNE 12

Dear Diary,

God, I miss her. No messages from my Euny yet, no reply to my entreaty to move here and let me take care of her with garlicky carcasses of eggplant, with my grown man's practiced affections, with what's left of my bank account after Howard Shu docks me 239,000 yuan-pegged dollars. But I'm persevering. Every day I take out my handwritten checklist and remember that Point No. 3 implores me to Love Eunice until the dreaded "Dear Lenny" letter pops up on GlobalTeens and she runs off with some hot Credit or Media guy, some mindless jerk so taken with her looks he won't even recognize how much this miniature woman in front of him is in need of consolation and repair. Meanwhile, on the other side of the ledger, the Abramovs keep leaving all these desolate messages on GlobalTeens with illiterate subject lines reading "me and momee sad" and "me worry" and "without son laif lonely," reminding me that Point No. 5, Be Nice to Parents, has almost come due. I just need to feel a little more secure about myself and my life and especially my money— a sore subject with the thrifty Abramovs—before I head off to Long Island to visit them in their vibrant right-wing habitat.

Speaking of money, I went to my HSBC on East Broadway, where a pretty Dominican girl with a set of dying teeth gave me a rundown of how my financial instruments were performing. In a word, shittily.

My AmericanMorning portfolio, even though it had been pegged to the yuan, had lost 10 percent of its value because, unbeknownst to me, the idiot asset managers had stuck the failing ColgatePalmoliveYum!BrandsViacomCredit albatross into the mix, and my low-risk BRIC [Brazil, Russia, India, China]-A-BRAC High-Performing Nations Fund had registered only 3 percent growth because of the April unrest near Putingrad in Russia and the impact of America's invasion of Venezuela on the Brazilian economy. "I feel like I'm going to shit a BRIC," I told Maria Abriella, my account representative.

Ms. Abriella bade me look at an old computer screen. I ignored the flickering capricious dollar amounts and focused on the steady yuan- and euro-pegged denominations. I had something like 1,865,000 yuan to my name, a figure that had been close to 2.5 million yuan before I had left for Europe. "You got top credit, Mr. Lenny," she said, in her husky, pack-an-hour voice. "If you want to be patriotic, you should take out a loan and buy another apar'men' as an inves'men'."

Another apartment? I was *hemorrhaging* funds. I turned away from Ms. Abriella's beautiful seagull-shaped lips as if slapped, and let death wash over me, the corned-beef smell of my damp neck giving way to an old man's odor rising from my thighs and armpits like steam, and then the final past-due stench of the Arizona hospice years, the orderly swabbing me down with detergent as if I were some sickly elephant.

Money equals life. By my estimation, even the preliminary beta dechronification treatments, for example, the insertion of SmartBlood to regulate my ridiculous cardiovascular system, would run three million yuan per year. With each second I had spent in Rome, lustily minding the architecture, rapturously fucking Fabrizia, drinking and eating enough daily glucose to kill a Cuban sugarcane farmer, I had paved the toll road to my own demise.

And now there was only one man who could turn things around for me.

Which brings me back to Point No. 1: Work Hard for Joshie. I think I'm doing all right on that front. The first week back at Post-

Human Services is over and nothing terrible happened. Howard Shu hasn't asked me to do any Intakes yet, but I've spent the week hanging out at the Eternity Lounge, fiddling with my pebbly new äppärät 7.5 with RateMe Plus technology, which I now proudly wear pendant-style around my neck, getting endless updates on our country's battle with solvency from CrisisNet while downloading all my fears and hopes in front of my young nemeses in the Eternity Lounge, talking about how my parents' love for me ran too hot and too cold, and how I *want* and *need* Eunice Park even though she's so much prettier than I deserve—basically, trying to show these open-source younguns just how much data an old "intro" geezer like me is willing to share. So far I'm getting shouts of "gross" and "sick" and "TIMATOV," which I've learned means Think I'm About to Openly Vomit, but I also found out that Darryl, the guy with the SUK DIK bodysuit and the red bandana, has been posting nice things about me on his GlobalTeens stream called "101 People We Need to Feel Sorry For." At the same time, I heard the ticka-ticka-ticka of The Boards as Darryl's mood indicator fell from "positive/playful/ready to contribute" to "annoying the heck out of Joshie all week." His cortisol levels are a mess too. Just a little more stress on his part and I'll get my desk back. Anyway, all this passes for progress, and soon I'll be hitting the Intakes, proving my worth, trying to corner the market in Joshie's affection and reclaim my big-man-on-campus status in time for the Labor Day tempeh stir-fry. Also, I've spent an entire week without reading any books or talking about them too loudly. I'm learning to worship my new äppärät's screen, the colorful pulsating mosaic of it, the fact that it knows every last stinking detail about the world, whereas my books only know the minds of their authors.

In the meantime, the weekend came and hallelujah! I decided to dedicate Saturday night to Point No. 4: Care for Your Friends. Joshie's right about one thing: Good relationships make you healthier. And the point is not just being cared for, but learning to return that care.

In my case, learning to overcome an only child's reluctance to commit fully to the world of others. Now, I haven't seen my buddies since I've been back, because, like anyone who's still employed in New York, they're working insane hours, but we finally made plans to get together at Cervix, the newly hip bar in newly hip Staten Island.

Before I left the 740 square feet of my apartment, I put the name of my oldest Media pal, Noah Weinberg, into my äppärät and learned that he would be airing our reunion live on his GlobalTeens stream, "The Noah Weinberg Show!," which made me nervous at first, but, then, this is exactly the kind of thing I have to get used to if I'm going to make it in this world. So I put on a pair of painful jeans and a flaming-red shirt with a bouquet of white roses embroidered along my chest. I wished Eunice were around to tell me if this was age-appropriate. She seems to have a good sense of life's limits.

Down in the lobby, I noticed the ambulances were silently flashing their lights out on Grand Street, which meant another death in the building, another invitation to sit shiva at a grieving son's house in Teaneck or New Rochelle, another apartment for sale on the community board. A wheelchair stood lonely amidst the antiseptic 1950s cream-on-cream décor of our building's lobby. We're all about immobility here in the Naturally Occurring Retirement Community, and so I prepared myself for an intergenerational encounter, thinking I might have to wheel the old fellow out into the early-evening sunshine, produce a few words of my grandmother's Yiddish.

I backed away. A body badly sheathed in an opaque plastic bag sat in the wheelchair, its head crowned with a pointy pocket of air. The body bag clung vehemently to a pair of slim male hips, and the deceased was huddled forward slightly, as if engaged in the fruitless act of Christian prayer.

An outrage! Where were his caregivers? Where were the EMT workers? I wanted to get down on my knees and, against my better instincts, to offer solace to this former being growing cold in his sickening plastic robe. I beheld the tiny pocket of air above the dead man's head, as if it were the visualization of his very last breath, and felt vomit rising from my breadbasket.

Dizzy, I walked out into the stifling June heat toward the ambulance guys, the both of them enjoying a smoke by the flashing vehicle bearing the legend "American Medicle [sic] Response." "There's a dead person in my lobby," I said to them. "In a fucking *wheel-chair*. You just left it there. Some respect, guys?"

Their faces were negligible, compromised, vaguely Hispanish. "You next of kin?" one said, nodding at my vicinity.

"Does it matter?"

"He's not going anywhere, sir."

"It's disgusting," I said.

"It's just death."

"Happens to everybody, Paco," the other added.

I tried to contort my face into anger, but whenever I try to do that I'm told I look like a crazy old woman. "I'm talking about your *smoking*," I said, my retort dying swiftly in the humidity around us.

Nothing on Grand could offer me solace. Nothing could make me Celebrate What I Have (Point No. 6). Not the inherent life inside the barely clothed Latino children or the smell of freshly cooked *arroz con pollo* wafting out of the venerable Castillo del Jagua II. I projected "The Noah Weinberg Show!" again, listened to my friend making fun of our armed forces' latest defeat in Venezuela, but I couldn't follow the intricacies. Ciudad Bolívar, Orinoco River, pierced armor, Blackhawk down—what did it mean to me, now that I saw one possible end to my life: alone, in a bag, in my own apartment building, hunched over in a wheelchair, praying to a god I never believed in? Just then, passing by the ochre grandiosity of St. Mary's, I saw a pretty woman, a little chunky and wide of hip, cross herself in front of the church and kiss her fist, her Credit ranking flashing at an abysmal 670 on a nearby Credit Pole. I wanted to confront her, to make her see the folly of her religion, to change her diet, to help her spend less on makeup and other nonessentials, to make her worship every biological moment she was offered instead of some badly punctured deity. I also wanted to kiss her for some reason, feel the life pulsing in those big Catholic lips, remind myself of the primacy of the living animal, of my time amongst the Romans.

I had to cool my stress levels by the time I got to see my buddies. On the way down to the ferry, I chanted Point No. 4, Care for Your Friends, Care for Your Friends, because I needed them by my side when the American Medicle [sic] Response ambulance trundled up to 575 Grand Street. In contravention of my belief that any life ending in death is essentially pointless, I needed my friends to open up that plastic bag and take one last look at me. Someone had to remember me, if only for a few more minutes in the vast silent waiting room of time.

My äppärät pinged.

CrisisNet: DOLLAR LOSES OVER 3% IN LONDON TRADING TO FINISH AT HISTORIC LOW OF 1€ = $8.64 IN ADVANCE OF CHINESE CENTRAL BANKER ARRIVAL U.S.; LIBOR RATE FALLS 57 BASIS POINTS; DOLLAR LOWER BY 2.3% AGAINST YUAN AT 1¥ = $4.90

I really needed to figure out what this LIBOR thing was and why it was falling by fifty-seven basis points. But, honestly, how little I cared about all these difficult economic details! How desperately I wanted to forsake these facts, to open a smelly old book or to go down on a pretty young girl instead. Why couldn't I have been born to a better world?

The National Guard was out in force at the Staten Island Ferry building. A crowd of poor office women wearing white sneakers, their groaning ankles covered with sheer hose, waited patiently to walk past a sandbagged checkpoint by the gate to the ferry. An American Restoration Authority sign warned us that "IT IS FORBIDDEN TO ACKNOWLEDGE THE EXISTENCE OF THIS CHECKPOINT ('THE OBJECT'). BY READING THIS SIGN YOU HAVE DENIED EXISTENCE OF THE OBJECT AND IMPLIED CONSENT."

Occasionally, some of us were pulled aside, and I worried about the otter flagging me in Rome, the asshole videotaping me on the plane, the asterisk that still appeared when my mighty credit score flashed on the Credit Poles, the continued disappearance of Nettie Fine (no response to my daily messages, and if they could get my American mama, what could they do to my *actual* parents?). Men in civilian clothes zapped our bodies and our äppäräti with what looked like a small tubular attachment of an old-school Electrolux vacuum cleaner and asked us both to deny and to imply consent to what they were doing to us. The passengers seemed to take the whole thing in stride, the Staten Island cool kids especially silent and deferential, shaking a little in their vintage hoodies. I overheard several young men of color whispering to one another "deee-ny and *imply*," but the older women quickly shushed them with bites of "Restoration 'thority!" and "Punch you in the mouth, boy."

Maybe it was Howard Shu's doing, but somehow I got through the checkpoint without being stopped.

Once disembarked on the Staten Island side, I braced myself for a walk. The main drag, Victory Boulevard, ramps uphill with a San Franciscan vigor. These parts of Staten Island, St. George and Tompkinsville, were once completely off the grid. Immigrants used to wash up here from Poland, Thailand, Sri Lanka, and especially Mexico. They worked the storefronts of their respective ethnic restaurants and also ran dusty groceries, check-cashing places, and twenty-centavo-a-minute phone booths. Outside the stores, black men used to lounge in puffy jackets, tottering sleepily over milk crates. I remember this 'hood well, because when my buddies and I were right out of college we'd all take the ferry to raid this spicy Sri Lankan joint, where for nine bucks you could eat an insane shrimp pancake and some kind of ethereal red fish while baby roaches tried to clamber up your trouser leg and drink your beer. Now, of course, the Sri Lankan place, the roaches, the somnolent minorities were gone, replaced by half-man, half-wireless bohemians ramming their baby strollers up and down the hump of Victory Boulevard, while kids from nearby New Jersey cruised past the outrageously priced Victorians in their Hyundai rice rockets, wishing they could work Media or Credit.

Cervix is exactly what you would expect from yet another stupid

Staten Island old man's bar cleaned up and turned into a hangout for Media and Credit types, fake oily paintings from basement rec rooms of yore, hot women in their early twenties looking to supplement their electronic lives, so-so men in desperately cool clothes scratching the upper-thirty limit and pushing deep into the next decade. My boys fit the bill exactly. There they were, crowded around a table, their äppäräti out, speaking into their shirt collars while thumbing Content into their pearly devices, two curly, dusky heads completely lost to the world around them: Noah Weinberg and Vishnu Cohen-Clark, fellow alumni of what used to be called New York University, that indispensable local educator of bright-enough women and men, fellow romantic sufferers, fellow lovers of spicy words and endless arcana, fellow travelers down the under-lubricated craphole of life.

"My Nee-groes!" I cried. They did not hear me. "My *Nee*-groes!"

Noah jumped up, not in the way he used to back in school, with an ambitious sprinter's leap, but quick enough to nearly upset the table. With that stupid, inevitable smile, those blazing teeth, that spinning, lying mouth, those gleaming enthusiast's eyes, he turned the camera nozzle of his äppärät my way to record my lumbering arrival. "Heads up, *manitos,* here he comes!" he shouted. "Get out your butt plugs and get ready to groove. This is a 'Noah Weinberg Show!' *exclusive*. The arrival of our personal number-one Nee-gro from a year of bullshit self-discovery in Rome, Italia. We're streaming at you live, folks. He's walking toward our table in real time! He's got that goofy 'Hey, I'm just one of the guys!' smile. One hundred sixty pounds of Ashkenazi second-generation, 'My parents are poor immigrants, so you gotta love me' flava: Lenny 'freak *and* geek' Abramov!"

I waved to Noah, and then, hesitantly, to his äppärät. Vishnu came at me with open arms and with nothing but joy on his face, a man possessed of roughly the same short-to-average height (five foot nine) and moral values as myself, a man whose choice in women—a tempered, bright young Korean girl named Grace who also happens to be a dear friend of mine—I can only second. "Lenny," he said, lingering over the two syllables of my name, as if they mattered. "We missed you, buddy." Those simple words made me tear up and stammer something mildly embarrassing into Vishnu's ear. He had on the same SUK DIK bodysuit as my young co-worker at Post-Human Services, although his muzzle was gray and unshaven and his eyes looked tired and ITP, lending him a proper age. The three of us hugged one another close, in a kind of overdone way, touching buttocks and flailing at each other genitally. We all grew up with a fairly tense idea of male friendship, for which the permissive times now allowed us to compensate, and often I wished that our crude words and endless posturing were code for affection and understanding. In some male societies, slang and ritualistic embraces form the entire culture, along with the occasional call to take up the spear.

As I hugged each boy and patted him on the shoulder, I noticed that we were surreptitiously sniffing one another for signs of decay, and that Vishnu and Noah were wearing some kind of spicy deodorant, perhaps as a way to mask their changing scent. We had each embarked on our very late thirties, a time when the bravado of youth and the promise of glorious exploits that had once held us together would begin to fade, as our bodies began to shed, slacken, and shrink. We were still as friendly and caring as any group of men could be, but I surmised that even the shuffle toward extinction would prove competitive for us, that some of us might shuffle faster than others.

"Harm Reduction time," Vishnu said. I still couldn't figure out what the hell Harm Reduction meant, although the youth in the Eternity Lounge couldn't shut up about it. "What does the wandering Jew-Nee-gro want? Leffe Brune or Leffe Blonde?"

"Blonde me," I said, tossing a twenty-dollar bill bearing the silver authenticity stripe and the holographic words "Backed by Zhongguo Renmin Yinhang/People's Bank of China," hoping the drinks were unpegged to the yuan, so that I could collect some serious change. The money was promptly thrown back at me, and I enjoyed Vishnu's kind smile.

"Nee-gro, please," he said.

Noah took an orator's deep, rehearsed breath. "Okay, *putas* and *huevóns*. I'm still streaming right at you. Eight p.m. on the dot. It's Rubenstein time in America. It's a motherfucking Bipartisan evening here in the People's Republic of Staten Island, and Lenny Abramov has just ordered a Belgian beer for seven yuan-pegged dollars."

Noah aimed his äppärät's camera nozzle at me, marking me as the subject for his evening news segment. "The Nee-gro must tell all," Noah said. "The returning Nee-gro must eh-*jew*-muh-cate our viewers. Start with the women you've done in Italy." He switched to a falsetto voice: " 'Fuck-ah me-ah, Leonardo! Fuck-ah me now-ah, you beeg-ah heeb-ah!' Then give us the pasta lowdown. Verbal at me, Lenny. Shoot me an Image of a lonely Abramov slurping up noodles at the neighborhood trat. Then the whole return-of-the-prodigal-Nee-*gro* shit. What's it like to be a gentle, unsuspecting Lenny Abramov just back to Rubenstein's one-party America?"

Noah hadn't always been this angry and caustic, but there was something disproportionate about his efforts these days, as if he could no longer keep track of how his personal decline paralleled that of our culture and state. Before the publishing industry folded, he had published a novel, one of the last that you could actually go out and buy in a Media store. Lately he did "The Noah Weinberg Show!," which had a grand total of six sponsors, whom he struggled to mention casually throughout his rants—a medium-sized escort service in Queens, several ThaiSnak franchises in Brownstone Brooklyn, a former Bipartisan politician who now ran security consulting for Wapachung Contingency, the well-armed security division of my employer, and I can't remember the rest. The show got hit about fifteen thousand times a day, which put him somewhere in the lower-middle echelon of Media professionals. His girlfriend, Amy Greenberg, is a pretty well-known Mediawhore who spends about seven hours a day streaming about her weight. As for Vishnu, my buddy does Debt Bombing for ColgatePalmoliveYum!BrandsViacomCredit, hanging around street corners and zapping people's äppäräti with Images of themselves taking on more debt.

Courtesy of the Debt Bomber, three wheaty beers, high in triglycerides, were smacked on the table. I began my debriefing, trying to entertain the boys with stories of my funny, dirty, crosscultural romance with Fabrizia, drawing with my fingers the outlines of her bush. I sang lyrical about the fresh garlic tang of old-world *ragù* and tried to inculcate them with a love of the Roman arch. But the truth was, they didn't care. The world they needed was right around them, flickering and bleeping, and it demanded every bit of strength and attention they could spare. Noah, the one-time novelist, could probably think of Rome in nonimmediate terms, could conjure up Seneca and Virgil, *The Marble Faun* and *Daisy Miller*. But even he seemed unimpressed, glancing impatiently at his äppärät, which was alive with at least seven degrees of information, numbers and letters and Images stacked on the screen, flowing and eddying against one another as the waters of the Tiber once did. "We're losing hits," he whispered to me. "Ix-nay on the Rome-ay, okay?" And then, in a really low voice: "Humor and politics. Got it?"

I cut short a description of the Pantheon's empty space drenched with early-morning sunlight, as Noah pointed the clumped remains of his frontal hair at me and said: "All right, here's the situation, Nee-gro. You have to fuck either Mother Teresa or Margaret Thatcher. . . ."

Vishnu and I laughed just the right amount and smiled at our leader. I raised my hands in defeat. This is the only way men could talk anymore. This is how we told one another that we were still friends and that our lives were not entirely over. "Maggie Thatcher if it's missionary," I said. "Definitely Mother Teresa from behind."

"You are *so* Media," Noah said, and we smacked fists.

From there the conversation moved on to *Threads,* a cult BBC nuclear-holocaust film, then over to the music of early Dylan, then a new way of fighting genital warts with a kind of smart foam, Secretary of State Rubenstein's latest bungling in Venezuela ("nothing more oxymoronic than a Jewish strongman, am I right, *pendejos?*" Noah said), the near collapse of AlliedWasteCVSCitigroupCredit, the ensuing failed bailout by the Fed, our faltering portfolios, the "wah-wuh" sound of the doors closing on the 6 train versus the resigned "sheeesh" sound on the L, the life and bizarre death of the deviant comic known as Pee-wee Herman, and finally, inexhaustibly, the fact that, like most Americans, we would probably lose our jobs soon and be thrown out onto the streets to die.

"I could eat, like, a dozen of those ThaiSnak Issan larb chicken salads right about now," Noah said, in deference to one of his sponsors.

As the retro sound system went into an old Arcade Fire tune, I let myself get cozy with another glass of foaming ale, observing the boys on a meta-level. Noah had aged worst of all. The weight had seemingly trickled from his thick, brainy forehead down into his jowls, where it jiggled inopportunely, giving him an afterglow of anger and dissatisfaction. At one time he was clearly the most handsome and successful of our number, he had introduced us to half the girlfriends we ever had (not that many, to be sure), had given us our edgy racial vocabulary, and had kept us updated with a dozen messages an hour on how we should act and what we should think. But with every year it was getting harder to keep me and Vishnu in check. The almost-forties, once the fulcrum of adulthood, was now a time of exploration, and each of the boys had struck out on his own.

Vishnu was settling into the life of a smart, fancy loser, the SUK DIK bodysuit and vintage Bathing Ape sneakers that must have cost five hundred yuan, an overeagerness to laugh too hard at others' jokes with a strange new honking sound that had developed in my absence—ha-*huh,* ha-*huh*—a laughter born of a life of diminishing returns that, I've been told, would miraculously end in marriage to a loving, forgiving woman named Grace.

As for me, I was now the odd man out. It would take a while for my boys to get used to my return. They glanced at me strangely, as if I had unlearned English, or repudiated our common way of life. I was already something of a weirdo for living all the way out in Manhattan. Now I had wasted an entire year and a good chunk of my savings in Europe. As a friend, a well-respected member of the technological elite, and, yes, a fellow "Nee-gro," I needed to reclaim my prime position among the boys as a kind of alternate Noah. I needed to replant myself on native soil.

The three things I had going for me: an inbred Russian willingness to get drunk and chummy, an inbred Jewish willingness to laugh strategically at myself, and, most impressively, my new äppärät. "Damn, *cabrón*," Noah said, eyeing my pebble. "Whuddat, a 7.5 with RateMe Plus? I'm going to stream that shit fucking *close*-up."

He filmed my äppärät with his äppärät, while I swallowed another mug of triglycerides. Some Staten Island girls had shown up, wearing trendy retro clothes from some point in my youth, looking very Media in their sheepy Ugg boots and rhinestone-encrusted bandanas, a few of them mixing the old-school duds with Onionskin jeans which clung transparently to their thin legs and plump, pink bottoms, revealing to us all of their shaven secrets. They were also looking our way, scrolling their devices, one of them a pretty brunette with beautiful sleepy eyes.

"Let's fuck," Vishnu said, pointing in their direction.

"Jeez, cool it, Nee-gro," I said, already slurring my words. "You've got a little cutie at home." I looked directly into the camera nozzle of Noah's äppärät: " 'Sup, Grace. Long time no see, baby girl. You watching this live?"

The boys laughed at me. "What an idiot!" Noah cried. "Did you hear that, beloved cocksucking audience? Lenny Abramov thought Vishnu Cohen-Clark just said, 'Let's *fuck*.' "

"It's F-A-C," Vishnu explained. "I said, 'Let's FAC.' "

"What does that mean?"

"He sounds like my granny in Aventura!" Noah was bellowing. " 'FAC? What's that? Who am I? Where's my diaper?' "

"It means 'Form A Community,' " Vishnu said. "It's, like, a way to judge people. And let them judge you." He took my äppärät, and slid some settings until an icon labeled "FAC" drifted onto the screen. "When you see FAC, you press the EmotePad to your heart, or wherever it can feel your pulse." Vishnu pointed out the sticky thing on the back of my äppärät that I thought could be used to attach it to a dashboard or a fridge. Wrong again.

"Then," Vishnu continued, "you look at a girl. The EmotePad picks up any change in your blood pressure. That tells her how much you want to do her."

"All right, Mediastuds and Mediawhores," Noah said. "We're streaming live here as Lenny Abramov tries to FAC for the first time. This is a future-reference event, folks, so widen your bandwidth. This is like the Wright brothers learning to fly, except neither of them was mildly retarded like our boy Lenny here. JBF, Nee-gro. Tell me if I'm going too far. Or wait. There's no such thing as *too far* in Rubenstein's America. Too far is when you're shot in the back of the head somewhere Upstate and the National Guard burns your body to a crisp and flushes the ashes down a cold winter's port-a-potty at some Secure Screening Facility in Troy. Lenny's looking at me like *What are you talking about?* Here's the breakdown on what you've missed during your 'junior year abroad,' Lenny-boy: The Bipartisans run the American Refund Agency, or whatever the fuck it's called, the ARA runs the infrastructure and the National Guard, and the National Guard runs *you*. Oops. Not supposed to mention *that* on GlobalTeens. Maybe I *have* gone too far!"

I noticed Vishnu moving his head out of the frame of Noah's äppärät's camera nozzle at the mention of the ARA and the Bipartisans. "Okay, Nee-gro," he said to me. "Set up your Community Parameters. Make it 'Immediate Space 360'—that'll cover the whole bar. Now look at a girl, then press the pad to your heart." I looked at the pretty brunette, at the hairless crotch glowing from within her see-through Onionskin jeans, at the lithe body crouched imperiously atop a set of smooth legs, at her worried smile. Then I touched my heart with the back of my äppärät, trying to fill it with my warmth, my natural desire for love.

The girl across the bar laughed immediately without even turning my way. A bunch of figures appeared on my screen: "FUCKABILITY 780/800, PERSONALITY 800/800, ANAL/ORAL/VAGINAL PREFERENCE 1/3/2."

"Fuckability 780!" Noah said. "Personality 800! *Leeeetl* Lenny Abramov's got himself a *beeeeeg* crush."

"But I don't even know her personality," I said. "And how does it know my anal preferences?"

"The personality score depends on how 'extro' she is," Vishnu explained. "Check it out. This girl done got three thousand–plus Images, eight hundred streams, and a long multimedia thing on how her father abused her. Your äppärät runs that against the stuff you've downloaded about yourself and then it comes up with a score. Like, you've dated a lot of abused girls, so it knows you're into that shit. Here, let me see your profile." Vishnu slid some other functions, and my profile shimmered on my warm pebbly screen.

LENNY ABRAMOV ZIP code 10002, New York, New York. Income averaged over five-year-span, $289,420, yuan-pegged, within top 19 percent of U.S. income distribution. Current blood pressure 120 over 70. O-type blood. Thirty-nine years of age, lifespan estimated at eighty-three (47 percent lifespan elapsed; 53 percent remaining). Ailments: high cholesterol, depression. Born: 11367 ZIP code, Flushing, New York. Father: Boris Abramov, born Moscow, HolyPetroRussia; Mother: Galya Abramov, born Minsk, Vassal-State Belarus. Parental ailments: high cholesterol, depression. Aggregate wealth: $9,353,000 non-yuan-pegged, real estate, 575 Grand Street, Unit E-607, $1,150,000 yuan-pegged. Liabilities: mortgage, $560,330. Spending power: $1,200,000 per year, non-yuan-pegged. Consumer profile: heterosexual, nonathletic, nonautomotive, nonreligious, non-Bipartisan. Sexual preferences: low-functioning Asian/Korean and White/Irish American with Low Net Worth family background; child-abuse indicator: on; low-self-esteem indicator: on. Last purchases: bound, printed, nonstreaming Media artifact, 35 northern euros; bound, printed, nonstreaming Media artifact, $126 yuan-pegged; bound, printed, nonstreaming Media artifact, 37 northern euros.

"You've got to stop buying books, Nee-gro," Vishnu said. "All those doorstops are going to drag down your PERSONALITY rankings. Where the fuck do you even find those things?"

"Lenny Abramov, last reader on earth!" Noah cried. And then, staring directly into his äppärät's camera nozzle: "We're FACing pretty hard now, people. We're getting Lenny's RateMe on."

Streams of data were now fighting for time and space around us. The pretty girl I had just FACed was projecting my MALE HOTNESS as 120 out of 800, PERSONALITY 450, and something called SUS-

TAINABILIT¥ at 630. The other girls were sending me similar figures. "Damn," Noah said. "The prodigal Nee-gro Abramov is getting creamed here. Looks like the *chicas,* they no likey that big Hebraic snorkel our boy was born with. And those flabby Hadassah arms. Okay, rank him up, Vish."

Vishnu worked my äppärät until some RANKINGS came up. He helped me navigate the data. "Out of the seven males in the Community," he said, gesturing around the bar, "Noah's the third hottest, I'm the fourth hottest, and Lenny's the seventh."

"You mean I'm the ugliest guy here?" I ran my fingers through the remnants of my hair.

"But you've got a decent personality," Vishnu comforted me, "and you're second in the whole bar in terms of SUSTAINABILIT¥."

"At least our Lenny's a good *providah,*" Noah said. I remembered the 239,000 yuan-pegged dollars I owed to Howard Shu and became even more depressed by the prospect of being deprived of them. Money and Credit was about all I had at this point. That, and my sparkling PERSONALITY.

Vishnu was pointing at the girls with his index finger, interpreting the data streams that were by now the sum total of our attention: "The one on the left, with the scar on her ankle and that little landing strip on her muff, Lana Beets, she went to Chicago Law, now has a Retail internship at Saaami Bras, making eighty thousand yuan-pegged. The one with the labia stud, name's Annie Shultz-Heik, works in Retail, she's got the smart foam for the genital warts and is on the pill, *and* last year she gave three thousand yuan to the Bipartisan Party's Young Future Leaders of America Together We'll Surprise the World Fund."

Annie was the girl I had FACed first. The one who had been allegedly abused by her dad and ranked my MALE HOTNESS a meager 120 out of 800.

"That's right, Annie," Noah said into his äppärät. "Vote Bipartisan and your warts will melt away faster than our country's sovereign debt rating. They'll disappear like our troops down in Ciudad Bolívar. Rubenstein time in America, folks. Rubenstein time."

I went to get some beers, passing the girls on the way, but they were too busy looking at rankings. The bar was filling up with Senior Credit guys in tapered chinos and oxfords. I felt superior to them, but my MALE HOTNESS was swiftly falling to last place out of thirty-seven, thirty-eight, thirty-nine, forty males. Walking past Annie, I clicked on her Child Abuse Multimedia, letting the sound of her screaming vibrate my eardrums as a pixelated disembodied hand hovered above an Image of her naked body and the screaming segued into what sounded like a hundred monks chanting the mantra "He *touched* me here, he *touched* me here, he *touched* me here, *he touched me here*."

I turned in Annie's direction with my left lip crinkled in sadness and my brow heavy with empathy, but the words "Look away quickly, dork," appeared on my äppärät. "Hair-transplant time for RAG?" another girl wrote. ("Rapidly aging geezer," according to my electronic pebble.) "I can smell the DO from here." ("Dick odor," my äppärät helpfully told me.) And the slightly consoling: "Nice ¥¥¥, Pops."

The bar was now utterly aflash with smoky data spilling out of a total of fifty-nine äppäräti, 68 percent of them belonging to the male of the species. The masculine data scrolled on my screen. Our average income hovered at a respectable but not especially uplifting 190,000 yuan-pegged dollars. We were looking for girls who appreciated us for who we were. We had absent fathers, who sometimes were not absent enough. A man ranked uglier than me walked in and, ascertaining his chances, turned right around. I wanted to follow his bald, creased head out of the bar into the all-forgiving summer air, but instead got a double whiskey for myself, along with two Leffe Brunes.

"After getting his ass *handed* to him by the RateMe Plus, Lenny Abramov is turning to drink," Noah intoned. But upon seeing the deep hamster funk of my expression, he said, "It's going to be okay, Lenny. We'll get you all fixed up with the bitches. You'll find the mercy in this rude data stream."

Vishnu had his hand on my shoulder and was saying, "We really care about you, buddy. How many of these Senior Credit assholes can say that? We'll get your rankings up, even if we have to slice an inch off your nose."

Noah: "And add one to your Johnson."

"Ha-*huh*," Vishnu laughed, sadly.

I appreciated the sentiments, but I felt bad receiving their kindness. The point was for *me* to care for *them*. That would help lower my stress profile and do wonders for my ACTH levels. Meanwhile, the double whiskey and the slow triglyceride death it portended had sunk into the last compartment of my stomach, and the world was projecting at me in an angry way. "Eunice Park!" I wailed into Noah's äppärät. "Eunice, honey. Can you hear me out there? I miss you so much."

"We're streaming these emotions live, folks," Noah said. "We're streaming Lenny's love for this girl Eunice Park in real time. We're 'feeling' the many levels of his pain just as he feels them."

And I started to blabber about how much she meant to me. "We were sitting in this restaurant in Via Giulia, or someplace. . . ."

"Losing hits, losing hits," Noah whispered. "No foreign words. Cut to chase."

". . . And she just. She *really* listened to me. She paid attention to me. She never even looked at her äppärät while I was speaking to her. I mean we were mostly eating. *Bucatini all'* . . ."

"Losing hits, losing hits."

"Pasta. But when we weren't eating, we were saying *everything* about ourselves, who we were, where we come from. She's an angry girl. You'd be too if you were her. All the shit she's had to put up with. But she wants to get to know me better, and she wants to help me, and I want to care for her. I think she weighs, like, seventy pounds. She should eat more. I'll make her eggplant. She showed me how to brush my teeth."

"Streaming these emotions live," Noah repeated. "You're the first to hear them, *patos*. Straight from the Abramov's mouth. He's verballing. He's emoting. But I'm getting a message from a hoser in Windsor, Ontario. He wants to know, did you fuck her, Lenny? Did you stick your thingie inside her tight snatch? Fifteen thousand souls absolutely need to know right now or they'll get their news else-where."

"We're such an unlikely couple, so unlikely," I was crying, "be-cause she's beautiful, and I'm the fortieth-ugliest man in this bar. But so what! So what! What if someday she lets me kiss each one of her freckles again? She has like a million. But every one of them means something to me. Isn't this how people used to fall in love? I know we're living in Rubenstein's America, like you keep saying. But doesn't that just make us even more responsible for each other's fates? I mean, what if Eunice and I just said 'no' to all this. To this bar. To this FACing. The two of us. What if we just went home and read books to each other?"

"Oh God," Noah groaned. "You just halved my viewer load. You're killing me here, Abramov. . . . Okay, folks, we're streaming live here in Rubenstein's America, zero hour for our economy, zero hour for our military might, zero hour for everything that used to make us proud to be ourselves, and Lenny Abramov won't tell us if he fucked this tiny Asian chick."

In the bathroom next to a graffito encouraging the pisser to "Vote Bisexual, Not Bipartisan," and the quizzical "Harm Reduction Re-duced My Dick," I let go of several ounces of Belgian ale and the five glasses of alkalized water I'd had before leaving my house.

Vishnu sidled up to me. "Turn off your äppärät," he said.

"Huh?"

He reached over and yanked my pendant into the off position. His eyes locked with mine, and even through the mist of my own drunkenness I noticed that my friend was basically sober. "I think Noah may be ARA," he whispered.

"What?"

"I think he's working for the Bipartisans."

"Are you crazy?" I said. "What about 'It's Rubenstein time in America'? What about the zero hour?"

"I'm just telling you, watch what you say around him. Especially when he's streaming his show."

My urination stopped of its own accord, and my prostate felt very sore. *Care for your friends, care for your friends,* the mantra repeated itself.

"I don't understand," I muttered. "He's still our friend, right?"

"People are being forced into all kinds of things now," Vishnu said. He lowered his voice even further. "Who knows what they got him for. His Credit ranking's been going to shit ever since he started doing Amy Greenberg. Half of Staten Island is collaborating. Everyone's looking for backing, for protection. You watch, if the Chinese take over, Noah will be sucking up to them. You should have stayed in Rome, Lenny. Fuck that immortality bullshit. Ain't going to happen for you anyway. Look at us. We're not HNWIs."

"We're not Low Net Worth either!" I protested.

"That don't matter. We're poster children for Harm Reduction. This city has no use for us. They privatized the MTA last month. They're going to knock down the projects. Even your fancy Jew projects. We'll be living in Erie, Pennsylvania, by the time this decade's over."

He must have noticed the lethal unhappiness disfiguring my expression. He zipped up and patted my back. "That was some good emoting about Eunice in there," he said. "That'll get your PERSONALITY ranking higher. And who knows about Noah? Maybe I'm wrong. Been wrong before. Been wrong lots, my friend."

Before my melancholy could get the best of me, Vishnu's girlfriend, Grace Kim, showed up to drag him homeward, to their pleasant, air-conditioned Staten Island abode, making me pine in a heartbreaking way for Eunice. I stared at Grace with a need bordering on grief. There she was: intelligently, creatively, timidly dressed (no Onionskin jeans to show off *her* slender goods), full of programmed intentions and steady, interesting plans, hardwired for marriage to her lucky beau, ready to bear those beautiful Eurasian kids that seem to be the last children left in the city.

Along with Noah, I was invited to Vishnu and Grace's house for a nightcap, but I claimed jet lag and bade everyone farewell. They were sweet enough to walk me to the ferry station, although not sweet enough to brave the National Guard checkpoint with me. I was duly searched and poked by tired, bored soldiers. I denied and implied everything. I said, in answer to some metaphysical question, "I just want to go home." It wasn't the right answer, but a black man with a little golden cross amid his paltry chest hairs took pity on me and let me board the vessel.

The rankings of other passengers swept across the bow, the ugly, ruined men emoting their desire and despair over the rail and into the dark, relentless waves. A pink mist hovered over the mostly residential area once known as the Financial District, casting everything in the past tense. A father kept kissing his tiny son's head over and over with a sad insistence, making those of us with bad parents or no parents feel even more lonely and alone.

We watched the silhouettes of oil tankers, guessing at the warmth of their holds. The city approached. The three bridges connecting Brooklyn and Manhattan, one long necklace of light, gradually differentiated themselves. The Empire State extinguished its crown and tucked itself away behind a lesser building. On the Brooklyn side, the gold-tipped Williamsburg Savings Bank, cornered by the half-built, abandoned glass giants around it, quietly gave us the finger. Only the bankrupt "Freedom" Tower, empty and stern in profile, like an angry man risen and ready to punch, celebrated itself throughout the night.

Every returning New Yorker asks the question: Is this still my city?

I have a ready answer, cloaked in obstinate despair: It is.

And if it's not, I will love it all the more. I will love it to the point where it becomes mine again.

FIRE UP THAT EGGPLANT
FROM THE GLOBALTEENS ACCOUNT OF EUNICE PARK

JUNE 13

LEONARDO DABRAMOVINCI *TO* EUNI-TARD ABROAD:

Oh, hi there. It's Lenny Abramov. Again. I'm sorry to be bothering you. I teened you a little while back and I didn't hear from you. So I guess you're busy and there must be all these annoying guys bothering you all the time and I don't want to be another dork who sends you glad tidings every minute. Anyway, I just wanted to warn you that I was on my friend's stream called The Noah Weinberg Show! and I was really really WASTED and I said all those things about your freckles and how we had bucatini all'amatriciana together at da Tonino and about how I pictured us reading books to each other one day.

Eunice, I am so sorry to drag your name through the mud like this. I just got carried away and was feeling pretty sad because I miss you and wish we could keep in touch more. I keep thinking about that night we spent in Rome, about every minute of it, and I guess it's become like this foundation myth for me. So I'm trying to stop it and think about other things like my job/financial situation, which is very complicated right now, and my parents, who are not as difficult as yours but let's just say we're not a happy family either. God, I don't know why I just constantly want to open up to you. Again, I'm sorry if I embarrassed you with that ridiculous stream and with the stuff about you reading books.

(Still) Your Friend (hopefully),

Lenny

JUNE 14

EUNI-TARD ABROAD *TO* LEONARDO DABRAMOVINCI:

Okay, Leonard. Fire up that eggplant, I think I'm coming to New York. It's "Arrivederci, Roma" for this girl. Sorry I've been out of touch for so long. I've been sort of thinking about you too, and I really look forward to staying with you for a little while. You're a very sweet and funny guy, Len. But I want you to know that my life blows major testes these days. I just broke up with this guy who was really my type, stuff with my parents, blah, blah, blah. So I may not always be the best company and I may not always treat you right. In other words, if you get sick of me, just throw me out on the curb. That's what people do. Hahaha!

I'll send you the flight info soon as I can. You don't have to pick me up or anything. Just tell me where to go.

I hope this doesn't make you uncomfortable, Lenny Abramov, but my freckles really miss you.

Eunice

P.S. Have you been brushing like I showed you? It's good for you and cuts down on bad breath.

P.P.S. I thought you were pretty cute on your friend Noah's stream but you should really try to get off "101 People We Need to Feel Sorry For." That guy with the SUK DIK overalls is just being cruel to you. You are not a "greasy old schlub," whatever that means, Lenny. You should stand up for yourself.

TOTAL SURRENDER
FROM THE DIARIES OF LENNY ABRAMOV

JUNE 18

Dear Diary,

Oh my God, oh my God, Oh My God! She's here. Eunice Park is in New York. Eunice Park is in my apartment! Eunice Park is sitting NEXT TO ME on my couch while I'm writing this. Eunice Park: a tiny fragment of a human being in purple leggings, pouting at something terrible I may have done, anger in her wrinkled forehead, the rest of her absorbed by her äppärät, checking out expensive stuff on AssLuxury. I am close to her. I am surreptitiously smelling the garlic on her breath, diary. I'm smelling a lunch of Malaysian anchovies and I think I'm about to have a heart attack. Oh, what's wrong with me? Everything, sweet diary. Everything is wrong with me and I am the happiest man alive!

When she teened me she was coming to NYC, I rushed out to the corner bodega and asked for an eggplant. They said they had to order it on their äppärät, so I waited twelve hours by the door, and when it came my hands were shaking so bad I couldn't do anything with it. I just stuck it in the freezer (by accident) and then went out on the balcony and started to weep. From joy, of course!

On the morning of the first day of my real life, I threw out the frozen eggplant, and put on my cleanest, most conservative cotton shirt, which became a monsoon of nervous sweat before I even left for the door. To dry off a little and gain perspective, I sat down and pondered Point No. 3: Love Eunice, the way my parents always sat down before a long trip to pray for a safe journey in their primitive Russian way. *Lenny!* I said aloud. *You are not going to screw this up. You've been given a chance to help the most beautiful woman in the world. You must be good, Lenny. You must not think of yourself at all. Only of this little creature before you. Then you will be helped in turn. If you don't pull this off, if you hurt this poor girl in any way, you will not be worthy of immortality. But if you harness her warm little body to yours and make her smile, if you show her that adult love can overcome childhood pain, then both of you will be shown the kingdom. Joshie may slam the door on you, may watch your heartbeat stutter to a stop in some public hospital bed, but how could anyone deny Eunice Park? How could any god wish her less than eternal youth?*

I wanted to meet Eunice at JFK, but it turns out that you can't even get close to the airport without a plane ticket anymore. The cabbie left me at the third American Restoration Authority checkpoint on the Van Wyck, where the National Guard had set up a greeting area, a twenty-foot camouflaged tarp beneath which a crowd of poor middle-class folk huddled in anticipation of their relatives. I almost missed her flight because a part of the Williamsburg Bridge had collapsed and we spent an hour trying to turn around on Delancey Street next to a hasty new ARA sign that said "Together We'll Repare [sic] This Bridge."

While we were pulling up to the checkpoint, my äppärät came through with another bit of wonderful news. Nettie Fine is alive and well! She teened me, using a new secure address. "Lenny, I'm so sorry if I brought you down when I saw you in Rome. My kids tell me sometimes I can be a real 'Nervous Nettie.' I just wanted to let you know things aren't so bad! There's good news on my desk all the time. There's real change back home. The poor people thrown out of their homes are getting organized just like in the Great Depression. These ex–National Guard boys are building cabins in the parks and protesting that they don't have their Venezuela bonuses. I can just feel a burst of bottom-up energy! Media isn't covering it, but you go take a look in Central Park and tell me what you see.

Maybe the reign of Jeffrey Otter is finally behind us! xxx, Nettie Fine." I teened her right back, telling her that I would go see the Low Net Worth people in the park and that I was in love with a girl named Eunice Park who (I anticipated Nettie's first question) wasn't Jewish but was perfect in every other way.

Filled with good tidings about my American mama, I waited for the UnitedContinentalDeltamerican bus, pacing nervously until the men with the guns began to look at me funny, then retreated into a makeshift Retail space by a dumpster, where I bought some wilting roses and a three-hundred-dollar bottle of champagne. My poor Eunice looked so tired when she huffed off the bus with her many bags that I nearly tackled her in a rejuvenating embrace, but I was careful not to make a scene, waving my roses and champagne at the armed men to prove that I had enough Credit to afford Retail, and then kissed her passionately on one cheek (she smelled of flight and moisturizer), then on the straight, thin, oddly non-Asian nose, then the other cheek, then back to the nose, then once more the first cheek, following the curve of freckles backward and forward, marking her nose like a bridge to be crossed twice. The champagne bottle fell out of my hands, but, whatever futuristic garbage it was made of, it didn't break.

Confronted with this kind of crazy love, Eunice didn't withdraw, nor did she return my ardor. She smiled at me with those full, purple lips of hers and those tired young eyes, abashed, and made a motion with her arms to indicate that the bags were heavy. They were, diary. They were the heaviest bags I've ever carried. The spiky heels of ladies' shoes kept stabbing my abdomen, and a metal tin of unknown provenance, round and hard, bruised my hip.

The cab ride passed in near silence, both of us a little ashamed of the situation, each probably feeling guilty of something (my relative power; her youth), and mindful of the fact that we had spent less than a day together in total and that our commonalities had yet to be determined. "Isn't this ARA shit totally crazy?" I whispered to her, as yet another checkpoint slowed us to a crawl.

"I don't really know much about politics," she said.

She was disappointed by my apartment, by how far it was from
the F line and how ugly the buildings were. "Looks like I'll get some
exercise walking to the train," she said. "Ha ha." This was what her
generation liked to add to the end of sentences, like a nervous tic.
"Ha ha."

"I'm really glad you're here, Eunice," I said, trying to keep everything I said both clear and honest. "I really missed you. I mean, it's
kind of weird. . . ."

"I missed you too, nerd-face," she said.

That single sentence hung in the air between us, the insult wedded
to the intimacy. She had clearly surprised herself, and she didn't
know what to do, whether to add a "ha!" or a "ha ha" or just to
shrug it off. I decided to take the initiative and sat down next to her
on my chrome-and-leather couch, the kind that once graced luxury
cruise ships in the 1920s and '30s and made me wish I was someone
else. She looked at my Wall of Books with a neutral expression, although by now my volumes mostly stank of Pine-Sol Wild Flower
Blast and not their natural printed essence. "I'm sorry you broke up
with that guy in Italy," I said. "You said on GlobalTeens he was
really your type."

"I don't want to talk about him right now," Eunice said.

Good, I didn't either. I just wanted to hold her. She was wearing
an oatmeal sweatshirt, beneath which I could espy the twin straps of
a bra she did not need. Her rough-hewn miniskirt made out of some
kind of sandpaper fiber sat atop a pair of bright-violet pantyhose,
which also seemed unnecessary given the warm June weather. Was
she trying to protect herself from my roving hands? Or was she just
very cold at her center? "You must be tired from the long flight," I
said, putting my hand on her violet knee.

"You're sweating like crazy," she said, laughing.

I wiped at my forehead, coming away with the sheen of my age.
"Sorry," I said.

"Do I really excite you that much, nerd-face?" she asked.

I didn't say anything. I smiled.

"It's nice of you to let me stay here."

"Indefinitely!" I cried.

"We'll see," she said. As I squeezed her knee and made a slight movement upward, she caught my hairy wrist. "Let's take it easy," she said. "I just had my heart broken, remember?" She thought it over and added, "Ha ha."

"Hey, I know what we can do," I said. "It's, like, my favorite thing when the summer comes."

I took her to Cedar Hill in Central Park. She seemed disturbed by the ragged project-dwellers walking and wheeling their way down my stretch of Grand Street, the old Dominicans leering at her and shouting "*Chinita!*" and "You better spend some money, China honey!" in what I hoped was a not-too-threatening way. I made sure to avoid the block where our resident shitter did his business.

"Why do you live here?" Eunice Park asked, perhaps not understanding that real estate in the rest of Manhattan was still grossly unaffordable, despite the last dollar devaluation (or perhaps because of it; I can never figure out how currency works). So, to compensate for my poor neighborhood, I paid the extra ten dollars each at the F train stop and got us into the business-class carriage. As Vish had drunkenly told me the other night, our city's dying transit is now run on a for-profit basis by a bunch of ARA-friendly corporations under the slogan "Together We'll Go Somewhere." In business class, we had the run of the cozy, already slightly browned sofas and the bulky äppäräti chained to a coffee table and dusted with fingerprints and spilled drinks. Heavily armed National Guardsmen kept our carriage free of the ubiquitous singing beggars, break-dancers, and destitute families begging for a Healthcare voucher, the ragtag gaggle of Low Net Worth Individuals who had turned the regular cars into a soundstage for their talents and woes. In business, we were allowed a thousand discrete moments of underground peace. Eunice scanned *The New York Lifestyle Times,* which made me happy, because even though the *Times* is no longer the fabled paper of yore, it's still more text-heavy than other sites, the half-screen-length essays on certain products sometimes offering subtle analysis of the greater world, a piece on a new kohl applicator giving way to a paragraph-long snapshot of the brain economy in the Indian state of Kerala. There was no denying that the woman I had fallen for was thoughtful and bright. I kept my eyes on Eunice Park, at her sun-browned little arms floating above the projected data, ready to pounce when an item she coveted was unfurled on the screen, the green "buy me now" icon hovering beneath her busy index fingers. I watched her so intently, the overlit subway stops flashing meaninglessly outside the windows, that we missed our own stop and had to double back.

Cedar Hill. This is where I start my walks in Central Park. Many years ago, after a violent breakup with an earlier girlfriend (a sad Russian I had dated out of some kind of perverse ethnic solidarity), I used to go to a young, recently accredited social worker just one block over on Madison. For under a hundred dollars every week, someone cared for me in these parts, even if, in the end, Janice Feingold, M.S.W., could not cure me of my fear of nonexistence. Her favorite question: "Why do you think you would be happier if you could live forever?"

After my sessions, I would decompress slowly with a book or an actual printed newspaper amidst the brilliant greenery of Cedar Hill. I would try to assimilate Ms. Feingold's therapeutic view of me as someone worthy of the colors and graces of life, and this particular stretch of Central Park nicely brought home the point of all her good work. Depending on your viewing angle, the Hill can appear a collegiate New England lawn or a dense coniferous forest, gray rocks spread out glacially, cedars cautiously intermingling with pines. The Hill descends eastward to a tiny green valley, unfurling a cast of strollers, long-haired dachshunds wearing polka-dot bandanas, dexterous Anglo-Saxon children in full swing, dark-skinned caregivers, tourists on ethnic blankets enjoying the weather.

What a day it was! The middle of June, the trees coming into their own, the boughs filling abundantly. Everywhere youth for the taking. How to contain the natural reflex to stand up on one's hind legs and sniff poignantly for the warmth of the sun? How to keep one's mouth from finding Eunice's and burrowing inside?

I pointed out a park sign that said "Passive Activities Encouraged." "Funny, huh?" I said to Eunice.

"*You're* funny," she said. She looked at me directly for the first time since she'd landed. There was her customary sneer curling the left side of her lower lip, but, per the sign's directions, it was entirely passive. She put her hands forward, and the sun stroked them before they met the shadow of my own. We held hands briefly and then she looked away from me. *Small doses,* I thought. *This is enough for right now.* But then my mouth started talking. "Boy," it said, "I could really learn to love—"

"I don't want to hurt you, Lenny," she interrupted me.

Easy. Easy does it. "I know you don't," I said. "You're probably still in love with that guy in Italy."

She sighed. "Everything I touch turns to shit," she said, shaking her head, her whole face suddenly older and unforgiving. "I'm a walking disaster. What's *that?*"

It hurt my eyes to part company with her face. But I looked as directed. Someone had built a little wooden shack at the crest of the hill, adding to its rustic appeal. We languidly went up to investigate, I relishing the opportunity to observe her behind, which sat humbly, almost unnecessarily, atop two sturdy legs. I wondered how she would survive in the world without an ass. Everyone needs a cushion. Maybe I could be that for her.

The cabin wasn't wooden actually, just some corrugated metal that had lost so much texture and paint it appeared primordial. A sunflower had been painted on it along with the words "my name aziz jamie tompkins I worked bus driver kicked out of home two days ago this is my space dont shoot." A black man sat on a brick outside the shanty, gray sideburns like my own, an affected cap that on second examination proved to belong to the former Metropolitan Transportation Authority, and the rest of him unremarkable—white T-shirt, golden chain with an oversized yuan symbol—except for the expression on his face. Stunned. He sat there looking to the side, his mouth open, gently breathing in the beautiful air like an exhausted fish, utterly removed from the small crowd of New York natives who had formed respectfully a few yards away to watch his poverty, and the äppäräti-toting tourists just another few yards behind them, jostling for a sightline. From time to time, one could hear the fall of a metal pan inside his shanty, or the opening bars of an obsolete computer trying to boot up, or a woman's low, displeased voice, but the man ignored it all, his eyes blank, one hand poised in midair as if practicing some quiet martial art, the other one scratching miserably at a patch of dead skin spreading along his calf.

"Is he poor?" Eunice asked.

"I guess so," I said. "Middle-class."

"He's a bus driver," a woman said.

"Was," said another.

"They cleared him out for the central banker dude's visit," said a third.

"The *Chinese* Central Banker." This was the first person, an older woman in an odorous T-shirt who clearly belonged to the marginal classes (what was she doing in this part of Manhattan anyway?). Several of her cohorts looked at Eunice, not in a friendly way. I wondered if I should declare to the gathering crowd that my new friend was not Chinese, but Eunice was absorbed by something on her äppärät, or pretending to be. "Don't be scared, sweetie," I whispered to her.

"He was living by the Van Wyck," said the marginalized know-it-all. "They don't want the *Chinese* banker seeing no poor people on the way from the airport. Make us look bad."

"Harm Reduction," a young black man said.

"What the hell's he doing *in the park*?"

"Restoration 'thority not going to like this. Uh-uh."

"Hey, Aziz," the black man yelled. There was no response. "Hey, brother. Better scoot out of here before the National Guard comes." The man in the MTA cap continued to sit there, scratching and meditating. "You don't want to end up in *Troy*," the younger man added. "They'll get your lady too. You *know* what they'll do."

This Aziz guy must have been part of the new "bottom-up" Great Depression movement Nettie Fine was talking about. Only a few hours together, and Eunice and I were already witnesses to history! I took out my äppärät and started to take Images of the man, but the young black man yelled, "What the fuck you doing, son?"

"A friend of mine asked me to take an Image," I said. "She works for the State Department."

"*State Department*? Are you fucking kidding me? You better put that thing away, Mr. 1520-Credit-ranking got-me-a-bitch-twenty-year-younger Bipartisan motherfucker!"

"I'm not a Bipartisan," I said, although I did as I was told. Now I was completely confused. And a little scared. Who *were* these people all around me? Americans, I guess. But what did that even mean anymore?

The conversation behind me was turning to the sensitive subject of China-Worldwide. "Damn China banker," someone was shouting. "When he comes, I'm going to cut up all my credit cards and throw them at him like confetti. I'm gonna shoot his lo mein ass."

The Chinese tourists on the outer perimeter were starting to disband, and I thought it would be wise to move Eunice along too. I looped myself around her shoulders and gently walked her down the hill, away from anyone who could cause her harm, and toward the Model Boat Pond. "I'm okay, I'm okay," she said, squeezing out of my embrace.

"Some of those folks looked a little street," I said.

"And you were going to put your *nerd* moves on them?" Eunice said, laughing brightly.

Some vestigial teenage memory ran up and down my gut, making me cramp. I was perhaps the least popular child in secondary school. I never learned how to fight or carry myself like a man. "Stop calling me that, please," I whispered, rubbing my stomach.

"Ha! I love it when my nerd feigns defiance."

I growled a bit, taking note of her use of the possessive. *My* nerd. Would she really take ownership of me?

We walked slowly and meditatively, neither of us speaking, both of us a little unhappy and a little content. Early-summer evening was settling over the city. The sky was the color of ghosts. The atmosphere, warm but breezy, reeking of pollinated sweetness and baked bread. Crowding around the boat pond were young Euro couples, playful as children, amorous as teenagers, pressing devalued dollars into the hands of T-shirt and trinket vendors, excited by the twilight country around them. Asian kids, learning to be loud and impetuous, chased one another's radio-controlled sloops across the still, gray waters of the pond.

Up above, three military helicopters, evenly spaced, rumbled across the put-upon sky. The fourth, barely tagging along, seemed to hold a giant spear in its maw; the spear glowed yellow at its tip. Only the tourists looked up. I thought of Nettie Fine. I had to believe in her optimism. She had never been wrong before, whereas my parents had been wrong about *everything*. Things were going to get better. Someday. For me to fall in love with Eunice Park just as the world fell apart would be a tragedy beyond the Greeks.

We were walking hand in hand now along the vast grassy Sheep Meadow, which felt comfortable and familial, like a worn rumpus-room carpet or a badly made bed. Beyond it, on three sides, lay the constellation of once-tall buildings, the old ones mansard-topped and stoic, the new ones covered with blinking information. We passed a white-and-Asian couple enjoying an early-summer picnic of prosciutto and melon, which made me squeeze Eunice's hand. She turned around and brushed my graying hair with her moisturized hands. I prepared myself for a comment on my age and looks. I prepared myself to become Chekhov's ugly merchant Laptev again. I knew this hurt so well, it actually had left a strange foretaste in my mouth, that of almonds and salt.

"My sweet emperor penguin," she said instead. "You're so beauticious. You're so smart. And giving. So unlike anyone I've met. So *you*. I bet you can make me so happy, if I just let myself be happy." She kissed me quickly on the lips, as if we had already exchanged a hundred thousand kisses before, then ran into a passing field of green and did three graceful somersaults—one after the other after the other. I stood there. Delirious. Taking in the world in tiny increments. Her simple body parting the air. The parabola of her spine in motion. The open mouth breathing hard after the light exhaustion. Facing me. Freckles and heat. I steeled my chest against what it expected of me. I would not cry.

Gray clouds bearing some kind of industrial remnant moved into the foreground; a yellow substance etched itself into the horizon, became the horizon, became the night. As the sky darkened, we found ourselves enclosed on three sides by the excess of our civilization, yet the ground beneath our feet was soft and green, and behind us lay a hill bearing trees as small as ponies. We walked in silence, as I sniffed the sharp, fruity facial creams that Eunice wore to fight off age, mixed in with just a hint of something alive and corporeal. Multiple universes tempted me with their existence. Like the immutability of God or the survival of the soul, I knew they would prove a mirage, but still I grasped for belief. Because I believed in her.

It was time to leave. We headed south, and when the trees ran out the park handed us over to the city. We surrendered to a skyscraper with a green mansard roof and two stark chimneys. New York exploded all around us, people hawking, buying, demanding, streaming. The city's density caught me unprepared, and I reeled from its imposition, its alcoholic fumes, its hubris, its loud, dying wealth. Eunice looked at some shop windows on Fifth Avenue, her äppärät crawling with new information. "Euny," I said, trying out a shorter version of her name. "How are you feeling right now? Are you jet-lagged?"

She was looking at an alligator skin stretched into a meaningfully large object and failed to answer me.

"Do you want to go to our house?"

Our house?

She was busy scanning the dead amphibian with her äppärät as if it contained an answer. Her lower face was now covered with a smile that was a smile in name only. But when she turned away from the store window, when she appraised me, there was nothing on her face. She was looking into the smooth white emptiness of my neck.

"Don't rub your eyes," she said into that emptiness, sucking the words through her lips, shredding each syllable. "You're killing the cells around your eyes when you rub so hard. That's why there's so much dark skin. It makes you look older." I was hoping she would add "nerd-face," so that I would know it was all right, but she didn't. I didn't understand. What had happened to the somersaults? What had happened to "my sweet emperor penguin"? To that wonderful, utterly unexpected word: "beauticious"?

We walked back to the subway without a syllable between us, her stare covering the ground ahead of her like a beam of negative light. The silence continued. I breathed so hard I thought I would faint. I didn't know how to bring us back to where we were before. I didn't know how to restore us to Central Park, to Cedar Hill, to the Sheep Meadow, to the kiss.

Back in my apartment, with the hollow "Freedom" Tower glowing extra bright behind the thick curtains, and the sound of an empty M22 bus lowering itself for an elderly insomniac, Eunice and I had our first fight. She threatened to move back with her parents.

I was on my knees. I was crying. "Please," I said. "You can't go back to Fort Lee. Just stay here with me a little longer."

"You're pathetic," Eunice said. She was sitting on my couch, hands in her lap. "You're so *weak*."

"All I said was 'I'd like to meet your parents someday.' You're more than welcome to meet mine next week. In fact, I *want* you to meet them."

"Do you know what that means for me? To meet my parents? You don't know me at all."

"I'm trying to know you. I've dated Korean girls before. I understand the families are conservative. I know they're not crazy about whiteys like me."

"You don't understand *anything* about my family," Eunice said. "How could you even *think* . . ."

I lay in my bed, listening to Eunice teening furiously on her äppärät in the living room, probably to her friends in southern California or to her family in Fort Lee. Finally, three hours later, the birds picking up a morning tune outside, she came into the bedroom. I pretended I was asleep. She took off most of her clothes and got in bed next to me, then pressed her warm back and behind into my chest and genitals, so that I ended up spooning her warm body. She was crying. I was still pretending to be asleep. I kissed her in a way that was consistent with my being supposedly asleep. I didn't want her to hurt me anymore that night. She was wearing those panties that snap right off when you press a button on the crotch. Total Surrender, I think they're called. I held on tighter to Eunice, and she pressed deeper into me. I wanted to tell her that it was okay. That I would bring her joy whenever I could. I didn't need to meet her parents right away.

But it wasn't true. This was another thing I had learned about Korean women. The parents were the key to Eunice Park.

SOMETHING NICE IS GROWING INSIDE ME
FROM THE GLOBALTEENS ACCOUNT OF EUNICE PARK

JUNE 18

EUNI-TARD *TO* GRILLBITCH:

Dear Precious Pony,

Sup, my little Busy Bee-iotch? I'm baaaaaaack. America the beautiful. Wow, I still can't believe that everyone's speaking English and not Italiano around me. Well, in Lenny's ghetto neighborhood it's mostly Spanish and Jewish, I guess. But whatever. I'm home. Things are quiet over in Fort Lee, at least for the time being. I'm seeing my parents soon, but I think my dad just quiets down when he knows I'm across the river. I get the feeling that I'm never going to be able to be more than a couple of miles away from my family, which is sad. Also, I think my dad has this radar, and anytime something good happens to me, like meeting Ben in Italy, he starts acting up and I have to drop everything and come back home. I am so sick of my mother saying "You older sister. You have responsibility." Sometimes I try to picture myself without them, just as my own person and doing things on my own, the way I tried to in Rome. But I don't really see it happening.

And now that Sally's getting all Political I feel like I have double responsibility to make sure she doesn't do anything stupid. To be honest, I kind of think it's all bullshit. She never cared about Politics before. When I left for Elderbird it was all Reverend Cho said this, and Reverend Cho said that, and Reverend Cho said it's okay if Daddy dragged Mommy out of bed by the hair because Jesu totally HEARTS sinners. This Politics crap is just another way to act out. Her and my mom and my dad, they all want attention like a bunch of little brats.

I miss Ben a lot. There was something so compatible about me and him. Like we didn't have to say much to each other, we could just lie there in bed for hours, doing whatever on our äppäräti, with the lights turned off. It's different with Lenny. I mean there are so many things wrong with him, and I guess I just have to fix them all. The problem is he's not young, so he thinks he doesn't have to listen to me. His teeth are in so much better shape since I got him to brush correctly and his breath is fresh like a daisy. If only he would take care of his gross feet! I'm going to make him set up an appointment with a podiatrist. Maybe my dad. JBF! My dad would freak if I told him I had a very old white, um, "friend." Ha ha. And then he dresses awful. This Korean girl pal of his named Grace (I haven't met her but I already hate the bitch) goes shopping with him once in a while and she finds all these like old-school hipster outfits with the wide collars and these awful acrylic shirts from the 70s. I hope there's a smoke detector in our apartment cause he just might set himself on fire one day. Anyway, I told him from the start: Look, you're THIRTY-NINE years old and I'm living with you, so now you've got to dress like a grown-up. He got all pissy, my little nerd, but next week we're going shopping for stuff actually made out of ANIMAL PRODUCTS like cotton and wool and ca$hmere and all that good stuff.

So on my first day back we went to the park (Lenny paid for business class on the subway! he can be so thoughtful) and there were all these like little shacks for the homeless people in Central Park. It was really sad. These people are getting kicked out of their homes along the highway because the Chinese central banker is coming and Lenny says the Bipartisans don't want us to look poor in front of our Asian creditors. And this poor black guy was just sitting out front of one of those shacks and he looked like he was so ashamed of what he's become, like when my father thought he was going to lose his practice because now there's no more medicare left. It just takes away dignity from a man when he can't take care of his family. I swear to god I almost started bawling, but I didn't want to give Lenny the impression that I cared about something. And they had this old computer in the shack, not even a real äppärät, I could even hear it starting up it was so loud. I'm not going to get Political on you, Pony, but I don't think it's right that our country doesn't take care of these people. That's one thing about our families, even if things get really bad, they'll always take care of us because they lived through much worse in Korea. You know what's funny. Lenny keeps a journal of all the things he's "celebrating." It's dorky, but I wonder about all the things I should be celebrating and maybe it's the fact that I'm not living in a tin can in Central Park and that you love me and maybe my sister and mom love me too and maybe I have an actual boyfriend who wants a HEALTHY, NORMAL, LOVING relationship with me.

Anyway, then me and Lenny kissed in the park. Nothing more than that for now, but it felt really good, like something nice was growing inside me. I'm trying to take it really slow and get to know him better. Right now I still see us as this mismatched pair. Honestly, I'm afraid to see our reflection when we pass by a mirror, but I think the more time I spend with him the more it feels right. He already told me he loves me, and that I'm the one for him, the one he's been waiting for all his life. And he takes his time with me. He'll listen to me talk about what my father did to me and Sally and Mom and he'll take it in, and sometimes he'll even cry (he cries a lot), and after a while I just start to trust him with everything and I open up the way I would to a girlfriend. And he kind of kisses like a girl too, all quiet and with his eyes closed. HA HA. So far my favorite thing is just walking down the street with him. He'll tell me all these things I never even learned at Elderbird, like that New York used to be owned by the Dutch (what were they even doing in America?), and whenever we see something funny like a cute weenie dog we'll both just totally break out laughing, and he'll hold my hand and sweat and sweat and sweat because he's still so nervous and so happy to be with me.

We fight a lot. I guess it's mostly my fault because I don't appreciate his great personality and just keep focusing on how he looks. Then there's the fact that he desperately wants to meet my parents and there's no effing way that's ever going to happen. Oh, and he said he'll take me to Long Island to meet HIS PARENTS! Like next week. What is wrong with him? He just keeps pushing me and pushing me on the parents issue. I told him I was leaving him and going back to Fort Lee and then my poor sweet nerd got down on his knees and started crying and saying how much I meant to him. He was so pathetic and so cute. I felt so sorry for him that I took off all my clothes, except for my TotalSurrenders and just got in bed with him. He felt me up a little but we fell asleep pretty fast. Damn, Precious Pony. I'm just one chatty ass-hookah these days. I'm going to sign off, but here's an Image of me and Lenny at the zoo in Central Park. He's to the left of the bear. Don't gag!!!!

GRILLBITCH *TO* EUNI-TARD:

Dear Precious Panda,

Welcome back, sticky bun! OK, I gotta run to the Pussy sale again, but really quickly, um, I saw the Image you sent and I really don't know about this Lenny. It's not like he's the most disgusting guy I've ever seen, but he's just not the kind of person I pictured you with. I know you're saying he has all these other qualities but, like, can you imagine how your parents would react if you brought him to their house or to church? Your father would just stare at him, clearing his throat all night long, "ahem, ahem," and then when he left he'd call you a whore or worse. I'm not saying one way or another, I'm just saying you're really beautiful and thin so don't settle. Take your time!

Oh God, I went to my cousin Nam Jun's wedding and I had to say this like totally vomitatious speech to him and his fat halmoni bride. She's like five years older than him and has ankles like redwoods. Slap a green visor and a perm on her, that ajumma is done! And the thing is they really love each other, all they kept doing is crying in each other's arms and she kept feeding him ddok. Sick, I know, but I wonder how I could learn to love somebody like that. Sometimes I walk around as if in a dream, like I'm on the outside looking in, and Gopher and my parents and my brothers are just these ghosts floating past me. Oh, and at the wedding there were all these adorable little girls all painted like cats and wearing little gowns and they kept chasing this little boy around and trying to wrestle him down and I thought of your little cousin Myong-hee. She must be what three by now? I miss her so much I may just drop by your cousin's house and squeeze her to death! Anyway, welcome home, sweet poontang of mine. Big California kiss your way.

JUNE 19

EUNI-TARD: Sally, are you bidding on the gray ankle boots on Padma?

SALLYSTAR: How did you know?

EUNI-TARD: Duh, you're my sister. And they're size 30. Anyway, stop bidding, we're completing against each other.

EUNI-TARD: Oops. COMPETING against each other.

SALLYSTAR: Mom wanted the olive ones, but they didn't have her size.

EUNI-TARD: I'm going to check out the Retail Corridor at Union Square. Don't get the olive. You have an apple-shaped body so you should wear only dark below the waist and NEVER, NEVER wear empire-waist tops, which make you look totally top-heavy.

SALLYSTAR: You're back in the States?

EUNI-TARD: Don't sound so excited. Are you in D.C.?

SALLYSTAR: Yeah, we just got off the bus. It's crazy here. There are all these National Guard troops that just got back from Venezuela and they didn't get the Service Bonus they were promised so they're marching on the Mall with all their guns.

EUNI-TARD: WITH THEIR GUNS??? Sally, maybe you should like LEAVE.

SALLYSTAR: No, it's okay. They're actually pretty nice. It's not fair what the Bipartisans are doing to them. Do you know how many of them died in Ciudad Bolivar? And do you know many of them are like mentally and physically screwed up for life? So what if the government's broke? What are they going to do about our troops? They have a responsibility. This is what happens when there's only one party in charge and we live in a police state. Yeah, I know, I'm not supposed to talk like that over Teens.

EUNI-TARD: Sally, this is ridiculous. Why can't you march in New York? I'll march with you if you want, but I don't want you doing these crazy things by yourself.

SALLYSTAR: Have you been to the house yet? I didn't hear anything from Mommy.

EUNI-TARD: No. Soon. I don't want to see dad just yet. Has he been talking about me?

SALLYSTAR: No, but he's sulking for some reason and we can't figure out why.

EUNI-TARD: Who cares?

SALLYSTAR: I think Uncle Joon is coming.

EUNI-TARD: Great, dad will have to give him money and he'll just go to Atlantic City and blow it all. Like dad's practice has been doing so well that he can afford it.

SALLYSTAR: Where are you staying?

EUNI-TARD: Remember that girl Joy Lee?

SALLYSTAR: From Long Beach? The one who had the armadillo?

EUNI-TARD: She lives downtown now.

SALLYSTAR: Fancy.

EUNI-TARD: Not really. It's by some projects. But don't worry, it's safe.

SALLYSTAR: Reverend Suk's Crusade is next month. You should come.

EUNI-TARD: I hope you're joking.

SALLYSTAR: If you don't want to come to the house you can at least see your family. And maybe you can meet someone. There's tons of Korean guys at the Crusade.

EUNI-TARD: How do you know I'm still not with Ben?

SALLYSTAR: The white guy from Rome?

EUNI-TARD: Yeah WHITE guy. Wow, Barnard's really opened your mind.

SALLYSTAR: Don't be sarcastic. I hate that.

EUNI-TARD: Can't I just see you and talk to you without having to go to some stupid Geejush event? When are you coming home?

SALLYSTAR: Tomorrow. Want to have dinner at Madangsui tomorrow?

EUNI-TARD: Minus dad.

SALLYSTAR: K.

EUNI-TARD: Love you, Sally! Call me the minute you get out of DC and let me know you're safe.

SALLYSTAR: I love you too.

EUNI-TARD *TO* LABRAMOV:

  Lenny,

  I'm going out shopping, if you come home and the delivery comes, can you please make sure the milk is antibiotic-free not just fat-free this time and that they didn't forget the Lavazza Qualità Oro Espresso. Then put the veal and the whole branzino in the fridge and set the white peaches out on the countertop, I'll take care of them later. Don't forget to put the fish and veal in the fridge, Lenny! And if you're going to do the dishes please wipe down the countertop. You always leave water all over the place. You're worried about roaches and water bugs, what do you think they're attracted to? Have a good day, nerd-face.

　Eunice

THE NUCLEAR OPTION
FROM THE DIARIES OF LENNY ABRAMOV

JUNE 25

Dear Diary,

I learned how to say "elephant" in Korean this week.

We went to the Bronx Zoo, because Noah Weinberg said on his stream that the ARA was going to close the place down and ship all the animals to Saudi Arabia "to die of heatstroke." I never know which part of Noah's streams to believe, but, the way we live now, you can never be too sure. We had fun with the monkeys and "José the Beaver" and all the smaller animals, but the highlight was this beautiful savannah elephant named Sammy. When we ambled up to his humble enclosure, Eunice grabbed my nose and said, "*Kokiri.*"

"*Ko,*" she explained, "means 'nose.' *Kokiri.* Long nose. 'Elephant' in Korean."

"I hab a long dose because I'm Jewish," I said, trying to pull her hand off my face. "Dere's duthing I can do aboud it."

"You're so sensitive, Lenny," she said, laughing. "I heart your nose *so much.* I wish I *had* a nose." And she started kissing my comma of a snout in full view of the pachyderm, going gently up and down the endless thing with her tough little lips. As she did so, I locked eyes with the elephant, and I watched myself being kissed in the prism of the elephant's eye, the giant hazel apparatus surrounded with flecks of coarse gray eyebrow. He was twenty-five, Sammy, at the middle of his lifespan, much like I was. A lonely elephant, the only one the zoo had at the moment, removed from his compatriots and from the possibility of love. He slowly flicked back one massive ear, like a Galician shopkeeper of a century ago spreading his arms as if to say, "Yes, this is all there is." And then it occurred to me, lucky me mirrored in the beast's eye, lucky Lenny having his trunk kissed by Eunice Park: *The elephant knows.* The elephant knows there is nothing after this life and very little in it. The elephant is aware of his eventual extinction and he is hurt by it, reduced by it, made to feel his solitary nature, he who will eventually trample his way through bush and scrub to lie down and die where his mother once trembled at her haunches to give him life. Mother, aloneness, entrapment, extinction. The elephant is essentially an Ashkenazi animal, but a wholly rational one—it too wants to live forever.

"Let's go," I said to Eunice. "I don't want *kokiri* to see you kissing my nose like that. It'll only make him sadder."

"Aw," she said. "You're so sweet to animals, Len. I think that's a good sign. My dad had a dog once and he really took care of her."

Yes, diary, so many good signs! Such a positive week. Progress on every front. Hitting most of the important categories. Lov[ing] Eunice (Point No. 3), Be[ing] Nice to Parents (Within Limits) (Point No. 5), and Work[ing] Hard for Joshie (No. 1). I'll get to our (yes, *our*!) visit with the Abramovs in a second, but let me give you a little breakdown on the work situation.

Well, the first thing I did at Post-Human Services was march into the Eternity Lounge and talk to the guy in the red bandana and SUK DIK suit, who put me on his stream "101 People We Need to Feel Sorry For," Darryl from Brown, who stole my desk while I was in Rome. "Hey, guy," I said. "Look, I appreciate the attention, but I got this new girlfriend with 780 Fuckability"—I had made sure to put an Image of Eunice I had taken at the zoo front and center on my äppärät screen—"and I'm kind of, like, trying to play it real coolio with her. So would you mind taking me off your stream?"

"Fuck you, Rhesus," the young fellow said. "I do whatever I

want. You're not, like, my parent. And even if you so *were* my parent I'd still tell you to go plug yourself."

As before, cute young people were laughing at our interaction, their laughter slow and thick and full of educated malice. I was frankly too stunned to reply (I was of the opinion that I was slowly befriending the SUK DIK guy), and even more stunned when my co-worker Kelly Nardl stepped out from behind the fasting-glucose tester, her arms crossed over the redness of her neck and chest, her chin glistening with alkalized water. "Don't you dare talk to Lenny like that, Darryl," she said. "Who do you think you are? What, just because he's older than you? I can't wait to see you hit thirty. I've seen your charts. You've got major structural damage from when you were into heroin and carbs, and your whole stupid Boston family is predisposed to alcoholism and whatever the fuck. You think your metabolism is just going to keep you skinny like that forever? Minus the exercise? When was the last time I saw you working out at ZeroMass or No Body? You are going to age *fast*, my friend." She took me by the arm. "Come on, Lenny," she said.

"It's just because he used to be a buddy of Joshie's," Darryl shouted after us. "You think that gives you a right to defend him? I'm going to tell on both of you to Howard Shu."

"He didn't *used* to be a buddy of Joshie's," Kelly growled at him, and how delightful she looked when enraged, those fierce American eyes, the forthrightness of her tremendous jaw. "They're *still* friends. If it weren't for Original Gangsters like Lenny, there would be no Post-Human Services and you wouldn't have your fat salary and benefits, and you'd probably be getting an M.F.A. in so-called *art and design* at SUNY Purchase right about now, you little turd. So be thankful to your elders or I will *fuck you up*."

We both left the Eternity Lounge proud and confused, as if we had stood up to some crazed, violent child, and I ended up thanking Kelly for half an hour, until she kindly told me to shut up. I worried that Darryl would tell Howard Shu, who would tell Joshie, who would get upset that Kelly was stressing Darryl out, the stressing out of Darryl types a big no-no in our organization. "I don't care," she said, "I'm thinking about quitting anyway. Maybe I'll move back to S.F." The idea of leaving Post-Human Services, of giving up on Indefinite Life Extension and eking out a small hairy lifetime in the Bay Area, seemed to me tantamount to plunging off the Empire State Building with such mass and velocity that the myriad of safety nets would snap beneath you until your skull knew the pavement. I massaged Kelly's shoulders. "Don't," I said. "Don't even think about it, Kel. We're going to stick by Joshie forever."

But Kelly never got reprimanded. Instead, when I walked into our synagogue's main sanctuary one humid morning, Little Bobby Cohen, the youngest Post-Human staffer (I think he's nineteen years old at the most), approached me wearing a kind of saffron·monk getup. "Come with me, Leonard," he said, his Bar Mitzvah voice straining under the profundity of what he was about to do.

"Oh, what's all this?" I asked, my heart pumping blood so hard my toes hurt.

As he led me to a tiny back office where, judging by the sweet-briny smell, the former synagogue's gefilte-fish supply was stored, Little Bobby sang: "May you live forever, may you never know death, may you float like Joshie, on a newborn's breath."

My God! The Desking Ceremony.

And there it was, surrounded by a dozen staffers and our leader (who hugged and kissed me)—my new desk! As Kelly fed me a ceremonial garlic bulb, followed by some sugar-free niacin mints, I surveyed all the pretty young people who had doubted me, all those Darryls and friends of Darryls, and I felt the queasy, mercurial justice of the world. I was back! My Roman failures were near-erased. Now I could begin again. I ran out into the synagogue's sanctuary, where The Boards were noisily registering my existence, the droning but comforting sound of the letters "LENNY A." flipping into place at the very bottom of one of the boards, along with my last blood work—not so hot—and the promising mood indicator "meek but cooperative."

My desk. All three square feet of it, shiny and sleek, full of text and streams and Images rising up from its digital surface, a desk probably worth the 239,000 yuan-pegged dollars I still owed Howard Shu. Ignoring the Eternity Lounge as if it were now beneath me, I spent the bulk of my working week at my desk, opening up several data streams at once so that I resembled a man too busy to bother with socializing.

Affecting a god-like air—my Eunice-kissed proboscis pointed toward the ceiling, both hands caressing the data in front of me, as if ready to make man out of clay—I scanned the files of our prospective Life Lovers. Their white, beatific, mostly male faces (our research shows that women are more concerned with taking care of their progeny than with living forever) flashed before me, telling me about their charitable activities, their plans for humanity, their concern for our chronically ill planet, their dreams of eternal transcendence with like-minded yuan billionaires. I guessed that the last time they had been so painfully dishonest was when they penned their applications to Swarthmore forty years earlier.

I picked out the profiles that appealed the most to me, some for the usual financial, intellectual, or "durability" (health) reasons, but others because they could not keep the fear out of their eyes, the fear that, for all the wealth and sinecures they had amassed, for all their supplicating children and grandchildren, the end was irreversible, the lapse into the void a tragedy before which all tragedies were scandalously trite, their progeny a joke, their accomplishments a drop of fresh water in a salty ocean. I scanned the good cholesterol and the bad, the estrogen buildups and the financial crack-ups, but mostly I was looking for the equivalent of Joshie's funny limp: An admission of weakness and insignificance; an allusion to the broad unfairness and cosmic blundering of the universe we inhabit. And an intense desire to set it right.

One of my Intakes, let's call him Barry, ran a small Retail empire in the Southern states. He looked suitably cowed by what Howard Shu must have told him before he was handed over to me. We accepted, on average, 18 percent of our High Net Worth applicants, our dreaded rejection letter still sent out by actual post. The Intake lasted a while. Barry, trying to subdue any remaining trace of his Alabama drawl, wanted to sound knowledgeable about our work. He asked about cellular inspection, repair, and reconstruction. I painted him a three-dimensional picture of millions of autonomous nanobots inside his well-preserved squash-playing body, extracting nutrients, supplementing, delivering, playing with the building blocks, copying, manipulating, reprogramming, replacing blood, destroying harmful bacteria and viruses, monitoring and identifying pathogens, reversing soft-tissue destruction, preventing bacterial infection, repairing DNA. I tried to remember how enthusiastic I had been upon first joining Joshie's enterprise as an NYU senior. I used my hands a lot, the way the faded Roman actors had done at da Tonino, the restaurant where I had taken Eunice and fed her the spicy eggplant. "How soon?" Barry asked, visibly excited by *my* excitement. "When will all this be possible?"

"We're almost there," I said, despairing. The 239,000 yuan-pegged dollars I owed Howard Shu would be deducted on the first of the next month. That money was supposed to be my deposit for the first of many beta dechronification treatments. Forget my name on The Boards. The train was pulling out of the station and I was running behind it, my suitcase half open, white underwear spilling comically along the platform.

I took Barry all the way over to the wasteland of York Avenue to our research center, the ten-story slab of concrete that once served as an adjunct to a large hospital. It was time for him to meet out Indians. We have this Cowboys and Indians theme going on at Post-Human Services. At the Life Lovers Outreach division we call ourselves Cowboys; the "Indians" are the actual research staff, mostly on loan from the Subcontinent and East Asia, housed at an eighty-thousand-square-foot facility on York and at three satellite locations in Austin, Texas; Concord, Massachusetts; and Portland, Oregon.

The Indians keep things pretty simple. There really isn't much to see in the areas to which visitors are allowed—basically the same thing you see in any office—young people with äppäräti, immune to the rest of the world, maybe the occasional glass cage filled with mice or some kind of spinning thingamabob. Two of our most sociable guys, both named Prabal, came out to greet him from the cancer and viral labs and burdened him with yet more terminology while letting out a few practiced promos: "We're past the alpha testing, Mr. Barry. I'd say we're definitely at the beta stage."

Back at the synagogue, I gave Barry the willingness-to-live test. The H-scan test to measure the subject's biological age. The willingness-to-persevere-in-difficult-conditions test. The Infinite Sadness Endurance Test. The response-to-loss-of-child test. He must have sensed how much was at stake, his sharp WASP-y beak aquiver as the Images were projected against his pupils, the results streaming on my äppärät. He would do anything to persevere. He was saddened by life, by the endless progression from one source of pain to another, but not more than most. He had three children and would cling to them forever, even if his present-day bank account would not be able to preserve more than two *for eternity*. I entered "Sophie's Choice" on my intake äppärät, a major problem as far as Joshie was concerned.

Barry was exhausted. The Patterson-Clay-Schwartz Language Cognition Test, the final barometer for selection, could await another session. I knew already that this perfectly reasonable, preternaturally kind fifty-two-year-old would not make the cut. He was doomed, like me. And so I smiled at him, congratulated him on his candor and patience, his intellect and maturity, and with a tap of my finger against my digital desk threw him onto the blazing funeral pyre of history.

I felt shitty about Barry, but even shittier about myself. Joshie's office was crammed with people all day long, but during a quiet moment I found him by the window, staring quizzically at a sky of untrammeled blue, just a fat lone military helicopter trudging toward the East River, its armored beak pointed downward as if it were a predatory bird hunting for food. I sidled up to him. He nodded, not unfriendly, but with some tired reserve. I told him the story of Barry, stressing the man's innate goodness and his problem of having too many children, whom he loved, and not enough money to save all of them, which elicited a shrug on his part. "Those who want to live forever will find a means of doing so," Joshie said, a cornerstone of the Post-Human philosophy.

"Hey, Grizzly," I said, "do you think you can put me in for some of the dechronification treatments at a reduced rate? Just basic soft-tissue maintenance, and maybe a few bio years shaved off?"

Joshie regarded the nine-foot fiberglass Buddha that furnished his otherwise empty office, its blissed-out gaze emitting alpha rays. "That's only for clients," he said. "You know that, Rhesus. Why do you have to make me say it out loud? Stick with the diet and exercise. Use stevia instead of sugar. You've still got a lot of life left in you."

My sadness filled the room, took over its square, simple contours, crowding out even Joshie's spontaneous rose-petal odor. "I didn't mean that," Joshie said. "Not just *a lot* of life. Maybe forever. But you can't fool yourself into thinking that's a certainty."

"You'll see me die someday," I said, and immediately felt bad for saying it. I tried, as I had done since childhood, to feel nonexistence. I forced coldness to run through the natural humidity of my hungry second-generation-immigrant body. I thought of my parents. We would all be dead together. Nothing would remain of our tired, broken race. My mother had bought three adjoining plots at a Long Island Jewish cemetery. "Now we can be together forever," she had told me, and I had nearly broken down in tears at her misplaced optimism, at the notion that she would want to spend her idea of eternity—and what could her eternity *possibly* comprise?—with her failure of a son.

"You'll see me extinguished," I told Joshie.

"That would be a big heartbreak for me, Lenny," Joshie said, his voice broken with exhaustion, or maybe just boredom.

"Three hundred years from now, you won't even remember me. Just some flunky."

"Nothing is guaranteed," Joshie said. "Even *I* can never be sure of whether my personality will survive forever."

"It will," I said. A father should never outlive his child, I wanted to add, although I knew Joshie would disagree on principle.

He put his hand on the side of my neck and squeezed lightly. I leaned in to him a little, hoping for more of his touch. He massaged softly. There was nothing special in that; we Post-Human staffers massage one another regularly. Still, I soaked in his warmth and believed it was only for me. I thought of Eunice Park and her pH-balanced body, healthy and strong. I thought of the warm early-summer day gathering in force outside the bay window, the New York of early summers past, the city that used to hold so many promises, the city of a million IOUs. I thought of Eunice's lips on my nose, the love mixed in with the pain, the foretaste of almonds and salt. I thought of how it was all just too beautiful to ever let go.

"We're only getting started, Lenny," Joshie said, his strong hand squeezing like a clamp at my tired flesh. "For now, diet and exercise. Focus on the work to keep your mind busy, but don't overthink or give in to anxiety. There's going to be loads of *tsuris* ahead. *Trouble*," he clarified, when I didn't catch on to the Yiddish word. "But also loads of opportunities for the right kind of people. And, *hey*, be happy you got your desk back."

"The LIBOR rate's fallen fifty-seven basis points according to CrisisNet," I said knowledgeably.

But he was looking into my äppärät, at an Image of Eunice flashing hard above the other data streams. She was pictured at a wedding of one of her ridiculously young Elderbird College friends in southern California, wearing a black polka-dotted dress that clung to her frame, desperately trying to coax out the preliminaries of an adult woman's body. Her skin glowed in the warm afternoon sun, and her look was one of coy pleasure. "That's Eunice," I said. "That's my girl. I think you'll really like her. Do you like her?"

"She looks healthy."

"Thank you," I said, beaming. "I can forward you an Image of her if you'd like. She's like a poster child for eternity."

"That's okay," he said. He looked at the Image some more. "Good boy, Lenny," he said. "Well done."

. . .

The next day, Eunice and I took the Long Island Rail Road to West-bury, Long Island, to meet the Abramovs. The love I felt for her on that train ride had a capital and provinces, parishes and a Vatican, an orange planet and many sullen moons—it was systemic and it was complete. I knew Eunice was not ready to meet my parents, but she was doing it anyway, and she was doing it to please me. This was the first major kindness she had shown me, and I was drowning in appreciation.

My sweet girl was nervous almost to the point of quaking (how many times could she reapply her lip gloss and wipe the shine off her nose?), which showed that she cared about me. She was dressed for the occasion, an extra pinch of conservatism in her outfit, a sky-blue blouse with a Peter Pan collar and white buttons, pleated wool skirt reaching down below the knees, a black ribbon tied around the neck—from certain angles, she looked like one of the Orthodox Jewish women who have overrun my building. The usual Korean elder-worship and elder-fear brought out a strange immigrant pride in me. With Eunice sweating so handsomely on her orange pleather commuter-train seat, I could project the natural longevity of our re-lationship, and, for a moment at least, the feeling that we were ful-filling our natural roles as the offspring of difficult parents from abroad.

There was something else too. My first love for a Korean girl de-veloped on the Long Island Rail Road some twenty-five years ago. I had been a freshman at a prestigious math-and-science high school in Tribeca. Most of the other kids were Asian, and although techni-cally you had to live within the confines of New York City to attend, there were more than a few of us who faked our residency and com-muted from various parcels of Long Island. The ride to Westbury amidst dozens of fellow nerd-students was a particularly difficult one, because it was public knowledge at the science high school that my weighted average was a dismal 86.894, while at least 91.550 had been recommended for entry into Cornell or the University of Pennsylvania, the weakest of the Ivy League schools (as immigrant children from high-performing nations, we knew our parents would slap us across the mouth for anything less than Penn). Several of the Korean and Chinese boys who took the railroad with me—their spiky hair still haunts my most literal dreams—would dance around me singing my average, "Eighty-six point eight nine four, eighty-six point eight nine four!"

"You won't even get into Oberlin with that."

"Have fun at NYU, Abramov."

"See you at the University of Chicago! It's the teacher of teachers!"

But there was one girl, another Eunice—a Eunice Choi, to be exact—a tall, quiet beauty, who would pry the boys away from me while shouting, "It's not Lenny's fault he can't do well in school! Remember what Reverend Sung says. We're all different. We all have different abilities. Remember the Fall of Man? We're all fallen creatures."

And then she'd sit down with me and, unbidden, help me with my impossible chemistry homework, moving the strange letters and numbers around my notebook until the equations were, for some reason, deemed "balanced," while I, utterly unbalanced by the magical girl next to me, her silken skin glowing beneath her summer gym shorts and orange Princeton jersey, tried to catch a brief smell of her hair or a brush of her hard elbow. It was the first time a woman had risen to defend me, had given me the inkling of an idea that I should actually be defended, that I wasn't a bad person, just not as skilled at life as some others.

At Westbury, Euny and I disembarked before an armored personnel carrier sitting by the squat station house, its .50-caliber Browning gun bouncing up and down, tracking the departing train as if waving a fond, spirited farewell. National Guardsmen were checking the äppäräti of the diverse crowd, Salvadorans and Irish and South Asians and Jews and whoever else had chosen to make this corner of central Long Island the rich, smelly tapestry it has now become. The troops appeared angrier and more sunburned than usual; perhaps they had just been rotated out from Venezuela. Two men—one brown-skinned, one not—had been taken off the line and were being pushed into the APC. All you could hear were the whirs and clicks of our äppäräti being downloaded and the competing chirping of the cicadas emerged from their seven-year slumber. And the looks on the faces of my countrymen—passive heads bent, arms at their trousers, everyone guilty of not being their best, of not earning their daily bread, the kind of docility I had never expected from Americans, even after so many years of our decline. Here was the *tiredness* of failure imposed on a country that believed only in its opposite. Here was the end product of our deep moral exhaustion. I almost teened Nettie Fine a message, begging her to lend me some of that sparkling native-born hope. Did she really think things were going to get better?

A paunched, goateed *muzhik* in a camouflaged helmet scanned my äppärät with an unhappy display of teeth and a gust of morning breath that had lasted well into the afternoon. "Malicious *per*vision of data," he barked at me in an accent that I placed somewhere between Appalachia and the deeper South, the word "data" now a three-syllable wonder. (How did this faux-Kentuckian become a *New York* National Guardsman?) "What the heck, son?" he said.

I deflated immediately. The world momentarily retreated into its contours. More than anything, I was scared to be scared in front of Eunice. I was her protector in this world. "No," I said. "No, sir. That's being fixed. That's a mistake. I was on a plane from Rome with a seditious fat man. I told the otter 'Some Italians' but I guess he thought 'Somalians.' "

The soldier held up a hand. "You work for Staatling-Wapachung?" he asked, mispronouncing the complicated name of my employer at at least four junctures.

"Yes, sir. Post-Human Services division, sir." The word "sir" felt like a broken weapon at my feet. Again I wished my parents were nearer to me, even though they were less than two miles away. I thought of Noah for some reason. Could he really be collaborating with the ARA, as Vishnu had suggested? If so, could he help me right now?

"Deny and imply?"

"What?"

The man sighed. "Do you deny the *ex*-istence of our conversation and imply consent?"

"Yes. Of course!"

"Fingerprint here." I grazed the pad of his thick brown äppärät with my thumb.

A flick of the wrist. "Move along." And as I did so, a legend on the armored personnel carrier caught my eye: "WAPACHUNG CONTINGENCY EQUIPMENT LEASE/OWN." Wapachung Contingency was the frighteningly profitable security branch of our parent company. What the hell was going on here?

We took a cab to my parents' house, passing various examples of modest two-story capes covered with aluminum siding, New York Yankee pennants streaming from every other door—the kind of striving neighborhood where all the money goes into the forty-by-hundred-foot lawns, which even in the overripe heat of the East Coast summer bristle with carefully cultivated greenness. I felt a little embarrassed, because I knew that Eunice's parents were much better off than mine, but I was pleased at how things had worked out with that twanging National Guardsman, at the appearance of power and grace that had been bestowed upon me as an employee of the mighty Staatling-Wapachung Corporation, which was now apparently arming the National Guard. "Were you scared back there, Euny?" I asked.

"I know my *kokiri* isn't some deviant criminal," she said, rubbing my nose and leaning forward so that I could kiss her brow, celebrate the fact that she could make jokes in these difficult times.

In a few minutes we reached the corner of Washington Avenue and Myron, the most important corner of my life. I could already see my parents' brownish half-brick, half-stucco cape, the golden mailbox out in front, the faux nineteenth-century lamp beside it, the cheap lawn chairs stacked on the island of cement that passed for the front porch, a black horse-and-carriage motif across the steel screen door (I do not mean to besmirch their taste; all this junk came with the house), and the gigantic flags of the United States of America and SecurityState Israel billowing in the hazy breeze from two flagpoles. The flavorful husk of Mr. Vida, my parents' neighbor and my father's best friend, waved from the porch across the street, and shouted something encouraging at me and possibly salacious at Eunice. Both my dad and Mr. Vida had been engineers in their homelands reduced to working-class life: big callused hands, small horny bodies, clever brown eyes, a thickly landscaped conservatism, and striving, hustling children, three for Mr. Vida to my father's one. His son Anuj and I went to NYU together, and now the little bastard was a senior analyst at AlliedWasteCVSCitigroup.

I took Eunice's arm and led her over my parents' pristine lawn. At the door my mother appeared in her usual outfit—white panties and utilitarian bra—a woman who since taking her retirement had committed herself to intensive housebound living and whom I haven't seen in proper dress for years.

She was about to throw her arms around my neck in typically overblown fashion when she noticed Eunice, let out some Russian garble of amazement, and retreated inside the house, leaving me, per the usual, with the visuals of her thick gravity-pulled breasts and white little round of belly. My father, shirtless, in stained beige shorts, soon took her place, also gaped at Eunice, ran his hand against his naked muscular breasts perhaps out of embarrassment, said "O!" then hugged me anyway. There was hair against my new dress shirt, the gray carpet that my father wore with an odd touch of class, as if he were a royal in some tropical country. He kissed me on both cheeks and I did the same, feeling the flood of intimacy, of sudden closeness with a person who usually orbited so far away from me. The instructions, the Confucian-like code of Russian father-son relations, spooled in my mind: Father means I have to love him, have to listen to him, can't offend him, can't hurt him, can't bring him to task for past wrongs; an old man now, defenseless, deserving of all I can offer.

My mother reappeared in shorts and a wife-beater. *"Sinotchek"* ("Little son"), she shouted, and kissed me in the same meaningful way. "Look who's come to us! *Nash lyubimeits*" ("Our favorite").

She shook Eunice's hand, and both of my parents swiftly evaluated her, affirmed that she was, like her predecessors, not Jewish, but quietly approved of the fact that she was thin and attractive with a healthy black mane of hair. My mother unwrapped her own precious blond locks from the green handkerchief that kept them safe from the American sun and smiled prettily at Eunice, her skin gentle and pale, aged only around the frantically moving mouth. She began talking in her brave post-retirement English about how glad she was to have a potential daughter-in-law (a perennial dream—two women against two men, better odds at the dinner table), filling in the contours of her loneliness with rapid-fire questions about my mysterious life in faraway New York. "Does Lenny keep clean house? Does he vacuum? Once, I came to college dormitory, okh, awful! Such smell! Dead ficus tree! Old cheese on table. Socks hanging in window."

Eunice smiled and spoke in my favor. "He's very good, Ms. Abramov. He's very clean." I looked at her with endearment. Somewhere beneath the bright suburban skies I felt the presence of a .50-caliber Browning gun swiveling toward an incoming Long Island Rail Road train, but here I stood, surrounded by the people who loved me.

"I got Tagamet from the discount pharmacy," I said to my father, taking five boxes out of the bag I'd brought.

"Thank you, *malen'kii*" ("little one"), my father said, taking hold of his beloved drug. "Peptic ulcer," he said to Eunice gravely, pointing at the depth of his tortured stomach.

My mother had already grabbed hold of the back of my head and was madly stroking my hair. "So gray," she said, shaking her head in an exaggerated way, as if she were an American comedic actress. "So old he gets. Almost forty. Lyonya, what is happening to you? Too much stress? Also losing hair. Oh my God!"

I shook her off. Why was everyone so concerned about my decline?

"You are named Eunice," my father said. "Do you know where it come from, such name?"

"My parents . . ." Eunice gamely began.

"It from the Greek, *yoo-nee-kay.* Meaning 'victorious.' " He laughed, happy to demonstrate that, before he was forced to be a janitor in America, he had served as a quasi-intellectual and minor dandy on Moscow's Arbat Street. "So I hope," he said, "that in life you will be victorious also!"

"Who cares about Greek, Boris," my mother said. "Look at how she is beautiful!" The fact that my parents admired Eunice's looks and capacity for victory brightened me quite a bit. All these years, and I still craved their approval, still longed for the carrot and stick of their nineteenth-century child-rearing. I instructed myself to lower the heat of my emotions, to think without the family blood bursting at my temples. But it was all for nought. I became twelve years old as soon as I passed the mezuzah at the front door.

Eunice blushed at the compliments and looked at me with fear and surprise, as my father began to lead me to the living-room couch for our usual heart-to-heart. My mother rushed over to the couch with a plastic bag which she draped over the place where I was about to sit in my compromised Manhattan outerwear, then took Eunice to the kitchen, chatting gaily to the potential daughter-in-law and ally about how "guys can be so dirty, you know," and how she had just built a new storage device for her many mops.

On the couch, my father draped his arm around my shoulders— there it was, the closeness—and said, "*Nu, rasskazhi*" ("So, tell me").

I breathed in the same breath as he did, as if we were connected. I felt his age seep into mine, as if he were the forward guard of my own mortality, although his skin was surprisingly unwrinkled, and he bore an odor of vitality on his skin, along with an afterthought of decay. I spoke in English with the tantalizing hints of Russian I had studied haphazardly at NYU, the foreign words like raisins shining out of a loaf. I mentally recorded some of the harder words for consultation with my non-digital Oxford Russian-English dictionary back home. I spoke about work, about my assets, about the 239,000 yuan-pegged dollars I owed Howard Shu (*"Svoloch kitaichonok"* ["Little Chinese swine"], my father rendered his opinion), about the

most recent, fairly positive valuation of my 740-square-foot apartment on the Lower East Side, about all the monetary things that
kept us fearful and connected. I gave him a photocopy of who I was,
without telling him that I was unhappy and humiliated and often,
just like him, all alone.

He held up the pendant of my new äppärät. "How much?" he
said, turning the thing over, varicolored data pouring over his hairy
fingers. When I explained that the device was gratis, he made a
happy snort and said in pure English: "Learn new technology for
free is good."

"How's your Credit?" I asked him.

"Eh." He waved the thought away. "I never go near those Poles,
so who cares?"

The floor beneath my feet was clean, immigrant clean, clean
enough so that you understood that somebody had done their best.
My father had two old-fashioned *televizor* screens stapled to the
walls above my mother's fanatically waxed mantelpiece. One was set
to a FoxLiberty-Prime stream, which was showing the growing tent
city in Central Park, now spreading from the backyard of the Metropolitan Museum, over hill and dale, all the way down to the Sheep
Meadow (*"Obeyziani"* ["Monkeys"], my father said of the displaced and homeless protesters). On the other screen, FoxLiberty-
Ultra was viciously broadcasting the arrival of the Chinese Central
Banker at Andrews Air Force Base, our nation lying prostrate before
him, our president and his pretty wife trying not to shiver as a bleak
Maryland downpour scoured the heat-cracked tarmac.

When I asked my father how he was feeling, he pointed at his
heartburn and sighed. Then he began to talk about the news on "the
Fox." Sometimes when he spoke I surmised that, at least in his own
mind, he had already ceased to exist, that he thought of himself as
just an empty spot cruising through a ridiculous world. Speaking in
the complicated Russian sentences that English had denied him, he
praised Defense Secretary Rubenstein, talked about all that he and
the Bipartisan Party had done for our country, and how, with
Rubenstein's blessing, SecurityState Israel should now use the nu-

clear option against the Arabs and the Persians, "in particular against Damascus, which, if winds are properly positioned, *s bozhei pomochu* ['with the help of God'], will carry poison clouds and fall-outs in direction of Teheran and Baghdad," as opposed to Jerusalem and Tel Aviv.

"You know I saw Nettie Fine in Rome," I told him. "At the embassy."

"And how is our American mama? Does she still think we are 'cruel'?" He laughed, somewhat cruelly.

"She thinks the people in the parks are going to rise up. The ex–National Guardsmen. There's going to be a revolution against the Bipartisans."

"*Chush kakaia!*" ("What nonsense!") my father shouted. But then he thought about it for a few moments and spread his arms. "What can be done about someone like her?" he finally said. "*Liberalka.*"

I felt my father's breath against my cheek for twenty minutes as he talked about his complex political life, then excused myself, unwound from his humid embrace, and went to the upstairs bathroom, as my mother shouted to me from the kitchen: "Lenny, don't take your shoes off in upstairs bathroom. Papa has *gribok*" ("athlete's foot").

In the contaminated bathroom, I admired the strange blob of plastic with wooden spokes that kept my mother's serious mop-collection in ready-to-access mode. Although my parents never had a good word to say about HolyPetroRussia, the hallways were hung with framed sepia-toned postcards of Red Square and the Kremlin; the snow-dusted equestrian statue of Prince Yuri Dolgorukiy, founder of Moscow (I had learned just a bit of Russian history at my father's knee); and the gothic Stalin-era skyscraper of prestigious Moscow State University, which neither of my parents had attended, because, to hear them tell it, Jews were not allowed in back then. As for me, I have never been to Russia. I have not had the chance to learn to love it and hate it the way my parents have. I have my own dying empire to contend with, and I do not wish for any other.

My bedroom was nearly empty; all the traces of my habitation, the posters and little bits of crap from my travels, my mother had stowed away in carefully labeled boxes in the closets. I reveled in the smallness, the coziness of an upstairs bedroom in a traditional American Cape Cod house, the half-floor that forces you to duck, to feel small and naïve again, ready for anything, dying for love, your body a chimney filled with odd, black smoke. These square, squat, awkward rooms are like a fifty-square-foot paean to teenage-hood, to ripeness, to the first and last taste of youth. I cannot begin to tell you how much the purchase of this house, of each tiny bedroom, had meant to my family and to me. I still remember the signing at the real-estate lawyer's office, the three of us beaming at one another, mentally forgiving one another a decade and a half worth of sins, the youthful beatings administered by my father, my mother's anxieties and manias, my own teenage sullenness, because the janitor and his wife had done something right at last! And it would all be okay now. There was no turning back from this, from the glorious fortune we had been granted in the middle of Long Island, from the carefully clipped bushes by the mailbox (our bushes, **ABRAMOV** bushes) to the oft-mentioned Californian possibility of an aboveground swimming pool in the back, a possibility that never came true, because of our poor finances, but which could never be decisively put to bed either. And this, my room, whose privacy my parents had never respected, but where I would still find a summer's hot sanctuary on my glorified army cot, my little teenaged arms doing the only nonmasturbatory thing they were capable of, hoisting aloft a big red volume of Conrad, my soft lips moving along with the dense words, the warped wood-paneled walls absorbing the occasional clicks of my tongue.

Out in the hallway, I caught sight of another framed memento. An essay my father had written in English for the newsletter of the Long Island scientific laboratory where he worked (it had made it onto the paper's front page, to our family's pride), and which I, as an undergraduate NYU English major, had helped to proofread and refine.

THE JOYS OF PLAYING BASKETBALL

By Boris Abramov

Sometimes life is difficult and one wishes to relieve oneself of the pressures and the worries of life. Some people see a shrink, others jump in a cold lake or travel around the world. But I find nothing more joyful than playing basketball. At the Laboratory we have many men (and women!) who like to play basketball. They come from all over the world, from Europe, Latin America, and everywhere else. I cannot say I am the best player, I am not so young anymore, my knees hurt, and I am also pretty short and this is a handicap. But I take the game very seriously and when a big problem comes up in my life and I feel like I do not want to live, I sometimes like to picture myself on the court, trying to throw a ball from a great distance into the hoop or maneuvering against an agile opponent. I try to play in a smart way. As a result, I find that I am often victorious even against a much taller or faster player, from Africa or Brazil, let's say. But win or lose, what's important is the spirit of this beautiful game. So if you have time on Tuesday or Thursday at lunchtime (12:30), please join me and your colleagues for a good, healthy time in the physical education center. You'll feel better about yourself and the worries of life will "melt away"! *Boris Abramov is a custodian in the Buildings and Grounds division.*

I remember trying to get my father to take out the part about being "pretty short," and the bit about the pained knees, but he said he wanted to be honest. I told him in America people liked to ignore their weak points and to stress their incredible accomplishments. Now that I think about it, I felt guilty about being born in Queens and having lots of nutritious food on my plate, food that allowed me to grow to a semi-normal height of five feet and nine inches, whereas my father had barely scraped the five-and-a-half-foot mark. It was he, the athlete, not I, the soft and stationary one, who needed those extra inches to sail the basketball past some Brazilian pituitary giant.

The familiar cry of my mother resounded downstairs: *"Lyonya, gotovo!"* ("Lenny, dinner is ready!")

Down in the dining room, with the shiny Romanian furniture the Abramovs had imported from their Moscow apartment (the totality of it could be squeezed into one small American room), the table was laid out in the hospitable Russian manner, with everything from four different kinds of piquant salami to a plate of chewy tongue to every little fish that ever inhabited the Baltic Sea, not to mention the sacred dash of black caviar. Eunice sat, Queen Esther–like in her Orthodox getup, at the ceremonial end of the table, upon a fluffed-up Passover pillow, frowning at the attention, unsure how to deal with the strange currents of love and its opposite that circulated in the fish-smelling air. My parents sat down, and my father proposed a seasonal toast in English: "To the Creator, who created America, the land of free, and who give us Rubenstein, who kill Arab, and to love which is blooming in such times between my son and Yooo-neee-kay, who [big wink to Eunice] will be victorious, like Sparta over Athens, and to the summer, which is most conducive season to love, although some may say spring. . . ."

While he went on in his booming voice, a vodka shot glass of some weird garage-sale provenance shaking in his troubled hand, my mother, bored, leaned over to me and said: *"Kstati, u tvoei Eunice ochen' krasivye zuby. Mozhet byt' ty zhenishsya?"* ("By the way, your Eunice has very pretty teeth. Maybe you will marry?")

I could see Eunice's mind absorbing the basics of my father's speech (Arabs—bad; Jews—good; Chinese Central Banker—possibly okay; America—always number one in his heart), while gauging the intent on my mother's face as she spoke to me in Russian. Eunice's mind moved so quickly through feelings and ideas, but the fear on her face reflected a life rushing by faster than she could make sense of it.

The toast put to rest, unraveled in some happy political mumbling, we shoveled in the food without reservation, all of us from countries historically strangled by starvation, none of us strangers to salt and brine. "Eunice," my mother said, "perhaps you can answer for me this. Who is Lenny by profession? I never can figure out. He went to NYU business school. So he is . . . businessman?"

"Mama," I said, letting out some air, "please."

"I am talking to Eunice," my mother said. "Girl talk."

I had never seen Eunice's face so serious, even as the tail end of a Baltic sardine disappeared between her glossy lips. I wondered what she might say. "Lenny does very important work," she told my mother. "It's, I think, like, medicine. He helps people live forever."

My father's fist slammed the dining table, not hard enough to break the Romanian contraption, but enough to make me draw into myself, enough to make me worry that he might hurt me. "Impossible!" my father cried. "It break every law of physics and biology, for one. For two, immoral, against God. Tphoo! I would not want such thing."

"Work is work," my mother said. "If stupid rich American want to live forever and Lenny make money, why you care?" She waved her hand at my father. "Stupid," she said.

"Yes, but how Lenny knows about medicine?" My father lit up, brandishing a fork capped by a marinated mushroom. "He never study in high school. What is his weighted average? Eighty-six point eight nine four."

"NYU Stern Business School rated number eleven for marketing, which was Lenny specialization," my mother reminded him, and I warmed to her defense of me. They took turns attacking and defending me, as if each wanted to siphon off only so much of my love, while the other could stab at the crusted-over wounds. My mother turned to Eunice. "So Lenny tell us you speak perfect Italian," she said.

Eunice blushed some more. "No," she said, lowering her eyes and cupping her knees. "I'm forgetting everything. The irregular verbs."

"Lenny spend one year in Italy," my father said. "We come to visit him. *Nothing!* Bleh-bleh-bleh. Bleh-bleh-bleh." He moved his body as if to imitate my walking through the Roman streets while trying to talk to the natives.

"You are liar, Boris," my mother said casually. "He bought us beautiful tomato in market Piazza Vittorio. He brought down price. Three euro."

"But tomato is so simple!" my father said. "In Russian *pomidor*, in Italian *pomodoro*. Even I know such thing! If he maybe negotiate for us cucumber or squash . . ."

"Zatknis' uzhe, Borya" ("Shut up already, Boris"), my mother said. She readjusted her summer blouse and bored her eyes into mine. "Lenny, neighbor Mr. Vida show us you appear on stream '101 People We Need to Feel Sorry For.' Why do you do it? This dick-sucking boy, he makes fun of you. He says you are fat and stupid and old. You don't eat good food and you do not have profession and your Fuckability rankings are very low. Also he says *tebya ponizili* ['you have been demoted'] at the company. Papa and I are very sad about this."

My father looked away in some shame, while I curled and uncurled my toes beneath the table. So this was at the heart of their anger with me. I had told them *so many times* not to look at any streams or data about me. I was a private person with my own little world. I lived in a Naturally Occurring Retirement Community. I had just learned to FAC. Why couldn't they find a better use for their retirement years than this painful scrutiny of their only child? Why did they stalk me with their tomatoes and high-school averages and "Who are you by profession?" logic?

And then I heard Eunice speak, her straightforward American English ringing against the smallness of our house. "I told him not to appear in it too," she said. "And he won't anymore. You won't, right, Lenny? You're so good and smart, why do you need to do it?"

"Exactly," my mother said. "Exactly, Eunice."

I did not tell them that I had regained my desk. I did not say anything. I leaned back and watched the two women in my life look across a glossy Romanian table groaning beneath a plastic cover and twenty gallons of mayonnaise and canned fish. They were eyeing each other with a placid understanding. Sometimes mothers and girlfriends compete against one another, but that has never been my experience. It is quite easy for two smart women, no matter what the gap in their ages and backgrounds, to come to a complete agreement about me. *This child,* they seemed to be saying . . .

This child still needs to be brought up.

TEMPERANCE, CHARITY, FAITH, HOPE
FROM THE GLOBALTEENS ACCOUNT OF EUNICE PARK

JUNE 25

EUNI-TARD *TO* GRILLBITCH:

Hi Precious Pony,

Sup, meathole? Oh, man. Or, "oy, man," as my Jewish boyfriend would say. I'm feeling so weird these days. Wish you could fly over and we could go to Padma and get our hair done. Mine is getting so long and freaky looking. Ugh. Maybe I should get one of those ajumma perms like our moms have, you just blow dry them in the morning and they settle into a helmet. I'm also getting those famous ajumma hips too! Great, huh? I look like my aunt Suewon crossed with a duck. And my ass is SO FUCK-ING HUGE it's getting bigger than Lenny's, which is one of those crushed middle-aged asses, not to gross you out again. See, we're perfect for each other! Just call me Fatty McFatty, okay?

Oh, Pony of mine. What am I doing with Lenny? He's so, like, brain-smart, it's intimidating me. I was intimidated by Ben in Rome because of his looks and I never felt super-secure in bed because of that. With Lenny it's easier. I can be myself, because everything he does is so sweet and honest. I gave him a half-gag CIM blow job and he was so grateful he ac-tually started to cry. Who does that? I guess sometimes I just want to want him as much as he wants me. He's already talking of marriage, my darling little dork! And I just want him to relax and maybe not always be so cute and caring and trying to please me, so that maybe I can pursue him a little myself. Does that make any sense?

So I went to Long Island to meet his parents. He basically guilted me into going. His dad's weird and hard to understand, but I like his mom.

She doesn't take crap from Lenny or her husband. We even talked about ways Lenny could dress better and be more assertive at work, and she actually kissed me when I told her I was taking Lenny shopping for breathable fabrics. She's so emotional, which kind of reminds me of Lenny. Um, what else? They live in a pretty poor house. It looks like the kind of place my dad's Mexican patients used to have in L.A. Remember Mr. Hernandez, the deacon with the gimp leg? They'd invite us to their little teensy house in South Central after church. I think his daughter Flora died of leukemia.

Anyway, what kind of freaked me out was that I saw Len reading a book. (No, it didn't SMELL. He uses Pine-Sol on them.) And I don't mean scanning a text like we did in Euro Classics with that Chatterhouse of Parma I mean seriously READING. He had this ruler out and he was moving it down the page very slowly and just like whispering little things to himself, like trying to understand every little part of it. I was going to teen my sister but I was so embarrassed I just stood there and watched him read which lasted for like HALF AN HOUR, and finally he put the book down and I pretended like nothing happened. And then I snuck a peek and it was that Russian guy Tolsoy he was reading (I guess it figures, cause Lenny's parents are from Russia). I thought Ben was really brain-smart because I saw him streaming Chronicles of Narnia in that cafe in Rome, but this Tolsoy was a thousand pages long BOOK, not a stream, and Lenny was on page 930, almost finished.

And he's too nice and humble to flaunt the fact that he knows so much, so it's not like I'm getting it in my face, but sometimes he'll talk about Politics or Credit or something and I'm like what? I'm just DREADING the day when I have to see his Media friends and they'll all be talking like that, even the girls. I guess if I went to law school like my mother wants I'd learn to be like that too, but who the hell wants to go to law school? Maybe I should go back to doing Images like I did at Elderbird. Prof Margaux in Assertiveness Class said I had "super talent" and even at Catholic the nuns all freaked out over my "spatial skills."

It's weird because things are so nice with Lenny, but a lot of the times I feel like I'm alone. Like I have nothing to say to him and he just thinks I'm an idiot behind my back. He says I'm smart because I learned Italian but that wasn't really so hard. It's just memorization and then copying the way Italians act, which is easy to do if you're from an immigrant family, because when you go to nursery school for the first time and you don't speak any English it's all about copying what others do. I know it's still sweet of Lenny to try to build up my self-esteem by saying I'm smart, but sometimes I just want to get out of his life and move back to Ft. Lee where I belong and try to help my family, so it's not all just Sally and my mom dealing with that black hole in the living room a.k.a my dad. Oh, and if Lenny mentions meeting my parents ONE MORE TIME I swear I'm going to nunchuk his ass. He just doesn't get it sometimes. And he doesn't WANT to get it, which is why I get so angry at him. He thinks we're both from "difficult families" as he likes to say, which just isn't true at all. I've met his and there's just no comparison.

So I had lunch and went Real Time Shopping with Sally and now I'm kind of worried for her. She has this like blank stare and everything I talked about she was like "uh-uh." She has, like, no idea who she is. On the one hand she wants those Saaami nippleless bras and on the other hand she wants me to go to some stupid church group at Barnard. And she gained a lot of weight, not just the freshman fifteen, and she looks sad and dumpy with her weight on, so I told her she better watch what she eats, and she just looked at me like I wasn't there. The only thing that floats her boat is Politics. She and these other fat girls are all into protesting and talking about Rubenstein and how we're not a free country anymore. And when I remind her how she's supposed to be religious not Political she just says that Christianity is an "activist's creed." I think I want to meet whoever told her to say that and punch him in the face. I love her so much, Precious Pony, I think next to mom she's the most important person in my life, and I don't know how to help her, because it's not like I'm some great role model myself, right?

Anyway, I went with Sally to this really pretty park in the East Village called Tompkins Square and there are all these Low Net Worth Individuals there and they're camped out with all their dirty things and they don't have food or clean water and they have all these really old computers they try to boot up but really they have no Images or streams. So after Sally left I ran home and got all my old äppäräti and I gave them out to a bunch of people in the park, so maybe this way they can look for jobs or contact their families. They were so happy to have my old ghetto stuff that it made me sad because this is what their lives have become and just last year some of them worked in Credit or were engineers. There was this one man who was actually quite handsome, tall and Germanic-looking, but he didn't have all his teeth. He was in the National Guard and they sent him to Venezuela and when he came home they didn't pay him his bonus. His name was David. He was really nice and he hugged me and said we were all in this together. And I thought, I wish things were better for you, but we're not all in this together. Then when I was leaving I saw this old fountain that had like a gazebo with four corners and on each there was a word, "Temperance, Charity, Faith, Hope." And I don't know why but something about those words made me think of my dad and how when I was young he used to put bandaids on my knees with those big thick fingers of his and say like he did to his patients who were children "All bettah now, all bettah now," and I just started to cry like an idiot. And then I thought of Lenny and this elephant we saw in the zoo and how I kissed his big nose and the look on his face. The look on his face, Pony! I don't know about temperance or faith, but what about charity and hope? Don't we all need that?

Ugh, why am I always whining to you? Sorry for being so down. When I see you I'm going to give you a big, big kiss right between your little titties, my one and only cum-slut, princess of all that is good and right in the world!

GRILLBITCH *TO* EUNI-TARD:

Dear Precious Panda,

Waka-waka, ass-sucka! Whut-a-happenin? Sorry, I'm a little hungover and depressed myself. I went to a party at Ha Ng's, that cute Vietnamese girl from Catholic who had her stomach stapled. We got wripped on Mai Tais and this flip girl from UGuangdong-Riverside threw up on herself. NASTY! So why I'm depressed is because I think Gopher is having an affair. And not with Wendy Snatch either, but with this Mexican betch that I saw blowing him in his car at this fish taco place in Echo Park. Yeah, I followed him, and then I figured out his password on Teens (it's "PORKadobo" in case you want to stream all his shit, ha ha!) and they've been sending each

other these illeterate love notes for three weeks now. He calls her chuleta
and all she can say in English is "Hi, babee." So I went on this new Teens
site called "D-base" where they can digitize you like covered in shit or getting fucked by four guys at once and I sent Gopher all these Images of myself getting fucked by four guys at once. It's like you said, I've got to own
my feelings about Gopher and that's the only way he's ever going to respect
me and not fuck around with some gross illegal immigrant fuck-tard who
probably rates 300 on a Credit Pole. I hope they deport her ass soon. Anyway, he came over to my parents house and fucked me in the ass, which I
guess is a good sign because we haven't done that in a while, and then it's
been three hours since he's responded to that bitch on Teens, so all I'm
doing is staring at my äppärät waiting for some more incriminating shit to
pop up.

What's wrong with us, Precious Panda? Why can't we find guys who
are just right for us? At least your Lenny loves you so much he'll never
ever cheat on you. I can't understand why you're feeling so insecure
about him. So he's brain-smart. Who cares??? It's not like he's some su-
perstar Media guy or VP at LandOLakes. So he REALLY, REALLY READS
instead of scans. Big whoop. Maybe you guys can read to each other in
bed or something. And then you can sew your own clothes. HA HA HA.
Anyway, looking good is the new smart, and I don't think you should have
kids with him because you'll have really ugly children.

I'm sorry you saw some poor people in the park, my sweet, sensitive
panda, but you're right we're not all in this together. I think what your sister is doing is cool though. Someone needs to stand up and say something
to these dumbasses in charge of everything. You go, Sally! Oh, shit. I
gotta subtract. Why does alcohol make you go so much? Is that a scientific thing?

JUNE 26

CHUNG.WON.PARK *TO* EUNI-TARD:

Eunhee,

Why you no respond to Mommy? Three times I call and right. We have
dinner with Uncle Joon I make dolsot bap just like you like with extra

crunchy rice from the pot bottom. When I was little girl we didn't eat rice from bottom because we are from good family and we only give nooroonggi to beggars, but now I know you like it so I always cook dolsot bap too long even when you not here because I miss you so much!! ☺ Ha, I try to make unhappy face, but it come out happy, so maybe Jesu telling me something! Be grateful and throw away of yourself because you are blessed in Christ. We are much more happy family now that you are close by and watching on Sally. Daddy love you very much but I have trouble in my heart. I see Joy Lee mother at H-Mart. You say you stay at Joy apartment in Manhattan but Mrs. Lee say it not true. Why you lie to Mommy? I find out everything anyway. Maybe you living now with some meeguk boy in dirty apartment? So shocking. So shocking. You come back home and live with us. Daddy much better now. Sally need you to be top roll model so you stay away from dirty meeguk boy. I know my english bad but you understand what I write I think.

I love you,

Mommy

Oh, what is 3200-yuan-peg-dollar "miscellaneous charge" on Allied-WasteCVS account?? This in addition to regular finance charge? I try to up-end link to new LSAT Prep Course in Fort Lee which Mrs. Lee say make Joy get best result. 174 and before she had 154. I ask other Mommies at Church what they got and this very good improvement.

EUNI-TARD: Lenny, I thought I asked you to clean the bathtub. This apartment is DISGUSTINGLY DIRTY. I've swiffered the kitchen floor and the bathroom floor already and vacuumed the carpet in the foyer too. Do it today! I don't like living in a pig-sty.
LABRAMOV: Euny, I'm sorry but we have to stay late at work today. There's a mandatory meeting about the Debt Crisis and the LNWI protest thing in Central Park and D.C. They think the Fed may default on the dollar this year (!) and not all our clients' money is totally yuan-pegged. I have to pull up like a thousand records by six o'clock. I think Joshie's going to meet the Chinese Central Banker! Anyway, it's pretty good for my career that they trust me with this kind of stuff.
EUNI-TARD: So? What does that have to do with the bathtub?

LABRAMOV: Maybe over the weekend we can have a little cleaning party.

EUNI-TARD: It's mostly your hair in the bathtub, you know. You're the one who sheds 24/7.

LABRAMOV: I know. I've never really cleaned the bathtub before, so maybe next time we can switch chores.

EUNI-TARD: I've shown you how to do it three times. You're brain-smart enough when it comes to dollar defaults or whatever but you can't clean the bathtub?

LABRAMOV: Maybe you can supervise me while I do it over the weekend.

EUNI-TARD: Never mind. I'll just do it myself. It's easier in the end to just do everything myself.

LABRAMOV: No, don't do it! Wait until I have some free time. I'm sorry it's so busy at work.

LABRAMOV: Hello! Are you there?

LABRAMOV: Are you mad at me?

LABRAMOV: Eunice!

EUNI-TARD: Ugh.

LABRAMOV: What?

EUNI-TARD: I hate this.

LABRAMOV: What can I do to make you feel better? I'll clean all weekend, top to bottom.

EUNI-TARD: Nothing. Nothing you can do. I can't change you. So I guess I just have to take on all these responsibilities myself.

LABRAMOV: That's not true, Eunice.

LABRAMOV: I AM changing. It just takes time.

LABRAMOV: Let's have a nice dinner at that Brazilian place in the village. My treat.

EUNI-TARD: Don't forget to pick up the TWO-PLY toilet paper on the way home.

LABRAMOV: I won't forget.

EUNI-TARD: You always forget. That's why you're a tuna-brain.

LABRAMOV: Ha ha. I'm glad you're not mad at me.

EUNI-TARD: Don't count your blessings, nerd.

LABRAMOV: I'm not counting anything.

EUNI-TARD: I just want a nice, clean apartment, Lenny. Don't you want to

come home to a nice, clean apartment too? Don't you want to be proud
of where you live? Isn't that what being an adult is about? It's not just
about reading Tolsoy and sounding smart. Big whoop.

LABRAMOV: Reading who? Big what?

EUNI-TARD: Forget it. I got to run to the laundry. Who else is going to pick
up your undies? By the way, you should wear boxer briefs not just plain
old regular briefs. They provide more support. You always complain that
your balls hurt after a long walk, well why do you think that is?

LABRAMOV: Because I wear bad underwear.

EUNI-TARD: Who loves you, *kokiri*?

AMY GREENBERG'S "MUFFINTOP HOUR":
FROM THE DIARIES OF LENNY ABRAMOV

JUNE 30

Dear Diary,

So, after the huge success with my parents, I asked Eunice to come out with me to Staten Island to meet my friends. I guess my intentions were self-aggrandizing and superficial. I wanted to introduce Eunice to my boys, impress them because she was so young and pretty. And I wanted to impress *her* because Noah and his girlfriend, Amy, were so Media.

The first part worked—you can't really meet Eunice without appreciating her youth and her cool, shimmering indifference. The second part not so much.

The night in question was what we called Family Night, when all the boys invited their respective partners to Cervix, the kind of night when I was usually minus girlfriend and feeling like a fifth wheel. But on that night it would be Noah and his emotive girlfriend, Amy Greenberg, Vishnu and Grace, and Eunice and me, the couple-in-progress.

Even on the way to the subway, walking arm in arm, I tried to show my girl off to the denizens of Grand Street, but the selection of Eunice-appreciators was a bit thin that day. A crazy white man brushing his teeth in broad daylight. A retired Jew throwing a plastic cup of Coke at a discarded mattress. A feuding Aztec couple hitting each other over the head with two plastic yellow daisies from within the unremitting brick façade of a housing project.

I had almost made it to the subway without incident. But by the razor-wire-surrounded lot next to the RiteAid, where our neighborhood's resident shitter would squat in the middle of the day, I noticed a curious thing. A new billboard had gone up, courtesy of my employer, the Staatling-Wapachung Corporation. It depicted a familiar latticework of glass and pomposity, a series of three-story apartments crashing into one another at odd angles like a bunch of half-melted ice cubes in a stirred drink. "HABITATS EAST," the sign proclaimed, beside the flags of the United Arab Emirates, China-Worldwide, and the European Union.

AN EXCLUSIVE TRIPLEX COMMUNITY FOR **NON–U.S. NATIONALS**
By Staatling Property

Seven TRIPLEX Living Units priced to move from 20,000,000 northern euros / 33,000,000 yuan

"Twenty million euros!" I said to Eunice. "That's fifty years of my salary. Even foreigners don't have that kind of money anymore!"

"Isn't this the place where that guy shits all the time?" Euny said nonchalantly, evidently inured to the vagaries of my *quartier.* I continued to read:

ATTENTION FOREIGN RESIDENTS!
BUY A TRIPLEX LIVING UNIT TODAY AND RECEIVE
- Exemption from American Restoration Authority (ARA) Cavity, Data & Property Searches
- Prize-winning security by Wapachung Contingency
- EXCLUSIVE Immortality Assistance from our Post-Human Services Division
- Free parking for first 6 months

Credit ranking of 1500+ only please
This Area COMPLETELY Zoned for Harm Reduction

"EXCLUSIVE Immortality Assistance"? Beg pardon? You had to *prove* you were worthy of cheating death at Post-Human Services. Like I said, only 18 percent of our applicants qualified for our Product. That's how Joshie intended it. Hence the Intakes I was supposed to perform. Hence the Language Cognition tests and the essays on outliving your children. Hence—the whole philosophy. Now they were going to bestow immortality on a bunch of fat, glossy Dubai billionaires who bought a Staatling Property "TRIPLEX Living Unit"?

I was about to start a healthy diatribe on the Subject of Everything (I think Eunice likes it when I teach her new stuff) when I noticed a familiar squiggle on the corner of the sign.

In a stenciled, bleeding-edge style that had been cool at the turn of the century, I saw—no, it couldn't be!—an arty reproduction of Jeffrey Otter, my inquisitor at the U.S. Embassy in Rome, in his stupid red-white-and-blue bandana, a smudge of what could have been a cold sore on his hairy upper lip. "Oh," I said, and actually backed away.

"*Kokiri?*" Eunice asked. "What's up, nerd-face?"

I made a breathing sound. "Panic attack?" she asked. I put up my hand to indicate a "time-out." My eyes ran up and down the graffito as if I were trying to scrub it into a different dimension. The otter stared back at me: curved, oddly sexual, pregnant with life, the fur smoothed into little charcoal mounds clearly warm and soft to the touch. It reminded me of Fabrizia. My betrayal. What had I done to her? What had *they* done to her? Who had drawn this? What were they trying to tell me? I looked at Eunice. She was using my forty-second pause to bury her head into her äppärät. What was I even doing with this sleek digital creature? I felt, for the first time since her arrival in my life, truly mistaken.

But the day wasn't finished with me yet.

When we got to the Cervix, my friend Grace was the one to object.

"She's too young for you," she whispered to me after Eunice had turned away from us and started AssLuxury shopping. There wasn't anything particularly antisocial about this—the boys were watching

Chinese Central Banker Wangsheng Li's visit to Washington on their own äppäräti, and Noah's girl, Amy, was setting up hand lotions and other sponsored products for a live stream of the "Amy Greenberg Muffintop Hour."

For a second I thought Grace was jealous of Eunice, and that was more than fine with me, because, to be honest, I've always had a crush on Grace. She wasn't particularly pretty, the eyes too widely set apart, her bottom teeth like an interstate pile-up, and she was, if it's at all possible, too thin from the waist up, to the point where she looked bird-like doing any activity, even walking up the stairs or passing a plate of Brie. But she was kind—so kind and forthright, and so well educated and serious about life, that when I thought I was in love with Fabrizia in Rome, all I had to do was think of Grace talking about her complex wintry childhood in the farthest reaches of Wisconsin State or the German artist Joseph Beuys, her passion, to know that everything about my relationship with poor, doomed Fabrizia was transitory and a lie.

"Why don't you like Eunice?" I asked Grace, hoping she would stutter and painfully confess her love for me.

"It's not that I don't like her," Grace said. "It just feels like she's got a lot of things to work out."

"I got a lot of things to work out too," I said. "Maybe Eunice and I can work them out together."

"Lenny." Grace rubbed my upper arm and flashed me her lower yellows (how I relished her imperfections). "If you're attracted to her physically, that's fine," she said. "There's nothing wrong with that. She's hot. Have a good time with her. Have a fling. But don't tell me, 'I'm in love with her.' "

"I'm worried about dying," I said.

"And she makes you feel young?" Grace said.

"She makes me feel bald." I ran my hand through what was left.

"I like your hair," Grace said, gently pulling at the clump standing armed sentinel over my widow's peak. "It's honest."

"I guess in some ridiculous way I think Eunice will let me live forever. Please don't say anything Christian, Grace. I really can't handle it."

"We're all going to die, Lenny," Grace said. "You, me, Vishnu, Eunice, your boss, your clients, everyone."

The boys were now hooting over their äppäräti, and Grace and I joined them. They were watching the stream of Noah's friend Hartford Brown, who did a political commentary show intermixed with his own hardcore gay sex. The esteemed Li—officially the Governor of the People's Bank of China-Worldwide, unofficially the world's most powerful man—was first shown chatting up our clueless Bipartisan leaders on the White House lawn. There was my father's idol, Defense Secretary Rubenstein, bowing from the waist, his bumbling incoherent rage turned to quiet obedience, his trademark white handkerchief flashing out of his suit pocket like a cheap surrender. Rubenstein presented Li with some sort of golden fish, which flopped into the air and miraculously opened up into an approximation of China's bulbous shape, a sign that America could still produce and *innovate*.

Then the positively ripped Hartford was mounted on top of what was announced as a yacht near the Dutch Antilles, fresh spray rainbowing his sunglasses, two hairy dark arms massaging his marbled chest and shoulders as his lover's thrusts pushed him into the frame of his äppärät. "Fuck me, brownie," he crooned to his sailing buddy, his lips so louche yet masculine, so full of life and heat that I found myself feeling happy for his happiness.

Then cut to Li and our youthful puppet leader Jimmy Cortez at the White House, the American President seated stiffly, the Chinese banker more at ease, impervious to the microphone booms crowding the air before him. "I totally *love* what the Chinaman is wearing," Hartford was saying over the White House visuals, intermittently groaning from being fucked by the Antillean. Viewers were reminded that Li had been picked the best-dressed man in the world by an informal multinational poll, with respondents particularly taken by "the simplicity of his suits" and "the glammy oversized glasses."

"We wish China to become a nation of consumers and not otters," President Cortez begged the banker.

Wait, what? A nation of *otters*? I replayed the stream on my own äppärät. "We wish China to become a nation of consumers and not savers," the president had actually said. Jesus Christ, I was losing it. "The American people need China-Worldwide to become a savior of our last manufacturers, large and small. China is no longer a poor country. It is time for the Chinese people to *spend.*" Mr. Li nodded distractedly and smiled his great big nothing of a smile. President Cortez then said some words in Chinese, which were interpreted as "O.K. to spend now! Go have fun!"

"Oh, shit," Vishnu said, pawing frantically at his äppärät. "Something's happening, Nee-groes!" We could hardly hear him above the roar of the bar. The young people were drinking more, and some women were getting nervously naked, even as Eunice Park tightened a light sweater around her shoulders, rubbing her nose from the air conditioning. "There's a riot in Central Park," Vishnu said. "This black dude is getting his ass kicked by the Guard and all these LNWIs are getting seriously whaled on."

News of the Central Park slaughter was spreading through the bar. No one was streaming live yet, but there were Images coming up on our äppäräti and on the bar's big screens. A teenager (or so he seemed, those awkward lanky legs), his face turned away from view, a red concavity cut from the midsection of his body, bundled up like road kill on the soft green hump of a protruding hill. The bodies of three men and a woman (a family?) lying on their backs, their naked black arms thrown wildly across their bodies, as if haphazardly hugging themselves. And one man whom I thought I recognized—the unemployed bus driver Eunice and I had seen on Cedar Hill. Aziz something. I remembered mostly what he had been wearing, the white T-shirt and the gold chain with the oversized yuan symbol. There it was—the strange confluence of having seen him alive, if even for a moment, combined with a dot the size of a five-jiao coin that had punctured the upper half of his elongated brown forehead, red bleeding into rust along the links of his heavy chain, teeth bitterly stamped together, the eyes already turned up in their sockets. It took me several moments to come up with a description of what I was seeing—*a dead man*—just as the screen switched to a shot of the sky above the park, the tail end of a helicopter lifted upward, its beak presumably lowered for execution, and a backdrop of red tracer fire illuminating the warm close of a summer day.

A silence overtook the Cervix. I could hear nothing but the sound of my Xanax bottle being instinctually opened by three of my be-numbed fingers, and then the scratch of the white pill descending my dry throat. We absorbed the Images and as a group of like-incomed people felt the short bursts of existential fear. That fear was tem-porarily replaced by a surge of empathy for those who were nomi-nally our fellow New Yorkers. What was it like to be one of the dead or the about-to-be-dead? To be strafed from above in the middle of a city? To receive the quick understanding that your family was dying around you? Finally, the fear and the empathy were replaced by a different knowledge. The knowledge that it wouldn't happen to us. That what we were witnessing was not terrorism. That we were of good stock. That these bullets would discriminate.

I teened Nettie Fine: "Did you see what's happening in the park????"

Despite the time difference in Rome (it must have been past 4 a.m.), she teened me back immediately: "Just saw it. Don't worry, Lenny. This is horrible, but it will BACKFIRE on Rubenstein and his ilk. They're shooting in Central Park because there aren't enough ex–National Guardsmen there. They'll never go after the former sol-diers. The real action is in Tompkins Square, which Media isn't cov-ering at all. You have to go there and meet my friend David Lorring. I used to do post-traumatic counseling in D.C. and he came to see me after two tours in Ciudad Bolívar. He's organizing a real resis-tance down there. Brilliant guy. Okay, I got to catch some zzzzz's, sweetie. Stay strong! xxx Nettie Fine. P.S. I follow your friend Noah Weinberg's stream religiously. When I'm back in the States I'd love to take him out to lunch."

I smiled when I read Nettie's missive. A woman in her sixties was still active, still trying to shape our country in the right way. Surely there was *some* hope. As if to confirm my thoughts, CrisisNet pinged with a new announcement: "LIBOR RATE RISES 32 BASIS POINTS; DOLLAR HIGHER BY 0.8% AGAINST YUAN AT 1¥ = $4.92."

Could the markets be right? Was the Central Park massacre really a turning point? Would it backfire on Rubenstein and his friends?

I re-read Nettie Fine's message. It was inspiring, but there was something off about the wording. *The real action is in Tompkins Square.* I tried to picture the words "real action" leaving Nettie's careful, intelligent lips. What had happened to her? *The otter.* I teened Fabrizia in Rome. "RECIPIENT DELETED." Okay, I had to stop worrying. There was a real massacre in front of me. Forget the Old World. I was not responsible for what happened to either Nettie or Fabrizia. I was responsible only for Eunice Park.

Meanwhile, at the Cervix, the stunned silence had already been replaced by a general mood of frivolity mixed with practiced outrage, people throwing around their near-worthless unpegged dollars and crowning themselves with Belgian ales. All I remember is feeling a little hot around the temples and wanting to be closer to Euny. Things had been rocky between us since I had relapsed and picked up a book, and she had caught me reading, not just text-scanning for data. With the violence just a few miles to our north, I wanted nothing to separate me from my sweetheart, certainly not a two-brick tome of Tolstoy's *W&P.*

Noah started streaming right away, but his girlfriend, Amy Greenberg, was already live. She lifted up her blouse to show the negligible roll of fat that crowned her perfect legs and spilled from her perfect jeans, her so-called *muffintop,* slapped at it, and delivered her signature line: "Hey, girlfriend, gots muffintop?"

"It's Rubenstein time in Central Park," Noah was saying. "It's Harm Reduction, giving away the store, everything must go, 'our prices are insane' time in America, and R-stein won't feel good until all the niggers and spics are cleared out of our city. He's dropping bombs on our moms like Chrissy Columbus dropped germs on the redman, *cabrónes.* First the shooting, then the roundup. Half the mamis and papis in the city are going to end up in a Secure Screening Facility in Utica before the week is over. Better keep your äppäräti away from those Credit Poles. . . ." He paused to look over the raw data streaming at him. And then he turned his tired, professionally animated face to us, unsure of what emotion to muster next but unable to contain the visceral thrill. "There's eighteen people dead," he said, as if he had surprised himself. "They shot eighteen."

And I wondered about the excitement in his voice: What if Noah was secretly pleased that all this was happening? What if we all were? What if the violence was actually channeling our collective fear into a kind of momentary clarity, the clarity of being alive during conclusive times, the joy of being historically important by association? I could already envision myself excitedly proclaiming the news of how I had seen this dead Aziz bus driver in Central Park, had maybe even exchanged a smile with him or an urban *whassup*. Don't get me wrong, I felt the horror too, but I wondered, for instance, what *were* these Secure Screening Facilities that Noah always talked about? Were people really shot in the back of the head without a trial? Once, I reminded Noah about how *The New York Lifestyle Times* used to have actual correspondents who would go out and report and verify, but he just gave me one of those "Old man, don't *even*," looks and went back to hollering Spanish slang into his camera nozzle. But, then again, Nettie Fine followed his stream *religiously*, so maybe I was missing something. Maybe Noah was as good as it got these days.

"Eighteen people dead!" Amy Greenberg was shouting. She put her hand on her make-believe muffintop, over the negligible waistline and the pretty serious musculature above, as if to scold Rubenstein and the administration, but this maneuver also allowed the outline of her left breast—which a random poll had publicly declared to be the better one—to spill out of her décolletage and frame the center of the shot. "Huge riot in Central Park, National Guard just shooting everyone, smashing up their little shacks, and I am so glad my man Noah Weinberg is right over my shoulder, because I *just cannot handle this anymore*. I mean, hello, stop me before I snack again. Noah, I am so blessed to have you in my life at this terrible moment, and I know I'm not perfect, but, okay, and this is like *total cliché alert,* but you mean the world to me, because you are so kind and sensitive and man-hot, you are *so* Media, and"—her voice started to shake, she started to blink voluntarily in a way that always hastened the tears—"I don't know how you can go out with a fat loser like me."

Grace and Vishnu were leaning in to each other as if they were two parts of an ancient ruin, while new death tolls appeared in the air around us, the numbers swelling. I recalled Point No. 4, Care for Your Friends, and again my friends were the ones who took care of *me*. Noticing me standing alone next to Eunice, who was deep into AssLuxury (was she too shocked by the violence to stop shopping?), they reached out and brought me into their circle, so that I could feel the warmth of their hands and the boozy comfort of their breath.

Noah and Amy were loudly streaming a few feet apart from each other, straining to be heard over the din of the bar.

"Rubenstein's making a point to Li," Noah was saying. "We may not be a great power anymore, we may be into you for sixty-five trillion yuan-pegged, but we're not afraid to use our troops if our spades act up, so watch out, or we'll go fucking *nuclear* on your yellow asses if you try to cash in your chips. Keep the credit *rolling, chinos.*"

Amy Greenberg: "Remember Jeremy Block, the guy I broke up with last Passover?" A stream of a naked, masturbating guy who resembled Noah was projected next to Amy's äppärät, and she scowled at the Image of his generous penis, her pretty post-bulimic face betraying the beginnings of a muzzle. "Remember how I couldn't count on that jerk-off when there was, like, trouble in the world? Remember how he wouldn't *explain* anything to me, even though he worked for LandOLakes? Remember how he made me *weigh* myself every morning? Remember how he . . ." Big pause, and then a bright, smiley face. ". . . *didn' respect the muffintop?*"

CrisisNet: RUBENSTEIN BLAMES CENTRAL PARK RIOT LEADER FORMER BUS DRIVER AZIZ JAMIE TOMPKINS FOR RIOTS. QUOTE: "ARA REPORTS IDENTIFIED 'AZIZ' AS HAVING TRAINED WITH HEZBOLLAH FORCES IN SOUTHERN LEBANON." QUOTE: "WE ARE DEALING WITH FRONTLINE ISLAMOFASCIST TERRORISM." QUOTE:

"NOW IS THE TIME FOR SPENDING, SAVING, AND UNITY.
ONE PARTY, ONE NATION, ONE GOD."

Vishnu had gone to get us more beer, and Eunice and Grace were
doing AssLuxury together. Grace said something that made Eunice
smile, and then they talked back and forth, Grace's eyes on Eunice,
Eunice's eyes mostly on her äppärät, but occasionally, shyly, on
Grace. I though I heard some words in Korean—"Soon-Dooboo"
(however it's spelled) is a tofu stew that Grace had ordered a lot on
32nd Street. I wanted to join their conversation, but Grace gently
pushed me away. Eunice was FACing a little with three of the other
Asian girls in the room, and her FUCKABILITY, I noticed with pride
and a little worry, was 795, although her PERSONALITY just 500
(maybe she wasn't extro enough). But one very young Filipina Mediawhore in a suburban cardigan, big clunky orthopedic-type shoes,
and Onionskin jeans streamed quietly by the jukebox rated several
points higher on the FUCKABILITY. "That girl has the perfect body,"
I heard Eunice saying to Grace. "God, I hate twenty-one-year-olds."

I looked sadly at my own rankings. Most of the men tonight were
wearing cool Mr. Rogers–like V-neck sweaters and were appraising
me coldly at best. Someone had written about my stubble, "That
dude next to the cute Asian spermbank has like pubic hair growing
out of his chin," and I was ranked fortieth out of the forty-three
guys in the room. Did Eunice care? I noticed that when I put my arm
around her my MALE HOTNESS shot up by a hundred points, and I
ranked a respectable thirty out of forty-three men. But what did that
say about me? That I needed Eunice just to be acknowledged in the
greater world? For one thing, I resolved to shave my stubble tomorrow. It only worked for a certain kind of very attractive guy.

Amy Greenberg, pointing to the little flaps of skin hanging between her armpits and breasts: "I've got wings! Thirty-four and I've
got wings like an angel. I can't believe *any guy* would want to feel
me up with all this *bra goo*! Look at me! Look at me!"

Noah Weinberg: "Thirty-three casualties in the Low Net Worth
riots as of nine-oh-four p.m. EST. And the Guard is still shooting up

in Central Park. But we've lost four hundred National Guardsmen in Ciudad Bolívar *alone* in the last two months. That's the Rubenstein strategy: The more Americans die, the less anyone cares. Redefine the normative down. Start digging the graves."

Amy Greenberg: "Let me break down what I'm wearing. The shoes are from Padma, the blouse is a Marla Hammond original, and the nippleless bra is a Saaami Wing Concealer—my mother got it for me on sale at the United Nations Retail Corridor."

Noah Weinberg: "And I'm not even talking about the LIBOR rate here. I'm talking—" He stopped and looked around. A trio of Staten Island girls were lustily humming a song whose only discernible lyric was "Mmmmmmm . . ." Noah started to say something, but in the end all he said was "You know what, *patos*? I—I have nothing more to say to any of you."

Amy Greenberg: "I just want to say, my mom is freaking *amazing*. When I was breaking up with Jeremy Block, she just like made me see through all his bullshit. We looked at his rankings together and we were like, who cares about his big dick and the fact that he can bone all night. He made me give him a rim job for his thirtieth birthday, and then he wouldn't kiss me afterwards. That really says *a lot* about a guy, when he won't kiss his girlfriend after she's licked out his junk. My mom, she's so cute, she was like 'You deserve so much better, Aimeleh. Be your *own* pimp, girl!' "

Grace took me aside. "Hey," she said. "I think Eunice has some real problems."

"Duh," I said. "Her father's a dickhead."

"I know this kind of girl," Grace was saying. "It's the worst kind of combination of abuse and privilege, and growing up in this, like, greenhorn southern-Californian Asian upper-middle-class ghetto, where everyone is *so* shallow and money-craven. I mean even shallower than Noah's girlfriends. At least Amy *Green*berg knows exactly what she's doing."

"But I love her," I said, quietly. "And I think she shops just because our society is *telling* Asian people to shop. You know, like it says on the Credit Poles. I actually heard one guy yelling to Eunice, 'Hey, ant, buy something or go back to China!' "

"Ant?"

"Yeah, like the ant that saves too much and the grasshopper that spends too much? Like on the ARA signs? Chinese and Latino? So fucking racist."

"Leonard, it's time to stop dating all these Asian and white-trash girls with serious problems," Grace said. "You're not doing them any favors, you know."

"You're really hurting me, Grace," I whispered. "How can you judge her so quickly? How can you judge *us*?"

And right away Grace softened. The Christianity and goodwill kicked in. She teared up. "I'm sorry," she said. "God, it's the times we live in. I'm becoming so harsh. Maybe I can hang out with her? Maybe I can be like a big sister?" I considered turning indignant, but then I considered who Grace was, the oldest of a brood of five well-adjusted kids, the inheritor of a set of doctor parents from Seoul whose immigrant anxieties and sense of Wisconsin alienation were high, but who nonetheless dispensed love and encouragement in the manner of the kindest, most progressive native-born. How could she even begin to understand Eunice? How could she comprehend what it was like between the two of us?

I hugged Grace for a few beats and kissed one warm cheek. When I looked back, I noticed that Eunice was staring at us, her lower face covered with that amphibian smile, the grin without qualities, the grin that cut me in the softness around my heart.

"Well, that's about it for the republic," Hartford was saying on his Antillean stream, his young friend toweling a spent geyser of semen off his back. "Yibbity-yibbity, that's all, folks."

We crossed back to Manhattan in silence. The National Guard checkpoints were practically abandoned, most of the troops likely ordered up to Central Park to quell the insurrection. Back in my apartment, I was on my knees and crying again. She was threatening to move back to Fort Lee again.

"Your friends are awful," she was saying. "They're *so* full of themselves."

"What did they do to you? You barely said a word to them all night!"

"I was the youngest person there. They were all ten years older than me. What did I have to say to them? They all work in Media. They're all funny and successful."

"First of all, they're not. And, second of all, you're still young, Eunice! You'll work in Media someday. Or Retail. And I thought you liked Grace. You were getting along so well. I saw you looking at AssLuxury together and talking about Soon-Dooboo."

"I hated *her* the most," Eunice Park hissed. "She's *exactly* who her parents want her to be and she's so fucking *proud* of it. Oh, and forget about meeting my family. You'll never meet them, Lenny. How can I trust you with them? You've blown it."

I lay in my bed alone; Eunice again in the living room with her äppärät, with her teening and shopping, as the night turned black around us, as I realized, with a quiet gnawing pain, that when you took away my 239,000 yuan-pegged dollars, when you took away the complicated love of my parents and the mercurial comforts of my friends, when you took away my smelly books, I had nothing but the woman in the next room.

My mind was full of sickening Jewish worry, the pogrom within and the pogrom without. I declined to think of Fabrizia, Nettie, or the otter. I stayed in the moment. I tried to find out what was happening in Central Park to the Low Net Worth protesters. Some of the rich young Media people on Central Park West and Fifth Avenue were streaming from balconies and rooftops, and a few had broken through the National Guard cordons and were emoting from deep within the park itself. I looked past their angry and excited faces screeching about their parents and lovers and weight gain, trying to catch sight of the helicopters floating behind them, firing into the green heart of the city. I thought of Cedar Hill—the new ground zero of my life with Eunice Park—and considered the fact that it was now covered in blood. Then I felt guilty for thinking about my own life with such Media obsessiveness, so readily forgetting the ranks of the new dead. Grace was right. The times we live in.

But one thing I knew: I would never follow Nettie's advice. I would never visit those poor people in Tompkins Square Park. Who knew what would happen to them? If the National Guard shot people in Central Park, why wouldn't they shoot them downtown? "Safety first," as they say around Post-Human Services. Our lives are worth more than the lives of others.

An armada of helicopters flew north. The whole building shook with their ferocity, china jiggling in the neighbor's kitchen cabinet, little children crying. That seemed to scare Eunice, and soon she was in bed next to me, trying to find a comforting fit with my larger body, pressing so deeply into me that it hurt. I felt scared, not because of the military operation outside (in the end, they would never hurt people with my assets), but because I knew that I could never leave her. No matter how she treated me. No matter how bad she made me feel. Because in her anger and anxiety there was familiarity and relief. Because I understood those greenhorn southern-Californian immigrant families better than I could Grace's right-hearted Midwestern kin, the craving for money and respect; the mixture of entitlement and self-loathing, the hunger to be attractive, noticed, and admired. Because after Vishnu told me that Grace was pregnant ("ha-*huh*," he laughed awkwardly while bearing the news) I realized that the last door had closed for me. Because, unlike the slick and sly Amy Greenberg, Eunice had no idea what the hell she was doing. And neither did I.

Sorry, diary, I'm such an emotional wreck today. Bad night's sleep. Even my best ear plugs can't help against the sound of rotor blades outside and Eunice mumbling loud Korean deprecations in her sleep, continuing her never-ending conversation with her *appa,* her father, the miscreant who is responsible for most of her pain, but without whose angry lashings I probably would never have fallen in love with her, or she with me.

But I realize that I'm also leaving some things out, diary. Let me describe some of the beautiful moments, at least before the LNWI riots started and the checkpoints went up by the F train.

We go to midtown Korean restaurants and feast on rice cakes swaddled in chili paste, squid drowning in garlic, frightening fish bellies bursting with salty roe, and the ever-present little plates of cabbages and preserved turnips and seaweed and chunks of delectable dried beef. We eat in the Asian fashion, eyes on our food, hearty slurps of tofu stew and little belches indicating our involvement with the meal, my hand reaching for a glass of alcoholic *soju,* hers for a dainty cup of barley tea. A peaceful family. No need for words. We love each other and feed each other. She calls me *kokiri* and kisses my nose. I call her *malishka,* or "little one" in Russian, a dangerous word only because it once spilled out of my parents' mouths, back when I was under three feet tall and their love for me was simple and true.

And the warmth of a Korean restaurant, the endless procession of plates, as if the meal cannot end until the whole world is eaten, the shouting and laughter after the meal is done, the unchecked inebriation of the older men, the giggly chatter of the younger women, and everywhere the ties of the family. It's no wonder for me that Jews and Koreans jump so easily into romantic relations. We were stewed in different pots, to be sure, but both pots are burbling with familial warmth and the easiness, nosiness, and neuroticism that such proximity creates.

While we were lunching at one of the louder places on 32nd Street, Eunice saw a man eating by himself and sipping a Coca-Cola. "It's so sad," Eunice said, "to see a Korean man without a wife or girlfriend to tell him not to drink that junk." She lifted up her cup of barley tea as if to show him a healthier alternative.

"I don't think he's Korean," I said to Eunice. "My äppärät says he's from Shanghai."

"Oh," she said, losing interest as soon as her bloodlines to the solitary Asian Coca-Cola drinker were cut.

When we were walking home, our stomachs filled with garlic and chili, the summer heat without and the pepper heat within covering our bodies with a lovely sheen, I started to ponder what Eunice had said. It was sad, according to her, that the Asian man did not have a wife or girlfriend to tell him not to drink the Coca-Cola. A grown man had to be *told* how to behave. He needed the presence of a girl-friend or wife to curb his basest instincts. What monstrous disregard for individuality! As if all of us didn't lust, on occasion, for a drop of artificially sweetened liquid to fall upon our tongues.

But then I started thinking about it from Eunice's point of view. The family was eternal. The bonds of kinship could never be broken. You watched out for others of your kind and they watched out for you. Perhaps it was *I* who had been remiss, in not caring enough for Eunice, in not correcting her when she ordered garlicky sweet-potato fries or drank a milkshake without the requisite vitamin boost. Wasn't it just yesterday, after I had commented on our age difference, that she had said, quite seriously, "You can't die before me, Lenny." And then, after a moment's consideration: "Please promise me that you'll always take care of yourself, even when I'm not around to tell you what to do."

And so, walking down the street, our breath ponderous with kim-chi and fizzy OB beer, I began to reconsider our relationship. I started to see it Eunice's way. We now had obligations to each other. Our families had failed us, and now we had to form an equally strong and enduring connection to each other. Any gap between us was a failure. Success would come when neither of us knew where one ended and the other began.

With that in mind, I crawled on top of her when we had reached home and pressed myself against her pubic bone with great urgency. "Lenny," she said. She was breathing very quickly. I'd known her for a month, and we had still not consummated our relationship. What I had seen as a sign of great patience and traditional morality on my part I now saw as a failure to connect.

"Eunice," I said. "My love." But that sounded too small. "My life," I said. Eunice's legs were spread, and she was trying to accommodate me. "You are my life."

"What?"

"You *are*—"

"Shhh," she said, rubbing my pale shoulders. "Shush, Lenny. Be quiet, my sweet, sweet tuna-brain."

I pressed myself inside her all the more, trying to wend my way into a place from which I would never depart. When I arrived there, when her muscles tensed and clasped me, when her collarbone jutted out, when the spectacular late-June twilight detonated across my simple bedroom and she groaned with what I hoped was pleasure, I saw that there were at least two truths to my life. The truth of my existence and the truth of my demise. With my mind's eye floating over my bald spot and, beneath that, the thick tendrils of Eunice's mane spilling over three supportive pillows, I saw her strong, vital legs with their half-moon calves and between them the chalky white bulk of me moored, righted, held in place for life. I saw the tanned, boyish body beneath me, and the new summertime freckles, and the alert nipples that formed tight brown capsules between my fingers, and felt the melody of her garlicky, sweet, slightly turned breath—and I began, with the kind of insistence that brings out heart attacks in men six years older than myself, to plunge in and out of Eunice's tightness, a desperate animal growl filtering out of my lungs. Eunice's eyes, wet and compassionate, watched me do what I needed to do. Unlike others of her generation, she was not completely steeped in pornography, and so the instinct for sex came from somewhere else inside her; it spoke of the need for warmth instead of debasement. She lifted up her head, enveloping me with her own heat, and bit the soft protuberance of my lower lip. "Don't leave me, Lenny," she whispered into my ear. "Don't please ever leave me."

THE QUIET AMERICAN
FROM THE GLOBALTEENS ACCOUNT OF EUNICE PARK

JULY 2

CHUNG.WON.PARK *TO* EUNI-TARD:

Eunhee,

We terrible worry right now because it sound like bad political situation in Manhattan. You should move back to Fort Lee and be family. This is more important than study for LSAT even. Remember we are old people and we see history. Daddy and I live through bad time in Korea when many people die on street, student young people like you and Sally. Make sure you no political. Make sure Sally no political. Some time she talk. We want come see you Tuesday coming up. Reverend Suk he was teacher to our Reverend Cho bring his special sinners crusade to madison square garden from Korea and we think all family should go and pray and we go to dinner later and meet this meeguk boy you say just Roommate. I am dissapoint you lie to me that you live with Joy Lee but I thank Jesu that you and Sally alive and safe. Even Daddy is so quiet now because he is Grateful and on his knee before God. This is difficult time. We come to America and now what happen to America? We worry. What it was all for? When we first come, before you were born, it was not so easy. You dont know how Daddy struggle for patient, even poor Mexican who has no insurance and he pay fifty dollar a hundred dollar. Even now he struggle. Maybe we make big mistake.

So please, make time for us Tuesday. Dress nice, nothing cheap or like "ho" but I always trust how you wear. Daddy say now there is road block on GW bridge and also holland tunnel. So how people from New Jersey suppose come?

Love you,

Mommy

EUNI-TARD: Sally, are you okay?

SALLYSTAR: Yeah. You? This is insane. We've been "advised" not to leave the campus. Some of the Midwestern first years are freaking out. I'm putting together an info session to help everyone deal.

EUNI-TARD: I do not want you doing ANYTHING Political! Do you hear me? This is the one time I think mom's like 100 percent right. Please, Sally, just promise me.

SALLYSTAR: Okay.

EUNI-TARD: This is SERIOUS. I am your older sister, Sally.

SALLYSTAR: I said OKAY.

SALLYSTAR: Eunice, why didn't you tell me you had a boyfriend?

EUNI-TARD: Because I have to be a "roll model" according to mom.

SALLYSTAR: That's not funny. It's like you're not even my sister if you can't tell me these things.

EUNI-TARD: Well, it's not like we're a normal family, right? We're a special family. Ha ha. Anyway, he's not really my bf. It's not like we're getting married. I told mom he's my roommate.

SALLYSTAR: What's he like? Is he muh-shee-suh?

EUNI-TARD: Does that matter? I mean, it's not really about looks with this guy. He's not Korean either, just so you know and can get judge-mental on me.

SALLYSTAR: I guess as long as he treats you well.

EUNI-TARD: Ugh, I don't want to be having this conversation.

SALLYSTAR: Is he coming to the crusade on Tuesday?

EUNI-TARD: Yes. So please act brain-smart. Do you know anything about Classics? I mean like texts?

SALLYSTAR: I just scanned Euro Classics but I don't remember a thing there were so many text pages. Something by this guy Grayham Green about a Vietnamese girl called Phuong, like the girl who worked at Lee's Banh Mi in Gardena. Why do we have to impress him?

EUNI-TARD: We don't. I just want him to know we're a smart family.

SALLYSTAR: I'm sure mom will act nice and then say really mean things behind his back.

EUNI-TARD: They'll just sit there and dad will drink and make those throat-clearing noises.

SALLYSTAR: Muhuuhuhuhuhmm.

EUNI-TARD: Hah! I love it when you imitate dad. I miss you.

SALLYSTAR: Why don't you come to dinner with Uncle Joon Friday? Maybe sans boyfriend.

EUNI-TARD: I like that "sans." That's brain-smart. I don't really want to see Uncle Joon. He's a fucking deadbeat.

SALLYSTAR: That's mean.

EUNI-TARD: He yelled at me last Thanksgiving when he visited from Korea because mom and I got a turkey that's too large. And his wife went shopping in Topanga and she bought Dad a pair of pliers for, like, sixteen bucks, not even yuan-pegged, and kept saying "Oh, make sure your dad knows this gift from me." Do you know how much money dad's given that idiot husband of hers and she bought him some pliers in return?

SALLYSTAR: They're family. And their taxi business isn't doing good. It's the thought that counts.

EUNI-TARD: They're the only people in Korea not making any money these days. Retards.

SALLYSTAR: Why are you so angry all the time? What's your bf's name?

EUNI-TARD: I'm just an angry person by nature. And I hate it when people take advantage of other people. His name is Lenny. I told you he's really not my bf.

SALLYSTAR: Did he graduate your year from college?

EUNI-TARD: Um, he's 15 years older.

SALLYSTAR: Oh, Eunice.

EUNI-TARD: Whatever. He's smart. And he takes care of me. And if you and mom are going to hate him then it's only going to make me like him more.

SALLYSTAR: I'm not going to hate him. Is he Christian or Catholic?

EUNI-TARD: Neither! He's circumcised. Ha ha.

SALLYSTAR: I don't get it.

EUNI-TARD: He's Jewish. I call him kokiri. You'll see why!

SALLYSTAR: That's interesting, I guess.

EUNI-TARD: What have you been eating?

SALLYSTAR: Just some mangoes with this fresh Greek yogurt they got at the cafeteria now.

EUNI-TARD: For lunch? Are you snacking?

SALLYSTAR: I had an avocado.

EUNI-TARD: They're good for you but they're fatty.

SALLYSTAR: OK. Thanks.

EUNI-TARD: Lenny says things to me that are so sweet but they don't make me vomit. Not like some Media or Credit guy who just wants to get laid and move on. Lenny cares. And he's there for me every day.

SALLYSTAR: I didn't say anything, Eunice. You don't have to defend him. Just make sure he takes off his shoes if he ever comes to the house.

EUNI-TARD: Ha ha. I know. White people are sick that way. They could have just stepped in poo or a homeless person.

SALLYSTAR: SICK!

EUNI-TARD: Lenny says I don't have any control over my emotions, because that's what dad is like. He says I crave negative attention.

SALLYSTAR: You told a stranger about dad????

EUNI-TARD: He's not a stranger. You have to get out of that mindset. That's what being in a relationship is about. Talking to the other person.

SALLYSTAR: That's why I'm never going to be in a relationship. I'm just going to get married.

EUNI-TARD: Do you ever miss CA? I miss In-N-Out. I'd kill for an Animal Style burger. Mmm. Grilled onions. Not that you should be eating red meat. I just sometimes want to go back to how things were when we were really young. You know what's the worst is when you're happy and sad at the same time and you can't figure out which is which.

SALLYSTAR: I guess. I got to study for chem. Don't talk about our family too much to others, okay, Eunice? They won't understand it and no one cares anyway.

EUNI-TARD: Please stay safe, Sally. Just study and eat healthy. I love you so much.

EUNI-TARD *TO* GRILLBITCH:

Dear Precious Pony,

What a week. I am SO fucked. My mother found out I wasn't living with Joy Lee, so I finally told her I had a white "roommate" who is also a BOY. So now she wants me to go to some stupid church thing so she can meet him. Ugh, this is like my worst nightmare. Lenny's been whining to meet my parents and now he'll think I'm caving in and he has the upper hand with me and can do whatever he wants, like not clean the apartment or make me leave the tip at restaurants even though he knows my Credit is MAXED. Yup my ranking just hit the magic number. Under 900! So much for "Chinese" people not spending. Ha ha.

And now my mom will know I'm dating an old hairy white guy. So I told Lenny he can't tell my mom that we're going out and he got really upset, like he thinks I'm ashamed of him or something. He says that I'm trying to push him away because I'm substituting him for my father, but that he won't let me, which is pretty ballsy for a nerd-face.

Things have been pretty up and down with us, although he finally had some Magic Pussy Penetration Time and it wasn't bad. What he lacks in looks he more than makes up for in passion. I thought he was going to explode! What else? The riots were pretty awful and now it takes forever to get around town. Lenny tries to act all gallant like he's going to protect me from those National Guard guys but it's not like they're going to shoot Asians, right?

Oh, I met his friends. This one guy Noah was cute, kind of tall and conventionally handsome. His girlfriend is this really hot woman Amy Greenberg, who has her own stream that gets like a million views. She has this really awesome pseudo-smart personality and a pretty hot face. She streams about not being petite, which is sad but she just wasn't built that way. Anyway I noticed Noah scoping me OUT and when I took off my sweater he just started STARING down my shirt and I was flattered, but it's not like I've got anything down there. Then he told me I had "acerbic wit" and I was just like "ha ha," although I couldn't help mentally cheating on Lenny a little. And then this Korean girl Grace was talking to me for hours. She's really sweet and tries to make you feel like she's on your side, but I think it's all just an act. She got all this information about how my father beats my mother because she spoilt the tofu under the guise of befriending me. I don't know why I told her any of it and I felt really vulnerable the whole night. Whatever. I hate all of them.

So the next day I went back to Tompkins Park with some cases of bottled water, because I heard they don't have any and the ARA shut down the water fountain and toilets in all the parks. There were all these hipsters running around streaming about the riots, but nobody's really helping out the LNWIs. I hung out with David, that cute guy who was in the National Guard in Venezuela. He has like four teeth in his mouth because he never had Dental and he was in an explosion. But it's still very inspiring to talk to him, because he always says what he means (unlike Lenny and his friends). Like he'll say "Shut up!" or "You're wrong, Eunice," or "You have no idea what you're talking about," or "That's just a High Net Worth way of looking at things." I like that, when people actually call you on your shit.

Anyway, I never thought I would care about Political stuff, but I can listen to David go on for hours. He says a lot of Guardsmen like him who didn't get their bonuses after Venezuela are thinking of getting together and they're going to fight back against the National Guard if they're attacked. He says the Guard these days are just a bunch of poor people hired from the south by this Wapachung Contingency thing Lenny works for and they don't care who they kill. Him and his friends are calling themselves Aziz's Army because of the bus driver who was shot in Central Park, the same one I saw with Lenny. I told David I don't want to be Political, but he wrote down all these supplies they need, like cans of tuna and beans and baby wipes and stuff, and I wonder if I should get it for them even though my AlliedWaste is completely maxed out. Maybe I should ask Lenny to help me, but for some reason I don't really want him knowing about David even though we're just friends.

The way they have it set up is pretty amazing. It's a tiny little park, but like every little bit of it is used for a purpose. Where there used to be a dog run all these ADORABLE and SURPRISINGLY CLEAN-LOOKING kids play soccer with an old basketball. I guess I should get them a real soccer ball at Paragon. There's recycling of all foods from garbage cans which is kind of gross, but basically people like Lenny throw out so much stuff that David said you can get like ten meals out of the typical dinner wasted by a Credit guy from the East Village. They're so organized here, it kind of reminds me of my family growing up. Everyone's assigned a role, no matter how young or old, and everyone has to do their part, even the snobby Credit and Media guys who lost their jobs and now live in the park. And if you don't do what you're told, tough luck, you're out.

It kind of made me miss helping out at that shelter for trafficked Albanian women in Rome. Lenny says he's proud of me for doing that, but then he always calls them ALGERIANS or AFRICANS instead of Albanians, like that sounds cooler. But David immediately knew what I was talking about. It's interesting how people who have been through a lot, they have this kind of childlike look on their face.

Anyway, David said I didn't need to take any more Assertiveness classes like I was planning to at Columbia, but I should just get busy and help out at the park. I said yes, but I kind of don't want to run into my sister up there, I don't know why. It's like being a saint is HER territory and I just want her to think of me as the protector of our family.

There's so much to do, it makes me dizzy. They got rid of most of the rodents, but Healthcare is the biggest problem, so in different corners of the park there's tents with signs saying "DIPHTHERIA" (TO-tally contagious), "TYPHOID" (red spots on the chest, eww), "PELLAGRA" (note to self: have to get vitamin B3 from Lenny), "ASTHMA" (get Lenny's old inhalers, some of them still have juice), "DEHYDRATION" (more bottled water ASAP), "CLOTHES WASHING AND SANITATION" (that's where I'm going to help out next week), "MALNUTRITION." Malnutrition is mostly pigeon peas and rice, because they're cheap and so many people here are Caribbean, but they're looking for donations of anything. They even have a GlobalTeens account under "aziz army" if you want to donate some ¥.

Maybe I should get my dad to come out and help them a little, cause he's an M.D.? When I was in high school I tried to help out at his office but he just said I was worthless even though I tried so hard and put all his charts on a computer because nobody can read his handwriting and I even cleaned the bathroom in the office top to bottom because my mother gets so distracted she misses corners.

You know, Lenny's so kind to me that sometimes I forget to keep my guard up and talk to him like a friend, but you're still my one and only bestest truest friend, Pony. And yet I'm so in love with him. Ugh. I said it. Sometimes I can spend half an hour in the morning just watching him sleeping, and I'll put my arm around him and draw him close to me and he looks so peaceful and darling, his little hairy chest going up and down like a puppy's. Oy vey. I hope you don't think I take you for granted, Precious P. I think about you all the time and you're still a MAJOR part of my life. Oh, and I saw the pics of that Mexican ho Gopher's been fucking and she has a totally broke-ass face! Pone, you are so super-pretty by comparison! Don't let that dicklick invalidate who you are. He's just trying to get to you because he knows you're out of his league. Okay, got to go and clean the bathtub because my super-smart boyfriend doesn't know how to. Talk to you later, sticky bun.

GRILLBITCH *TO* EUNI-TARD:

Panda, I'm off to Juicy for a vag rejuv, but what the hell is "acerbic wit"? I tried to look it up on Teens but all I got was "aerobic whip." Is that the same? Remember what Prof Margaux told us, beware of guys who try to sound too smart.

P.S. I looked up your Amy Greenberg and she COULD use to lose another twenty pounds, although she gets points for being old.

P.S.S. Are you going to stream American Spender tonight? Remember that girl with the herpes sty in her eye in bio Kelli Nozares? She is totally going to be on it and she's got all kinds of Credit I hear because ALL THREE of her brothers are Debt Bombers. If she wins I am seriously going to strangle somebody.

P.S.S.S. If things get dangerous there, maybe you SHOULD move out to CA. I see poor people hanging out in tents on the medians but it's not so bad still. Except my dad's business is doing really bad even though toilet plungers are supposed to be depression-proof, but I walked into my mom's bathroom and I caught her sitting on the floor crying with all her like twenty-year-old Golf Digests just lying all around. Oh God. Maybe I should move out of the house, huh? But then this is probably when they need me the most, and it's not like my brother's going to do anything. It's always on the girls to keep the family going. We're like the sacraficial lamps.

I'll thresh you later, Panda-ga-tor.

AZIZARMY-INFO *TO* EUNI-TARD:

Hi, Eunice. David here. Listen, it's the Fourth of July in two days and Cameron at Morale, Welfare & Recreation says we need 120 units of Hebrew National hot dog and also 120 hot dog buns, 90 cans of root beer (any brand), 50 units of AfterBite Original for the mosquitoes, and 20 units of Clinique Skin Supplies for Men M Protect, SPF 21. Can you bring all that over pronto?

Thought about our conversation re: parents and siblings. This is what I realized when I was an undergrad at UT and after I was in the Guard downrange in the Venezuelan swamplands eating grilled capybara with my troops and taking Bolívar flak 24/7: No matter what social arrangement we're in, we're always an army. You're an army and your father's an army, and you love each other, but you have to go to war in order to be something like a father and daughter.

OBJECT LESSON: My dad died about eighty klicks north of Karachi. He was a gunner and those are always the toughest assholes. But in the very last message I got right before they ambushed his ass he basically said, David, you are a dreamer and a disgrace and you'll never get your shit together, and I'll always fight everything you believe in, but I'll also never love anyone more than you, so if anything happens to me just keep going the way you are.

I think that's where we went wrong as a country. We were afraid to really fight each other, and so we devolved into this Bipartisan thing and this ARA thing. When we lost touch with how much we really hate each other, we also lost the responsibility for our common future. I think when the dust settles and the Bipartisans are history that's how we're going to live, as small units who don't agree. I don't know what we'll call it, political parties, military councils, city-states, but that's how it's going to be and we're not going to screw it up this time. It'll be like 1776 all over again. Act Two for America. Okay, Eunice, I'm off for the night. Don't forget the supplies for the Fourth.

Yours,

David

THE SINNERS' CRUSADE
FROM THE DIARIES OF LENNY ABRAMOV

JULY 7

Dear Diary,

I hate the Fourth of July. The early middle age of summer. Everything is alive and kicking for now, but the eventual decline into fall has already set itself in motion. Some of the lesser shrubs and bushes, seared by the heat, are starting to resemble a bad peroxide job. The heat reaches a blazing peak, but summer is lying to itself, burning out like some alcoholic genius. And you start to wonder—what have I done with June? The poorest of the lot—the Vladeck House project dwellers who live beneath my co-op—seem to take summer in stride; they groan and sweat, drink the wrong kind of lager, make love, the squat children completing mad circles around them by foot or mountain bike. But for the more competitive of New Yorkers, even for me, the summer is there to be slurped up. We know summer is the height of being alive. We don't believe in God or the prospect of an afterlife mostly, so we know that we're only given eighty summers or so per lifetime, and each one has to be better than the last, has to encompass a trip to that arts center up at Bard, a seemingly mellow game of badminton over at some yahoo's Vermont cottage, and a cool, wet, slightly dangerous kayak trip down an unforgiving river. Otherwise, how would you know that you have lived your summertime best? What if you missed out on some morsel of shaded nirvana?

Frankly, these days, knowing that immortality is further away from me than ever (the 239,000 is gone; only ¥1,615,000 to my name at last count), I prefer the wintertime, when all is dead around me, and nothing buds, and the truth of eternity, so cold and dark, is revealed to the unfortunate acolytes of reality. And most of all I hate this particular summer, which has already left a hundred corpses in the park.

"An unstable, barely governable country presenting grave risk to the international system of corporate governance and exchange mechanisms" is what Central Banker Li called us when his ass had landed safely in Beijing. We had been humiliated in front of the world. The Fourth of July fireworks were canceled. The parade to crown the "American Spender" winner put on hold because a section of Broadway near City Hall had buckled in the heat. The remaining streets were empty, the citizenry prudently staying home, the F running at one train per hour (not that different from its normal schedule, I must say). The only changes noticeable are the new ARA signs drooping off some of the Credit Poles featuring a tiger pawing at a miniature globe and the words "America is back! Grrrr . . . Don't write us of [sic]. Ain't No Stoppin' Us Now! Together We'll Surprise the World!"

Tuesday morning, after the long weekend, Post-Human Services sent a Hyundai Town Car to pick me up for work. It took forever to get up to the Upper East Side. Almost every block going up First Avenue was a barbed-wire-strewn checkpoint. Bleary-eyed, overworked Guardsmen with those thick Alabamississippi accents would pull us over, search the vehicle from engine to trunk, play with my data, humiliate the Dominican driver by making him sing "The Star-Spangled Banner" (I myself don't know the words; who does?) and then making him parade in front of a Credit Pole. "Soon the time'll come, grasshopper," one of the soldiers brayed at the driver, "for us to send your *chulo* ass home."

At the office, Kelly Nardl was crying over the riots, while the young folk in the Eternity Lounge were deep into their äppäräti, teeth grinding, sneaker-clad feet crossed, unsure of how to interpret all the new information pouring over them like warm summer pop, everyone awaiting Joshie's cue. The Guard had cleared a part of the park and let in Media. I was watching Noah's stream as he ambled up and down Cedar Hill, past the remnants of tarps and somber, amoeba-shaped pools of real-time blood on the tired grass, which made Kelly whimper all over her tempeh-covered desk. She was a touchstone of honest emotion, our Kelly. I took my turn petting her head and inhaling her. One day, if our race is to survive, we will have to figure out how to download her goodness and install it in our children. In the meantime, my mood indicators on The Boards went from "meek but cooperative" to "playful/cuddly/likes to learn new things."

Joshie had called a full organizational meeting, Cowboys and Indians. We walked to the Indians' auditorium on York Avenue, significantly larger than our synagogue's main sanctuary, Joshie leading us past the checkpoints with one hand raised up in the air, like a schoolteacher on a field trip. "Pointless loss of life," he said once installed at the dais, sipping eloquently from his thermos of unsweetened green tea, as we regarded him multiculturally from our plush reclining seats. "Loss of prestige for the country. Loss of tourist yuan. Loss of face for our leadership, as if they had any face to lose. And for what? Nothing has been achieved in Central Park. When will the Bipartisans realize that killing Low Net Worth Individuals will not reverse this country's trade deficit or cure our balance-of-payment problems?"

"Truth to power," Howard Shu brown-nosed behind him, but the rest of us remained quiet, perhaps too shocked by the latest turn of history to find succor even in Joshie's words. Nonetheless, I smiled timidly and waved, hoping he would notice me.

"The dollar has been grossly, fantastically mismanaged," Joshie went on, his usual bemused conversational face coiled by the kind of rage that wasn't allowed at Post-Human Services, a rage decidedly *pre*-human, parts of his chin shaking independently, so that from one angle he looked thirty years old and from another sixty. "The ARA has tried a dozen different economic plans in as many months. Privatization, deprivatization, savings stimulus, spending stimulus, regulation, deregulation, pegged currency, floating currency, controlled currency, uncontrolled currency, more tariffs, less tariffs. And the net result: *bupkis.* 'The economy has still not achieved traction,' to quote our beloved Fed chairman. As we speak, in HSBC-London, the Chinese and the EU are in final partnership talks. We are finally no longer critically relevant to the world economy. The rest of the globe is strong enough to decouple from us. We, our country, our city, our infrastructure, are in a state of freefall.

"But," Joshie said. And here he breathed in deeply, smiled sincerely, the dechronification treatments coming to life on his face, glowing eyes, glowing dome, glowing skin—we moved slightly to the edge of our seats, fingered our cup holders suggestively. "We have to remember that our primary obligation is to our clients. We have to remember that all those who died in Central Park over the last few days were, in the long run, ITP, Impossible to Preserve. Unlike our clients, their time on our planet was limited. We must remind ourselves of the Fallacy of Merely Existing, which restricts what we can do for a whole sector of people. Yet, even though we may absolve ourselves of responsibility, we, as a technological elite, can set a good example. I say to all the naysayers: The best is yet to come.

"Because we are the last, best hope for this nation's future.

"We are the creative economy.

"And we will prevail!"

There were murmurs of assent from the Cowboys, while the Indians were lowing to get back to their work. I confess my mind was elsewhere too, despite the importance of what Joshie was saying, despite the pride I felt at being a part of this creative economy (a pride verging on the patriotic), and despite the guilt I felt about the deaths of the poor people. That night I was going to meet Eunice Park's parents.

I had never dressed for church before, and my synagogue days were a quarter of a century behind me, Yahweh be praised. Not one of my friends had ever met exactly the right person (Grace and Vishnu excepted), so there was never a need to dress up for a wedding. I foraged deeply into the recesses of the one closet not ceded to Eunice's shoes to find a suit jacket made out of what may have been polyurethane, a silvery number I had used at speech and debate tournaments in high school, one that always won me sympathy points from the judges because I looked like an entry-level pimp from a degentrified part of Brooklyn.

Eunice scrutinized me with unbelieving eyes. I leaned over to kiss her, but she pushed me away. "Act like a roommate, okay?" she said.

The protocol of the meeting, the roommate charade, weighed on me, but I chose not to worry over it. The Parks were immigrant parents. I would convince them of my financial and social worth. I would press their emotional panic buttons with the briskness I reserve for entering my bank code. I would make them understand that in these troubled times they could count on a white guy like me to steward their daughter.

"Can I at least tell your sister that we're more than roomies?" I asked Eunice.

"She knows."

"She knows?" A small victory! I reached over and buttoned the silky white work shirt Eunice had put on, and she kissed me on both hands as I was fitting the buttons into the elaborate loops.

The worship service was to be held in one of the Madison Square Garden auditoriums, an overlit yet fundamentally dark amphitheater suitable for maybe three thousand persons, but today filled with half as many. The heavy use of lights exposed the dinginess of the place, the facilities barely swept from the last event, which may well have been a licorice convention. Most attendees were Korean, with the exception of the few Jewish and WASPish young men brought in by their girlfriends. Teenagers wearing bright-green sashes with the words "Welcome to Reverend Suk's Sinners' Crusade" greeted us and bowed to their elders. Crisply dressed kids, their äppäräti confiscated by their parents, horsed around quietly between our feet, playing simple coeducational games with thumbtacks and adhesive tape, a lone grandmother deputized to watch over the lot of them.

I felt my monstrous suit jacket glowing around my shoulders, but the middle-aged women with elaborate permed hair and shoulder-padded suit jackets, the ajummas, a sometimes derisive term for married women I picked up from Grace, made me feel better about myself. Together we all looked like we had been plucked from the distant decade of 1980–89 and deposited into this dull, awkward future, a bunch of poorly dressed sinners throwing ourselves at the mercy of Christ, who was always sharp-looking and trim, graceful in pain, kindly in Heaven. I'd always wondered if the Son of God didn't harbor a wide hatred for ugly people, his pleasant teachings notwithstanding. His liquid blue eyes had always hurt me to the quick.

Eunice and I walked to our seats, maintaining a "roommate-like" decorum, at least three feet of dusty atmosphere between us at all times. Middle-aged men, exhausted from ninety-hour work weeks, were slumped deep into their chests, shoes off, catching precious sleep before the onslaught of prayer began. I got the sense that these weren't the A-level Koreans, most of whom had returned to the motherland after the economic scales had tipped toward Seoul. These must have been people from the poorest provinces, those who couldn't gain admittance to the finer universities in their home country, or those who had broken horribly with their families. The era of the Korean greengrocers I had known as a child had pretty much come to a close, but the people around me were less assimilated, still close to the tremulously beating heart of the immigrant experience. They owned small businesses outside the golden zone of Manhattan and Brownstone Brooklyn, they struggled and calculated, they pushed their children over the edge of sleep deprivation—there would be no shameful 86.894 weighted averages among them, no talk of Boston-Nanjing Metallurgy College or Tulane.

I was nervous in a way I hadn't been since childhood. My last time in a place of worship, I had been chastised by the angry, aged audience at Temple Beit Kahane for singing the Mourner's Kaddish for my parents when they were quite obviously not dead, and in fact were standing blankly next to me, mouthing the Hebrew words none of us could begin to understand. "Wish fulfillment," my social worker had told me as I sobbed in her cramped Upper East Side office a decade later. "The guilt of wishing them dead."

My silvery jacket glided past the rows of exhausted Koreans. I had to keep myself from sweating further, because the reaction of salt and the poly-whatever-it-was of my jacket may well have hastened all of us into Jesus's waiting arms. And then I saw them. Sitting in a good row, heads bent forward either from a sense of shame or to get a head start on worship. The family Park. The tormentor, the enabler, the sister.

Mrs. Park looked twenty years older than the age Eunice had given me for her mother—just a little over fifty. I almost addressed her with another term I had picked up from Grace, "halmoni," but was pretty sure she was not the grandmother, that, in fact, Eunice's grandmother was already in the ground somewhere on the outskirts of Seoul. "Mommy, this is my roommate, Lenny," Eunice said, her voice like nothing I had heard before, a shouted whisper on its way to becoming a plea.

Mrs. Park had tweezed her brows to within an inch of their life, à la Eunice, and her round lips had a trace of rouge, but that was the extent of her beautification project. A great spidery web of defeat spread across her face—as if there lived below her neck a parasitic creature that gradually but purposefully removed all the elements that in human beings combine to form satisfaction and contentment. She was pretty, the features economical, the eyes evenly spaced, the nose strong and straight, but seeing her reminded me of approaching a reassembled piece of Greek or Roman pottery. You had to draw out the beauty and elegance of the design, but your eyes kept returning to the seams and the cracks filled with some dark cohesive substance, the missing handles and random pockmarks. It was an act of the imagination to see Mrs. Park as the person she had been before she met Dr. Park.

I bowed from the waist in greeting, not low enough to caricature the custom, but enough to show her that I knew the tradition existed. I shook hands with Dr. Park, feeling immediately ashamed and inferior before him. His hands were strong, as was the rest of him. He was a singularly handsome man, the one who had obviously bequeathed to Eunice her beauty. He was dressed down—at least by comparison with the other parishioners—in an Arnold Palmer polo shirt, a jacket slung over one arm. He had a thick entrepreneurial neck, and skin that still bore the leather of the California sun. I had never seen a chin so firm and set, so unmistakably manly, and a lower body that contained such an endless amount of propulsion. He had partly dark lenses in his glasses, another incongruity or maybe even a hint of blasphemy, which he lowered just slightly to take me in. Despite his race, his eyes were almost as light as Jesus's, and they regarded me with indifference. I sat down next to Sally Park, Eunice's sister, who shyly shook my hand.

Sally was pretty, but she had taken more of her mother's than her father's looks; in a sense, she opened a window onto how lovely the mother must have been. The flatter face and bulkier shoulders made her stand apart from her sister's easy glamour, at least as far as my own judgmental gaze was concerned, but the fact that she resembled her mother gave her an instant kindness. The shadows under her eyes spoke of studies undertaken, endless worry, and hard work. The imaginary parasitic creature that constrained her mother's and her sister's happiness had not burrowed beneath her neck. Eunice had told me Sally was the most tender and loving member of her family, and I could only believe this was true.

And yet Sally bothered me. Throughout the service, she and Eunice engaged in a dance of glances, like two divorced spouses who hadn't seen each other in years and were now sizing each other up. On the few occasions when Eunice had talked to me about Sally, she had lowered her voice to a defeated, mumbling register, as opposed to the high and smirky one she used to lay siege to her parents. When she talked of her sister, Eunice appeared scattered and unsure. Sometimes Sally came across as rebellious, sometimes as religious, sometimes as political and involved, sometimes as detached, sometimes as budding with sexuality, and always as overweight, which was to Eunice the deepest of shames, the most self-evident loss of face imaginable. Upon first inspection, Sally might have been all of these things (except fat) and something else too. The dance of glances between the sisters—Sally's thrusts and Eunice's parries—revealed it all. She was hurt and alone. She was in love with her sister, but unable to breach the walls that made of Eunice a stern, pretty castle amidst a landscape laid to waste.

We sat there silently. The family was embarrassed to say anything; without alcohol, Koreans can be a timid people. I felt proud of myself. I had known Eunice for a little over a month, and already I was sitting next to her kin. I was pacifying her as surely as she had domesticated me. How my life had changed in such a short amount of time! With just a few morning kisses on my eyelids, unbidden, welcome kisses, Euny could transform me for the rest of the day into the opposite of Chekhov's ugly Laptev. I would greet the food deliveryman in my boxer shorts, forgetting my usual timidity at showing my hairy legs, reveling in the idea that on the couch behind me this little girl was shopping, teening, watching a hated former classmate of hers scheme her way into new lines of credit on "American Spender," fully ensconced within her digital reality but also within the walls of *my* apartment. I would hand the deliveryman his ten yuan-pegged with my chest thrust forward, with a Joshie-grade smile on my face, the smile of one of life's easy champions. *I am a man, and this is my money, and here is my future wife, and this is my charmed life.*

The service began. A cellist, two oboists, several violinists, a pianist, and a small, adorable choir, the majority of them young women dressed in rather form-fitting gowns, mounted the stage and began to play a medley of songs that varied between the sacred and the bizarre. We got a Mahler violin concerto, then the stirring Korean pop anthem Alphaville's "Forever Young" sung by some exhausted-looking teenagers in bad haircuts and tight jeans, which they followed with a power-rock tribute to Ephesians that left the older half of the congregation visibly confused. We ended with "Softly and Tenderly Jesus Is Calling." It was this last song that roused all the parishioners who began to sing loudly and with gusto as a kind of PowerPoint presentation appeared on a large screen in both Korean and English against a backdrop of orchids floating down streams and a very visible copyright sign, which seemed to soothe our law-abiding natures. Everyone sang in tune, even the older folks mouthing the English words with more competence than my father and mother trying to wail Sh'ma Yisroel (Listen Up, Israel) at their synagogue.

I was caught unawares by the line "Why should we tarry when Jesus is pleading? / Pleading for you and for me?" The English language was dying around us, Christianity was as unsatisfying and delusional an idea as it had ever been, but the effectiveness of the sentence—its clever mix of kitsch, guilt, and heartbreaking imagery, Jesus *pleading* for the attention and love of these put-upon Asian people—made me shudder. The awful things was: They were beautiful words. For the first time in my life, I felt sorry for Jesus. Sorry that the miracles ascribed to him hadn't actually made a difference. Sorry that we were all alone in a universe where even our fathers would let us get nailed to a tree if they were so inclined, or cut our throats if so commanded—see under Isaac, another unfortunate Jewish shmuck.

I turned to Eunice, who was minding her conservative shoes, and then to Sally, who was earnestly trying to follow along, her mouth contorting to the words, staring at the screen, upon which more pastoral images appeared, an American deer leaping past two American birches. I could feel nothing but the mournful, hopeful waft of sound emerging from her mouth.

"O for the wonderful life He has promised / Promised for you and for me."

Some of the older people had started weeping, the kind of hemorrhaging, deep-seated sound that can only bring relief to the sufferer. Were they crying for themselves, for their children, for the future? Or was this crying just a matter of course? Soon, to everyone's dismay, the choir and the musicians left the stage, and Reverend Suk ascended the podium.

He was a dapper man with a deceptively kind face, broad shoulders filling out a dark-blue middle-class suit, and an innocent smile deployed after a harangue like a reward, like a father trying to recover his child's love after taking away her toy. He seemed like the perfect preacher for citizens of an insecure, rapidly developing nation, a nation that Korea had recently been.

Reverend Suk and some of his younger ministers took turns yelling at us in English and Korean. I glanced at Dr. Park, sitting mutely, hands folded over his lap, his dark glasses off to reveal deep creases and a touch of submerged anger. I wouldn't be surprised if he hated the Reverend, or thought himself more clever. Eunice had told me Dr. Park read the Scripture from four in the morning and boned up on the Koran and the Hindi texts as well. A smart man, she had said proudly, but then the dead smile came on, as if to say, *See how little "smart" means to me?*

"Why are so many empty seats?" Reverend Suk yelled at us, accusingly, for we had not done our job, for we were failures in his eyes and the eyes of God. "So many people in the streets, but so many empty seats! This nation once was deep in the Gospel! Now where is everyone?"

At home, cowering, I wanted to tell him.

"Do not accept your thoughts!" the Reverend shouted, the copper orbs of his eyes alight with a painless flame. "Accept world of Christ, not your thoughts! You must throw away of yourself. Why? Because we are dirty and we are wicked!" The audience sat there—subdued, restrained, compliant. I don't want to be literal here, but these immaculately coiffed and scrubbed women in their halo-like hairdos and shoulder pads sticking out like epaulets were the very opposite of dirty.

And yet even the antsy children, even the ones who couldn't speak, realized that they were sinners and this was a crusade; that they had done something immeasurably wrong, had soiled themselves at an inopportune moment, would soon fail their poor, hardworking parents in many ways. One little girl started to cry, a kind of hiccupping, snot-clogged cry that made me want to reach out and comfort her.

Reverend Suk went for the kill. Three words formed the arrows in his quiver: "heart," "burden," and "shame."

To wit, "My heart was very *burden*some."

"I have this kind of heart. Geejush, help me throw it away!"

"If you find me in a shameful position"—this must have been a direct translation from the Korean, the last word pronounced with difficulty as "poh-jee-shun"—"fill my burdensome heart with Your grace! Because only Geejush's grace will save you. Only Geejush's grace will save this fallen country and protect from Aziz Army. Because you are lazy. Because you do not appreciate. Because you are prideful. Because you are unworthy of Christ."

My eyes returned to the copyright sign below the screen imagery of bucking deer and floating orchids upon which key phrases from Reverend Suk's sermon ("THROW AWAY PRIDE," "JESUS GRACE SAVE YOU," "BIG SHAME") were superimposed in English and Korean. How comforting the copyright sign against the religious foreground. How assuring the idea that we were nominally a nation of laws.

I wondered if the young people manning the PowerPoint truly believed. I have always wished that I could better understand the Korean-Christian connection. A friend of mine from the Indian side of Post-Human Services, one of our best nanotechnologists and survivor of not one but two Korean Bible camps, once told me, "You have to realize that, compared with the Korean brand of Confucianism, Christianity is a walk in the park. Compared with what came before, Protestantism is almost a freaking liberation theology."

I thought of Grace, whose intelligence was unquestioned, but whose piety troubled me. "It's just a passing thing," Vishnu had told me about his girlfriend's beliefs. "It's like their way of assimilating into the West. It's like a social club. One more generation, it'll be over." I didn't want to think of Grace's deeply private experience, the heavily highlighted New Testament she once showed me, the weekly trips to an Episcopalian church full of Jamaicans, as just a form of assimilation, but I knew, instinctively, that the child she carried would not worship the Lord.

"Forget all the good you have done!" Reverend Suk was shouting. "If you pride the good, if you don't throw away the good, you will never stand in front of God. Do not accept the good before God. Do not accept your thoughts!" I looked at Eunice. She was playing with the straps of her tan JuicyPussy purse, the purse nearly as big as the rest of her, running the straps up and down her fingers, making brief outlines of red and white on her chalky skin, until her mother grabbed her hand and sent a brief, powerful snorting sound her way.

I wanted to get up and address the audience. "You have nothing to be ashamed of," I would say. "You are decent people. You are trying. Life is very difficult. If there is a burden on your heart, it will not be lifted here. Do not throw away the good. Take pride in the good. You are better than this angry man. You are better than Jesus Christ."

And then I would add: "We Jews, we thought all this stuff up, we invented this Big Lie from which all Christianity, all Western civilization, has sprung, because we too were ashamed. So much shame. The shame of being overpowered by stronger nations. The endless martyrdom. The wailing at the ancestors' graves. We could have done more for them! We let them down! The Second Temple burned. Korea burned. Our grandparents burned. So much shame! Get up off your knees. Do not throw away your heart. Keep your heart. Your heart is all that matters. Throw away your shame! Throw away your modesty! Throw away your ancestors! Throw away your fathers and the self-appointed fathers that claim to be stewards of God. Throw away your shyness and the anger that lies just a few inches beneath. Do not believe the Judeo-Christian lie! Accept your thoughts! Accept your desires! Accept the truth! And if there is more than one truth, then learn to do the difficult work—learn to choose. You are good enough, you are *human enough,* to choose!"

I was so deep in my own rage, a rage that might have been better summed up with the simple plea "Dr. Park, please do not hit your wife and daughters," that I had not noticed that the worshippers around me had sprung to their feet and were belting out "The Rose of Sharon." As it turned out, this was the last chapter of the Sinners' Crusade. My gaze skirted that of a fellow Hebrew itching to make his way out of there, away from the in-laws, and into his honey's arms. Tenderly, angrily, Jesus was pleading for our very souls, but we were too tired, too hungry, to hear him out, too hungry even to complete Reverend Suk's quick sermon quiz ("Only for fun, not graded!"), which the young people in sashes were passing down the rows.

We bowed our way out of Madison Square Garden and adjourned nearby to a new restaurant on 35th Street that specialized in *nakji bokum,* an octopus-tentacle dish inflamed with pepper paste and chili powder, among many other forms of debilitating heat. "Maybe too spicy for you?" Eunice's mother said, the usual question asked of the white.

"I've eaten this many times before," I said. "It's yummy." Mrs. Park looked at me with great suspicion.

We were taken to an empty little room where we were to remove our shoes and cluster, cross-legged, around a table. I realized, with toilet-inducing horror, that one of my socks featured a giant bull's-eye of a hole, through which my pale, milky flesh could be scrutinized by all. I turned to Eunice with a why-didn't-you-tell-me look, but she was too scared by the collision of her two worlds to notice my urgent stare. She threw off her pointy church shoes and made herself uncomfortable by the table. The grown-ups were clustered around one side of the table; Eunice and Sally faced us meekly from the other. Mrs. Park began to order, but her husband stopped her, unleashing a series of grunts at a pimply young waiter with a slick parabola of hair. A bottle of *soju,* the Korean alcohol, was immediately presented to Eunice's father. I tried to reach over and pour it for him, as the young are supposed to serve the old in this culture (as if the old are really any better than the rest of us, not merely closer to extinction), but he forcefully moved my hand away and did it himself. He picked up my glass, put it in front of him, and, with a precise, calibrated spill, topped me off. Then, with one index finger, he moved the glass in my direction. "Oh, thank you," I said. I waved the bottle toward Eunice and Sally. "Anybody want some of this good stuff?" They averted their eyes. Dr. Park swallowed his medicine without a word.

"Well, then," I said. "I've got to say, having Eunice as a roommate has been really great this past week, with all that's been going—"

"Hee-young!" Dr. Park ejaculated at Sally. "How are your studies?"

Sally blushed. A cube of cool, white radish slipped out from between her chopsticks. "I," she said. "I—"

"I, I," Dr. Park mimicked. He turned to me briefly as if I were his co-conspirator. I smiled at him, finding it impossible to ignore any gestures from this man, even if it meant siding with him against the innocent women at the table. That's what tyrants can do, I guess. They make you covet their attention; they make you confuse attention for mercy. "All that money for Elderbird, for Barnard, and for what?" the doctor said. "They have nothing to say. This one protests, this one spends my money." He spoke with the hint of a British accent, acquired during a residency in Manchester. The quality of his speech scared me all the more. He was a perfect little man, towering above us in his own special way.

"Actually," I said, "this is not a good time for speaking and writing. Younger people express themselves in different ways."

"Yes, yes." Mrs. Park nodded at me, one tiny hand held up before her equally minuscule face, blushing like her daughters, the other hovering nervously over her rice. "It is time we live in," she said. "These are final times." And then to her daughters: "Daddy only want best. You listen to him."

I ignored the scary biblical reference and continued to praise the woman I loved. "It may surprise you to know that Eunice is actually a great speaker of sentences. Recently we discussed—"

Dr. Park began to speak lowly, and in Korean, at Sally and Eunice. He spoke for twenty minutes from behind his dark glasses, stopping only to refill his glass and to knock it back within the space of a second. They sat there and blushed, looking at each other occasionally, each seeing how the other was taking her punishment. No one ate anything, except for me. I was hungry in a way I had never been, and felt myself growing faint, hypoglycemic. The waiters came, bearing immensities of smoking, steaming cuisine. A large pot of baby octopus came my way, hot and sweet, surrounded by *ddok,* a tubular rice cake that soaked up the spices like a sponge. I felt anxious with so much spice in my mouth, as words continued to spill out of Dr. Park's. I reached for a plate of pickles and egg custard to cool me down; the flavors of the squid, the green onions, the chili peppers, the orange-streaked onions soaked in sesame oil built in intensity. I couldn't stop eating. I tried to reach for the *soju* bottle, but Dr. Park swatted away my hand and poured my drink himself, while continuing to let loose at his tiny daughters across the wide wooden gulf of the table.

I thought I heard the word *hananim,* which I know means "God" in Korean, and the deeply insulting term *michi-nneyun,* which made Eunice exhale in such a sad, hurt, elongated, final way, it made me wonder if she would ever be capable of replacing that breath. Mrs. Park's hand continued to hover over her metallic rice bowl, occasionally touching its rim. In my experience, it was very unusual for Koreans to sit before food and not partake. I closed my eyes and let the lining of my mouth turn into pure heat. I floated over the table and out into the dense midtown air. I wished I were stronger and could help Eunice, or at least take my place in front of her and absorb some of the pain. I wanted to bury my face in the warmth of her hair, the musk and the oils of it, because it was home to me. Because I knew she was too small in body and spirit, too worshipful of her family and the idea of her family, to accept this kind of hurt alone. Was this why she had run off to Rome, learned Italian, found someone pliable and kind, if unbeautiful, to be her companion, tried to become a different person? But one can never outrun the Dr. Parks of the world. Joshie had asked us to keep a diary because the mechanicals of our brains were constantly changing and over time we were transforming into entirely different people. But that's what I wanted for Eunice, for the synapses dedicated to responding to her father to wither and be reborn, to be rededicated to someone who loved her unconditionally.

Something was drawing me back, a breath of coolness across my brow. When I opened my eyes, I saw Eunice looking at me, pleadingly, shyly, like the first time I saw her in Rome, talking to that ridiculous sculptor. How I loved her then, and how I loved her now. Rarely could affection be both so instant and so deep. We locked eyes for a millisecond, but it was enough time to download a million bits of sympathy, for me to tell her, *Soon you will be home and in my arms and the world will reconfigure itself around you and there will be enough compassion for you to feel scared by how much I care for you.* Meanwhile, Dr. Park was landing the plane of his soliloquy. The fight was leaving his body. He spat a few more things, then became quiet, so quiet that he appeared to have deflated before my eyes, leaving behind only the dense, poisoned marrow of those whose entire lives are reduced to the acts of hurting and being hurt. Who had done what to him, I wondered, or was it just the usual neurotransmitters run amok? Dr. Park inhaled another glass of *soju* and then leaned into the octopus and began to push large amounts of it into his mouth. The girls and Mrs. Park started to eat as well, and within five intense moments all the food was gone.

"So, Lenny," Mrs. Park said, as if nothing had happened, "Eunice tell me you have good job science."

Dr. Park snorted.

I wanted to build up my status with the Parks, but didn't want to push my position at Post-Human Services too much, because I knew that devout Christians were not enamored of the concept of eternal life here on earth, which made their celestial dreams pitifully invalid.

"I work for a division of Staatling-Wapachung," I said. "You might have seen some of our buildings going up in New York. That's Staatling Property. And then there's Wapachung Contingency, which is a huge security firm. Property and security and life extension I guess are the three things that we do. All very important in a time of crisis."

I went on in that vein for a while, careful to be nonpolitical, hewing to my parents' FoxLiberty-Prime conservatism. Sometimes when I spoke of Wapachung Contingency, Sally would look at me with ill-concealed annoyance, as if she was not overly enamored of my employer, but even in her displeasure she was graceful and mild, and I wanted to get rid of her parents and talk directly to her, debate her in a chummy, casual way. "Of course," I was saying to her father, "I am not a doctor, a man of science, in the way that you are, sir. What I try to do is synthesize commerce and—"

Dr. Park pointed his index finger at my foot, the white flesh peeking out from within the hole of my sock like a shameful bit of burlesque. "I see," he said, "that you have either a tissue or bone growth at the base of your metatarsophalangeal joint. Maybe the beginning of a bunion. You should buy different footwear, shoes that don't crowd the toes. This is a real pathology that you should take care of, because over time your only option will be surgery." He turned toward Eunice, who nodded.

"New shoes," she said.

"Take care of each other in difficult time," Mrs. Park said. "Good roommates, okay?"

"Thank you," I said. I wanted to return to my career, to how I was going to help Eunice weather the uncertainty ahead, but the screen over the ticket window had just dropped shut. "Um."

Mrs. Park took out an old äppärät and set it on the table between a newly arrived dish of baby ferns and one of salted beef. "Look," she said to Eunice and Sally. "Video of Myong-hee her mother just sent." To me she said: "Cousin from Topanga."

An Asian girl of no more than three ran toward the camera against a crowded background of cheap Californian townhouses and an aquamarine pool. She was wearing a bathing suit festooned with rubber daisies and wore a profoundly genuine smile across her broad face. "Hi, Eunice *Emo*. Hi, Sally *Emo*," she shouted at the screen. "I miss you, Eunice *Emo*," the girl yelled, showing us the full array of her nubby teeth.

"Look," Mrs. Park said. "She has a little bit of rice on top her eye." There *was* a grain of something above her brow. Everyone laughed, Dr. Park included, who said a few words in Korean, the first approving words of the evening, the first time his jaw had been unclenched, the war anthem silenced, the forward battalion called to barracks. Eunice was wiping her eyes, and I realized she wasn't laughing. She uncrossed her legs, sprang from the table in one motion, and ran from the room in bare feet. I started to get up to follow her, but Mrs. Park only said: "She miss her cousin in California. Don't worry."

But I knew it wasn't just the cute girl on the screen that had made Eunice cry. It was her father laughing, being kind, the family momentarily loving and intact—a cruel side trip into the impossible, an alternate history. The dinner was over. The waiters were clearing the table with resignation and without a word. I knew that, according to tradition, I had to allow Dr. Park to pay for the meal, but I went into my äppärät and transferred him three hundred yuan, the total of the bill, out of an unnamed account. I did not want his money. Even if my dreams were realized and I would marry Eunice someday, Dr. Park would always remain to me a stranger. After thirty-nine years of being alive, I had forgiven my own parents for not knowing how to care for a child, but that was the depth of my forgiveness.

I'LL LOVE HIM EVEN MORE

FROM THE GLOBALTEENS ACCOUNT OF EUNICE PARK

JULY 10

EUNI-TARD *TO* CHUNG.WON.PARK

Mom, you haven't written me back in a while. Are you still mad about Lenny? Stop worrying about the Mystery, okay? Worry about Sally instead. You have to watch her weight. Don't let her order "peejah." Make only food with lots of vegetables. I'm going to buy her some nice summer shoes from FootsieGalore, the kind she can wear to interviews too.

I'm too busy looking for Retail jobs to take the LSAT prep right now, but definately next summer. The miscellaneous charge on AlliedCVS must be this new "minimum aggregate APR" they're charging these days. It means we'll have to pay a little less for the monthly charge but we have to pay this new charge immediately or it gets tacked on to the principal, which then turns into a maximum aggregate, which will probably mean another six thousand or more in the next two billing cycles. I think it's time to switch out of AlliedWaste anyway and LandOLakes is running some special promotional rates this month although you have to borrow an extra ten thousand just to "switch in." I guess we should at least "do the math" and check it out.

EUNI-TARD *TO* GRILLBITCH:

Dear Precious Pony,

Hello out there in TV land! Oy. I guess I've been streaming too many old shows with Lenny. Weird. So now my mom is mad at me too. Dinner with la famiglia was a disaster, as you rightfully predicted. Why on earth did Lenny think he could charm my parents? You know, he is so FULL of himself sometimes. He has this American white guy thing where life is always fair in the end, and nice guys are respected for being nice, and everything is just HONKY-dory (get it?). He went on and on about how I can form sentences and how I always talk about taking care of Sally, and meanwhile my father is just flexing his fist under the table. Believe me, that flexed fist was all Sally and I could think about while old Len went on his little dietribe.

I know his heart is in the right place. It's always in the right place. But after a while, who cares, right? How can he not understand me? It's like he doesn't take time to put two and two together. He promised he would read less and spend more time taking care of our apartment, but his head is all caught up in these texts. I looked up War and Peace and it's about this guy Pierre who fights in France, and all this terrible stuff happens to him, but in the end because of his charm he gets to be with this girl he really loves, and who really loves him even though she cheated on him. That's Lenny's view on life in a nutshell, that in the end niceness and smartness always win.

But the worst was my mother. She just went OFF on me. Like, yeh, nuh moo heh ta. You could do so much better. He's old, he's unattractive, his skin looks unhealthy, he's got bad feet, he's not as tall as you said he was, he makes 25,000 yuan a month. If you want to date someone older, there's this gemologist from Palisades who makes close to a million a year and daddy says the Post Human place Lenny works for is a total scam and is going to fall apart completely. Mom kept teening me "Keep options open, keep options open."

I tried not to be hurt, but it was impossible. It's like in the same way Lenny doesn't see me, they don't see HIM. To them he's just this unattractive, not-rich person with a hole in his sock (I thought I was honestly going to kill him for that).

But then we went home and I got that sucky message from my mom and then I just started to feel like I loved Lenny even more. Like the more she detested him, the more I loved him. He was so tired from the dinner and the stupid church service, he just conked out and fell asleep on the couch and he even snored like he never does. He had obviously put so much of himself out there, my sweet, caring tuna-brain, he had tried so hard as he does to be nice to my parents and to defend me against my ass-wipe of a dad, and it had just taken everything out of him. And I thought, if someone can't recognize what a good man he is then what good are they to me? I guess what I'm saying is I'm not as turned off by Lenny's vulnerabilities anymore and I have my cuh-ragee mom to thank for that epiphany. That's the thing with Lenny, if you spend time with him you realize he's just very yamjanae. I think that's a very Korean thing, to be able to sense someone so sweet and gentle and appreciate him for who he is.

Sorry to blah blah blah for so long. Things are really pretty good overall. We've been hanging out and talking and doing lots of fun stuff together. We saw some Images in a gallery and had some okay burgers at bürgr in Bushwick (why can't they have In-N-Out here in New York?). We had un-protected sex and he told me he could see us having a baby. I was like: WHAT??? But it kind of made sense. I WANT to have a baby with him, even if things are really bad in the world. I think I'd be the happiest fairy in the forest if we were a real family someday. Oh, and then we went to this Sri Lankan place for dinner and Lacy Twaät was sitting next to us. Remem-ber she used to do all those gagging and ass-to-mouth porns when we were kids? She was wearing a size two Parakkeet blazer with pearls and sheer Onionskin jeans which she can totally pull off even at her age. Over-all, a very classy, refined ass hookah look. And her date was this older Germanic-looking gentleman, very handsome.

Speaking of, I've been going to Tompkins Square with more supplies, doing some odd ends at CLOTHES WASHING AND SANITATION and just hanging out with David. He's so funny. He just grabbed me at one point and threw me over his shoulder and carried me around the whole park so that I could wave to everyone. It felt good to have a strong guy taking charge of me, and David is SO strong, and not just because he was a soldier in Venezuela. And he keeps his little hut so NEAT (not like you-know-who, ha ha), which is something he said he learned in the army. He's getting ready for when the Guard comes to clear them out, which is making me nervous. If you have any old äppäräti or even laptops, please send them to me, because these people are really desperate. I tried to get him to just have some lunch with me, but he won't leave the park. He's as dedicated to his people as my father is to his patients, and I guess I really admire that. I've been looking at his mouth, and there's something charismatic about him having lost some teeth. He's a rugged man who knows when to be physical and when to be smart. Anyway, I bet if he had Healthcare he could look even more handsome. Sometimes when he talks about what it's going to be like after the Bipartisans are overthrown, I'm like hmm, that doesn't sound bad. He's against the Credit people, but he thinks Retail is always going to be a part of our lives and that Retail girls can be Creative. His ideas are a little out there, but at least he believes in something, right?

Sigh. Okay, Princess P, I'm off to swiffer the balcony, which is covered with bird doo 24/7. This is New York and everyone always shits all over you. Ha ha.

JULY 12

GRILLBITCH *TO* EUNI-TARD:

I'm sorry I didn't get back to you right away, Panda. Something really BAD is happening here. These LNWIs ran into my father's factory when it was closed and took it over and they phased out the LAPD last month and the National Guard won't do anything and now it's like we're going to lose the business or something? I heard my mother and father just VERBALLING VERY QUIETLY in their bedroom and I got so scared, because I don't know what's happening, and I don't know what I'm supposed to do to help. Usually they tell me everything but the look on my father's face was like uhhhhhhhhhhhh and they were even talking about going back to Korea for a while. I tried to go to Padma and there was a road block on the 405 and they had people with their hands behind their heads, so I just turned off into a service station and sat there with the motor running and then I just started HITTING AND HITTING AND HITTING the steering wheel. WTF??????????? How can they not protect our business? How can they just let this Aziz's Army do what it wants? It's like they don't want us to feel safe anymore. I don't think you should hang out with this David guy, Eunice. He sounds like one of those dicks who's destroying my family. And I don't want to be with Gopher either because he's not one of us and he understands NOTHING and his parents have old-school money and it's all just a JOKE to him. I told him about my dad's factory and he was like "good let the poor people take over." I think this is the time for us to forget who we are and to be a part of our families and everything else is just that weird noise you hear when people you don't know are verballing. It's true, everyone is a ghost around me, except when I'm on the äppärät with you. This country is so stupid. Only spoiled white people could let something so good get so bad. I'm sorry you had a sucky dinner with your parents and I'm glad you're loving Lenny more than ever, but you should take into consideration what your parents say, because they've been around for so long. I'm not saying don't date Lenny, just balance in your mind what you feel for him and what you'll eventually have to do. I love you, sweet potato.

EUNI-TARD: Hi, Sally. Did you hear LNWIs took over the Kang's plunger business?

SALLYSTAR: No. That's terrible.

EUNI-TARD: That's all you have to say?

SALLYSTAR: What do you want me to say?

EUNI-TARD: Do you want to get burgers? You can have a little red meat if you promise to just do vegetables and yogurt for a week.

EUNI-TARD: Hello? Earth to Sally Park.

EUNI-TARD: You must be busy. You still haven't told me what you think of Lenny.

SALLYSTAR: Everyone's concerned about you.

EUNI-TARD: They're CONCERNED? That's really nice.

SALLYSTAR: Mommy and Daddy just don't want you to rush into anything.

EUNI-TARD: And you're their Media spokeswoman now?

SALLYSTAR: We're not a perfect family but we're still a family, right?

EUNI-TARD: I don't know. You tell me.

SALLYSTAR: We have to get new carpeting for the living room and new runners for the stairs. Do you want to come to NJ and help us pick it out?

EUNI-TARD: Can I bring Lenny?

SALLYSTAR: You can do whatever you want Eunice.

EUNI-TARD: I was kidding.

SALLYSTAR: So you'll come?

EUNI-TARD: I'll come. But I'm not going to sit next to Dad or say anything to him. Lenny uses the word truculent. Dad's like a truculent child, it's best to ignore him.

SALLYSTAR: Cut him some slack. He's trying. He's not completely well inside and that means we have to forgive him.

EUNI-TARD: Whatever.

SALLYSTAR: Seriously. You will feel so much better if you forgive him, Eunice. Then you can focus on what's happening on the rest of the planet. Maybe you can help me set up a food distribution committee for the tent cities we're doing with Columbia and NYU. Things are getting really bad at Tompkins Square.

EUNI-TARD: How do you know I'm not helping out already?

SALLYSTAR: Huh?

EUNI-TARD: Nothing. I'll forgive Dad when he's 70 years old and Uncle Joon has gambled all his money away and he's this raving homeless man who turns to me and Lenny for help. Then I'll be like, you treated me and Mommy and Sally like shit, but now here's some money so you don't starve.

SALLYSTAR: That's so horrible. I can't believe you would even think that.

EUNI-TARD: Hey, I'm kidding. Sense of humor?

EUNI-TARD: Sally, are you still there? I don't know what's wrong with me today. I really miss Myong-hee. Last time I was in LA I tried to braid her and she was squealing "No, Eunice emo!" like leave me alone, you're not the boss of my hair!!! She's such a cute little oinker. I bet next time we see her she'll be like four inches taller. I don't want her to grow up.

EUNI-TARD: Sally? Come on! Was it the thing I said about dad?

EUNI-TARD: Fine. My BOYFRIEND is almost home and we're going to make a branzino together.

EUNI-TARD: Sally, do you love me?

SALLYSTAR: What?

EUNI-TARD: I'm serious. Do you really love me? I mean like a person. Not just an older sister you're supposed to look up to.

SALLYSTAR: I don't want to talk about this. Of course I love you.

EUNI-TARD: Maybe I didn't do enough.

SALLYSTAR: What are you talking about? Would you please just SHUT UP ALREADY. I'm so sick of you. THE PAST, THE PAST, THE PAST!!!

SALLYSTAR: Hello? Eunice.

SALLYSTAR: Eunice?

SALLYSTAR: Hello.

ANTI-INFLAMMATION
FROM THE DIARIES OF LENNY ABRAMOV

JULY 20

Dear Diary,

Noah told me there's a day during the summer when the sun hits the broad avenues at such an angle that you experience the sensation of the whole city being flooded by a melancholy twentieth-century light, even the most prosaic, unloved buildings appearing bright and nuclear at the edge of your vision, and that when this happens you want to both cry for something lost and run out there and welcome the decline of the day. He made it sound like an urban rapture, his aging face taking on a careful glow, as if he was borrowing some of the light of which he spoke. I thought he was emoting when he said it, but his äppärät was at standby, he wasn't streaming: This was real enough. We were sitting in some crappy St. George café, oddly moved by the fact that there were still cafés out in the world, much less on Staten Island. "I'd love to see that," I said. "When does it happen exactly?"

"We missed it," Noah said. "It was late in June."

"Next year then," I said.

And then, like a perfect Media drama queen, Noah told me he expected to be dead by the next year. Something about the Restoration Authority, the Bipartisans, the price of biofuel, the decline of the tides—who can keep up anymore? That kind of ruined the effect of what he was saying about the light hitting the avenues just so. I wanted to tell him that he didn't have to strain for me, that I liked him exactly as he was: perfectly above average, angry but decent, just smart enough. I thought of Sammy the Elephant in the Bronx Zoo, his calmly depressive countenance, the way he approached extinction with both equanimity and unobtrusive despair. Maybe this was what Noah was jabbering about when he followed the light across the city. The fading light is us, and we are, for a moment so brief it can't even register on our äppärät screens, beautiful.

Speaking of the light, I had one luminous moment with Eunice this week. I caught her looking at my Wall of Books with some curiosity, specifically at a washed-out old cover of a Milan Kundera paperback—a bowler hat floats over a Prague cityscape—her index fingers raised above the book as if ready to tap at the BUY ME NOW symbol on her äppärät, her other fingers massaging the book's back, maybe even enjoying its thickness and unusual weight, its relative quiet and meekness. When she saw me approach she slid the book back on its shelf and retreated to the couch, smelling her fingers for book odor, her cheeks in full blush. But I knew she was curious, my reluctant sentence-monger, and I chalked up yet another victory— the second after what I thought was a very successful dinner with her parents.

Life with Euny has been okay. Exciting, sometimes upsetting. We argued daily. She never backed down. A fighter to the very last. This is how a human being is forged after an unhappy early life. This is the independence of growing up, of standing up for yourself, even if against a phantom enemy.

Mostly we fought about social commitments. She'd be fine with her Elderbird friends who just moved back to New York. They seem like decent girls, effervescent but unsure of themselves, lusting after big-ticket items and some measure of identity, confusing one for the other, but basically in no great hurry to grow up. One girl who actually ate food scored only in the low 500s on her Fuckability, so the other girls would give her tips on how to lose weight. They'd reach over and pinch her all the time, coat her in creams until she glowed sadly on my living-room couch, and weigh her as if she were a prized albacore hanging over a Tokyo wharf. Another girl was going for that new Naked Librarian look, very little covering her body except glasses as thick as my storm windows, which I thought was funny because even a fine institution like Elderbird had recently closed its physical library, so what the hell was this girl even referencing? Then they'd get trashed on rosé out on our (our!) balcony, those cute, bloated, drunken faces of theirs, as they told these long, circular stories that were supposed to be funny but instead proved highly disturbing, narratives of a cheap, ephemeral world where everyone let everyone down as a matter of course and women sometimes got pissed on in front of others. I felt both jealous of their youth and scared for their future. In short, I felt paternal and aroused, which is not a good combination.

I had told Eunice, offhandedly and wearing my cutest platypus grin, that the next two weeks would prove busy on the social front. Joshie had been begging to meet her and expected us on Saturday at his house. Grace and Vishnu were having a party in Staten Island on the Monday after that to officially announce Grace's pregnancy. "I know you're not, like, the biggest socializer," I said.

But she had already turned away from me, the angry spires of her shoulder blades staying my comforting hand.

"Your boss," she said, "wants to meet *me*?"

"He loves young people. He's turning into a teenager himself."

"That bitch Grace wants us over? Why? So she can laugh at me some more?"

"Are you kidding? Grace loves you!"

"Probably wants to be my big sister. No thanks, Len."

"She does care about you, Eunice. She wants to find you a job in Retail. She said her Princeton roommate might know of an internship at Padma." The three times we had briefly, tangentially, touched upon the subject of Eunice procuring employment and helping out with the escalating air-conditioning bill ($8,230 unpegged, just for the month of June), she had mentioned working in Retail. All her Elderbird friends wanted the same. No big surprise there. *Credit for boys, Retail for girls.*

"You don't under*stand*, Leonard."

The phrase I hate the most in the world. I *do* understand. Not everything, but a lot. And what I don't understand, I certainly want to learn more about. If Eunice ever asked me to I would take an entire week off from work, claim some family-related emergency (which is essentially what this is), and listen to her talk. I would put a box of tissues and some calming miso broth between us, take out my äppärät, write it all down, pinpoint the hurt, make reasonable suggestions based on my own experiences, become completely versed in all things Park. "I'm broke," she said.

"What?"

"I have nothing to wear. And my butt is fat."

"You weight eighty-three pounds. Everyone on Grand Street stares at your ass in wonder. You have three closets' worth of shoes and dresses."

"Eighty-six. And I have nothing for the *summer*, Lenny. Are you even listening to me?"

We fought some more. She went to the living room and started teening, legs crossed, the dead smile on her face, forceful sighs, my entreaties rising in pitch. Eventually we reached a kind of compromise. We would go to the United Nations Retail Corridor and buy new clothes for the both of us. I would contribute 60 percent of the cost of her outfits, and she would cover the rest with her parents' Credit. Like I said, a compromise.

I'd never been to the UNRC. I've always been intimidated by Retail Corridors, and this one was supposed to be the biggest yet. When I went to the Corridor they carved out of Union Square two years ago, everyone looked better and way younger than I did. I love going to these little offbeat boutiques in Staten Island with Grace, even if the clientele is older and grayer, folks who came of age in the grand Brooklyn neighborhoods of Greenpoint and Bushwick, and who have now been forced to retreat to Staten Island.

I started panicking the moment we got to the UN: the crush of humanity pouring out of the seven layers of underground parking; the floor samples emitting info that flooded my äppärät with impulsive data; the Debt Bombers singling me out for my impressive Credit ranking; the giant ARA "America Celebrates It's [sic] Spenders" banners, which now featured this girl Eunice actually knew from high school who finagled all these Credit lines and managed to buy six spring collections and a house.

The afterglow of the setting sun rushed through the glass roof of the UNRC, the steel trellises hundreds of feet above us gleaming like the ribs of a fearsome animal. I think this is where the Security Council used to meet, although I could be wrong. Since my sabbatical in Rome, it seems that America had learned her lesson on overhead, had shuttered her traditional malls. These thrifty Retail Corridors were supposed to mimic North African bazaars of yore, their only purpose a quick exchange of goods and services, minus the plangent cries of the sellers and the whiffs of tangerine sweat.

Eunice didn't need a map. She led and I followed past the merchandise crowding the endless floor space in haphazard fashion, one store running into another, rack after rack after rack, each approached, surveyed, considered, dismissed. Here were the famous nippleless Saaami bras that Eunice had shown me on AssLuxury and the fabled Padma corsets that the Polish porn star wore on AssDoctor. We stopped to look at some conservative JuicyPussy summer cocktail dresses. "I'm going to need two," Eunice said. "One for your boss's party and one for that bitch Grace."

"With my boss it's not really a party," I said. "We'll drink two glasses of wine and eat some carrots and blueberries."

Eunice ignored me and set about her task. She did some äppärät work to get a sense of how things were selling around the world. Then she went over to a circle of black, identical-looking dresses and started clicking through them. Click, click, click, each hanger hitting the preceding one, making the sound of an abacus. She spent less than a full second on each dress, but each second seemed more meaningful than the hours she spent on AssLuxury viewing the same merchandise; each was an encounter with the real. Her face was steely, concentrated, the mouth slightly open. Here was the anxiety of choice, the pain of living without history, the pain of some higher need. I felt humbled by this world, awed by its religiosity, the attempt to extract meaning from an artifact that contained mostly thread. If only beauty could explain the world away. If only a nippleless bra could make it all work.

"They either don't have a size zero," Eunice said, upon clicking through the last of the JuicyPussy summer dresses, "or there's this weird embroidery on the hem. They're trying to make themselves more classy than TotalSurrender, which has the slit down the crotch. Let's go to Onionskin."

"Aren't those the sheer jeans?" I said. I imagined Eunice with her labia and behind exposed to passersby as she crossed an especially busy Delancey Street, drivers of cars with Jersey plates rolling down their tinted windows in disbelief. I felt protective of her minimalist package, but there was a frisson of eroticism as well, not to mention social positioning. Others would see her little landing strip and think highly of me.

"No, jerk-face," Eunice said. "I wouldn't be caught dead in those jeans. They make normal dresses too."

"Oh," I said. The fantasy came to an end, and I found myself oddly happy with the conservative girl by my side. We wended our way through a half-kilometer of racks and hit upon the Onionskin outlet. True enough, there were several racks of cocktail dresses, a bit revealing around the bosom, but certainly not see-through. Women, tired and aggrieved, were plowing through the brand's signature transparent jeans, hanging like rigid, empty skins in the center of the Retail space.

As Eunice started clicking through the dresses, a Retail person came over to talk to her. My äppärät quickly zoomed in past the data outflows spilling out from the customers like polluted surf falling upon once-pristine shores and focused on McKay Watson. She was beautiful, this Retail girl. A tall, straight-necked creature whose eyes, clear and present, spoke of native-born honesty, as if to say, *With a background like mine, who needs self-invention?* I caressed McKay's data, even as I took in the Onionskin jeans that clung to her slight if bottom-heavy body—she wore the semi-translucent kind that partly obscured her nether regions and gave them an impressionistic quality, the kind you had to step back to admire. She had graduated from Tufts with a major in international affairs and a minor in Retail science. Her parents were retired professors in Charlottesville, Virginia, where she grew up (baby Images of an oblivious but affectionate McKay hugging a container of orange juice). She didn't have a boyfriend at present but enjoyed the "reverse cowgirl" position with the last one, an aspiring young Mediastud from Great Neck.

Eunice and McKay were verballing each other. They were discussing clothes in a way I couldn't fully appreciate. They were discussing the finer points of a particular dress *not* made of natural fibers. The waists, stretched, unstretched. Composition—7 percent elastane, 2 percent polyester, a size three, 50 percent rayon viscose.

"It's not treated with sodium hydroxide."

"I bought the one with the slit to the left and it stretched."

"Coat the inside of the hem with petroleum jelly."

Eunice had put one hand on the shiny white arm of the Retail girl, a gesture of intimacy I had seen only extended to one of her Elderbird friends, the plump, matronly girl with the low Fuckability ranking. I heard some funny retro expressions like "JK," which means one is "just kidding," and "on the square," which means one is not. I heard the familiar "JBF" and "TIMATOV!" but also "TPR!" and "CFG!" "TMS!" (temporary motion sickness?), "KOT!," and the more universal "Cute!" This is just how people talk, I thought to myself. Feel the wonder of the moment. See the woman that you love reaching out to the world around her.

She bought two cocktail dresses for 5,240 yuan-pegged dollars, of which I covered three thousand. I could feel my debt load groaning a little, shedding a few points, immortality slipping a few notches into the improbable, but nothing like the 239,000-yuan-pegged-dollar punch I had recently taken in the balls from Howard Shu.

"Why didn't you ask that girl if she could get you a job at Onionskin?" I asked Eunice when we had walked away from the Retail space.

"Are you kidding?" Eunice said. "Do you know what kind of *grades* you have to have to work UNRC? And she had the perfect body too. A nice round butt, but a totally boyish top. That's so hot right now."

I hadn't thought of it that way. "Your grades or looks aren't any worse than hers," I said. "Anyway, at least you could have gotten her Teens address. She seems like a good friend to have."

"Thanks, Dad," Eunice said.

"I mean—"

"Okay, shhhh . . . It's your turn to shop. Breathable fabrics are going to do wonders for my *kokiri*."

We hit the glowing, mahogany-paneled insinuation that was the JuicyPussy4Men store. "You have a weak chin," Eunice told me, "so all these shirts you wear with the huge, high collars just show-case your chin and accentuate how weak it is. We're going to get you some V-necks and some solid-colored tees. Striped cotton shirts a bit on the roomy side are going to make your flabby breasts less notice-able, and do yourself a favor, okay? Cashmere. You're worth it, Len."

She made me close my eyes and feel different fabrics. She dressed me in nontight JuicyPussy jeans and stuck a hand down my crotch to make sure my genitals had room to breathe. "It's about comfort," she said. "It's about feeling and acting like a thirty-nine-year-old. Which is what you are, last time I checked." I could feel her family inside her—rude, snide, unsupportive, yet getting the job done, act-ing appropriately, making sure there was room for my genitals, sav-ing face. Beyond the mountains, according to the old Korean proverb Grace had once told me, were more mountains. We'd only just begun.

When I went into a changing room, one of the teenaged sales clerks said to me, "I'll tell your daughter you're in there, sir," and in-stead of taking offense at being mistaken for Eunice's presumably adoptive father, I actually felt in awe of my girl, in awe of the fact that every day we were together she ignored the terrible aesthetic differences between us. This shopping was not just for me or for her. It was for us as a couple. It was for our future together.

I left JuicyPussy with the equivalent of ten thousand yuan's worth of goods. My debt load was blinking frantically with the words RE-CALCULATION IN PROGRESS, which scared off the swarms of Debt Bombers looking to give me more money. When I walked by a Credit Pole on 42nd Street, I registered a ranking of 1510 (down ten points). I may have been poorer, but you couldn't confuse me for the overaged faux-hipster that had entered the UNRC three hours ago. I was what passed for a man now.

There was more. I looked healthier. The breathable fibers took about four years off my biological age. At work, Intakes asked if I was undergoing dechronification treatments myself. I took a physical, and my statistics started flapping on The Boards, my ACTH and cortisol levels plummeting, my designation now "a carefree and inspiring older gent." Even Howard Shu came down to my desk and asked me to lunch. By this point, Joshie was sending Shu down to Washington on his private jet every week. Rumor had it Shu was bound for the White House or even higher up than that. "Rubenstein," people hiccuped, covering their mouths. We were negotiating with the Bipartisans themselves! Over what, though, I still couldn't tell.

But I was no longer scared of Shu. At our lunch meeting, I stared him down as I played with the cuffs of my striped cotton shirt, which indeed gave cover to my incipient man-breasts. We sat in a busy canteen drinking Swiss water we had alkalinized ourselves at the table and eating a few pellets of something fishy.

"I'm sorry we got off on the wrong foot when you came back from Rome," Shu allowed, his full-bore eyes floating through the data fog of his äppärät.

"No big," I said.

"I'm going to tell you something for your ears only."

"Whatevs," I said. "Verbal me, friend."

Shu wiped his mouth as if I had just spat in it, but then resumed his collegial air. "There's a good chance there's going to be a disturbance. A realignment. Bigger than with the last riots. Not sure when. It's what we're picking up from Wapachung Intelligence. Just playing out some war games."

"Safety first," I said, looking bored. "What's going on, Shu-ster?"

Shu descended into another äppärät reverie. I did the same, pretending it was something serious and work-related, but really I was just GlobalTracing Eunice's location. She was, as always, at 575 Grand Street, Apt. E-607, my home, deep into her own äppärät, but subconsciously saturated by the presence of my books and mid-twentieth-century-design furniture. It pleased me, in a parochial way, the fact that I could always count on her being there. My little house-wife! She tracked me moment by moment as well, getting suspicious if I veered off course from the daily set of my life, an impromptu meeting at a bar with Noah or Vishnu or a walk in the unbloodied part of Central Park with Grace. The fact that she was suspicious of me, the fact that she cared—that pleased me too.

"Let's not talk about what *might* happen," Shu said. "I just wanted you to know that Post-Human Services values you." He swallowed too much water and coughed into his hand. He had had the same educational and work background as I had, but I noticed the callused tips of his fingers, as if he volunteered at a knitting factory during the weekends. "And we want you to be safe."

"I'm touched," I said, and I meant it. A high-school memory resurfaced, the day I found out that a wispy freshman girl whom I fancied, complete with an attractive limp and a penchant for poetry, liked me as well.

Howard nodded. "We've updated your äppärät. If you see any National Guard troops, point your äppärät at them. If you see a red dot, that means they're Wapachung Contingency personnel. You know"—he tried to smile—"the good guys."

"I don't get it," I said. "What happened to the *real* National Guard?"

But Shu never answered me. "That girl you have on your äp-pärät," he said, pointing to an Image of Eunice I had floating all over my screen.

"Eunice Park. My gf."

"Joshie says to make sure you're with her in any emergency."

"Duh," I said. But it was nice that Joshie remembered I was in love.

Shu picked up his glass of alkalinized water and made a jokey toast with it. Then he leaned back and drank it down in such forceful gulps that our veined marble table shook, and the business people who shared the premises looked at this small brown almond of a man in their midst and tried to snicker at his display of strength. But they too were afraid of him.

After my Shu lunch, I walked from the Essex Street F stop to my far-flung riverside co-op with a renewed sense of grandeur. Since Eunice had picked out my new duds, I had started obsessively FACing every girl in sight: pretty, average, thin, skeletal, white, brown, black. It must have been my confidence, because my PERSONALITY was hitting the 700s and my MALE HOTNESS skirted into the 600s—so that, in an enclosed space like the M14 bus, with its small herd of trendoids grazing amidst the dying old people, I could sometimes emerge in the middle range of attractiveness, say the fifth-cutest man out of nine or ten. I would like to describe this utterly new feeling to you, diary, but I fear it will come out in purely evangelical terms. It felt like being born again. It felt like Eunice had resurrected me on a bed of cotton and wool.

But getting Eunice to meet Joshie was not easy. On the night before we were to go over to his place, she couldn't sleep. "I don't know, Len," she whispered. "I don't know, I don't know, I don't know."

She was wearing a long satin twentieth-century sleeping gown, a gift from her mother that left everything to the imagination, instead of her usual TotalSurrenders.

"I feel like you're making me do this," she said.

"I feel like I'm being pushed."

"I feel like things are moving too fast."

"Maybe I should move back to Fort Lee."

"Maybe you need to be with a real adult."

"We both knew I was going to hurt you."

I gently pawed her back in the dark. I did my patented cornered-rat-tapping-his-foot-in-distress noise against the mattress and made an ambiguous animal sound.

"Stop that," she said. "The zoo is closed."

I whispered what was required of me. Various pop-psych gems. Encouragements. I assumed the debt and the blame. It wasn't her fault. Maybe it was my fault. Maybe I was just an extension of her father. The night was dedicated to her sighs and my whispers. We finally fell asleep just as the sun rose over the Vladeck housing projects, an exhausted American flag slapping itself in the summer wind. We awoke at 5 p.m., having nearly missed the car Joshie had sent to help us ascend to the Upper West Side. We dressed in silence, and when I tried to take her hand in the sparkling new Hyundai Town Car, possibly on its maiden voyage, she flinched and looked away. "You look beautiful," I said. "That dress."

She said nothing. "Please," I said. "It's important for Joshie to meet you. It's important for me. Just be yourself."

"What's that? Dumb. Boring."

We cut through Central Park. Armed choppers were making their weekend rounds above us, but the traffic below was light and easy, the humid breeze rocking the tops of the immortal trees. I thought of how we had kissed in the Sheep Meadow on the day she moved in with me, how I had held her tiny person to me for a hundred slow beats, and how, for that entire time, I had thought death beside the point.

Joshie's building was on a street between Amsterdam and Columbus—a twelve-story Upper West Side co-op, unremarkable save for the two National Guardsmen who stood on either side of the entrance, shunting passersby off the sidewalk with their rifles. An ARA sign at the mouth of the street urged us to deny its existence and imply consent. Joshie had told me these men were keeping tabs on him, but even I understood they served as protection. A red dot appeared on my äppärät, along with the words "Wapachung Contingency." The good guys.

The tiny lobby was filled by an affably heavy Dominican man in a faded gray uniform and the difficult breath coming out of him. "Hello, Mr. Lenny," he said to me. I used to see him all the time when Joshie and I were more regular friends, when our work was not yet all-consuming and we would think nothing of sharing a bagel in the park or catching some exhausting Iranian flick at Lincoln Center.

"This is where the Jewish intelligentsia used to live, a long, long time ago," I told Eunice in the elevator. "I think that's why Joshie likes it here. It's a kind of nostalgia trip."

"Who were they?" she said.

"What?"

"Jewish intelligentsia."

"Oh, just Jews who thought a lot about the world and then wrote books about it. Lionel Trilling and those guys."

"They started your boss's immortality business?" Eunice asked.

I could have almost kissed her cold, rouged lips. "In a sense," I said. "They came from poor, hardy families and they were realistic about dying."

"See, this is why I didn't want to come," Eunice said. "Because I don't know any of this stuff."

The old-fashioned elevator doors opened symphonically. By Joshie's door, a muscular young man in T-shirt and jeans was dragging out a heavy garbage bag with his back to me, the dull interior light of the Upper West Side glistening off his shaved head. A cousin, if I remembered correctly. Jerry or Larry from New Jersey. I stuck out my hand as he began to turn around. "Lenny Abramov," I said. "I think we met at your dad's Chanukah party in Mamaroneck."

"Rhesus Monkey?" the man said. The familiar black pelt of his mustache twitched in greeting. This was no cousin from Matawan. I was looking at dechronification in action. I was looking at Joshie

Goldmann himself, his body reverse-engineered into a thick young mass of tendons and forward motion. "Jesus Christ," I said. "Someone's been hitting the Indians. No wonder I haven't seen you at the office all week."

But the rejuvenated Joshie was no longer noticing me. He was breathing both heavily and evenly. His mouth opened slowly. "Hiya," the mouth said.

"Hi," Eunice said. "Lenny," she started to say.

"Lenny," Joshie echoed, absently. "Sorry. I'm—"

"Eunice."

"Joshie. Come in. Please." He examined her as she passed through the door, preyed on the lightly tanned shoulders beneath the black cocktail-dress straps, then looked at me with numb understanding. Youth. A seemingly untrammeled flow of energy. Beauty without nanotechnology. If only he knew how unhappy she was.

We passed into the living room, which I knew to be as humble as the rest of the apartment. Art Deco couches in blue velvet. Posters from his youth—science-fiction films with big-haired women and deep-jawed men—framed conservatively in oak, as if to say they had withstood the test of time and emerged, if not masterpieces, then at least potent artifacts. The names alone. *Soylent Green. Logan's Run.* Here were Joshie's beginnings. A dystopian upper-class childhood in several elite American suburbs. Total immersion in *Isaac Asimov's Science Fiction Magazine.* The twelve-year-old's first cognition of mortality, for the true subject of science fiction is death, not life. It will all end. The totality of it. The self-love. Not wanting to die. Wanting to live, but not sure why. Looking up at the nighttime sky, at the black eternity of outer space, amazed. Hating the parents. Wanting their love. Already an anxious sense of time passing, the staggered bathroom howls of grief for a deceased Pomeranian, young Joshie's stalwart and only best friend, felled by doggie cancer on a Chevy Chase lawn.

Eunice stood there, in the middle of the living room, blushing intensely, the blood coming in waves. I did something I hadn't quite expected of myself. I breached decorum, came over and kissed her on the ear. For some reason I wanted Joshie to understand just how much I loved her and how that love was not just predicated on her youth, probably the only thing he appreciated about her. The two people who formed my universe looked away from me, embarrassed. "I'm so glad," Joshie muttered. "I'm so glad to finally meet you. Jeez. Lenny talks so much about you."

"Lenny just talks a *lot*," Eunice successfully joked.

I put my hand around her shoulders and felt her breathe. Joshie straightened up and I could see the muscle tone, the deep-veined reality of what he was becoming, the little machines burrowing inside him, clearing up what had gone wrong, rewiring, rededicating, resetting the odometer on every cell, making him shine with a child's precocious glow. Among the three of us in the room, I was the one who was proactively dying.

"Okay, let's get some of that yummy good wine," Joshie said. He laughed with uncharacteristic fakeness, then ran off into the well-stocked galley kitchen.

"I've never seen him like this," I said to Eunice.

"He reminds me of you," Eunice said. "A big nerd." I smiled at that, pleased that she could conceive of our commonalities. The idea occurred to me that we could form a family, although I was unsure of what role I would play. Eunice picked a few hairs from my face, her face warm with attention, then glossed my lips with chap. She pulled down on my short-sleeved shirt so that it aligned better with my light cashmere V-neck sweater. "Go like this with your arms," she said, shaking her own. "Now pull on the sleeves."

Joshie returned to hand Eunice a glass of wine; I got a mug's worth of purple aroma. "Hope you don't mind the mug, Lenny," he said. "My cleaning woman got stopped at the ARA checkpoint on the WB."

"The *what*?" I said.

"Williamsburg Bridge," Eunice clarified. Both she and Joshie rolled their eyes and laughed at my slow ways with abbreviations. "You have such a pretty apartment," Eunice said. "Those posters must be worth a billion. Everything's so old."

"Including the owner," Joshie said.

"No," Eunice said. "You look great."

"You look great too."

I pulled on the sleeves of my shirt an extra time. "Let me show you around," Joshie said. "Two-minute house tours my specialty."

We went into his cluttered "creative study." I noticed Eunice had finished most of her Pinot and was already improvising a way to remove the purple from her lips with her finger and a translucent green jelly she squeezed out of a tube. "These are stills from my one-man show," Joshie said, as he pointed out a framed Image of himself dressed in prison stripes with a giant stuffed albatross hanging from his neck. Standing before me, he looked thirty years younger today than in the Image, which was at least ten years old. He had lost forty years. A half-life gone.

"The play was called *Sins of the Mother*," I said helpfully. "Very funny and very deep."

"Was it on Broadway?" Eunice asked.

Joshie laughed. "Yeah, right," he said. "Didn't make it past this sucky supper club in the Village. But I didn't give a damn about success. Creative thinking, working with your mind, that's my number-one prescription for longevity. If you stop thinking, if you stop wondering, you die. That simple." He looked down at his feet, perhaps realizing he sounded more like a salesman than a leader. Eunice made him nervous, I could tell. We had no shortage of attractive women at Post-Human Services, but their self-assuredness made them bleed into one personality. Anyway, Joshie had always said that he had no time for romance until immortality was "a done deal."

"Did you draw this yourself?" Eunice asked, pointing to a watercolor of an old, naked woman shattered into three by an unnamed force, her empty breasts flying in all directions, a dark pubic mound holding the thirds together.

"Very beautiful," I said. "Very Egon Schiele."

"This one's called *Splinter Cell*," Joshie said. "I did about twenty variations of it, and they all look exactly the same."

"She kind of resembles you," Eunice said. "I like the shading around her eyes."

"Yes, well . . ." Joshie said, and made a shy croaking sound. I always felt embarrassed when looking at Joshie's paintings of his mother, as if I had walked into a bathroom and caught my own mother lifting her tired hindquarters off the toilet seat. "You paint yourself?"

Eunice coughed. The Great Discomfort Smile came on, the shame bringing her freckles into strong relief. "I took a class," she barely breathed out. "At Elderbird. A drawing class. It was nothing. I sucked."

"I didn't know that," I said. "That you took a drawing class."

"That's because you never listen to me, jerk-face," she whispered.

"I'd love to see something you've drawn," Joshie said. "I miss painting. It really calmed me down. Maybe we can get together one day and practice a little."

"Or you could take some classes at Parsons," I suggested to Eunice. The idea of the two of them—alive and deathless—creating something together, an Image, a "work of art," as they used to say, made me feel sorry for myself. If only I had had a proclivity to draw or paint. Why did I have to suffer that ancient Jewish affliction for words?

"Maybe we can *both* take some classes at Parsons," Joshie said to Eunice. "You know, together."

"But who has the time?" I ventured.

We returned to the living room, with Joshie and Eunice landing on one cozy, curvaceous sofa, while I hunched over an opposing leather ottoman. "Cheers," Joshie said, clinking his mug with Eunice's long-stemmed glass. They smiled at each other, and then Eunice turned to me. I had to abandon the ottoman and walk over to them to complete the ritual. Then I had to sit back down again. Alone.

"Cheers," I said, nearly demolishing Joshie's mug. "To the people I love the most."

"To being fresh and young," Joshie said.

They started talking. Joshie asked her about her life, and she replied in her usual inconsequential manner—"Yeah," "I guess so," "Sort of," "Maybe," "I tried," "I'm not good," "I suck." But she was pleased to be engaged, as attentive as I had ever seen her, one open palm buffering a clump of hair spilling down her shoulder. She didn't know how to conduct a conversation with a man properly, without anger or flirtation, but she was trying, filtering, giving away as little as possible, but wanting to please. She would look at me worriedly, her eyes crinkling with the pain of having to think and respond, but the worry receded as Joshie kept pouring wine—we were all above the two-glasses-of-resveratrol maximum—and fed her a plate of blueberries and carrots. He volunteered to boil some pot in a kettle of green tea, something I hadn't seen him do in years, but Eunice politely told him that she didn't smoke marijuana, that, perversely enough, it made her sad.

"I wouldn't mind some," I said, but the offer had clearly floated off the table.

"Why do you call Lenny 'Rhesus Monkey'?" Eunice asked.

"He looks like one," Joshie said.

Eunice gave her äppärät a spin, and when the animal in question appeared, she actually threw her head back and laughed the way I had only seen her laugh with her best Elderbird friends, with honesty as well as mirth. "Totally," she said. "Those long arms and that, like, bunched-up middle. It's so hard to shop for him. I always have to teach him how to . . ." She couldn't describe it, but made some stretching motions with her arms.

"Dress," I concluded for her.

"He's a quick learner," Joshie said, looking at her, one arm reaching absently for a second bottle of wine sitting obediently by his legs. I presented my mug for a refill. We continued to drink heavily. I pushed myself down into the moist leather ottoman, marveling at how little Joshie cared about his surroundings. He hadn't bought a new piece of furniture in the years I'd known him. All those years, alone, no children, no American overabundance, devoting himself to only one idea, the personification of which sat half a foot away from him, one leg tucked under her, a sign that her distress was abating. One thing Joshie could always communicate was the fact that he wasn't going to hurt you. Even when he did.

They were talking youthfully: AssDoctor, girl-threshing, Phuong "Heidi" Ho, the new Vietnamese porn star. They used words like "ass hookah" and teenaged abbreviations like TGV and ICE that brought to mind high-speed European trains. The wrinkle-free, wine-blushing Joshie, his body run through with new muscles and obedient nerve endings, leaned forward like a missile in mid-arc, his mind likely flooding with youthful instincts, the need to connect at any cost. I wondered, heretically, if he would ever miss being older, if his body would ever long for a history.

"I really want to draw, but I'm no good," Eunice was saying.

"I bet you're good," Joshie said. "You have such a sense of— style. And economy. I get that just by looking at you!"

"This one teacher in college said I was good, but she was just this dyke."

"OMFG, why don't you doodle something right now?"

"No freaking way."

"Totally. Do it. I'll get some paper." He pumped his fists into the sofa, propelled himself into the air, and was running for his study.

"Wait," Eunice shouted after him. "Holy crap." She turned to me. "I'm too scared to draw, Len." But she was smiling. They were playing. We were drunk. She ran after Joshie, and I heard a sharp youthful yell—I could barely tell which of them was responsible. I went over to the abandoned sofa and sat in Joshie's space, savoring the warmth my master had left behind. It was getting dark. Out the window I traced water towers and the unadorned backs of once-tall buildings leading up to the glass-and-cement scrim of development that lined both banks of the Hudson River, like two sets of dirty mirrors. My äppärät patiently provided information on various real-estate valuations and compared them with HSBC-London's and Shanghai's. I pressed the wine bottle to my lips and let the resveratrol flood my system, hoping, praying for a few more years added to the countdown clock of my life. Joshie came back into the living room. "She wouldn't let me watch," he said.

"She's actually drawing?" I said. "By hand? Not on an äppärät?"

"Hell's yeah, home-slice! Don't you know your own gf?"

"She's so modest around me," I said. "FYI, no one really says 'home-slice' anymore, Grizzly."

Joshie shrugged. "Youth is youth," he said. "Talk young, live young. How are your pH levels anyway?"

She came out, blushing but happy, clutching a sketchpad to her chest. "I can't," she said. "It's stupid. I'm going to tear it up!"

We raised the appropriate protests, outdoing each other with our thundering baritones, Joshie rapping his mug on the coffee table like some coarse fraternity brother. Shyly, but with a hint of flirtation probably borrowed from an old television series about women in Manhattan, Eunice Park handed Joshie her sketchpad.

She had drawn a monkey. A rhesus monkey, if I wasn't mistaken. A bulbous gray-haired chest, long heart-shaped ears, perfectly dark little paws holding on tenuously to a tree branch, a whirl of gray hair on top, below an expression of playful intelligence and contentment. "How meticulous," I said. "How detailed. Look at those leaves. You're wonderful, Eunice. I'm so impressed."

"She's got you down, Len," Joshie said.

"Me?" I looked at the monkey's face once more. The red, cracked lips and rampant stubble. The overstated nose, shiny at the tip and bridge, the early wrinkles dashing up to the naked temples; the bushy eyebrows that could count as separate organisms. If you looked at it from a different angle, if you moved the sketchpad into half-shadow, the contentment I had previously discerned on the monkey's slightly fat face could pass for want. It was a picture of me. As a rhesus monkey. In love.

"Wow," Joshie said. "That is *so* Media."

Eunice said it was awful, that twelve-year-olds could do a better job, but I could tell she wasn't entirely convinced. We each hugged him farewell. He kissed her cheeks for a while, then slapped me quickly on the shoulders. He offered us a digestif and some Upstate-sourced strawberries for the road. He offered to go down in the elevator with us and deal with the armed men outside. He stood in the doorway, clutching on to the doorpost, watching the last of us. During that final moment, the moment of letting go, I saw his face in profile, and noticed the confluence of purpled veins that made him look momentarily old again, that produced a frightening X-ray of what burbled up beneath that handsome new skin tissue and gleaming young eyes. That stupid male shoulder-slap wasn't enough. I wanted to reach out and comfort him. If Joshie somehow failed at his life's work, which of us would be more heartbroken, the father or the son?

"See, that wasn't so bad," I said in the Town Car as Eunice put her sweet, alcohol-reeking head on my shoulder. "We had fun, right? He's a nice man."

I heard her breathing temperately against my neck. "I love you, Lenny," she said. "I love you so much. I wish I could describe it better. But I love you with all I've got. Let's get married." We kissed each other on the lips, mouth, and ears as we passed through seven ARA checkpoints and the length of the FDR Drive. A military helicopter seemed to follow us home, its single yellow beam stroking the whitecaps of the East River. We talked about going to City Hall. A civil ceremony. Maybe next week. Why not make it official? Why ever be apart? "You're the one I want, *kokiri,*" she said. "You're the only one."

OLD MAN SPUNKERS
FROM THE GLOBALTEENS ACCOUNT OF EUNICE PARK

JULY 20

GOLDMANN-FOREVER: Hi, Eunice. It's Joshie Goldmann. Whasss'uuuup?

EUNI-TARD: Joshie?

GOLDMANN-FOREVER: You know, Lenny's boss.

EUNI-TARD: Oh. Hi, Mr. Goldmann. How'd you get my info?

GOLDMANN-FOREVER: Just teened around for it. And what's with the Mr. Goldmann? That's my dad's name. Call me Joshie. Or Grizzly Bear. That's what Lenny calls me.

EUNI-TARD: Ha ha.

GOLDMANN-FOREVER: So I'm writing to remind you of our little date.

EUNI-TARD: We had a date?

GOLDMANN-FOREVER: We were going to take an art class together. Duh!

EUNI-TARD: We were? I'm sorry. I've been so busy this week. I should be applying for Retail jobs and stuff.

GOLDMANN-FOREVER: A lot of our clients are in Retail. What kind of job are you looking for? The guy from Ass something just came in. That's confidential, actually.

EUNI-TARD: Oh, I couldn't impose.

GOLDMANN-FOREVER: Stop! Who's imposing? Ha! I'm sure we can hook you up with some mad-ass job.

EUNI-TARD: Okay. Thank you.

GOLDMANN-FOREVER: So I got us into a summer drawing class at Parsons-Ewha.

EUNI-TARD: That's very nice of you, but the summer session's already started.

GOLDMANN-FOREVER: They're making an exception. It's just the two of us. Although maybe you shouldn't tell that to Lenny. Ha ha.

EUNI-TARD: Thank you so much but I really can't afford it.

GOLDMANN-FOREVER: WTF? I got it covered.

EUNI-TARD: That's very kind of you, Mr. Goldman. But I think I need to concentrate on getting a job this week.

GOLDMANN-FOREVER: What did you call me?

EUNI-TARD: Sorry!!!! I meant Joshie.

GOLDMANN-FOREVER: Duh! Anyway, that rhesus monkey painting was so good I don't want your talent to go to waste, Eunice. You're super-gifted. This may sound weird, but you kind of remind me of me when I was younger. Except you're sweeter. I was a very angry young man until I realized I didn't have to die. Some of us are so special, Eunice, we don't have to succumb to the Fallacy of Merely Existing. Maybe you're special too, huh? Anyway, I can help you get a job, so you don't have to worry about that part. And I'll take a class with you. It'll be so great!!!! You can make more animal drawings of Lenny and then give them to him for his birthday in the fall.

EUNI-TARD: I've been wondering what to get him actually.

GOLDMANN-FOREVER: Poifect! OK, gotta jet, but get back to me soon about the classes. They're flying in some teacher from Paris just for us.

EUNI-TARD *TO* GRILLBITCH:

Dear Precious Pony,

HOLY FUCKING SHIT!!! Okay, you've got to help me, jizz-monkey. Okay, are you sitting down? So we go over to Lenny's boss's place and it's this like adorable old-school apartment, like something out of Paris. So smartly decorated and not too typical Mediastud either, like he's put a lot of thought into it. They even had the street closed off for him. And his boss is SOOOO adorable. He runs this huge company that makes people look a lot younger. And he's in his seventies but he looks like he could be Lenny's younger, handsomer brother. Remember those porns we used to watch when we were in kindergarten? With the old man who molests teens on the beach. What was it called? Old Man Spunkers or something? That's sort of what he looks like, with the shaved head, but cuter and younger.

Anyway, Lenny's boss says he has these micro-robots inside him that repair his dead cells, but that sounds like bullshit. I bet he's just had a lot of
plastic surgery and he also takes care of himself and works out three times
a day (UNLIKE LENNY!). So when we hung out I drunk more wine than
I've had since Rome, and I got a little tipsy, and this guy, Mr. Goldman, he
kept looking at me with this kind of sweet, lustful face, like he wants to
whore me out, but gently, like I'm his daughter and his sex toy at the
same time. He's so goofy and dorky (he had a one-man show on a live
stage and he drew all these funny paintings of an old woman with massive pubic hair—SICK!), I just wanted to jump on his lap or something. It
kind of made me a little wet, how disarming he was and how smart and
easygoing and just plain old FUN, the way Lenny never really is anymore.
I was starting to sweat a little, and I get SO self-conscious. It's like my
freaking thighs are so fat they're rubbing against each other and making
this wet kissing sound. MWAH! MWAH! TIMATOV!!!! I need to lose
weight NOW, no excuses. I am so through with proteins and carbs, although Mr. Goldman was talking a lot about peak proteins. Anyway, this
week I'm just going to eat those lo-cal red-bean icicle pops from the Korean mart and drink five cups of water for dinner.

And then I go home with Lenny and I make out with him and we do
Magic Pussy time and all that, but all the time I'm thinking about Joshie
Goldman. GAH! What is wrong with me. It's like Lenny's not old enough?
I have a real "ha ra buh gee" complex! Ha ha! I should ask Sally if I can
intern at the geriatric ward of this hospital where she volunteers. And I
guess I felt so guilty that I kept telling Lenny I want to get married to him!
Anyway, the next day I get a message from Joshie (that's what he wants
me to call him) saying that WE SHOULD TAKE THIS ART CLASS TO-
GETHER at Parsons, where it's just me and him and some French art
teacher. And that I should keep that secret from Lenny that it's just the
two of us. Does that sound like a come-on do you think? What do I do?
He's my boyfriend's boss, Pony!

Oh, and he said he could get me a job in Retail, like maybe at AssLuxury or something. He's a really powerful man. The thing is, though he's
like 40 years older than Lenny he's still a bit like a child, but like a totally
advanced child. He's fun loving and in control and I bet he can pay off my

AlliedWaste bills—HA HA HA! Totally kidding. But on the other hand it's like I can communicate with him easier than I can with Lenny even though he doesn't wear an äppärät for some reason and I can't get his profile. Jesus Christ, pussy pinyata. Please just tell me I'm a bad person and set me straight before I geezer again.

So I guess the other major thing is that I saw my dad and it was weird, but at the same time it kind of healed my heart a little. He really has no patients anymore, so he asked Sally if he could help out in one of the LNWI camps in the parks and she sent him to Tompkins Square, and then Sally sort of "arranged" that we should meet there. She always has to play the role of the good daughter bringing the family together.

It was raining so hard all of a sudden, all the food on the dinner tables was completely washed away and someone had donated three hams, so people were crying. This old woman died last week of a heart attack and no ambulances will even come down there anymore and plus no one has Healthcare vouchers. So it was like Dad to the rescue. He spent a whole afternoon just giving free checkups in the tents. And at first David would like bark orders at him, saying this is a priority or that's a priority, but Dad would just look at him quietly, the same way he stares at me, only without saying anything. And David was like okaaaay. Dad brought all his medical stuff with him, and it was so strange to just see him as this little old ha ra buh gee walking through the park, carrying this huge brown leather bag mommy got him for his 60th birthday, so harmless and innocent, and I was thinking THIS is the man who ruined my life?

He said there was serious malnutrition going on, so we went to the new H-Mart on Second Ave and we got all this stuff that wouldn't spoil, like 1,000 ddok and packets of kim (the not so good kind) and those nori crackers by like the wagonload and we brought it all back to the park in a cab. It was weird because I used to be so ashamed of having all that food in my lunchbox in kindergarten and now we're feeding it to poor Americans. It was fun to go shopping with dad, he never yelled at me once. And you know how great he is around poor patients. He even played with all the children in the Activities tent the way he plays with Myong-hee when we're in CA, pretending he's a plane flying back to Seoul and she climbs on board and then she's strapped in, and then the meal is served (more ddok!)

and then when it comes to a landing he says, "Thank you for flying Air Uncle. Make sure you have ALL personal belongings, okay?" He and David talked about scripture for like ten hours, and I could tell David was impressed by my dad just spouting Romans and all that crap, about how helping LNWIs is like "going unto Jerusalem to minister unto the saints," and I liked that saying because it made David and all these poor people sound like saints, much better than the stuck-up Media jerks Lenny hangs around with. They had to get out all the spare tarps to protect the leftover Fourth of July corn from the rain, and David was trying to get other people to help him, but my dad was this obstanate little bulldog and he refused any help and it was just him and David doing all the work, like two reliable strong men, even though I was worried Dad would catch a cold.

It's weird but I almost thought that maybe this could be my family, without mom or Sally. Maybe I should have been born a guy, huh? I know you don't like David and the whole Aziz's Army, but after they finished, my dad told me he thought David was really smart and that it was a shame what this country was doing to men like him, sending him to Venezuela and then not giving him his bonus or Healthcare.

I have to say I think in some ways my dad has more in common with David than with Lenny. It's like because our dads grew up in Korea after the war they know what it's like to not have anything and how to survive off their smarts. Anyway, I was really worried Dad would bring up Lenny, and at one point I thought he was about to, because we were all alone and he really changes when we're alone, the mask just drops off and it's all about how I've failed him and mom, but all he said was "How are you, Eunice?"

And I almost freaking started to cry, because he never asked me that in my life. I was just like, "Uh-huh, fine, uh-huh," and then it was like I couldn't breathe, and I couldn't tell if it was because I was happy or just scared because it seemed so final for him to ask me that, like he'd never see me again. I wondered what he would do if I just threw my arms around him. I get so scared whenever I have to leave my parent's house to go away for a while, because he always attacks me at the last minute, he always says something terrible in the car on the way to the airport, but I also wonder if secretly he just wants to have some kind of contact with me before I fly off and abandon him for someone like Lenny. That's how it felt when we were walking out of the park and I just blurted out, "Bye, Daddy, I love you," and I ran down to our apartment and thank god Lenny wasn't there because I bawled for three hours until he came home for dinner and I really didn't want to spend any time with him that night.

Anyway, I don't want to think about this too much, because it depresses me. What's new with you, my little churro frito? Did your father get his plunger biz back? How was the vag rejuv? Fuck-tard Gopher? I miss you more and more each day we're apart. Oh, my mom STILL won't respond to my messages. It's like punishment for dating Lenny. Maybe I should bring my new seventy-year-old friend Joshie GOLDMAN to church! Ha ha.

JULY 22

GRILLBITCH *TO* EUNI-TARD:

Dear Precious Panda,

I really can't talk right now. We can't find my dad. He had gone to the factory and that's the last GlobalTrace of him I had on my äppärät. We thought he had snuck into the building even though it's surrounded by National Guards and there are LNWIs inside doing whatever they want. Mommy and I tried to get through the checkpoint but they wouldn't let us and when my mom started hollering at one of the soldiers he punched her. We're home and I'm changing the compresses on her now, because her eye is swollen and she won't go to the hospital. We don't know what's happening anymore. Some Media guy Pervaiz Silverblatt of the Levy Report is streaming that there's a fire at the factory, but I've never heard of him. I'm sorry I'm a bad friend and can't help you with your problems right now. You have to be strong and do whatever you have to do for your family.

EUNI-TARD: Sally, did you hear what's happening in California? To the Kangs?
SALLYSTAR: Ask your boyfriend.
EUNI-TARD: What?
SALLYSTAR: Ask him about Wapachung Contingency.

EUNI-TARD: I don't get it.

SALLYSTAR: Don't worry about it.

EUNI-TARD: Fuck you, Sally. Why do you have to be like that? What has Lenny ever done to you or to mom? And FYI Lenny doesn't work for Wapachung Whatever, he works for Post Human Services. I met his boss and he's really nice. It's just a company that helps people look younger and live longer.

SALLYSTAR: Sounds pretty egotistical.

EUNI-TARD: Right, because only you and dad can be saints ministering unto Jerusalem.

SALLYSTAR: Huh?

EUNI-TARD: Look it up, it's in your bible. You probably have it highlighted in twenty different colors. Guess what? I've been helping too, Sally. I've been at the park the last few weeks. And I've become friends with David who thinks you're just a spoiled little Barnard girl.

SALLYSTAR: How much longer are you going to go on just being a little ball of anger, Eunice? One day your looks are going to fade and all these stupid old white men won't be chasing after you and then what?

EUNI-TARD: Nice, Sally. Well, at least your being honest for the first time in your life.

SALLYSTAR: I'm sorry, Eunice.

SALLYSTAR: Eunice? I'm sorry.

EUNI-TARD: I have to go see David in the park. I'm getting them Men's Biomultiples because they need to be strong in case there's an attack.

SALLYSTAR: Okay. I love you.

EUNI-TARD: Sure.

SALLYSTAR: Eunice!

EUNI-TARD: I know you do.

JULY 24

AZIZARMY-INFO *TO* EUNI-TARD:

Hi, Eunice. Good meeting your dad and talking to him. He reminds me of you, in the sense that you're both hardcore. I'm glad you said being together at Tompkins Square Nation has brought you closer. Seeing your dad made me miss mine. When we were growing up they were even tougher on us than they had to be and that means their kids became stronger than they had to be. OBSERVATION: You bitch and whine a lot, Eunice, that's your SOP, but you're still a very strong woman, scary strong sometimes. Use that strength for good. Move on.

It is COLD with the rain tonight. Everyone's asleep and the only sound is Marisol's little girl Anna singing old R&B by the water fountain. I'm worried about Force Protection. My MPs say there's no ARA activity around the park perimeter, which doesn't feel right for a Friday. I'm going to send a unit downrange to the Laundromat on St. Mark's. Maybe the Bipartisans see the writing on the wall. Maybe we really are going to get our Venezuela bonuses this time.

OBSERVATION: You're very lucky overall, Eunice, you know that? It would be helpful if you were here with me right now so that we could talk in the quiet of the tent (I tried to verbal you, but you're probably asleep) and it would be just like in college all over again, only no one at Austin was as pretty as you. FYI, Chauncey at Malnutrition says we need 20 cans of mosquito repellent and if we get a 100 more avocado and crabmeat units from H-mart that would really up our nutritional profile.

Hope you're staying dry and that your mind and body are in a good place. Don't give in to High Net Worth thinking this week. Perform useful tasks that your dad would be proud of. But also: Relax a little. Whatever happens, I got your back.

David

THE RUPTURE
FROM THE DIARIES OF LENNY ABRAMOV

JULY 29

Dear Diary,

Grace and Vishnu had their pregnancy-announcing party on Staten Island. On the way to the ferry terminal, Euny and I saw a demonstration, an old-school protest march down Delancey Street and toward the broken superstructure of the Williamsburg Bridge. It was sanctioned by the Restoration Authority, or so it seemed, the marchers freely chanting and waving misspelled signs demanding better housing: "Peeple power!" "Houssing is a human right." "Don't throw us off the peir." "Burn all Credit Pole!" "I am no a grasshopper, *huevón*!" "Don call me ant!" They were chanting in Spanish and Chinese, their accents jamming the ear, so many strong languages vying to push their way into our lackadaisical native one. There were small Fujianese men, big-backed Latina mothers, and, sticking out of the fray, gangly white Media people trying to stream about their own problems with condo down payments and imperious co-op boards. "We are being overruled by real estate!" the more erudite marchers shouted. "No more threats of deportation! Boo! Space for LGBT youth is not for sale! In unity there is power! Take back our city! No justice! No peace!" Their cacophony calmed me. If there could still be marches like this, if people could still concern themselves with things like *better* housing for transgendered youth, then maybe we weren't finished as a nation just yet. I considered teening Nettie Fine the good news, but was preoccupied by the travails of just getting to Staten Island. The National Guard troops at the ferry terminal checkpoints weren't Wapachung Contingency according to my äppärät, so we submitted to the usual half-hour "Deny and Imply" humiliations like everyone else.

Grace and Vishnu lived on one floor of a Shingle Style manse in the hipster St. George neighborhood, the house's Doric columns declaring an overbearing historicity, the turret providing comic relief, stained-glass windows a pretty kind of kitsch, the rest of it sea-weathered and confident, a late-nineteenth-century indigenous form built on an island at a tiny remove from what was then becoming the most important city in the most important country in the world.

They weren't rich, my Vishnu and Grace—they had bought the house for almost nothing two years ago, when the last crisis was hitting its peak—and the place was already a mess, even without the impending baby, a flurry of broken Shaker furniture that Vishnu would never find the time to fix, and truly smelly books from another lifetime he would never read. Vishnu was out on the back porch grilling tofu and turning over vegetables. The porch deck elevated their apartment beyond the mundane, a full view of downtown Manhattan rising through the midsummer heat, the skyline looking tired, worn, in need of a bath. Vishnu and I did the Nee-gro slap and hug. I hovered around my friend, chatting him up with great care like I would a woman at a bar when I was young and single, while Eunice stood timidly in the distance, a glass of Pinot something-or-other tight in her fist.

CrisisNet: CREDIT MARKET DEBT EXCEEDS 100 TRILLION NORTHERN EURO BENCHMARK.

I wasn't sure what that meant. Vishnu gazed distractedly into the middle distance, while a root vegetable fell between the slats of the grill and issued a mild report.

The deck began to fill up. There was Noah, looking flushed and summer-weary but ready to emcee the announcement of Vishnu and Grace's little girl soon to come, fully indebted, into our strange new world, and Noah's girlfriend, Amy Greenberg, the comic relief, streaming hard on her "Muffintop Hour," filled with bursts of spasmodic laughter and not-so-subtle anger at the fact that Noah wasn't planning to get her pregnant, that all she had was her hard-driven *career.*

My friends. My dear ones. We chatted in the typically funny-sad way of people in their very late thirties about the things that used to make us young as Amy passed around a real joint, seedless and moist, the kind that only Media people get. I tried to get Eunice involved, but she mostly stayed by the edge of the deck with her äppärät, her stunning cocktail dress like something out of an old movie, the haughty princess no one can understand but one man.

Noah came over to Eunice and started charming her retro ("How ya doin', little lady?"), and I could see her mouth turning to form little syllables of understanding and encouragement, a terminal blush spreading like a rash across the gloss of her neck, but she spoke too quietly for me to hear her over the spitting din of vegetables being grilled black, the communal laughter of old friends.

More people showed up: Grace's Jewish and Indian co-workers, Retail women-lawyers who effortlessly switched from friendly to stern, quiet to volatile; Vishnu's summer-pretty exes, who still kept in touch because he was so swell a guy; and a bunch of people who went to NYU with us, mostly slick Credit dudes, one with a fashionable Mohawk and pearl earring who was trying to match Noah in pitch and importance.

I had a quick succession of vodka shots with Noah, who, turning off his äppärät, confided in me that Grace's pregnancy was "totally making [him] nervous," that he didn't know what to do with himself next, and that his alcoholism, while charming to most, was starting to worry Amy Greenberg. "Do what feels right," I glibly told him, advice from an era when the first Boeing Dreamliner, still flying under the American flag, lifted off the soil and broke the leaden Seattle skies.

"But *nothing* feels right anymore," Noah set me straight, his eyes lazily scanning Eunice's tight form. I poured him a bigger shot, vodka overflowing and moistening my grill-blackened fingers. I was happy that at least he wasn't talking politics today, happy and a little surprised. We drank and let the passing joint add a tasty green humidity to our uncertain moods, danger pulsing behind my cornea, yet the field of vision bright and clear as far as my affections were concerned. If I could have my friends and my Eunice forever and ever I would be fine.

A fork clanged against a champagne glass, the only nonplastic glass in the couple's possession. Noah was about to make his well-rehearsed "impromptu" speech. Vishnu and Grace stood in our midst, and my sympathies and love for them flowed in unabashed waves. How beautiful she looked in her featureless white peasant top and nontransparent jeans, that kind, awkward goose of a woman, and Vishnu, his dark features growing ever more Hebraic under the weight of upcoming responsibilities (truly our two races are uniquely primed for reproduction), his wardrobe more calm and collected, the youthful SUK DIK crap replaced by slacks of no vintage and a standard-issue "Rubenstein Must Die Slowly" T-shirt. Grace and Vishnu, my two adults.

Noah spoke, and although I thought I was going to hate his words, the surface nature of them, that always-streaming quality that Media people are unable to correct for, I didn't. "I love this Nee-gro," he said pointing to Vishnu, "and this here bride of Nee-gro, and I think they are the only people who should be giving birth, the only peeps *qualified* to pop one out."

"Right on!" we call-and-responded.

"The only peeps sure of themselves enough so that, come what may, the child will be loved and cared for and sheltered. Because they're good people. I know folks say that a lot—'They're good peeps, yo'—but there's the kind of plastic good, the kind of easy 'good' any of us can generate, and then there's this other, deep thing that is so hard for us to find anymore. Consistency. Day-to-day. Moving on. Taking stock. Never exploding. Channeling it all, that anger, that huge anger about what's happened to us as a people, channeling it into whatever-the-fuck. Keeping it away from the children, that's all I'm going to say."

Eunice was appraising Noah with warm eyes, unconsciously closing her fingers around her äppärät and the pulsing AssLuxury in
front of her. I thought Noah was finished speaking, but now he had
to make some jokes to balance out the fact that we all loved Grace
and Vishnu yet were immensely scared for them and their two-
months-in-the-oven undertaking, and Amy had to laugh at the
jokes, and we all had to follow suit and laugh—which was fine.

The joint returned, passed by a slender, unfamiliar woman's
hand, and I toked harshly from it. I settled into a memory of being
maybe fourteen and passing by one of those then newly built NYU
dormitories on First or Second Avenue, those multi-colored blobs
with some kind of chicken-wing-type modernity pointedly hanging
off the roof, and there were these smartly dressed girls just being
young out by the building's lobby, and they smiled in tandem as I
passed—not in jest, but because I was a normal-looking guy and it
was a brilliant summer day, and we were all alive. I remember how
happy I was (I decided to attend NYU on the spot), but how, after I
had walked half a block away, I realized they were going to die and
I was going to die and that the final result—nonexistence, erasure,
none of this mattering in that "longest" of runs—would never ap-
pease me, never allow me to enjoy fully the happiness of the friends
I suspected I would one day acquire, friends like these people in
front of me, celebrating an upcoming birth, laughing and drinking,
passing into a new generation with their connectivity and decency
intact, even as each year brought closer the unthinkable, those waking hours that began at nine post meridian and ended at three in the
morning, those pulsing, mosquito-bitten hours of dread. How far I
had come from my parents, born in a country built on corpses, how
far I had come from their endless anxiety—oh, the blind luck of it
all! And yet how little I had traveled away from them, the inability
to grasp the present moment, to grab Grace by the shoulders and
say, "Your happiness is mine."

CrisisNet: CHINA INVESTMENT CORPORATION QUITS
U.S. TREASURIES.

I saw Vishnu blink several times as the latest news scrolled on our äppäräti, and some of the Credit guys were whispering stuff to one another. Vishnu gripped his fiancée and cupped her still-small belly. We returned to the business of laughing at Noah's rendition of Vishnu's freshman year at NYU—a hayseed from Upstate, he had been partially run over by a light truck and had to be hospitalized with tread marks on his chest.

Two lines of helicopters, like a broken V of geese, were massing over what I imagined to be the Arthur Kill on one side and the poetic curve of the Verrazano Bridge on another. We all looked up from the speech Grace was tearfully giving us—how we meant the world to her, how she wasn't worried about anything, as long as she had us—

"Holy fuck," two of the Credit guys said to each other, their Coronas shaky in their hands.

CrisisNet: CHINESE CENTRAL BANKER WANGSHENG LI ISSUES CAUTIONARY STATEMENT: "WE HAVE BEEN PATIENT."

"Let's just—" Vishnu said. "Never mind it. Let's just enjoy the day. People! There's another joint going around this way!"

Our Credit rankings and assets started to blink. RECALCULATION IN PROGRESS. The gentleman with the Mohawk was already making his way for the exit.

CrisisNet: URGENT: AMERICAN RESTORATION AUTHORITY RAISES THREAT LEVEL FOR NEW YORK, LOS ANGELES, DISTRICT OF COLUMBIA TO RED++IMMINENT DANGER.

We were all shouting at one another now. Shouting and grabbing on to one another, the excitement of what we always suspected would happen tinged with the reality that we were actually, finally, in the middle of the movie, unable to leave the cineplex for the safety of our vehicles. All of us were looking into one another's eyes, our *real* eyes, sometimes blue and hazel but mostly brown and black, as if gauging our alliances: Would we be able to survive together, or would it be better apart? Noah craned his neck upward, ever upward, as if both to get a grip on the situation and to assert his primacy as a tall man. "We have to stick together," I was saying to Amy Greenberg, but she was in a different place, a place where calculations were made and the data and Images flowed like *vino verde* in July. I worked through my own data as I tried to find Eunice.

CrisisNet: SIGNIFICANT SMALL ARMS COMBAT IN PROGRESS NEW YORK CITY, AREAS IMMEDIATELY UNDER NATIONAL GUARD QUARANTINE, CENTRAL PARK, RIVERSIDE PARK, TOMPKINS SQUARE PARK.

URGENT MESSAGE FROM AMERICAN RESTORATION AUTHORITY MID-ATLANTIC COMMAND (6:04 p.m., EST) Text follows—Insurgent attacks have been launched on the Borrower-Spender-Financial-Residential Complex in Lower Manhattan. Residents MUST report to primary residence for further instructions/relocation. *By reading this message you are denying its existence and implying consent.*

There were streams now. From the Media people living in the tenements around Tompkins Park, gingerly leaning their äppäräti out their windowsills. The rectangle of green was choked in smoke; even the sturdiest trees had been denuded by the scale of the artillery, their bare branches shuddering wordlessly in the helicopter wind. The LNWIs had been surrounded. Their leader, now listed by Media as David Lorring, two "r"s, one "n," was badly wounded. Guardsmen were carrying him out of the park and toward an armored personnel carrier. I couldn't see his face beyond the meaty red lump peering out from behind a hasty bandage, but he was still wearing his own jungle-green Venezuela-vintage uniform, one arm dangling off the stretcher at an inhuman angle, as if it had been torn away and reattached by psychotics. Through the smoke, I caught snatches of bodies too compromised to categorize, the outlines of men with guns at their side breaching further into the chaos, and everywhere the pop of exploding plastic water bottles. A sign bearing the surprising word "DIPHTHERIA" billowed right into the camera nozzle of someone's äppärät.

Eunice swiftly came up to me. "I want to go to Manhattan!" she said.

"We all want to go home," I said, "but look at what's happening."

"I have to go to Tompkins Park. I know someone there."

"Are you crazy? They're killing people there."

"A friend of mine's in trouble."

"A lot of people are in trouble."

"Maybe my sister's there too! She helps out in the park. Help me get to the ferry."

"Eunice! We're not going *anywhere* right now."

The dead smile came on with such full force that I thought a part of her cheekbone had cracked. "That's fine," she said.

Grace and Vishnu, who were loading bags full of food for people who did not cook in their homes, predicting the siege-like situation to come with their forebears' canniness. My äppärät started to warble. I was being hit with a serious data package.

TO: Post-Human Services Shareholders and Executive Personnel
FROM: Joshie Goldmann
SUBJECT: Political situation.
BODY OF MESSAGE FOLLOWS: We are in the process of a profound change, but we urge all members of the Post-Human family to remain both calm and vigilant. The expected collapse of the Rubenstein/ARA/Bipartisan regime presents us with great possibilities. We at Staatling-Wapachung are reaching out to other nations' sovereign wealth funds looking for investment and alliance. We anticipate social changes that will benefit all shareholders and top-level personnel. In the initial stages of the transformation our primary concern is the safety of all shareholders and co-workers.

If you are currently located outside New York, please make haste to return to the city. Despite appearances of lawlessness and collapse in certain sections of downtown and midtown, your safety can be best guaranteed if you are in your own Triplexes, houses, or apartments within Manhattan and Brownstown Brooklyn. Wapachung Contingency personnel have been instructed to protect you from rioting Low Net Worth Individuals and rogue National Guard elements. Please contact Howard Shu at Life Lovers Outreach if you have any questions or require immediate assistance. If regular äppärät transmissions cease for any reason, please look for Wapachung Contingency emergency scrolls and follow the directions given. An exciting time is about to begin for us and the creative economy. We are all fortunate, and, in an abstract sense, blessed. Onward!

Eunice had turned away from me and was crying intermittent but voluptuous tears that curled around her nose and beaded, gathering volume and strength. "Eunice," I said. "Sweetheart. It's going to be all right." I put one arm around her, but she shook it off. The ground echoed nearby, and I picked up an entirely surreal sound beyond the unkempt hedges of Grace and Vishnu's little palazzo—the sickening contralto of middle-class people screaming.

CrisisNet: UNIDENTIFIED SOURCES: VENEZUELAN NAVY MISSILE FRIGATES MARISCAL SUCRE & RAUL REYES PLUS SUPPORT SHIPS REPORTED 300 MILES OFF NORTH CAROLINA COAST. ST. VINCENT'S OTHER NEW YORK AREA HOSPITALS ON HIGH ALERT.

The few of us who were from Manhattan and Brownstone Brooklyn were lining up before Vishnu and Grace, trying to get a place to crash in their house; other Staten Islanders were offering fold-out cots and oven-warm spaces in their attics. The names and numbers of car service companies were bouncing around from äppärät to äppärät, and people were trying to figure out if the Verrazano Bridge was still passable.

My own äppärät squealed again, and without warning Joshie's voice, as urgent as I've ever heard it, filled my head. "Where are you, Len?" he said. "GlobalTrace is showing Staten Island."

"St. George."

"Is Eunice with you?"

"Yeah."

"You've got to make sure she's all right."

"She's all right. We're going to bed down in Staten Island, wait for the worst to pass."

"Bed down? You didn't get the memo? You've got to get back to Manhattan."

"I got it, but it doesn't make any sense. Aren't we safer here?"

"Lenny." The voice paused, allowing my name to ring in my lower consciousness, as if it were God calling me to him. "These memos don't come from nowhere. This is straight from Wapachung Contingency. Get off Staten Island *now*. Go home immediately. Take Eunice with you. Make sure she's safe."

I was still stoned. The windows to my soul were foggy and red. The transition from relative happiness to complete fear made no sense. Then I remembered the source of that relative happiness. "My friends," I said. "Will they be okay if they stay on Staten Island?"

"It depends," Joshie said.

"On what?"

"Their assets."

I did not know how to respond to this. I wanted to cry. "Your friends Vishnu and Grace are going to be fine where they are," Joshie said. *How did he know the names of my friends? Had I told him?* "Your main focus should be getting Eunice back to Manhattan."

"What about my friends Noah and Amy?"

There was a pause. "I've never heard of them," Joshie said.

It was time to move out. I kissed Vishnu on both cheeks, Nee-gro–slapped the others, and accepted a small container of kimchi and seaweed wrap from Grace, who begged us to stay.

"Lenny!" she cried. Then she whispered into my ear, careful not to let Eunice overhear: "I love you, sweetie. Take care of Eunice. Both of you take care."

"Don't say it like that," I whispered back. "I'll see you again. I'll see you tomorrow."

I found Noah and Amy streaming next to each other, him shouting, her crying, the air dense with panic and Media. I reached over and turned off Noah's äppärät. "You and Amy have to come with us to Manhattan."

"Are you crazy?" he said. "There's fighting downtown. The Venezuelans are on their way."

"My boss says we've got to get to Manhattan. He said we're safer there. He heard it from Wapachung Contingency."

"Wapachung Contingency?" Noah shouted. "What, are you Bipartisan now?" And for once I wanted to smack the indignation out of my friend.

"We need to keep safe, asshole," I said. "There's a major riot on. I'm trying to save your life."

"And what about Vishnu and Grace? If it's not safe here, why don't they come with us?"

"My boss told me they'd be okay here."

"Why, because Vishnu's collaborating?"

I grabbed his arm in a way that I never had, his thick flesh twisting in my strong grip, but also in a way that connoted that for once I was in charge between us. "Look," I said. "I love you. You're my friend. We've got to do this for Eunice and Amy. We've got to make sure they don't get hurt."

He looked at me with the easy hatred of the righteous. I had always been unsure of his affection for Amy Greenberg, and now I had no reason to doubt. He didn't love her. They were together for the obvious and timeless reason: It was slightly less painful than being alone.

CrisisNet: UNIDENTIFIED SOURCES: 18 CREDIT POLES SET ON FIRE BY LOW NET WORTH PROTESTERS IN MANHATTAN CREDIT DISTRICT. NATIONAL GUARD TO RESPOND WITH "SWIFT ACTION."

We walked out on beautiful, leafy, Victorian St. Mark's Place, like two fine couples, Noah's arms around Amy, mine around Eunice. But the pretty coupledom and the handsome, drooping willows of the street formed a lie. A sickening Caucasian fear, mowed grass and temperate sex mixed with a surprising shot of third-world perspiration, crowded the borough's most elegant street, the hipsterish white young humanity rushing back toward the Staten Island Ferry, toward Manhattan and then Brooklyn, while another crowd was trying to fight its way back onto Staten Island—neither side knowing if they had the right idea; to hear the Media chatter off our äppäräti, the entire city seemed engulfed in violence, either real or invented. We stalked past one another, the Media people streaming in motion, Amy giving off a précis of her wardrobe and her recent frustrations with Noah, Eunice watching her surroundings with one careful eye, while her formidable Fuckability rankings fluttered in the wind around us. A fresh armada of helicopters flew over us, just as a real storm was beginning to announce itself.

I got an emergency teen from Nettie Fine: "LENNY, ARE YOU SAFE? I'M SO WORRIED! WHERE ARE YOU?" I wrote her that Noah and Eunice and I were on Staten Island trying to get back to Manhattan. "LET ME KNOW WHAT'S HAPPENING EVERY STEP OF THE WAY," she wrote, calming my fears. Everything was going to hell, but my American mama was still looking out for me.

I bore left onto Hamilton Avenue, the Staten Island Ferry terminal but a rapid descent to the bay. We were almost knocked down by a running Mediastud, all teeth and sunburn and opened guayabera shirt. "They're shooting at Media people!" he was projecting into his äppärät and at anyone who would listen.

"Where?" we shouted.

"Here. In Manhattan. Brooklyn. The LNWIs are burning down the Credit Poles! The Guard is firing back! The Venezuelans are sailing up the Potomac!"

Noah pulled us back, his arms around Eunice and me, his relative strength and the solidity of his dumb bulk squeezing us tight, making me hate him. "We've got to loop around!" he shouted. "There's no way we can make it down Hamilton. It's covered in Credit Poles. The Guard's going to start shooting." I saw Eunice looking at him with a smile, congratulating his cheap decisiveness. Amy was streaming about her beloved mother—a sun-worn prototype of a contemporary Mediawhore—at present vacationing in Maine, how she missed her, how she wished she had gone up to see her this weekend, but Noah, *Noah,* had insisted they go to Grace and Vishnu's party, and now life really sucked, didn't it?

"Can you get me to Tompkins Park?" Eunice asked Noah.

He smiled. In the middle of the hysteria, *he smiled.* "Let's see what I can do."

"Are you all insane?" I shouted. But Noah was already dragging Eunice and Amy in the direction of Victory Boulevard. There were people running there, fewer than on Hamilton Avenue, but still at least a few hundred, scared and disoriented. I reached Eunice and tore her from Noah's grasp. My body, flabby but real and nearly double Eunice's weight, huddled fully around her and angled us against the flow, my arms bearing the brunt of the advancing horde, the parade of young, scared people, the frontal mass of their floral body washes, the denseness of their inability to survive. Ahead of us, two Credit Poles smoldered in the gray pre-storm heat, their LED counters knocked out, sparks flying from their electronic innards.

I pushed my way forward, innate Russianness, ugliness, Jewishness, beating through my system—emergency, emergency, emergency—while inuring my precious cargo against any harm, as her Padma cosmetics bag jammed into my ribs, misting my eyes with the pain of its sharp edges.

I was whispering to Eunice: "Sweetie, sweetie, it's going to be okay."

But there was no need. Eunice was okay. We linked hands. Noah led Amy, Amy led Eunice, and Eunice led me through the screaming crowd, which was turning in one direction and then another, rumors flashing around with äppärät speed. The sky changed as if to taunt us further, a strong wind lashing us from the east and then from the west.

Behind the old courthouse, a municipal area had become a National Guard staging ground, choppers taking off, armored personnel carriers, tanks, Browning guns in mid-swing, a small area cordoned off into a holding pen where some older black people were interred.

We ran. It meant nothing. It all meant nothing. All the signs. The street names. The landmarks. Even here, amidst the kingdom of my fear, all I could think about was Eunice not loving me, losing her respect for me, Noah the decisive leader in a time when she was supposed to need *me*. Staten Island Bank & Trust. Against Da' Grain Barber Shop. Child Evangelism Fellowship. Staten Island Mental Health Society. The Verrazano Bridge. A&M Beauty Supplies. Planet Pleasure. Up and Growing Day Care. Feet, feet. Shards of data all around us, useless rankings, useless streams, useless communiqués from a world that was no longer to a world that would never be. I smelled the garlic on Eunice's breath and on her body. I confused it with life. I felt the small heft of a thought that I could project at her back. The thought became a chanted mantra: "I love you, I love you, I love you."

"Tompkins Park," she said, her stubbornness clawing at me. "My sister." A surge of black humanity from the ungentrified neighborhood just beyond St. George merged with ours, and I could feel the hipsterish component trying to separate themselves from the blacks, an American survival instinct that dated back to the arrival of the first slave ship. Distance from the condemned. Black, white, black, white. But it didn't matter either. We were finally one. We were all condemned. A new squall of rain blanketing our faces, a rolling wave of heat following the rain, Noah's weathered face staring into mine, cursing my slowness and indecision, Amy streaming just one word, "Mommy," over and over again into the satellites above us, into the breezy reality of her mother's Maine, Eunice, her face level and straight, her arms around me, all of her in my arms.

Noah and Amy ran into the ferry terminal through a portal of finely shredded glass. Eunice had grabbed my arm and was pulling me toward our goal. Two ferries had just disgorged their last screaming Manhattan passengers. Who was piloting these ferries? Why were they still crossing the bay? Was there safety in constant motion? Was there any safe place left to dock?

"Lenny," she said. "I'm telling you right now that if you don't take me to Tompkins I'm just going to go with Noah. I've got to find my sister. I've got to try to help my friend. *I know I can help him.* You can go and be safe at our house. I'll come back, I promise."

One ferry, the *John F. Kennedy,* had begun to chortle in the water in preparation for departure, and we headed for its open hold. Noah and Amy had already clambered on board and were huddled beneath a sign that read "ARA Transport—Ain't That America, Somethin' to See, Baby."

You can go and be safe at our house. I had to say something. I had to stop her, or she would be shot just like the LNWI protesters. Her Credit was bad enough. "Eunice!" I shouted. "Stop it! Stop running away from me! We have to stick together right now. We have to go *home.*"

But she shook off my arm and was running toward the *Kennedy* just as the ramp of the ferry had started lifting. I grabbed her by one tiny shoulder, and, with the intense fear of dislocating it, of hearing the crunch that meant I had hurt her, pulled her toward a second, waiting boat, its bridge bearing the legend *Guy V. Molinari.*

A black chopper circled overhead, its armed golden beak pointing in our direction and then at the island bristling with skyscrapers in the immediate distance. "No!" Eunice shouted, as the *Kennedy* pulled away, my friends, her new hero Noah, aboard.

"It's okay," I said. "We'll meet them on the other side. Come on! Let's go!" We clambered onto the *Molinari,* elbowing our way through the young people and the families, so many families, full of new tears and drying tears and makeshift embraces.

"LENNY," Nettie Fine teened me, "WHERE ARE YOU NOW?" Despite all the confusion, I quickly teened her that we were on a ferry to Manhattan and safe for the moment. "YOUR FRIEND NOAH SAFE WITH YOU?" she wanted to know, sweet, solicitous Nettie Fine, concerned even about people she had never met. She was probably GlobalTracing us in real time. I wrote her he was on a different ferry but as safe as we were. "WHICH FERRY?"

I told her we were on the *Guy V. Molinari* and Noah was on the *John F. Kennedy,* just as stray gunfire opened up behind us, thundering up and down Hamilton Avenue, the resulting screams sneaking into my earlobes and momentarily turning them off. Deafness. Complete silence. Eunice's mouth twisted into cruel words I couldn't understand. The *Guy V. Molinari*'s oblong snout cut into the warm summer water, and we displaced ourselves furiously in the direction of Manhattan, and now more than ever I hated the false spire of the "Freedom" Tower, hated it for every single reason I could think of, but mostly for its promise of sovereignty and brute strength, and I wanted to cut my ties with my country and my scowling, angry girlfriend and everything else that bound me to this world. I longed for the 740 square feet that belonged to me by law, and I rejoiced in the humming of the engines as we sailed toward my concept of home.

A single raven appeared above Noah and Amy's ferry. It lowered its golden beak, and its golden beak turned orange. Two missiles departed in rapid succession. One explosion, then two; the helicopter casually turned and flew back in the direction of Manhattan.

A moment of nonscreaming, of complete äppärät silence, overtook the *Guy V. Molinari,* older people holding tight to their children, the young people lost in the pain of suddenly understanding their own extinction, tears cold and stinging in the sea breeze. And then, as the flames bloomed across the ferry's upper decks, as the *John F. Kennedy* reared up, split into two, disintegrated into the warm waters, as the first part of our lives, the false part, came to an end, the question we had forgotten to ask for so many years was finally shouted by one husky voice, stage left: *"But why?"*

SECURITY SITUATION IN PROGRESS
FROM THE DIARIES OF LENNY ABRAMOV

AUGUST 7

Dear Diary,

The otter came for me in a dream. Not the cartoon otter that interrogated me in Rome, not the graffito otter I saw on Grand Street, but a true-to-life otter, a high-definition mammal, whiskers, fur, the dampness of the river. He pressed his wet plush black nose into my cheek, into my ear, kissing me with it, blessing my hungry face with his hot familiar and familial salmon breath, his little muddy paws destroying the clean white dress shirt I had put on for Eunice, because in my dreams I wanted her to love me again, because I wanted her back. And then he spoke to me in Noah's voice, in that edgy, improper, but basically humane voice, the voice of a thwarted scholar. "You know Americans get lonely abroad," he said, pausing to gauge the look on my face. "Happens all the time! That's why I never leave the brook where I was born." Staring me up and down to see if I found him entertaining. "Did you meet any nice foreign people while you were abroad." Not a question, but a statement. Noah had no time for questions. "I'm still waiting for that name, Leonard or Lenny." I felt my dream mouth move to betray Fabrizia yet again, but this time I couldn't pry it open. The Noah-otter smiled as if he knew exactly what kind of man I was and wiped his whiskers with a human paw. "You said 'DeSalva.' "

Noah. Three days after the Rupture. Instead of mourning, instead of grief, shallow memories of us sharing a joint on the gravel mounds of Washington Square, our early friendship as tenuous and goofy as a young love affair. Politics on our tongues, girls on our minds, just two guys from the suburbs, freshmen at NYU, Noah's already working on one of the last novels that will ever see print, I'm working on being the friend of someone like Noah. Are these memories even real? This is my life now. Dreams, nothing but dreams.

I've been sleeping on the couch. Eunice and I have barely spoken since I dragged her home and away from her goddamn Tompkins Park, from whatever or whomever she thought she could save. Her mysterious male friend? Her sister? What the hell would Sally be doing in the middle of a battlefield?

"I don't think this is going to work," I had told Eunice of our relationship after she had sulked in the bedroom for the better part of that blood-soaked day. "If we can't take care of each other *now,* when the world is going to shit, how are we ever going to make it? Eunice! Are you even listening to what I'm saying? I've lost one of my best friends. Don't you want to, like, comfort me?" No response, dead smile, retreat to the bedroom. *E basta.*

The booms, big and small, faraway and close, the pounding in my head, tracer rounds against the overcast moon, tracer rounds lighting up the secret, hidden parts of the city, an entire building of crying babies, and, even scarier, the temporary absence of those wails. Relentless. Relentless. Relentless. You can see the magenta flashes even against the fully closed curtains, you can hear them on your skin. At night, the sound of metallic scraping coming off the river, like two barges slowly crashing against each other. When I open a window, the strange bloom of flowers and burnt leaves hits my nose—a sweet, dense rot, like the countryside after a storm. Oddly enough, no car alarms. I listen for the comfort-food sounds of ambulances presumably rushing to keep people alive—every few minutes the first day after the Rupture, then every few hours, then nothing.

My äppärät isn't connecting. I can't connect. No one's äppäräti are working anymore. "It's an NNEMP," all the thirtysomething Media wizards hanging out in the lobby of our building are saying with finality. A Nonnuclear Electromagnetic Pulse. The Venezuelans must have detonated it high above the city. Or the Chinese. Like anyone knows. Like there's any difference between the quality of "news" since the Media's gone out.

Venezuelans detonating something other than an arepa.

*Whate*ver, as Eunice would say, if she still spoke to me.

I point my äppärät out the half-opened window, trying to catch a signal. I can't reach my parents. I can't connect to Westbury. I can't connect to Vishnu. I can't connect to Grace. And nothing from Nettie Fine. Complete radio silence since Noah's ferry exploded. All I have is the Wapachung Contingency emergency scroll. "SECURITY SITUATION IN PROGRESS. REMAIN IN DOMICILE. WATER: AVAILABLE. ELECTRICITY: SPORADIC. KEEP ÄPPÄRÄT FULLY CHARGED IF POSSIBLE. AWAIT INSTRUCTIONS."

In the next room, she's crying.

I'm so scared.

I have no one.

Eunice, Eunice, Eunice. Why must you break my heart, again and again?

Five days after the Rupture, instructions.

WAPACHUNG CONTINGENCY EMERGENCY MESSAGE: SECURITY SITUATION LOWER/MID-MANHATTAN IMPROVED. PLEASE REPORT TO YOUR DIVISION HEADQUARTERS.

I put on a shirt and pants, feeling both scared and celebratory. The air conditioner had gone out and I had been living in my underwear, which made the pants feel like armor and the shirt like a shroud. Eunice was sitting by the kitchen table, staring absently at her nonfunctional äppärät. I have never smelled unwashed hair off her, but there it was, as strong as anything in the half-dead refrigerator. And that softened me for some reason, made me want to for-give her, to find her again, because whatever happened between us had nothing to do with me. "I have to go to work," I said, kissing her on the forehead, not afraid to inhale what she had become.

She looked up at me for the first time in a hundred hours, eyes crusted over. "To see Joshie?" she said.

"Yes," I said. She nodded. I stood there like a Japanese salaryman in my overwarm pants and stifling shirt, waiting for more. But it wouldn't come. "I still love you," I said. No response, but no dead smile either. "I think we both really tried to make this work. But we're just too different. Don't you think?" And then, before she could summon an emotion and deny it in the same breath, I left.

Outside, the streets were nearly empty. All the cabs had fled to wherever cabs come from, and that absence of moving yellow made Manhattan feel as still and silent as Kabul during Friday prayers. The Credit Poles were burned up and down Grand Street, and they looked like prehistoric trees after the glaciers retreated, their colored lights sagging down in a row of inverted parabolas, the racist Credit signs atop them torn down and ripped apart, coating the windshields of cars like old washrags. An old Econoline van with a bumper sticker that read "My Daughter Is a U.S. Marine in Venezuela" had also been torched for some reason—it lay on its back in the middle of the street, imitating a dead water bug. The A-OK Pizza Shack was open but had boarded up its windows, as had the local Arab bodega, the words "WE ACCEPT ONLY YUAN SORRY BUT WE ALSO HALF TO EAT" stenciled along each bit of cardboard. But, otherwise, the neigh-borhood looked remarkably intact, the looting minimal. The deep hush of the morning after a failed third-world coup seeped up from the streets and coated the silent towers. I was proud of New York, now more than ever, for it had survived something another city would have not: its own rage.

The F train entrance was stuffed with garbage, the subways clearly out. I walked up Grand, a lone man feeling the density of Au-gust along with the strange hunger of being alive, wondering what would come next. For one thing, I needed real money, not dollars.

Outside my Chinatown HSBC branch, a dragon's tail of poor middle-class Chinese folk waited to hear the verdict on their life savings. I wondered if these ruined older men and women, the Tai Chi practitioners of Seward Park with their three-yuan trainers and mottled bald spots, could find a way to repatriate to the now wealthier land of their birth. Would they even be welcomed back? Would Eunice's parents be if they decided to return to Korea?

I stood in line for an hour, listening to a Caribbean man dressed in head-to-toe denim, his cracked skin glistening with patchouli, sing to us his take on the world. "All these Wapachung people, all these Staatlin people, they takin the money and runnin. They messin up the economy, they messin up our pockets. This is extortion. This is Mafia doin. Why they shoot that ferry down? Who control who? That's what I askin you. And you know we never fine out the answer, because we little people."

I wanted to give the man an answer he could live with, but my throat remained blank, even as my mind was running. Not now, not now. Save the questions for Joshie.

My bank account was still big enough to warrant a special teller, an old Greek woman imported from a ransacked Astoria branch, who laid it all out for me. Everything I owned that had been yuan-pegged was relatively intact, but my AmericanMorning portfolio—LandOLakes, AlliedWasteCVS, and the former conglomeration of cement, steel, and services that had once formed an advanced economy—no longer existed. Four hundred thousand yuan, two years of self-denial and bad tipping at restaurants, all gone. Together with the Eunice-related expenditures of the past month, I was down to 1,190,000 yuan. From the standpoint of immortality, I was already on the mortuary slab. From the standpoint of survival, the new gold standard for all Americans, I was doing just fine. I took out two thousand yuan, Chairman Mao's solid face and remarkable hairline staring back at me from the hundred-note currency, and hid the bills in my sock. "You're the richest man in Chinatown," the teller snorted. "Go home to your family."

My family. How were they surviving? What had happened on

Long Island? Would I ever hear the warble of their anxious birdsong again? On a street corner I saw a man flagging down a car, then bargaining over the price of a ride. My father had told me this is how he used to get around Moscow when he was young, once even flagging down a police car, its captain looking to make a ruble. I stuck out my hand, and a Hyundai Persimmon decked out in all things Colombian pulled up to me. I negotiated twenty yuan to the Upper East Side, and for the next few minutes the city slid past me, demure and empty against the outrageously joyous salsa that colored the inside of the Hyundai. My driver was something of an entrepreneur and on the way over sold me a hypothetical bag of rice that would be delivered to my apartment by his cousin Hector. "I used to be scared of things before," he said, pulling down his sunglasses to show me his sleepless eyes, their brown orbs swimming in the colors of the first and last bars of the Colombian flag, "but now I see what our government is. Nothing inside! Like wood. You break it open, *nothing*. So now I'm going to live my life. And I'm going to make some money. Real money. *Chinese* money." I tried to be his friend and economic confidant for the duration of the ride, saying, "Mhh-mm, mhh-mm," in the usual noncommittal tone I use with people I have nothing in common with, but when we got to my destination, he hit the brakes. "*Salte, hijueputa!*" he shouted. "Out! Out! Out!" I clambered out of the car, which squealed immediately in the opposite direction, the fare left uncollected.

The street was full of National Guard.

I had not seen any military on the streets since I left my apartment, but the Post-Human Services synagogue was entirely surrounded by armored personnel carriers and Guardsmen, whom my äppärät cheerfully identified as Wapachung Contingency. (In fact, upon closer inspection, the National Guard flags and insignia were almost completely scraped off their vehicles and uniforms; now these men were pure Wapachung.) They were protecting the doors of the building from a riotous horde of young people, apparently our just-fired employees, our beautiful Daltons, Logans, and Heaths, our Avas, Aidens, and Jaidens, who had tormented me in the Eternity Lounge and were now massed against Joshie's synagogue, the very source of their identity, their ego, their dreams. My nemesis Darryl, the SUK DIK guy, was jumping around like a locust on fire, trying to get my attention. "Lenny!" he shouted to me, as I walked up to the Guardsmen at the door, had my äppärät scanned, and was curtly nodded admission. "Tell Joshie this isn't fair! Tell Joshie I'll work for half-salary. I'm sorry if I hurt your feelings! I was going to stand up for you at the Miso Pig-Out in November. Come on, Lenny!"

I glanced at them from the top step of the synagogue's entrance. How perfect they looked. How absolutely striking and up-to-the-minute and young. Even in the middle of calamity, their neuro-enhanced minds were working with alacrity, trying to solve the puzzle, trying to get back in. They had been prepared from an evolutionary perspective to lead exalted lives, and now civilization was folding up around them. Of all the rotten luck!

And then I was inside, the main sanctuary jammed by further Guardsmen in full battle regalia. The Boards were ticking madly as the bulk of our staff were getting their TRAIN CANCELED. The sound of flaps turning on five boards at once made it sound as if gangs of pigeons had flown into our headquarters to engage in winged combat. I stood before one of the stained-glass windows depicting the tribe of Judah, represented here by a lion and crown, and for the first time considered the fact that to several thousand people this had once been a temple.

A small remnant of our staff still haunted the offices, but their conversations were funereal and dense. No mention of pH levels or "SmartBlood" or "beta treatments." The word "triglyceride" did not echo in the bathroom where we Post-Human Services men took our lengthy organic shits, straining to be free of whatever greenery tormented us. On the way up to Joshie's, I stopped by Kelly Nardl's desk. Empty. Gone. I reached instinctively for my äppärät to shoot her a message, but then realized all outside transmissions had ceased. Apropos of nothing, I felt scared for my parents again.

Two National Guardsmen stood outside Joshie's office. The emergency feed of my äppärät must have alerted them to my importance, because they stepped aside and opened the door for me. There he was. Joshie. Budnik. *Papi chulo.* Under siege in his minimalist office as the young voices outside brayed for *his* SmartBlood. I made out the uncreative and juvenile "Hey, hey / Ho, ho, / Joshie Goldfuck's gotta go," and the much more hurtful "Our jobs are gone, / Our dream's been sold, / But one day, jerk, / You will get old." Joshie was wearing a gold yuan symbol around his neck, trying to look young, but his posture looked embattled, the skin of his earlobes sagged in a peculiar way, and a Nile delta of purple veins ran down the left side of his nose. When we hugged, the slight tremor of his hands beat against my back. "How's Eunice?" he said immediately.

"She's upset," I said. "She thinks her sister may have been in Tompkins Park, for some reason. She can't get in touch with her family in Jersey. There's a checkpoint at the George Washington. They're not letting anyone pass. And she's angry with me. I mean, we're actually not speaking to each other."

"Good, good," Joshie mumbled, staring out the window.

"What about you? How are you taking all this?"

"Minor setback," he said.

"Minor setback? It's the fall of the Roman Empire out there."

"Don't be dramatic, chipmunk," Joshie said. "I'm going to pay off these young bucks with preferred stock, and when we're back on our feet I'll rehire them all."

As he spoke, his energy returned, his earlobes actually tightened up and moved into position. "Hey, listen, Rhesus!" he said. "I bet this is going to be good for us in the long run. This is a controlled demise for the country, a planned bankruptcy. Liquidate labor, liquidate stocks, liquidate everything but real estate. Rubenstein's just a figurehead at this point. The Congress is just for show: 'Look, we still have a Congress!' Now more responsible parties are going to step in. All that stuff about Venezuelan and Chinese warships is all bunk. Nobody's going to invade. But what *will* happen, and I got this from reliable sources, is that the International Monetary Fund will skedaddle from D.C., possibly to Singapore or Beijing, and then they're going to make an IMF recovery plan for America, divide the country into concessions, and hand them over to the sovereign wealth funds. Norway, China, Saudi Arabia, all that jazz."

"No more America?" I asked, not really caring about the answer. I just wanted to be safe.

"Fuck that. A *better* America. The Norsemen, the Chinese, they're going to want returns on their investment. They're going to want to clear out our trophy cities of all the riffraff with no Credit and make them real lifestyle hubs. And who's going to profit from that? Staatling-Wapachung, that's who. Property, security, and then us. Immortality. The Rupture's created a whole new demand for not dying. I can see StatoilHydro, the Norwegians, getting together with Staatling. Maybe a merger! Yeah, that's the way to do it. The Norwegians have euros and renminbi to burn."

"What do you mean, get rid of all the riffraff with no Credit?"

"Relocate them." He took an excited sip of green tea. "This town's not for everyone. We have to be competitive. That means doing more with less. Balancing our ledgers."

"A black man at my bank said it's all Staatling-Wapachung's fault," I said, trying to tap into the liberal hierarchy of "a black man said."

"What's our fault?"

"I don't know. We bombed the ferry. Three hundred dead. My friend Noah. Remember what you told me right before the Rupture. That Vishnu and Grace were going to be okay. But you said you didn't know who Noah was."

"What are you saying?" Joshie leaned in, elbows on his desk. "Are you accusing me of something?"

I kept quiet, played the role of the hurt son.

"Look, I'm sorry that your friend is dead," Joshie went on. "All these deaths were tragic. The ferry, the parks. Obvi. But at the same time, who *were* all these Media people, what did they bring to the table?"

I coughed into my hand, a painful chill across my body, as if an iceberg had stabbed me in the anus.

I had never told Joshie that Noah was Media.

"Spreading useless rumors. Secure Screening Facilities Upstate. Yeah, right. Rubenstein's government couldn't organize a clambake on a mussel shoal. Lenny, you know the score. You're not dumb. We're working on something important here. We've put so much into this place. You and I. And look at it now. It's a real game-changer. Whoever's in charge tomorrow, Norwegians, Chinese, they want what *we* got. This isn't some stupid äppärät app. This is eternity. This is the *heart* of the creative economy."

"Fuck the creative economy," I said, without thinking. "There's no food downtown."

One instant. His hand. My cheek. The parameters of the world moving sixty degrees to the left and then buzzing into stillness. I felt my own hand rising to my face without knowing I had moved it.

He had slapped me.

I suppose the memory of the first paternal slap surfaced somewhere in the back pocket of my soul, Papa Abramov's hand parting the air before it, the wide boxer stance of his feet as if he were going after a two-hundred-pound bruiser and not a nine-year-old kid, but for some reason all I could think about was that I would turn forty in November. In three months I would be a forty-year-old man who had just been slapped by his friend, his boss, his secondary father.

And then I was upon him. Across the desk, its sharp ridges slicing at my stomach, the scruff of his silky black T-shirt in both of my hands, his face, his humid, scared face thrust into mine, the gentle brownness of his eyes, the expressiveness, that funny Jewish face that could turn sad on a dime, everything we had done together, all those battle plans hatched over trays of safflower-oil-fried vegan samosas.

One hand let go of his T-shirt, a fist was cocked. I either did this or didn't. I either chose this final path or put my fist down. But what did I have other than Joshie? Could he still pull this together after everything that had happened? Didn't the Renaissance eventually follow the fall of Rome?

Could I really punch this man?

I had waited too long. Joshie was gently removing my remaining hand from his T-shirt. "I'm sorry," he said. "I'm so sorry. Oh my God. I can't believe I did that. It's the stress. I'm stressed. My cortisol levels. Jesus. Trying to put on a brave face. But of course I'm scared too."

I backed off. Moved to the edge of the room like a punished child, felt the alpha rays of Joshie's fiberglass Buddha stroking my being. "Okay, okay," Joshie was saying. "Go home for the day. Give my love to Eunice. Tell Joe Schechter outside I can take him back at half-pay, but Darryl is finished. Come back tomorrow. We're got so much work ahead. I need you too, you know. Don't look at me like that. Of course I need you."

I stopped by the A-OK Pizza Shack, and cleared out the few things they had left, three precious pizzas and calzones warm to the touch, all for sixty yuan. As I stepped outside, the light hit me, the Noah light, the light that floods the city and leaves nothing but itself, the urban rapture. I closed my eyes, thinking that when I opened them the last week would simply fall away. Instead, what I saw was that abominable creature. That fucking *otter,* right in the middle of Grand Street, chewing on something in the asphalt. I grabbed a heavy calzone, ready to club my furry antagonist. But no, it wasn't an otter. It was just someone's escaped pet rabbit enjoying the new solitude, feasting on his street meal while spasmodically brushing back his ears with one paw, reminding me of Noah enjoying the fullness of his hair. The clouds came, and Noah's urban light turned to shadow the density of slate. My friend was gone.

A pair of shoe-filled suitcases awaited me by the door, but Eunice herself was in neither the living room nor the bedroom. Was she finally moving out? I searched 700 of the 740 square feet that constituted my nest—nothing. Finally, I was clued in by the running water in the bathroom and, once I strained my hearing beyond the whir of a passing helicopter, the soft wailing of a broken woman.

I opened the door. She was shuddering and hiccupping, two bottles of spent Presidente beer by her feet and the remainder of a half-drained bottle of vodka. Do not give in to pity, I told myself. Hold the anger of the past week, hold it tight in your chest. Rise above the ritual humiliations. You're the richest man in Chinatown. She has done nothing for you. You can do better. Let the world fall apart, there is more to be gained in solitude now. Untether yourself from this eighty-six-pound albatross. Remember how she wouldn't comfort you after Noah had died.

"I thought we weren't supposed to drink anything grain-based," I told Eunice, nodding at the spent alcohol, the most I have ever seen her drink.

The "fuck you" I had expected didn't come. Her shaking continued, steady as a dying animal thumping against the cheaply tiled bathroom floor. She was whispering in English and Korean. "*Appa, why?*" she beseeched her father. Or maybe it was merely her non-functioning äppärät. I never realized the similarity between the device that ruled our world and the Korean word for "father." The T-shirt she was wearing, an ironic "Baghdad Tourist Authority" tee, was my own, and that strange connection—Eunice covered in my own garb—made me want to fold my own arms around her, made me want to feel myself on her. I picked her up—even the small weight of her pinched my prostate, but the rest of me felt blessed—and carried her to our bed, catching a whiff of her alcohol breath along with the strawberry integrity of her just-washed hair. She had washed for me. "I brought pizza," I said. "And spinach calzones. That's all that's out there right now. Nothing organic."

She was shuddering with such intensity that I grew worried from a medical standpoint. Her body, that *nothing*, shook in little round motions of spent energy. I touched her blazing forehead.

"It's okay," I said. "Have some Motrin. Eat a pizza. Drink water. Alcohol makes you dehydrated."

"I know that," she whispered in between shudders, and I hoped that maybe it was a sign of her displeasure returning. But she continued to quiver, her face a pale freckled mask twisted to the left as if by seizure. A child, just a child. "Len," she spoke. Water pooled inside the dimple of her chin. "Lenny. I'm . . ." She was sorry. Just like Joshie. A decision was drawing upon me. A final one. My lips pursed to form the first words of a fateful sentence. I held them pursed for now. I suppose I could have started telling her about all the different ways in which she needed to change in order for us to be happy together, but it would be pointless. I had either to accept the girl cradled in my arms, or to spend the rest of my time searching for something else.

Her trembling increased, and she turned around in my grasp, letting me feel the heavy beating of her spine against my chest. I could see her bones draped within my T-shirt, and in her convulsions I made out the dynamic aspects of her skeleton. She wailed from a place so deep that I could only connect it with somewhere across the seas, and from a time when our nations were barely formed. For the first time since we'd met, I realized that Eunice Park, unlike others of her generation, was not completely ahistorical. I cradled the softness of her behind, her one concession to being a woman. It steadied her, my open-palmed touch. I moved down and popped off her TotalSurrenders. The taste was the same as always—not sweet like honey, as urban musicians may claim, but musky and thick and vaguely urinary. I put my mouth around her, and just lay there motionless, waiting for the tremors to subside, for sleep to come to both of us, forgetting the pizza-hunger gnawing at my center. I was thinking about the word "truth." Whatever else could be said of Eunice Park, she was perfectly true.

DATING TIPS
FROM THE GLOBALTEENS ACCOUNT OF EUNICE PARK

AUGUST 4

EUNI-TARD *TO* AZIZARMY-INFO:

David, are you there? Oh my god! I saw the last Media streams. You were bleeding. Your face. And your arm. My poor David. I almost passed out. I tried to get to Tompkins Square, I swear I did, but I just couldn't. They wouldn't let me through. Are you okay? WAS MY SISTER IN THE PARK WITH YOU??? I know she goes on the weekends sometimes. Please get back to me as soon as you can. I still believe in you. I still think of what you taught me about my life and about my father, your Object Lessons and your Observations. You were right about everything. I'm not going to give in to High Net Worth thinking. I'm going to do things to make you proud. I'm a fighter and I'm never going to stop fighting. David, talk to me!

Love, Eunice

GLOBALTEENS AUTOMATIC ERROR MESSAGE 01121111:

We are SO TOTTALY sorry for the inconvenience. We are experiencing connectivity issues in the following location: NEW YORK, NY, U.S.A. Please be patient and the problem should resolve itself like whenever.

Free GlobalTeens Dating Tip: Guys love it when you laugh at their jokes. But nothings less sexy than when you try to outdo them by being a laff-hog yourself! When he makes a joke, smile so that he can see your teeth and how much you "want" him, then say, "You're so funny!" You'll be sucking crotch in no time, betch.

EUNI-TARD *TO* GRILLBITCH:

Pony, are you there? What's going on? I've been trying to verbal you for a week, my äppärät can't connect on TALK or STREAM, all I get is some error message which is freaking me out. Write me back. I miss you. I'm worried about you. I miss you SO much. What's happening over there? Was there shooting in Hermosa too? What happened to your dad's factory? Write to me NOW! I'm worried, Jenny Kang. Talk to me, sweet Precious Pony. All I'm doing now is crying. I don't know what's happening with my family. I don't know what happened to my friend David. I think Lenny doesn't want me anymore. I think we've totally broken up, only he can't send me packing because of the situation. Please write or TALK me back. I don't want to be alone and I'm scared. You're my best friend.

GLOBALTEENS AUTOMATIC ERROR MESSAGE 01121111:

We are SO TOTTALY sorry for the inconvenience. We are experiencing connectivity issues in the following location: HERMOSA BEACH, CA, U.S.A. Please be patient and the problem should resolve itself like whenever.

Free GlobalTeens Dating Tip: Don't ever fold your arms in front of your date. That says that you don't fully agree with what he's saying or maybe you're not into his data. Instead put your hands out in front of you, palms open, like you want to be cupping his balls! Get a degree in Body Language, girlfriend, and you'll be giving head to the class.

EUNI-TARD *TO* CHUNG.WON.PARK:

Mom! Hello there. Mom, I'm worried. I tried to verbal you and Sally, but I can't connect. I just wanted you to know that I'm fine. They weren't ever shooting our building which is Jewish. I need you right now, Mom. I know you're still mad at me because of Lenny, but I need to know that you're all right. Just tell me you and Dad and Sally are all right.

GLOBALTEENS AUTOMATIC ERROR MESSAGE 01121111:

We are SO TOTTALY sorry for the inconvenience. We are experiencing connectivity issues in the following location: FORT LEE, NJ, U.S.A. Please be patient and the problem should resolve itself like soon.

AUGUST 8

EUNI-TARD *TO* GRILLBITCH:

Hi Jenny. I guess I'm just going to get an error message after I send this, but I want to write to you anyway in the hope that you'll get it, if not now, then someday. I won't believe that you're gone like Lenny's friend Noah. I can't and I won't, because you mean so much to me. So let me tell you what's going on with my life.

It's been very hard here, but I think I've forgiven Lenny. I just have to accept the fact that David and everyone else in the park is gone, even though I know, I just KNOW, that Sally wasn't there. I have to accept that there was nothing I could have done to save David and his people, and that it wasn't Lenny's fault, he was just trying to get us to safety. Oh, sweet Precious Pony. I think I loved David in a way that I can't really even describe. Of course we were completely mismatched, but Lenny and I are mismatched too. My dad was kind to me after he saw me and David in the park, because all three of us were in it together, doing something for a greater good, and it's like my dad SAW that no matter how fucked up I am I'm basically good too and there's no reason to hate me. It's so Christian-sounding, but I guess I have it too, this thing that Sally does. An instinct to help, I guess.

I don't know, I don't know, but yesterday, when Lenny and I had sex, I couldn't look him in the eyes. He was poking me with his chubby stomach and I kept thinking about how much I've lost and how much I'm still going to lose, and I felt SORRY before David, like I was cheating on him. And that made me want to cheat on Lenny, I guess.

It's not like Lenny's been doing anything bad. He's got yuan in the bank, so there's pizza and calzones and my ass is actually getting even fatter. We're surviving and it's all thanks to Lenny. I hope, sweet Pony, that someone is caring for you the way he's been caring for me. There are also all these old mostly Jewish people in the building and no one really looks out for them and it's like 100 degrees this week and there's not enough electricity for the AC so we have to go around and get them water. I'm trying to get Lenny to help me buy up bottles from the bodegas because there's rationing. He's trying to help I guess, but he's too timid to get the job done. White people don't really care about old people, except for David who tried to help everyone. And then they shot him like a dog.

GLOBALTEENS AUTOMATIC ERROR MESSAGE

WAPACHUNG CONTINGENCY EMERGENCY MESSAGE:
Sender: Joshie Goldmann, Post-Human Services, Administrative
Recipient: Eunice Park
Eunice, I'm going to be sending you these messages on an emergency frequency, which we're piggybacking on Lenny's äppärät. This is just between you and me, okay? Don't even tell Lenny, he's got enough on his plate. At this point I want you to confirm that you're getting this message and that you're safe. Let me know if there's ANYTHING I can do for you. xo Joshie

AUGUST 20

EUNI-TARD *TO* GRILLBITCH:
Sorry I haven't written in a while. I guess I'm a little depressed. Things are much better between me and Lenny, but still I feel like the tables have turned. Now that Lenny almost dumped me, I feel out of control. It's like I'm naked or something, without armor. I worry that he's going to punish me for all the times I didn't fully love him. Maybe I should punish him first? His boss Joshie keeps sending me messages on this Wapachung emergency frequency checking up on me, but I don't know what to do. The thing is, I kind of find Joshie attractive in a manly, older way. I guess I'm physically attracted to his kind of strong personality. He's like David, always ready to take charge when the people he loves are threatened. Anyway, I spend half the day waiting for an emergency message from Joshie. Is that totally wrong? I'm such a bad girlfriend.

But I've also been thinking. Maybe David was wrong about everything in the end? Maybe there isn't going to be an Act Two for America like he said. Maybe you were right about him. Maybe he was just a dreamer and would never be able to look out for me and my family. But if not him, then who? Lenny?

Sometimes I feel guilty that I'm not more of an accomplished person, because then I could help my sister and my mother. Maybe I should ask Joshie about what I should do, if he can check up on my family somehow. Ugh, how fucked am I? Tell me please. Write me or verbal me. Anytime, day or night, whenever you get this, whenever it's safe to write or holler back. I need to hear your voice, Pony of my heart. Tell me I'm not alone.

GLOBALTEENS AUTOMATIC ERROR MESSAGE

AUGUST 22

EUNI-TARD *TO* CHUNG.WON.PARK:

Hi, Mommy. I bet I'm going to get an error message after I write this, but I feel like I have to write this anyway. If you get this someday, I just wanted you to know that I'm sorry. You're so close and yet I can't help you and Sally and dad. I know you raised me better than that. I know that if this were Korea you'd figure out a way to help your parents no matter what the personal sacrafice. I'm just not a good person. I don't have any strength and I don't have any accomplishments under my belt and I'm so so sorry I didn't do better on my LSAT. I wish I knew what my special path was, as Reverend Cho likes to say. If Sally's with you, please tell her I'm sorry I failed her as a sister too.

Your useless daughter,

Eunice

GLOBALTEENS AUTOMATIC ERROR MESSAGE

WAPACHUNG CONTINGENCY EMERGENCY MESSAGE:

Sender: Joshie Goldmann, Post-Human Services, Administrative
Recipient: Eunice Park

Hi, Eunice. How are you doing? Listen, I know there are some food shortages downtown, so I'm going to send you a big care package. Look for a black Staatling-Wapachung Service Jeep at 575 Grand around 4pm tomorrow. Any special requests? I know you girls totally heart organic peanut butter and lots of soy milk and cereal, right?

Listen, things are going to get better very soon, I promise. This whole situation is clearing right up. Hint: Brush up on your Norwegian and Mandarin. JBF. And guess what? That art teacher is going to come from Paris, so we can start practicing together at my place! Parsons is out of business. I can't wait to see you again. We're gonna have so much fun, Eunice. As always, please let's keep this our little secret. We've got a very sensitive Rhesus Monkey on our hands and he might misconstrue, if you know what I mean. Ha ha.

.

AUGUST 23

WAPACHUNG CONTINGENCY EMERGENCY MESSAGE:

Sender: Eunice Park

Recipient: Joshie Goldmann, Post-Human Services, Administrative

Hi Joshie. I got your sweet message. I'm really excited about the food package. We've been eating nothing but carbs and fats for the last week. Tap water is pretty hit or miss and our local bodega ran out of bottled last week. Also there are some old people in the building who need water and supplies and the heat is really bad for them, although I worry what will happen when winter comes if there's not ENOUGH heat. Thanks so much! Yes, I totally heart cereal (Smart Start is my favorite) and organic PB. I'm sorry to bother you about this stuff, but could you please find out if my parents are okay? I haven't heard from them since my GlobalTeens went off and I'm super worried. Dr. Sam Park and Mrs. Chung-won Park, 124 Harold Avenue, Fort Lee, NJ 07024. Also, I haven't heard from my best friend Jennifer Kang, who's at 210 Myrtle Avenue, Hermosa Beach, CA, I don't know the zip code. Also, my friend David Lorring was in Tompkins Square when all this stuff happened, maybe there's some way you can check to see if he's okay. Again, I'm so sorry to impose on you like this, but I'm scared out of my mind.

I think it would be great to draw with you, but I wonder if we should let Lenny know. He is a very sensitive Rhesus Monkey, as you say, but I think if he ever found out he would be very angry with me. And he IS my boyfriend. Thanks for understanding.

Yours, Eunice

WAPACHUNG CONTINGENCY EMERGENCY MESSAGE:

Sender: Joshie Goldmann, Post-Human Services, Administrative

Recipient: Eunice Park

Smart Start! Wow, that's my favorite cereal too! I'm glad we have so much in common. You really take care of yourself and it shows in how beautiful and young you look. There's a real overlap between our philosophies on life and staying younger and taking care of oneself, something I think we've both been trying to instill in Lenny, but ultimately I think Lenny's immune to that. I've been trying to get him to think about health choices, but he's just really focused on his parents and worried about THEIR death, without really understanding what it means to want to live life to the fullest, to the freshest, to the youngest. In some ways, you and I are really from the same generation of people and Lenny is from a different world, a previous world that was obsessed with death and not life, and was consumed with fear and not positivism. Anyway, I'm going to totally load up a couple of jeeps with supplies so you can have lots of food for yourself and also feed and hydrate all those poor old people in your building.

I don't know if Lenny explained to you, but the Post-Human Services division I run is part of the same company as Wapachung Contingency. So I talked to some of the Contingency folks and they're going to make some inquiries about your parents. I know the situation in Fort Lee is very touch and go. Basically, the week after the Rupture no one had command & control over there, but it's not so bad as in other parts of the country, because it's right over the river from us. In other words, I'm sure they're okay. I couldn't get any info on Hermosa Beach, CA, except there were reports of very heavy small-arms fire during and after the Rupture. I'm sorry, Eunice. I don't know if your friend was in the area at the time of the fighting. I just want you to be prepared for the worst.

I feel a little stupid writing this, but I want to be completely honest. I really have strong feelings for you, Eunice. From the moment I met you, I felt so flustered, I thought my mind was about to go blank. It took me a good ten minutes just to open a bottle of resveratrol because my hands were shaking so much! When I saw you, I remembered some of the worst parts of my life, some things I shouldn't really be talking about over this emergency signal. Let's just say there were some difficult moments, moments that it may take several more lifetimes to get over (which is why I simply cannot die), and when I saw you, AFTER I started breathing again (ha ha), I felt some of that weight lift off my shoulders. I felt like I knew what I wanted, not just from eternity, but from the present moment too. And when things got bad recently, it was thinking of you that kept me going. What is that effect you have over people, Eunice? Where does it come from? How does your smile reduce one of the most powerful men in the hemisphere to a dopey teenager? It's like I feel that together we can redeem whatever misery we encountered on this planet, whatever awfulness we faced as children.

Anyway, I feel so totally, like, weird opening up my heart like this to you, because what I feel for YOU and for YOUR FAMILY IN FORT LEE AND THEIR WELL-BEING, is so strong and without reservation, that I fear it might make you run away from me. I'm sorry if that's the case. But if it's not, please let me know and we'll just do some drawing together, no strings attached. Better than hanging out at miserable 575 Grand Street, right? Ha ha ha.

Love,

Your Joshie

FIVE-JIAO MEN

FROM THE DIARIES OF LENNY ABRAMOV

SEPTEMBER 5

Dear Diary,

My äppärät isn't connecting. I can't connect.

It's been almost a month since my last diary entry. I am so sorry. But I can't connect in any meaningful way to anyone, even to you, diary. Four young people committed suicide in our building complexes, and two of them wrote suicide notes about how they couldn't see a future without their äppäräti. One wrote, quite eloquently, about how he "reached out to life," but found there only "walls and thoughts and faces," which weren't enough. He needed to be ranked, to know his place in this world. And that may sound ridiculous, but I can understand him. We are all bored out of our fucking minds. My hands are itching for connection, I want to connect to my parents and to Vishnu and Grace, I want to mourn Noah with them. But all I have is Eunice and my Wall of Books. So I try to Celebrate What I Have, one of my prime directives.

Work has been good. Kind of a blur, but even a blur is better than the slow churn of reality. Mostly I work alone at my desk with a half-turned bowl of miso by my side. I haven't really spent time with Joshie since The Slap. He's off somewhere, negotiating with the IMF or the Norwegians or the Chinese or whoever still gives a damn. Howard Shu, dork that he is, has become the standard-bearer for the few of us still left at Post-Human. He walks around with an old-fashioned clipboard and actually tells us what to do. Before the

Rupture, we would never have stood for anything so hierarchical, but now we're just glad to have instructions, even barked ones. My job for the time being is to send out Wapachung emergency frequency messages to our clients, making sure they're safe, but also subtly checking up on their businesses, their marriages, their children, their finances. Making sure *we're* safe and that our monthly dues keep coming.

It's not going to be easy. No one's working. The teachers aren't getting paid, is what I hear. No school. Children set loose and free into the difficult new city. I found a Vladeck House kid, maybe ten or twelve, sitting by the Arab bodega, licking out the inside of an empty bag of something called "Clük," which the packaging warned was "inspired by real chicken flava!" When I sat down next to him, he could barely lift his eyes up to mine. Out of instinct, I took out my äppärät and pointed it at the kid, as if that would make things right. Then I took out a brown twenty-yuan note and set it at his feet. Immediately, his hand darted for it. The bill was scrunched into his fist. The fist was hidden behind his back. His face slowly turned to face mine. The brown-eyed look he gave me was not one of gratitude. The look said: *Leave me alone with my newfound fortune or I will lash out at you with the last strength I have.* I left him there with his fist behind his back, his eyes on my departing feet.

I don't know what's going on. The city is either completely finished or already shooting for redemption. New signs are going up. "Tourism NYC: Are YOU Rupture-Ready?" and "New York Cit-ay *Edge:* Do U Have What It Takes 2 Survive?"

As far as I can tell, the most significant forms of employment around Manhattan are the "Staatling-Wapachung Works Progress" sites promising "One hour honest labor = 5-jiao coin. Nutritious lunch served." Rows of men cracking open asphalt, digging ditches, filling in ditches with cement. These five-jiao men roam the city, hands in pockets, useless vestigial äppäräti plugs in their ears, like a pride of voiceless lions. They're middle-aged to younger, sparse hair bleached by the sun, tyrannical sunburns on their face and neck, expensive T-shirts bought in happier days, new Antarcticas of perspi-

ration spreading down to the stomach. Shovels, picks, loud exhala-
tions, not even grunts anymore, to save energy. I saw Noah's old
friend Hartford Brown, who only a few months ago was getting
reamed on a yacht in the Antilles, working a five-jiao line on Prince
Street. He looked cracked, half of him bronzed, the other half peeling, that slightly pudgy face of his devoid of all texture, like a thick
slice of prosciutto. If they can make a fabulous gay man work like
that, I thought, what can they do to the rest of us?

I went up close to him as he swung his pick, felt his rank odor bat-
tering its way into my nostrils. "Hartford," I said. "It's Lenny
Abramov. Noah's friend." A terrible exhale from a terrible place inside him. "Hartford!" He turned away. Someone with a megaphone
was yelling, "Let's *do* get back to work, Brownie!" I handed him a
hundred-yuan note, which he accepted, also without thanks, and
then he went back to swinging his pick. "Hartford," I said. "Hey!
You don't have to work now. A hundred yuan is two hundred hours
of work. Take it easy. Get some rest. Get some shade." But he just
went on swinging mechanically, avoiding my presence, already back
into his world, which began with the pick behind his shoulder and
ended with the pick in the ground.

Back home, Eunice took charge of organizing the relief efforts for
the older people. I don't know why. The stirrings of her Christian
background? Sorrow over not being able to help her own parents?
I'm just going to take it at face value.

She went from floor to floor in each of our four co-op buildings,
a total of eighty floors, knocked on each door, and if there were
older people she took down their food and water needs and made
sure the supplies were brought down the next week in one of
Joshie's Staatling-Wapachung Service convoys. Why is he helping
us? I suppose he feels guilty about Noah and the ferry, or maybe
about The Slap. In any case, we need what he's got.

She delivered the water herself—with my sporadic help—to each
apartment, she made sure all the windows and doors were open to

improve circulation, she sat there and listened to the old people cry about their children and grandchildren who were scattered around the country and for whom they feared the worst, she asked me to interpret certain Yiddish words ("that *farkakteh* Rubenstein," "that *shlemiel* Rubenstein," "that little *pisher* Rubenstein"), but mostly she sat with them and hugged them as their tears pollinated the dusty throw rugs and embattled last-century carpets. When the older women (most of our aged residents are widows) smelled particularly bad, she would clean their dirty bathtubs, help the shaky old ladies inside, and wash them. It was a task I found particularly repulsive—how I feared one day having to care for my parents in so thoughtful and tactile a manner, as Russian tradition expected of me—but Eunice, who despised any alien smell coming from our refrigerator or the rankness of my toenails after several missed pedicures, did not flinch, did not turn away from the sunken, splotched flesh in her hands.

We saw a woman die. Or Eunice did anyway. I think it was a stroke. She couldn't get the words out of her mouth, this withered creature, sitting beside a coffee table littered with unusable remote controls, a photo of the Lubavitcher Rebbe showing off his beautiful beard framed behind her. "Aican," she kept saying, arcing spittle across Eunice's shoulders. And then, more emphatically: "Aican, aican, aican!"

Did she mean to say, "I can"? I left the apartment, because I couldn't bear to rekindle the memories of my own grandmother after her final stroke, in a wheelchair, covering up the dead parts of her body with her shawl, worried about looking helpless in front of the world.

I feared the old people, feared their mortality, but the more I did so, the more I fell in love with Eunice Park. I fell for her as hopelessly and thoroughly as I had in Rome, where I had confused her for a different, stronger person. My problem was that I couldn't help her find her parents and sister. Even with my Staatling connections, I couldn't find out what had happened to her family in Fort Lee. One day Eunice told me she could *feel* that they were still alive and doing well—a sentiment that floored me with its almost religious naïveté, but also made me wish I could believe the same thing about the Abramovs.

Aican, aican, aican.

So many things have happened since I've last written in you, diary, some of them awful, most of them mundane. I guess the main thing I can think of is the fact that things are getting better with Eunice, that through our mutual depression over what's happened to our city, our friends, and our lives we've become closer. Because we can't connect to our äppäräti, we're learning to turn to each other.

Once, after a long weekend of scrubbing and watering our elderly, she even asked me to *read* to her.

I went over to my Wall of Books and picked up Kundera's *The Unbearable Lightness of Being,* whose cover I had caught Eunice examining once before, tracing with her finger the depicted bowler hat flying over the Prague skyline. There were laudatory quotes for the author and his work on the first page of the book from *The New Yorker, The Washington Post, The New York Times* (the real *Times,* not the *Lifestyle Times*), even something called *Commonweal.* What had happened to all these publications? I remember reading the *Times* in the subway, folding it awkwardly while leaning against the door, caught up in the words, worried about crashing to the floor or tripping over some lightly clad beauty (there was always at least one), but even more afraid to lose the thread of the article in front of me, my spine banging against the train door, the clatter and drone of the massive machine around me, and me, with my words, brilliantly alone.

Reading Kundera's book, I felt a growing anxiety as the words on the crinkly yellow pages came out of my mouth. I found myself struggling for breath. I had read this book many times over as a teenager, had bent the topmost edges of many pages where Kundera's philosophy touched my own. But now even I had trouble understanding all the concepts, never mind what Eunice could understand. *The Unbearable Lightness of Being* was a novel of ideas set in a country that meant nothing to her, set in a time—the Soviet invasion of Czechoslovakia in 1968—that might as well not have existed as far as Eunice was concerned. She had learned to love Italy, but that was a far more digestible, stylish land, a country of Images.

In the first few pages, Kundera discusses several abstract historical figures: Robespierre, Nietzsche, Hitler. For Eunice's sake, I wanted him to get to the plot, to introduce actual "living" characters—I recalled this was a love story—and to leave the world of ideas behind. Here we were, two people lying in bed, Eunice's worried head propped on my collarbone, and I wanted us to feel something in common. I wanted this complex language, this surge of intellect, to be processed into love. Isn't that how they used to do it a century ago, people reading poetry to one another?

On page eight, I read a part I had underlined as a moody, unlaid teenager. "What happens but once . . . might as well not have happened at all. If we have only one life to live, we might as well not have lived at all." Next to this I had written in shaded block letters: "EUROPEAN CYNICISM or VERY SCARY TRUTH???" I re-read the lines again, slowly, with emphasis, directly into Eunice's pert, wax-free ear, and as I did so I wondered if perhaps it was this book that had launched my search for immortality. Joshie himself had once said to a very important client, "Eternal life is the only life that matters. All else is just a moth circling the light." He had not noticed my standing by the door to his office. I returned to my cubicle in tears, feeling abandoned to nothingness, moth-like, yet stunned by Joshie's unusual lyricism. The part about the moth, I mean. He never talked like that with me. He always underlined the positive things about my brief existence, the fact, for example, that I had friends and could afford good restaurants and was never completely alone for very long.

I read on, feeling Eunice's solemn breath against my chest. The main character, Tomas, started having sex with many attractive Czech ladies. I re-read several times a passage about Tomas's mistress standing in front of him, in panties and bra and a black bowler hat. I pointed to the black bowler hat on the cover. Eunice nodded, but I felt that Kundera had put too many words around the fetish for her to gain what her generation required from any form of content: a ready surge of excitement, a temporary lease on satisfaction.

By page sixty-four, Tomas's girlfriend Tereza and his mistress Sabina are taking photographs of each other naked, dressed only in that recurring black bowler hat. "She was completely at the mercy of Tomas's mistress," I read two pages later, winking at Eunice. "This beautiful submission intoxicated Tereza." I repeated the words "beautiful submission." Eunice stirred. She took off her To-talSurrenders with a snap of her finger and moved up to straddle my face between her legs. With the book still partly open in one hand, I cupped her behind with the other while using my tongue in the familiar motions against her opening. She pulled back for a while and let me look into her face. I mistook her expression for a smile. It was something else, a slight opening of the mouth, with the lower lip leaning rightward. It was astonishment: the astonishment of being fully loved. The miracle of not being hit. She returned to her position on top of me and let out a volley of grunts of a pitch and treble I had never heard. It was as if she were speaking a foreign language, one that had not kept up with history, one that was stuck on the primal sound "guh." I lifted her up, not sure she was enjoying herself. "Should we stop?" I asked. "Am I hurting you?" She forced herself down on my face and rocked her body faster.

Afterward, she returned to her perch on my collarbone, sniffing critically at the trail she had left on my chin. I read once more. I read loudly about the exploits of the fictional Tomas and his many lovers. I skipped around, looking for juicier bits to feed Eunice. The story moved from Prague to Zurich and then back to Prague. The little nation of Czechoslovakia was torn to shreds by the imperialist Soviets (who, the author had no way of knowing at the time of writing, would themselves be torn to shreds a negligible twenty-three years later). In the book, characters had to make political decisions that, in the end, meant nothing. The concept of kitsch was rightfully, if somewhat ruthlessly, attacked. Kundera forced me to ponder my mortality some more.

Eunice's gaze had weakened, and the light had gone out of her eyes, those twin black orbs usually charged with an irrepressible mandate of anger and desire.

"Are you following all this?" I said. "Maybe we should stop."

"I'm listening," she half-whispered.

"But are you *understanding*?" I said.

"I've never really learned how to read texts," she said. "Just to scan them for info."

I let out a small, stupid laugh.

She started to cry.

"Oh, baby," I said. "I'm sorry. I didn't mean to laugh. Oh, baby."

"Lenny," she said.

"Even I'm having trouble following this. It's not just you. Reading is difficult. People just aren't meant to read anymore. We're in a post-literate age. You know, a *visual* age. How many years after the fall of Rome did it take for a Dante to appear? Many, many years."

I blubbered on like this for a few minutes. She went to the living room. Alone, I threw *The Unbearable Lightness of Being* across the room. I wanted to tear it to pieces. I touched my chin, still wet with her. I wanted to run out of the apartment, into the impoverished Manhattan night. I missed my parents. In times of trouble, the weak seek the strong.

In the living room, Eunice had opened up her äppärät and was concentrating on the last shopping page stored in its memory before communications collapsed. I could see she had instinctively opened a LandOLakes Credit Payment stream, but every time she tried to input her account info, she ended up throwing her head back as if stung. "I can't buy anything," she said.

"Eunice," I said. "You don't have to buy anything. Go to bed. We don't have to read anymore. We don't have to ever read again. I promise. How can we read when people need our help? It's a luxury. A stupid luxury."

When the morning light was at full blast, Eunice finally curled up next to me, covered in sweat, defeated. We ignored the morning and we ignored the day. We ignored the following day as well. But when I woke up on the third day, the heat raking its way through the opened window, she was gone. I ran into the living room; no Eunice. I ran to the lobby. I asked the loitering old people about her where-abouts. I could feel my heart stopping and the blood draining from my feet and hands.

When she finally showed up, twenty hours later ("I went for a walk. I needed to get out of here. It's not *that* dangerous, Lenny. I'm sorry if you were worried"), I found myself on my knees in my usual position, begging her to forgive me for some ill-defined sin, praying for her real smile and her companionship, pleading for her never to leave me again.

Aican, aican, aican.

OH MY GOD, I'M SUCH A BAD GIRLFRIEND
FROM THE GLOBALTEENS ACCOUNT OF EUNICE PARK

SEPTEMBER 10

WAPACHUNG CONTINGENCY EMERGENCY MESSAGE:

Sender: Joshie Goldmann, Post-Human Services, Administrative

Recipient: Eunice Park

Hello there, my darling Ms. Eunice. How's tricks? Okay, I've got to admit, I can't stop thinking about our little time together last week. I am so totally HOOKED on you. Those twenty-four hours we spent drawing with Monsieur Cohen (ho ho ho, color theory, here we come!), rifling through what's left of Barneys, oysters at the Staatling canteen, a little, um, fun in bed, and then doing those stretches together, holy moly, that was like the perfect date. You were so cute when you walked into my apartment. I can't believe how your hands were shaking. I'm still picking up the glass shards off the floor (how did you manage to break TWO glasses?), but that's okay, because it just shows how real you are. Thank you, Eunice, for making me feel FINE and limber and ready to hit the ground running. And thanks for picking out all those clothes. You're right, there was something a little hippie-ish about the way I used to dress, and my mustache HAD to go. Over and done with. My only prob is that I miss you sooo much already. Can we do this again soon? Can we do this again like permanently? I can't seriously see my life go on without the little patter of your feet by my bedside. And I've got a lot of living to do, ha ha.

Well, it IS a big relief to know that your parents and sis are alive and doing as well as anyone else under the circumstances. I've passed on the relocation request to Headquarters, but the problem is that, even if they do get your family out of Ft. Lee, where are we going to put them? We're working out future arrangements with the IMF and I think the idea is to rebuild New York as a kind of "Lifestyle Hub" where wealthy people can do their thang, spend their money, live forever, blah blah blabbity BLAH. So every inch of space is going to be accounted for, and the prices are going to be absolutely PREMIUM. And the rest of the country's going to be carved up between a bunch of foreign sovereign wealth funds, with Wapachung Contingency taking over what's left of the National Guards and the army and doing security support (yay for us!). I'm not sure if the Chinese are going to be "in charge" of New Jersey, or if that's going to go to Norway or to the Saudi Arabian Monetary Agency, but in either case I'm sure things are going to be a lot better and safer than they are now. Tho maybe your sis can learn to wear a burka. Totally kidding. It's not going to be like that. They just want returns on investment.

Sigh. I miss you. I miss the very SCENT of you. I miss your sweet smiling face and your tight embrace. God, listen to me. Anyway, I might send Lenny on a weekend trip to visit his parents on Long Island (don't tell him yet, but according to Wap Contingency they survived), which means more quality time for us!!! Mwah! as you like to say. Mwah, my dear, dear Eunice, my brave young love. Isn't it exciting to be ALIVE these days?

SEPTEMBER 12

WAPACHUNG CONTINGENCY EMERGENCY MESSAGE:
   Sender: Eunice Park
   Recipient: Joshie Goldmann, Post-Human Services, Administrative
   Joshua,
   I got your message. Thanks. Yes, Monsieur Cohen is very interesting. Is he gay, or just French? I'm sorry if I seem to be holding us back in class, I'm such a perfectionist and I really don't think I'm very good. And if I'm as good as you and M. Cohen say then it's just a fluke and I'll come shattering back down to earth pretty soon, you can bet your bottom yuan. My father always said my hands were too weak to be an artist anyway.
   I know we spent some good times together and I will remember those hours, but I also feel like a very bad girlfriend to Lenny. And that's what I

am, I'm Lenny's girlfriend and I love him, and I'm really not able to explore anything more than friendship with you right now.

Thanks for finding out about my parents and sister. I miss my family very much and I wish there was some way to get them to Manhattan or even back to Korea. That's what I'm concentrating on right now. I've been reading some of the old messages from my friend Jenny Kang, the one who disappeared and who you can't seem to be able to find in Hermosa Beach, and one of the last things she wrote me was "I'm sorry I'm a bad friend and can't help you with your problems right now. You have to be strong and do whatever you have to do for your family." See, you don't have a family. And you never really wanted one from what I can gather. But throughout this whole Rupture thing I guess that's what I found out about myself, that my family matters the most to me and it always will.

Yours,

Eunice

WAPACHUNG CONTINGENCY EMERGENCY MESSAGE:

Sender: Joshie Goldmann, Post-Human Services, Administrative

Recipient: Eunice Park

I have to say I was a little hurt by your last message. If you didn't want to pursue a relationship, then why did you go home with me? I think you don't fully comprehend how I feel about you, Eunice. I've been trying to put my finger on it, and I think I've sort of come to some conclusions. You're very beautiful, but that doesn't really matter to me in the long run. Everything about you is so perfect, so squared away (from the way you dress to the minimum amount of words you use to express yourself), but that doesn't matter either. What matters to me is that I KNOW you are capable of love, that you cannot hide forever from the truth of being a full emotional human being with a need to connect, with a need to be with someone who can understand you and where you come from, respect you, and take care of you. And that's what I want to do, Eunice, to take care of you, forever and ever. I want to help you become a full-fledged artist, even if that means you have to spend time away from me, studying Art & Finance at HSBC-Goldsmiths in London. I want to get you a job in Retail, if that's what you want, once New York becomes a full Lifestyle

Hub and we start to get back on our feet. And yes, I want to help your family to resettle in the city, but please just give me some time to see what I can do. The situation is still very fluid.

You say Lenny is your boyfriend. I've known Lenny since he was a young adult like you. He's not a bad person, but he's also very conflicted, impotent, and depressive. Those are not the qualities you want to look for in a serious partner, not today, not with the world in the shape it's in. I want you to consider all these things, Eunice, and to know that, whatever you decide, I will always love you.

Joshie (never Joshua) G.

P.S. Just a heads-up, but there is going to be some activity in your area in a month or so, what the ARA used to call "Harm Reduction," in the Vladeck Houses. Nothing I have any control over, believe me, but there might be violence. I want you and Lenny to be safe. I'm thinking maybe that's when I'll send him to Long Island to see his folks and you and I can have a slumber party.

DEAF CHILD AREA
FROM THE DIARIES OF LENNY ABRAMOV

OCTOBER 12

Dear Diary,

Please forgive another month-long absence, but today I have to write in you with the greatest of news. My parents are alive. I found out five days ago, at 5:54 p.m. EST, the precise time Telenor, the Norwegian telecommunications giant, restored our communications and our äppäräti started whirring with data, prices, Images, and calumny; 5:54 p.m. EST, a time no one of my generation will ever forget. My parents' voices filled my ears immediately, the baritone insanity of my father's happy booms, the titter and laughter of my mother as they shouted: *"Malen'kii, malen'kii! Zhiv, zdorov? Zhiv, zdorov!"* ("Little one, little one! Alive and well? Alive and well!"). I hollered in such a way (*"Urá!"*) that Eunice became scared. She moved to the bathroom, where I could hear her verballing into her äppärät in a monotone English mixed together with an endless procession of passionate Korean honks directed at her mother: *"Neh, neh, umma, neh."* And so the two of us celebrated with our parents, reconnected to them so strongly that when Eunice came into the bedroom and we faced each other, there was almost nothing to say in our common tongue. We found ourselves laughing at our stunned, merry silence, me wiping my tears, her with her hands pressed to the hardness of her chest.

The Abramovs. Surviving, scavenging, setting up their own roadblocks with Mr. Vida and the other neighbors while the world came undone around them, being hard-boiled working-class immigrants, designed by an angry God for a calamity of precisely this magnitude. How could I have doubted their tenacious hold on life? According to the stressful GlobalTeens messages they sent me right after we finished verballing, the security situation in Westbury was relatively normal, but the pharmacy had been ransacked and the heavily guarded Waldbaum's supermarket was out of Tagamet, my father's remedy against heartburn and his chronic peptic ulcers. So it was a happy surprise when I got a note, a *handwritten note,* from Joshie:

Rhesus Monkey! Be a good son and go visit your parents. I'm reserving some crack Wapachung security people for you on Monday. They'll escort you out to Long Island. Stay away from those boiled Russian meats! And don't get too excited, okay? I'm looking out for your epinephrine levels like a hawk.

I was met outside the Post-Human Services synagogue by two armored Hyundai Persimmon jeeps sporting enormous hood-mounted weaponry, probably leftovers from our ill-fated Venezuelan adventure. Our expedition leader seemed to be of Venezuela vintage as well, one Major J. M. Palatino of Wapachung Contingency, a small but powerfully put-together man smelling of middle-class cologne and horses. He surveyed me with professional eyes, quickly concluded that I was soft and in need of protection, slapped his sides militarily, and introduced his team of two young armed guys, both remnants of the Nebraskan National Guard, one missing the better half of his hand.

"Here's the game plan," Palatino said. "We follow the major arteries and hope there haven't been any flare-ups along the way. We're talking about I-495 here, the old Long Island Expressway. Don't expect much trouble there. Then we swing over to the Northern and Wantagh Parkways. That could be trickier, depending on who's in charge at this point in the day."

"I thought that would be us," I said.

"There's still sporadic enemy-combatant activity after Little

Neck. Nassau warlords fighting Suffolk warlords. Ethnic stuff. Salvadorans. Guatemalans. *Nigerians.* Got to tread lightly. Anyway, we're armed to the teeth here, so no worries. We've got a heavy .50-caliber M2 Browning machine gun on the lead vehicle and AT4 anti-armor on both. Nothing even comes close out there. Expect we'll be in Westbury at 1400 hours."

"Three hours to drive thirty miles?"

"I didn't create this world, sir," Palatino said. "I'm just along for the ride. We've got Oslo Delight sandwiches for you in the back. You cool with lingonberry jam? Enjoy."

At the entrance to the expressway, Wapachung troops were screening cars for weapons and contraband, throwing unlucky five-jiao men on the ground, and prodding them with weapons, the whole scene oddly quiet and methodical and reminiscent of the near-distant past. "It's like the American Restoration Authority out here," I said to the major. "Nothing's changed but the uniforms."

"You don't just disband a force overnight," Palatino said. "We'd have a situation like out in Missouri."

"What's in Missouri?" I asked.

He waved his hand at me as if to say: *It's better not to know.* We turned our backs on Manhattan and rolled past the ugly gigantism of LeFrak City, a collection of buildings that, with their rows of balconies on both ends, resembled soot-covered accordions. These housing projects were riddled with Russian immigrants, and my parents had always thought that one more step down on the economic ladder would bring us directly to LeFrak, where, according to my mother, we would all be killed. She was something of a seer, Galya Abramov.

The grounds of the LeFrak development were littered with home-made tents. People were lying on mattresses on a pedestrian overpass, the acrid smell of bad meat being grilled wafting down below. As we passed LeFrak City ("Live a Little Better" its heartfelt mid-twentieth-century motto), the Manhattan-bound side of the Long Island Expressway became an endless jumble of cars slowly maneuvering around men, women, and children of all possible persuasions compliantly carting their belongings in suitcases and shopping trolleys. "Lots of folks going west," Palatino said, as we crawled forward past a gaggle of poor middle-class cars, tiny Samsung Santa Monicas and the like, children and mothers huddled over one another in back. "The closer to the city, the better. Even if you have to work a five-jiao line. Work is work."

"Where do you live?" I asked Palatino.

"Sixty-eighth and Lex."

"Nice area," I said. "Close to the park."

"My kids love the zoo. Wapachung's going to get us a panda."

I had heard of this.

Three hours later, we were driving down Old Country Road, the Champs-Élysées of Westbury, past the mostly boarded-up ghosts of Retail past, the Payless ShoeSource, Petco, Starbucks. A crowd of would-be consumers still congregated around the 99¢ Paradise store. The smell of sewage and a brown savage haze filtered through the windows, but I also heard the loud, screechy sound of human laughter and people yelling to one another on the street, friendly-like. It seemed to me that in some weird way a suburban place like Westbury, with its working- and middle-class folks, its Salvadorans and Southeast Asians and the like, was what New York City used to be when it was still a real place. There was something lovely about Old Country Road today, folks milling about, trading goods, eating papusas, young boys and girls wearing nothing, verballing one another with love. "They maintain pretty good security," Palatino seconded. "The good guys got all the weapons, and they've spread their assets out strategically." I had no idea what the hell he was talking about.

We turned off the commercial street and drove headlong into the residential peace of Washington Avenue. Despite the serenity of my parents' street, I found myself worried by a sign that said "Deaf Child Area." I tried to remember a deaf neighborhood child from my days in Westbury, but no such creature sprang to mind. Who was this deaf child, and what kind of a future would she have today?

We approached my parents' house, the gigantic flags of the United States of America and SecurityState Israel still fluttering obstinately. Huddled behind the screen door, I saw the Abramovs leaning in to each other. For a second it seemed like there was just one Abramov, for although my mother was delicate and pretty and my father was not, they appeared to take on a twin form, as if each was reflected in the other. What had happened in the past few months was unclear. They had aged, become grayer, but also it seemed as if some indeterminate part of each of them had been surgically taken out, leaving a kind of muddled transparency. When I approached them with my arms stretched out, with my bag of Tagamet ulcer remedy and other goodies banging against my hip, I saw a part of that transparency fill in; I saw their creased faces welcome in the joy of my survival, my physical presence, my indelible link to them, surprised that I stood in front of them, secretly hurt and ashamed that they could do less for me than I could for them.

We were surrounded by elements of one another: my mother's immaculateness, my father's unadulterated musk, and my own whiff of receding youth and passing urbanity. I can't remember if we revealed nothing—or everything—to one another in the foyer, but after my mother ceremonially draped the living-room couch with a plastic bag so that I wouldn't stain it with the foulness of Manhattan, my father followed through with his usual heartfelt request: "*Nu, rasskazhi*" ("So, tell me").

I told them as much as I could about what had happened during the past two months, skirting Noah's death (my mother had so enjoyed meeting "such a handsome Jewish boy" at our NYU graduation) but emphasizing how well Eunice and I were doing, and how I still had 1,190,000 yuan in the bank. My mother listened carefully, sighed, and went off to work on a beet salad. When I asked my father about how it had been for them, he turned up FoxLiberty-Prime, which was showing the deliberations of the Israeli Knesset, with Rubenstein, still nominally employed as the Defense Secretary of whatever entity we are becoming, lecturing the all-Orthodox parliament on ways to fight Islamofascism, the men in black nodding sympathetically, some staring off into deeply sacred space, playing with their bottles of mineral water. On the other screen, FoxLiberty-Ultra—where the hell were they still broadcasting this stuff from?—featured three ugly white men yelling at a pretty black man from all directions, while the words "Gays to wed in NYC" flashed beneath them.

Pointing to FoxLiberty-Ultra, my father asked me: "Is it true they are letting *gomiki* marry in New York?"

My mother quickly darted out of the kitchen, a plate of beet salad in hand. "What? What did you say? They are letting *gomiki* marry now?"

"Go back to the kitchen, Galya!" my father shouted with a measure of his usual depressed vitality. "I am talking to my son!" I confessed that I did not know what was happening in my hometown, nuptial-wise, and that we really had other things to worry about, but my father wanted to share more of his opinions on the matter. "Mr. Vida," he said, gesturing in the direction of his Indian neighbor, "believes that *gomiki* are the most disgusting creatures in the world and should be castrated and shot. But I don't know. They say, *naprimer* ['for example'], that the famous Russian composer Tchaikovsky was a *gomik*. That *on soblaznil* ['he corrupted'] little boys, even the Tsar's own son! And that when he died it was the Tsar who had pressured him to make suicide. Maybe this is true, maybe it is not." My father sighed and brought one hand to his face. His tired brown eyes were marked with a sadness I had seen only once before—at my grandmother's funeral, when he had emitted a howl of such unknown, animalistic provenance, we thought it had come from the forest abutting the Jewish cemetery. "But for me," he said, breathing heavily, "it doesn't matter. You see, for a genius like Tchaikovsky I could forgive anything, *anything*!"

My father's arm was still around me, holding me in place, making me his. I no longer had any idea what he was talking about. A bewildered part of me wanted to say, "Papa, there's an armored jeep guarding the 99¢ store on Old Country Road and you're talking about *gomiki*?" But I kept quiet. Whom would it help if I spoke? I felt the sorrow that flowed in all directions in this house, sorrow for him, for them, for the three of us—Mama, Papa, Lenny. "Tchaikovsky," my father said, each heavy syllable eliciting an unquantifiable pain in his deep baritone voice. He raised his hand in the air and silently directed a movement, from the depressive Sixth Symphony perhaps. "Pyotr Ilyich Tchaikovsky," my father said, lost in reverence for the homosexual composer. "He has brought me so much joy."

By the time my mother called me down to dinner—after I had taken a breather upstairs and noticed the replacement of my father's essay on "The Joys of Playing Basketball" with a gleaming poster of the Israeli fortress of Masada—I was nearly in tears myself. The dinner table would usually be covered lengthwise with meats and fish, but today it was nearly empty—just beet salad, tomatoes and peppers from the garden, a plate of marinated mushrooms, and some slices of a suspiciously white bread.

My mother noticed my chagrin. "There is a deficit at the Waldbaum's, and anyway we are afraid of the Credit Poles," she said. "What if they are still on? What if they try to deport us? Sometimes Mr. Vida takes us in the truck, but otherwise it is very hard to find food."

And then a different kind of truth appealed to me, reminded me of how self-involved I was, how residually angry I had remained at the Abramovs and their difficult household. The transparency I had noticed in my parents earlier, the way they had melded into each other—it was simply a matter of looking closely at their bodies and their stunted movements.

My parents were starving.

I walked into the kitchen and checked the nearly bare pantry—potatoes from the back garden, canned peppers, marinated mushrooms, four sliced pieces of moldy white bread, two rusted tins of some kind of Bulgarian cod-in-a-can. "This is terrible," I said to them. "We have the jeeps here. Let me at least take you to Waldbaum's."

"No, no," they shouted in unison.

"Sit down," my father said. "There's beet salad. There's bread and mushrooms. You have brought Tagamet. What more do we need? We're old people. Soon we will die and be forgotten."

They knew exactly what to say. I had been kicked in the stomach, or so it seemed, for I was now clutching my relatively full belly, and every brand of concern coursed through my digestive tract.

"We're going to the Waldbaum's," I said. I raised my hand in preparation for their weak protests. The decisive son speaks. "We're not going to discuss this. You need food."

We crammed into one jeep, the other serving as a lead escort, Palatino's men flashing their weapons at a gang of miscreants crowded around what used to be the Friendly's restaurant but was now apparently the headquarters of some local militia. Was this what Russia looked like after the Soviet Union collapsed? I tried, unsuccessfully, to see the country around me not just through my father's eyes but through his *history*. I wanted to be a part of a meaningful cycle with him, a cycle other than birth and death.

While my mother carefully wrote out a list of supplies they needed, my father told me about a recent dream he had had. A few of the "Chinese swine" engineers at the laboratory where he used to work accuse him of releasing radiation into the air during his morning custodial rounds, he is about to be arrested, but in the end he is vindicated when two Russian women janitors show up from Vladivostok and pin the radiation leak on some Indians. "When I wake up, my lip is bleeding from fear," my father said, his gray head still trembling from the memory.

"They say that dreams often have secret meanings," I said.

"I know, I know," he said, waving his hand in the air dismissively. "Psychology."

I patted my father's knee, wanting to impart comfort. He was wearing denims, old Reebok sneakers that I had bequeathed him, an Ocean Pacific T-shirt with a fading iron-on of some young southern-Californian surfers showing off their boogie boards (also from the Lenny Abramov teenage collection), along with plastic sunglasses covered by what looked like an oil slick. He was, in his own way, magnificent. The last American standing.

We pulled into the strip mall where the Waldbaum's supermarket huddled next to a boarded-up nail salon and a former sushi place which now sold "WATER FROM CLEAN PLACE, 1 GALLON = 4 YUAN, BRING YOUR OWN CAN." As the jeep pulled up directly to the Waldbaum's door, my parents looked at me with great pride—here I was taking care of them, honoring them, a good son at last. I refrained from throwing myself around their necks in gratitude. Look at the happy family!

Inside the brown-and-cream-colored supermarket, the lights had been turned down to create an even sadder shopping environment than I had known in the heyday of Waldbaum's, although Enya was still being piped through the sound system, warbling about the flow of the Orinoco and the cruelly phrased possibility of sailing away. I was also struck by a row of ancient photographs showing the walleyed, balding produce and deli managers of years past, a Westbury combination of striving Southeast Asians and Hispanics, under the fascistic slogan "If it's good for you, it's good for Waldbaum's."

My father took me to see the empty shelf where the Tagamet pills used to be stocked. "*Pozorno*" ("It is shameful"), he said. "No one care about the sick or the old anymore."

My mother was standing in the baked-goods aisle, next to an old Italian woman, deep into an angry monologue about the Mix-n-Match butter-pound-cake and angel-food-cake combo, which was priced at an exorbitant eighteen yuan. "Let's get the cakes, Mama," I said, mindful of my mother's sweet tooth. "I'm paying for everything."

"No, Lyonitchka," she said. "You have to save for your own future. And for Eunice's, don't forget. At least let's look for the red-dot special."

"Let's see if there's any fresh produce around," I said. "You need to eat healthy. No artificial or spicy flavors. Otherwise, all the Tagamet in the world isn't going to help Papa."

But the fresh produce was in short supply; most of the good stuff had long been diverted to New York. We filled our carts with twenty-eight-ounce containers of cheese balls (a red-dot special, plus

20 percent off) and a lifetime supply of seltzer, which was effectively cheaper than the four-yuan "water from clean place" they were selling out of the sushi joint. I drove my cart up and down every aisle. The lobster cage ("Any Fresher and They'd Be Alive!") was not only empty, but missing a glass side. My mother bought more mops and brooms in Household Supplies, and I got some decent whole-wheat bread out of the bakery and bought ten pounds of lean turkey breast for my father. "Use the fresh tomatoes from your garden to make a sandwich with the turkey breast and whole-wheat bread," I instructed. "Mustard, not mayonnaise, because there's less cholesterol."

"Thank you, *sinotchek*" ("little son"), my father said.

"*Zabotishsia ty o nas*" ("You are taking care of us"), my mother said, tearing up a little as she stroked the head of a new mop.

I blushed and looked away, wanting their love, but also careful about not drawing too close to them, not wanting to be hurt again. Because where my parents are from, openness can also mean weakness, an invitation to pounce. Find yourself in their embrace and you might not find a way out.

I paid over three hundred yuan at the only working checkout counter, and helped my father load the bags into the jeep. As we were about to drive back to their house, a loud thump of an explosion echoed from the north. Palatino's men pointed their guns at the perfectly blue sky. My father grabbed my mother and held her like a real man could. "Nigerians," he said, pointing toward Suffolk County. "Don't worry, Galya. I beat them on the basketball court, I'll beat them now. I'll kill them with my two hands." He showed us the strong little hands that used to dunk balls into hoops on given Tuesdays and Thursdays.

"Why does everyone blame the Nigerians?" I blurted out. "How many Nigerians are there on this side of the ocean?"

My father laughed and reached up to stroke my hair. "Listen to our little liberal," he said, with that familiar Fox-Ultra bombast in his voice. "Maybe he is a secular progressive too?" My mother joined in the laughter, shaking her head at my silliness. He came over and grabbed my head with two hands, then kissed me moistly on the forehead. "Are you?" he shouted in mock seriousness. "Are you a secular progressive, Lyon'ka?"

"Why don't you ask Nettie Fine about it?" I said loudly and in English. "I haven't heard a word from her. Even after the äppäräti started working again. Why don't you ask your Rubenstein? He's done so well by you, you've lost all your savings and pension and now you're scared to walk past a Credit Pole. When he says 'the boat is full' he's talking about you, you know."

My father looked at me quizzically and chuckled. My mother said nothing. I cooled my emotions. What was the point? Underneath it all, my parents were scared. And I was scared for them. After a meager family dinner of turkey breast, beet salad, and cheese puffs, I spent a restless, sexless night huddled in the spotless downstairs bedroom, scented with apples, clean laundry, and every other manifestation of my mother's close attention. I felt lonely and tried to teen and verbal Eunice, but she didn't respond, which was odd. I GlobalTraced her progress throughout the day—as soon as I left, she had headed up to the Union Square Retail Corridor, then she continued to head up to the Upper West Side, and then her signal just disappeared. What on earth was she doing on the Upper West Side? Was she crazy enough to try to cross into Fort Lee over the George Washington Bridge and see her family? I became acutely worried for her and even thought of rustling up Palatino and heading back to the city.

But I couldn't deny my parents a full visit. There they stood in the morning, waiting for me by the landing with the same worried, submissive smiles that had carried them through half a lifetime in America, staring at me as if no one and nothing else existed in the world. The Abramovs. Tired and old, romantically mismatched, filled to the brim with hatreds imported and native, patriots of a disappeared country, lovers of cleanliness and thrift, tepid breeders of a single child, owners of difficult and disloyal bodies (hands professionally scalded with industrial cleansers and gnarled up with carpal tunnel), monarchs of anxiety, princes of an unspeakably cruel realm, Mama and Papa, Papa and Mama, *na vsegda, na vsegda, na vsegda,* forever and ever and ever. No, I had not lost the capacity to care—incessantly, morbidly, instinctually, counterproductively—for the people who had made of me the disaster known as Lenny Abramov.

Who was I? A secular progressive? Perhaps. A liberal, whatever that even means anymore, maybe. But basically—at the end of the busted rainbow, at the end of the day, at the end of the empire—little more than my parents' son.

HOW DO WE TELL LENNY?
FROM THE GLOBALTEENS ACCOUNT OF EUNICE PARK

OCTOBER 13

GOLDMANN-FOREVER *TO* EUNI-TARD:

Good morning, my sweet, sweet girl, my tender love, my life. Yesterday was so much fun, I can't believe the weekend is upon us and I've got to surrender you to our little friend. I'm counting 52.3 hours until I see you again, and I don't know what to do with myself! I'm about as complete without you as a leopard without his claws. I'm working on all the things you said too. My arms need to improve more than the rest of my body, they're the hardest to fix in some ways, the depleted muscle tone, etc. And I'm sorry if we didn't do enough of the good stuff. I have to pace myself for my heart, because genetically I've really been dealt a poor hand there. The Indians tell me that in the next two years I'm going to have my heart removed completely. Useless muscle. Idiotically designed. That's this year's big project at Post-Human Services, we're going to teach the blood *exactly* where to go and how fast to go and then we'll just let it do all the circulating. Call me heartless. Hahaha.

So Howard Shu (he says "hi" by the way) has been doing a lot of research and I think he's hit upon something. We need to get your parents better credentialed, so they're not just your average American immigrants with bad Credit. It's hard to get Norwegian papers, but there's a Chinese "Lao Wai" foreigner passport that gives you a lot of the same privileges, and you can even leave New York for six out of twelve months a year. He's trying to qualify your father as essential personnel, because the podiatrist quota in NYC hasn't been completely filled yet. The new IMF plan is very methodical about occupations. The problem is that in order to qualify your dad's going to have to get a New York address, either in Manhattan or Brownstone Brooklyn, and the cheapest non-Triplex stuff in Carroll Gardens is going to go for about 750,000 yuan. So what I'm proposing is that I buy a place for your family, and if your dad ever makes enough money he can pay me back. We can get a student visa for Sally, and I can grandfather you in. So to speak. Ha ha. Anyway, it's a good investment and I don't mind doing it, because I love you. I know you hate it when Lenny reads to you, and I hate reading too, but there's a great line by an old poet Walt Whitman: "Are you the New person drawn toward Me?" I used to think that all the time when I walked the streets of Manhattan, but I don't think that anymore, because now I have you.

I wanted to bring something up and I feel like it's not really any of my beeswax. I know you want your family safe, but in some ways, does it make sense to have your father here, so close to you and your sister? Maybe I'm old-school, but when you talk about him walking into the shower when Sally is around, or how you watched him drag your mother out of bed by her hair, well, I think some people would call that physical and psychological abuse. I know there are cultural factors involved, I just want you and your sister protected from a man who obviously can't control his behavior, and should be under supervision and taking medication. The lack of boundaries is one thing, but the violence sounds like it contravenes even Chinese basic law, forget about whatever hippie-dippy Scandinavian shit the Norwegians have. I hope you'll move into my place soon (or we can get a bigger place if you feel claustrophobic), and then I'll make sure no one ever touches or hurts you again.

Okay, my little empress penguin, looks like I'll be working through the weekend, more Staatling internal stuff, but every seventh minute I look up at the ceiling or down at the floor and picture your open, honest face and feel completely serene and completely in love.

EUNI-TARD *TO* EUNI-TARD:

I'm writing this for me. One day I want to look back at this day and make peace with what I'm about to do.

All my life has been about doubts. But there's no room for them now. I know I'm too young to have to make this kind of decision, but this is how things are.

I miss Italy sometimes. I miss being a complete foreigner and having no ties to anyone. America might be gone completely soon, but I was never really an American. It was all pretending. I was always a Korean girl from a Korean family with a Korean way of doing things, and I'm proud of what that means. It means that, unlike so many people around me, I know who I am.

Prof Margaux in Assertiveness Class said, "You are allowed to be happy, Eunice." What a stupid American idea. Every time I thought of killing myself in my dorm room I thought of what Prof Margaux said and just started howling with laughter. You're ALLOWED to be happy. Ha! Lenny always quotes this guy Froid who was a psychiatrist who said that the best we can do is turn all our crazy misery, all our parents bullshit, into common unhappiness. Sign me up.

I wake up next to Joshie feeling that way. But also with a little thrill. We were doing brushstrokes with M. Cohen and I couldn't believe the concentration on Joshie's face. The way his lower lip was just hanging there like a little boy's and he was breathing really carefully, like there was nothing more important in the world than brushstrokes. There's something powerful in being able to let go and focus on something that's completely outside yourself. I guess Joshie has had a lot of privilege in his life and he knows what to do with it.

And then he noticed I was looking at him, and he just smiled like a little kid and pulled his lip in and tried to look his age, which I don't think he can anymore. And I thought, Okay, I'm going to leave Lenny and I'm going to spend my life waking up next to Joshie, getting older every day, while he gets younger. There's something right about that. It's like my punishment. Morning, afternoon, night, sex, dinner, shopping, whatever it is we're doing, I don't feel turned off by Joshie and I don't feel the opposite. I just want to do brushstrokes with him and hear that even, even breathing. He has these old slippers that are perfectly arranged by his bed just so he can slip right into them first thing in the morning, but they're too big for him. He waddles around like an old man in them. And that's something I can fix. I can fix him. I'm so glad he can take criticism. First thing I HAVE to do is get him new slippers. I guess I'm like a lucky version of my mother with Joshie. Like Froid said, common unhappiness.

Lenny. Will he ever forgive me?

I feel like a recycling bin sometimes, with all these things passing through me from one person to another, love, hate, seduction, attraction, repulsion, all of it. I wish I were stronger and more secure in myself so that I could really spend my life with a guy like Lenny. Because he has a different kind of strength than Joshie. He has the strength of his sweet tuna arms. He has the strength of putting his nose in my hair and calling it home. He has the strength to cry when I go down on him. Who IS Lenny? Who DOES that? Who will ever open up to me like that again? No one. Because it's too dangerous. Lenny is a dangerous man. Joshie is more powerful, but Lenny is much more dangerous.

All I wanted to do was have my parents take complete responsibility for how fucked up I am. I wanted them to admit that they did wrong. But that doesn't matter to me now.

Common unhappiness, as the doctor said, but also common responsibility.

I can't just be an abused little girl anymore. I have to be stronger than my father, stronger than Sally, stronger than Mommy.

I'm sorry, Lenny.

I love you.

EUNI-TARD *TO* GOLDMANN-FOREVER:

It sounds like you're one busy bee, sweetheart. I'm so turned on when you work so hard, Joshie. There's nothing sexier than a hardworking man, that's how I was brought up, and that part of my parents I am NOT ashamed of. So many emotions are going through me right now. It's not just gratitude for what you've done for my family, it is a deep, deep love. Am I the New person drawn toward You? Yes, I am, Joshie. I sometimes see men and women who are beautiful on the street, but they're beautiful in such an obvious Media way. And you're the real thing. Don't worry about the sex, darling. I'm not some sex monster. Holding you in my arms, taking a shower with you, scrubbing you HARD with a loofah, picking out stuff to wear, cuddling on the couch, making those fat-free blueberry pancakes, those are the most fulfilling things I've ever done with anyone. Just being in the same room with you is arousing. I miss you so much. You do NOT have old man arms. You're much stronger than Lenny, and you have such soft, gorgeous lips. All I need you to do is keep your neck in good shape, because you are going to be going down there a lot! Hahaha.

Re: my parents, I sometimes feel like I tell you too much. I know it's my fault, I feel like I need to blab about them to everyone I love. Unloading about my life is like the only thing that keeps me from spending the day inside the refrigerator and adding to my FAT ass. I just wonder if I'm being fair to them and to you when I bring up what happened to me and Sally and my mom. There were good times too, you know. When I was in Tompkins Park right before the Rupture, my father asked me how I was. I know deep down inside he's a good person, he's just had a hard life is all and that makes me sad. Sometimes when I miss you, I feel sad the same way, like my whole life has been rushing toward you and I can't wait for us to be together.

Ugh, I was just watching a stream of this Jamaican guy who was being deported from New York and he was crying and his whole family was in tears and he was telling his daughter that he'd be back and that it was best for them to stay in the city and be safe. I thought I was going to break down in tears too. Did I tell you I used to volunteer with trafficked Albanian women in Rome? I wish we didn't have to deport anyone. And I can't believe you said they're going to clear out our co-op buildings. Lenny put so much money into this apartment and he's got all these books. And what are they going to do with the old people? Where are they going to move them? They'll die. Is there something you can do, sweetheart? Okay, Lenny's coming back home right now. I can hear him huffing and puffing. I gotta run. Have a great weekend, Joshie. You're all I think about, dream about. I trust you and need you so much. No one has ever been so wonderful to me.

OCTOBER 21

CHUNG.WON.PARK *TO* EUNI-TARD:

Eunhee,

Today we got application for Lao Wai passport thank to you! Mr. Shu even call us and tell us that it just formal application and we already guarantee to move New York. Daddy and me so proud of you. Smart daughter! We always know. Even in Catholic when you get good grade and then go Elderbird. Remember how art teacher in school praise your spatial skill and we think she say SPECIAL skill and we always wonder what it is? ☺ We saw your new friend Joshie Goldman, and he is very handsome for old man much younger look than Roommate Lenny. We are proud also you have such important friend. Lenny he is not able to help you. He is Russian. Maybe he is communist? All Russians in old time were communist before oil. But if you like older man we know in Toronto Mrs. Choi's son who is 31, tall and very musheesuh and work good job in medical tool industry. Thank you Eunhee for thinking of your family. Please forgive you do not understand my English. God bless you always.

Love,

Mommy

OCTOBER 22

SALLYSTAR: I got the student visa. I don't know what to say, Eunice, just that I love you. I know you'll always have my back, and not just because you're my older sister. You don't want to hear this, but I pray for you every day. I pray that you're happy and at peace with yourself. Remember how happy we were as kids when we'd get H-Mart ddok and mandoo after church? Remember how you'd stuff your face and cry later because you thought you gained weight?

EUNI-TARD: You don't have to thank me, Sally. I'm just glad you're safe. I can't believe you had to hide in the basement for a whole week. I can't believe what happened to the Kim's daughter, what's her name?

SALLYSTAR: I don't think I want to talk about that right now.

EUNI-TARD: I just feel guilty that I wasn't there with you.

SALLYSTAR: It's the kind of thing that makes you focus. And now I know why I'm alive. For you and for Mommy and for Daddy. I'm going to be quiet, I'm not going to act out Politically, and I'm going to make sure that nothing like what happened to Sarah Kim is going to happen to any of us. You really are a "roll" model for me, Eunice, just like Mommy says.

EUNI-TARD: Are you going back to Barnard?

SALLYSTAR: They're closing Barnard for the year, but that's fine. I have to take more Mandarin and Norwegian classes all year long anyway.

EUNI-TARD: You'll do great, Sally. You can do anything you set your mind to.

SALLYSTAR: What about you?

EUNI-TARD: Huh?

SALLYSTAR: What do you think you want to do next with your life?

EUNI-TARD: I don't know. Joshie can get me a great Retail job, but I might do art-finance college in London.

SALLYSTAR: So things are pretty serious with him? Have you told Lenny yet?

EUNI-TARD: No.

SALLYSTAR: You shouldn't lie to him anymore, Eunice. I never told you this but I think Lenny's a very nice man, the one time I met him anyway. He really tried with Mom and Dad.

EUNI-TARD: I know. You don't have to tell me. But he's not perfect. He only cares about me when I'm pissed at him. Anyway, I'm sure he'll find another Korean girl, like the hundred he's already dated. A real nomo cha-keh girl, not like me. Oh, and I saw some Images of his exes broke-ass faces. Lenny's one of those white guys who can't tell a good-looking Asian girl from an ugly one. We all look the same to them.

SALLYSTAR: It's none of my business, but I think you should be really kind to Lenny, even if you break up with him. You want to be fair to him.

EUNI-TARD: I know, Sally. I'll be honest. I don't know if I CAN break up with him. I still love him. He's just so clueless. My poor Leonardo Dabramovinci. He's sitting next to me now and trimming his toenails, smiling at me for no good reason. I don't know why, but I think that's really sad when he smiles like that. And I get kind of angry too, that he can still have that kind of effect on me.

OCTOBER 24

GOLDMANN-FOREVER *TO* EUNI-TARD:

Eunice, we have to talk. I know you love me, but sometimes you really don't treat me well. One day you tell me I'm "the bestest boyfriend ever" and the next day you're not sure, you want us to take some time off from each other, you want to relax things a little. And that makes me feel like I'm some kind of needy asshole, pushing you to tell Lenny about us, pushing you to move in with me, pushing you to take this relationship as seriously as I take it. You seem to get me confused with Joshie Goldmann the high-profile guy who's trying to change the world and whom everyone worships. I'm a different man with you. I'm just a human being who's in love and nothing more.

I don't like it when you make me feel guilty about all the old people who are going to be thrown out of Lenny's buildings. That's not my department, Eunice. I can help you with your parents and your sister, but I can't exactly keep over a hundred unneeded people in New York. The IMF calls the tune now. I think I've done about all I can for them over the last months, sending down food and water.

Look, I know I'm asking you to take enormous steps, and I know Lenny represents a kind of "emotional" safety net, and that's why you're sticking up for him. But don't forget that I'm ultimately the one that can assure your safety. And I know that Lenny pursued you in this ridiculous overbearing way and I don't want to repeat that mistake. Though I may not act it sometimes, let's not forget that I'm seventy. And one thing I can tell you from my experience, Eunice, is that you'll only get one youth. And you better spend it with someone who can maximize it for you, who can make you feel good and cared for and loved and, in the long run, someone who won't die a long time before you, like Lenny will. (Statistically, given that he's a Russian male and you're an Asian female, he'll be gone about twenty years before you.)

Am I scared of how fast things are going with us? You better believe it! I look at us in the mirror sometimes and I can't believe who I am. Every week we come closer together, and then every week you do something to make me feel like I'm not deserving of you. You push me away. Why? Is it just in your nature to be cruel to men? Then maybe you can change that part of your nature before it's too late.

I think about you all the time, Eunice. Sometimes you're the only thing in this world that still makes sense to me. Now YOU have to start thinking of ME. I'm up here on the good old Upper West Side, thumping my chest and making sad ape sounds and dreaming of the day when you will treat me the way I deserve to be treated. We've got many years ahead of us, my sweet bumblebee. Let's not waste a moment of precious time. Sogni d'oro, as you like to say. Golden dreams to you.

FOREVER YOUNG

FROM THE DIARIES OF LENNY ABRAMOV

NOVEMBER 10

Dear Diary,

Today I've made a major decision: *I am going to die.*

Nothing of my personality will remain. The light switch will be turned off. My life, my entirety, will be lost forever. I will be nullified. And what will be left? Floating through the ether, tickling the empty belly of space, alighting over farms outside Cape Town, and crashing into an aurora above Hammerfest, Norway, the northernmost city of this shattered planet—my data, the soupy base of my existence uptexted to a GlobalTeens account. Words, words, words.

You, dear diary.

This will be my last entry.

A month ago, mid-October, a gust of autumnal wind kicked its way down Grand Street. A co-op woman, old, tired, Jewish, fake drops of jade spread across the little sacks of her bosom, looked up at the pending wind and said one word: "Blustery." Just one word, a word meaning no more than "a period of time characterized by strong winds," but it caught me unaware, it reminded me of how language was once used, its precision and simplicity, its capacity for recall. Not cold, not chilly, blustery. A hundred other blustery days appeared before me, my young mother in a faux-fur coat standing before our Chevrolet Malibu Classic, her hands protectively over my ears because my defective ski hat couldn't be pulled down to cover them, while my father cursed and fumbled with his car keys. The streams of her worried breath against my face, the excitement of feeling both cold and protected, exposed to the elements and loved at the same time.

"It *is* blustery, ma'am," I said to the old co-op woman. "I can feel it in my bones." And she smiled at me with whatever facial muscles she still had in reserve. We were communicating with words.

I returned from Westbury to find Eunice in one piece, but the Vladeck Houses turned into shells, their orange carapaces burned black. I stood in front of the houses with a posse of still-employed Media guys in expensive sneakers, as we evaluated the jagged lines of windows past, made poetry out of a lone Samsung air conditioner dangling back and forth on its cord in the shallow river breeze. Where were the project dwellers? The Latinos who had once made us so happy to say we were living in "downtown's last diverse neighborhood," where had they gone?

A Staatling truck full of five-jiao men pulled up. The men clambered out and were immediately presented with tool belts, which they eagerly, almost happily, tied around their shrunken waists. A rural log truck pulled up behind the first. But these weren't logs stacked five to a row, these were Credit Poles, blunt and round, lacking even the adornments of their predecessors. They were up within a day, a new slogan billowing from their masts, the outline of the new Parthenon-shaped IMF headquarters in Singapore, and the words:

"Life Is Richer, Life Is Brighter! Thank You, International Monetary Fund!"

I met Grace for a picnic lunch in the park. She was sitting on a comfortable rock outcropping in the Sheep Meadow, a glacier-era chaise longue. Less than half a year ago, the blood of a hundred had washed over the neighboring pillows of grass. In a white cotton dress loosely draping her shoulders, in a perfect curve of hair draping the concentration of her face, deeply pregnant yet elegant in repose, she seemed, from afar, a vision of something incomprehensibly right in the world. I walked toward Grace slowly, gathering my thoughts. Now I would have to figure out how to adjust our friendship to include someone else, someone even smaller and more innocent than her mother.

I could see the child already. Whatever her nature would impress upon him (I was told it would be a boy), he was sure to have at least some of Vishnu's furriness, his bumbling nature, his kindness and naïveté. It was strange for me to consider a child the product of *two* people. My parents, for all their temperamental differences, were so alike that at times I consider them a uni-parent, made heavy with child by a Yiddish Holy Ghost. What if Eunice and I had a child together? Would it make her happier? She seemed, in recent days, distant from me. Sometimes even when she was viewing her favorite anorexic models on AssLuxury, it would appear Eunice's gaze was boring right through them into some new dimension devoid of hip and bone.

Grace and I drank watermelon juice and ate freshly sliced kimbap from 32nd Street, the pickled daikon radish crunching smartly between our teeth, rice and seaweed coating our mouths with sea and starch. Normalcy, that's what we were going for. After some jokey preliminaries, she put on her serious face. "Lenny," she said, "there's something a little sad I have to tell you."

"Oh, no," I said.

"Vishnu and I got permanent residency in Stability. We're moving to Vancouver in three weeks."

I felt the rice expanding in my throat and coughed into my hand. I beheld the terms I was given. *Grace.* The woman who had loved me the most. Had listened to me for the past fifteen years, me with all that melancholy and dysthymia. *Vancouver.* A northern city, far away.

Grace's arms were around me, and I breathed in her conditioner and her impending motherhood. She was abandoning me. Did she *still* love me? Even Chekhov's ugly Laptev had an admirer, a woman named Polina, "very thin and plain, with a long nose." After Laptev marries the young and beautiful Julia, Polina tells him:

"And so you are married. . . . But don't be uneasy; I'm not going to pine away. I shall be able to tear you out of my heart. Only it's annoying and bitter to me that you are just as contemptible as every one else; that what you want in a woman is not brains or intellect, but simply a body, good looks, and youth. . . . Youth!"

I wanted Grace to hiss similar words at me, to confront me once again for loving someone so young and inexperienced, and to make me consider being with her instead of Eunice. But, of course, she didn't.

And that made me angry.

"So how did you guys get Canadian residency?" I asked her, not even bothering to modulate the acidity of my tone. "I thought it was impossible. The waiting list is over twenty-three million."

"We got lucky," she said. "And I have a degree in econometrics. That helps."

"Gracie," I pressed on, "Noah told me a while ago that Vishnu collaborated with the ARA, with the Bipartisans."

She didn't say anything, ate her kimbap. A man and woman conversing in a rolling foreign language walked behind a dirty mountain of a Saint Bernard whose tongue was dragging along the ground from the Indian-summer heat. Behind a scrim of trees a group of five-jiao men were digging a ditch. One had clearly disobeyed, because his leader was now approaching him bearing something glinty and long. The five-jiao guy was on his knees, his hands covering his long, matted blond hair. I tried to shield Grace's view with my plastic cup of watermelon juice and prayed there wouldn't be violence. "I'm sure it's not true," I continued, picking grass off my jeans as if this were any other conversation. "I know Vishnu's a good guy."

"I don't want to talk about these things," Grace said. "You know, the three of you were always pretty strange friends. *The boys.* Like in books. With all that swagger and camaraderie. But that was never going to work. When you were apart you were real people, but when you were together you were like a cartoon."

I sighed and put my head in my hands.

"I'm sorry," Grace said. "I know you loved Noah. That's no way to speak of the dead. And I don't know what happened with the ARA and who did what. I just know that there's no future for us here. And there's no future for you either, when you think about it. Why don't you come to Canada with us?"

"I don't seem to have your connections," I said, too roughly.

"You have a business degree," she said. "That could put you at the front of the list. You should try to get to the Quebec border. You can take an armored Fung Wah bus. If you make it across legally, the Canadians have a special category. I think it's something like 'Landed Immigrants.' We can hire a lawyer on the other side to get to work for you."

"They'll never let Eunice in," I said. "Her education is worthless. Major in Images, minor in Assertiveness."

"Lenny," Grace said. Her face was near mine, and her vocal breathing kept pace with the exhale of the wind and the trees. Her hand was upon my cheek, and all the worries of my life were cupped and held within. A dull thud echoed behind the trees, metal connecting with scalp, but there was no whimper, just the distant, mirage-like sight of a body fully lowering itself to the ground. "Sometimes," she said, "I think you're not going to make it."

Late October. A few days after my lunch with Grace, Eunice verballed me at work and told me to come down immediately. "They're throwing us all out," she said. "Old people, everyone. That asshole." I did not have time to ascertain who the asshole was. I hijacked a company Town Car and raced downtown to find my inglorious red-brick hulk of a building surrounded by flat-bottomed young men in khakis and oxfords, and three Wapachung Contingency armored personnel carriers, their crews lounging peaceably beneath an elm tree, guns at their feet. My aged fellow cooperators had filled the ample park-like grounds around our buildings with their helter-skelter belongings, heavy on decrepit credenzas, deflated black leather couches, and framed photographs of their chubby sons and grandsons attacking river trout.

I found a young guy in the standard-issue chinos and an ID that read "Staatling Property Relocation Services." "Hey," I said, "I work for Post-Human Services. What the fuck? I live in one of these units. Joshie Goldmann's my boss."

"Harm Reduction," he said, giving me an actual pout with those fat red lips.

"Excuse me?"

"You're too close to the river. Staatling's tearing these down tomorrow. In case of flooding. Global warming. Anyways, Post-Human has space for its employees uptown."

"That's bull crap," I said. "You're just going to build a bunch of Triplexes here. Why lie, pal?"

He walked away from me, and I followed through the jumble of old women propelling themselves out of the lobby on walkers, some of the more able-bodied babushkas pushing the wheelchair-bound, a collective crooning, heavier on depression than outrage, forming a kind of aural tent over the exile-in-progress. All the younger, angrier people who lived in the co-ops were probably at work. That's why they were throwing us out at noon.

I was ready to grab the young Staatling guy's head and to start bashing it against the cement of my beloved building, my homely refuge, my simple home. I could feel my father's anger finding a righteous target. There was something Abramovian in this buzz in my head, in the continual teetering between aggression and victimhood. "The Joys of Playing Basketball." Masada. Grabbing the young man by one skinny shoulder, I said to him, "Wait a second, friend. You don't own this place. This is *private property.*"

"Are you kidding, Grandpa?" he said, easily throwing off my

almost-forty-year-old grip. "You touch me again, I swear I'll ass-plug you."

"Okay," I said. "Let's talk about this like human beings."

"I *am* talking like a human being. You're the one being a bitch. You've got one day to get all your shit out or it's going down with the building."

"I've got books in there."

"Who?"

"Printed, bound media artifacts. Some of them very important."

"I think I just refluxed my lunch."

"Okay, what about *them*?" I said, pointing to my elderly neighbors, shuffling out into the sunlight, widows in straw boaters and sundresses with perhaps but a few years to live.

"They're being moved into abandoned housing in New Rochelle."

"New Rochelle? Abandoned housing? Why not just take them straight to the abattoir? You know these old people can't make it outside New York."

The young man rolled his eyes. "I can't be having this conversation," he said.

I ran into my familiar lobby, with the twin pines of the cooperative movement inlaid into the shiny, carefully waxed floor. Old people were sitting atop tied-up bundles, awaiting instructions, awaiting deportation. Inside the elevator, two uniformed Wapachung men were carrying out an old woman, Bat Mitzvah–style, on the very chair she had been sitting on, her puffy, sniffling visage too much for me to bear. "Mister, mister," some of her friends were chanting, withered arms reaching out to me. They knew me from the worst of the Rupture, when Eunice used to come and wash them down, hold their hands, give them hope. "Can't you do something, mister? Don't you know somebody?"

I could not help them. Could not help my parents. Could not help Eunice. Could not help myself. I ignored the elevators and ran up the six flights of stairs, stumbling, half alive, into the noontime light flooding my 740 square feet. "Eunice, Eunice!" I cried.

She was in her sweatpants and Elderbird T-shirt, heat rising from her body. The floor was covered with cardboard boxes she had assembled, some of them half filled with books. We hugged each other and I tried to kiss her at length, but she pushed me away and pointed to the Wall of Books out in the living room. She made me understand that she would put together more of these boxes and that I was to continue packing them with books. I went back to the living room to face the couch where Eunice and I had made love for the second and third time (the bedroom had won the first round). I walked up to the bookcase, picked up an armload of volumes, some of the Fitzgeraldian and Hemingwayesque stuff I had swallowed along with an imaginary glass of Pernod as an NYU undergrad; the musty, brittle Soviet books (average price one ruble, forty-nine kopecks) my father had given me as a way to bridge the unfathomable gap between our two existences; and the Lacanian and feminist volumes that were supposed to make me look good when potential girlfriends came over (like anybody even cared about texts by the time I got to college).

I dumped the books into the cardboard boxes, Eunice quickly moving over to repack them, because I was not placing them in an optimal way, because I was useless at manipulating objects and making the most out of the least. We worked in silence for the better part of three hours, Eunice directing me and scolding me when I made a mistake, as the Wall of Books began to empty and the boxes began to groan with thirty years' worth of reading material, the entirety of my life as a thinking person.

Eunice. Her strong little arms, the claret of labor in her cheeks. I was so thankful to her that I wanted to cause her just a tiny bit of harm and then to beg for forgiveness. I wanted to be wrong in front of her, because she too should feel the high morality of being right. All the anger that had built against her during the past months was dissipating. Instead, with each armful of books tumbling into their cardboard graves, I found myself focusing on a new target. I felt the weakness of these books, their immateriality, how they had failed to change the world, and I didn't want to sully myself with their weakness anymore. I wanted to invest my energies in something more fruitful and conducive to a life that mattered.

Instead of returning to the Wall of Books for a fresh batch, I walked into one of Eunice's closets. I went through her intimates, peered at their labels, mouthed what I read as if I were reciting a poem: 32A, XS, JuicyPussy, TotalSurrender, sky-blue gossamer velvet. In the shoe closet, I plucked two glittering pairs of shoes and a lesser set of some kind of shoe/sneaker hybrid that Eunice was fond of wearing to the park, and I carried them into the kitchen. I thrust them at Eunice with a smile. "We don't have that many boxes left," I said.

She shook her head. "Just the books," she said. "That's all we have room for. They're going to take us to a place uptown because you work for Joshie." She put down her packing tape and poured me a cup of coffee out of the French press, garnishing it with soy milk from what would soon no longer be my refrigerator.

"At least let's make sure we get all your Mason Pearson hairbrushes," I said, taking a sip, then passing it to her. She brushed her thick mane in acknowledgment. We kissed, two mouths, coffee breath. Her eyes were closed but I had opened mine; "No cheating!" she used to cry out when I would do that. I pressed my nose into the galaxy of freckles, some orange, some brown, some planet-sized, others the fine floating detritus of space. "How am I going to let you go?" I said.

She pulled away. "What do you mean?" she said.

"Nothing." What *did* I mean? There was heat in my temples, but my feet were ice. The elevators were full of old people and their stuff, but we managed to get our boxes downstairs to the lobby, Eunice making sure to help the older people with their sacks of medicine, their tangles of hosiery, and all those gilt-edged family photos of big and little Jews together. We kicked my boxed library out to the building's front lawn and toward the Hyundai Town Car.

The first of November. Or thereabouts. We were moved into two rooms on the Upper East Side, a boxy 1950s nurses' residence on

York Avenue that resembled a jigsaw puzzle left out in the rain. Other displaced Staatling-Wapachung youngsters shared the hallways, but once they peeked in and saw that every square inch of our two rooms was stuffed with books, they went into high avoidance mode, even skirting Eunice, their coeval in every way.

On the day Media showed the Grand Street co-op buildings, my sunburned brick beauties, coming down in a cloud of red bricks and gray ash, I started crying, and instead of comforting me Eunice became angry. She said when I got that emotional it reminded her of her dad whenever something bad happened to him, his loss of control, although her father would get violent instead of sad. I looked at her through swollen eyes and said, "Don't you see the distinction between the two things? Violent and sad."

She flared the dead smile at me. "I feel like I don't know you sometimes," she whispered in a way that was hardly a whisper.

"Eunice," I said. "My apartment. My home. My investment. I'll be forty in two weeks and I have nothing."

I wanted her to say, "You have me," but it was not forthcoming. I clenched into myself and waited for an hour, knowing her hatred of me would eventually change to a shade of pity. It did. "Come on, tuna-brain," she said. "Let's go to the park. I have an hour before work."

We walked into the warm, pleasant day hand in hand. I watched her. I reveled in the mallard way she threw her feet forward, the pedestrian awkwardness of the born southern Californian. I saw myself in the twin spheres of her sunglasses. I grasped the reflected smile on my own face. How many people are there on this earth who have never known what I had known in the past half a year? Not just a beautiful woman's love but her *inhabitance*.

Central Park was filled with people of at least two castes, tourists and occupiers, enjoying the day. The trees held fast, but the cityscape was in constant flux. The skyscrapers framing the lower half of the park looked tired of their history, stripped of commerce, the executive upper floors staring down into empty lobbies and concrete plazas where lamb kebabs and hummus spreads once fueled the world's most storied white-collar workforce. Soon they would be replaced with curt, smart residential units with Arab, Asian, and Norse designations.

"Do you remember," I said to Eunice, "the day you came back from Rome? It was June 17. Your plane landed at one-twenty. And the first thing we did was take a walk in the park. I think that was around six. It was getting dark, and we saw the first LNWI camp. The bus driver who later got killed. Aziz's Army. Whatever happened to that? Jesus. Everything changes so fast. Anyway, we took the subway uptown. I paid for business class. I was *so* trying to impress you. Do you remember?"

"I remember, Lenny," she said, briskly. "How could you think I would ever forget that, tuna?" We bought an ice cream from a man dressed like a nineteenth-century carnival barker, but it melted in our hands before we even opened it. Not wanting to waste the five yuan, we drank it straight from the paper wrap, then wiped the patches of chocolate and vanilla from each other's faces.

"Remember," I tried again, "the first place we went to when we came to the park?" I took her by the hand and led her past the throng-choked Bethesda Fountain, the *Angel of the Waters* statue, lily in hand, blessing the tiny lakes below. Once the familiar Cedar Hill was in our sights, she turned around so quickly my arm cracked within its socket. "What's the matter?" I said. But she was already taking me away from my nostalgia, walking toward safer emotional climes.

"What is it, honey?" I tried again.

"Don't, Lenny," she said. "You don't have to keep trying."

"We can get out of here!" I almost shouted. "We can go to Vancouver. We can get Stability-Canada residency."

"Why, so you can be with your *Grace*?"

"No! Because this place . . ." I gestured a full two hundred degrees with one spastic arm, trying to encompass the totality of what had become of my city. "We won't survive together in this place, Eunice. No one can anymore. Only people with blood on their hands."

"So dramatic," Eunice said. The way she said it, her tone not just compassionless but assured, made me fear the worst. She was in possession of something I didn't know about, or maybe knew too well.

We went in a southerly direction via a cemented road, avoiding the Sheep Meadow, where we had taken our first long kiss in New York, and all the other snug, green, tender-hearted places where we had found love. At Central Park South, before the row of reconfigured Triplexes that used to be the mansard-roofed Plaza Hotel, surrounded by the piles of horse shit that demarcated the grass and trees from the difficult city, we both looked back at the park.

"I have to go," she said.

"Let me take you to work." I stood there, not wanting to lose a minute with her, feeling the end drawing near. "Look, the cabs are back! Hallelujah! Let's get one. My treat."

I let her go at Elizabeth Street, at the Retail place where, courtesy of Joshie's connections, Eunice now sold recyclable leather wristbands featuring avant-garde representations of decapitated Buddhas and the words RUPTURE NYC for two thousand yuan apiece. I hid behind the trunk of an exhausted urban tree and watched. She worked alongside another girl, a dark-haired and voluptuous member of Boston's Irish diaspora, and the store's manager, a much older woman who intermittently showed up to stick her finger in the chests of her underlings and to growl at them in Argentine-accented English. I watched Eunice work—diligently sweeping the store with a lovely Thai straw broom, anticipating the questions of the adventurous Chinese and French tourists who stopped by, and parrying them with a toothy smile, tallying up the sales on an old äppärät at the end of the day, and then, when the last yuan and euro were accounted for, waiting for the store's shutters to close so that she could stop smiling and put on her usual face, the face of a grave and unmitigated displeasure.

A Town Car pulled up to the curb, aggressively stubbing its nose between two parked cars. A man sprang out from the back seat, powerful legs carrying him into the store. Was it him? The back of the head, shorn, globular, rosy. A cashmere sport coat, a little too formal and expensive. The gait? That uncertain balance that had first made me fall for him? I wasn't sure. But so what? So what if he had come to see her? He had got her the job after all. He was just checking up on his investment. In the store I saw her speaking to the man, looking up at him. Those eyes. When they took in important information they narrowed and refused to blink. Then there was the tilt of the chin. Worshipful.

I went to a neighboring bar, which boasted some kind of idiotic Gallic theme, and began to drink with some assholes, one of whom also had parents from the former Soviet Union and was also named Lyonya in Russian and Lenny in English. He was a gemologist with both Belgian and HolyPetroRussia citizenship, a big guy with oddly delicate hands and the kind of obvious humor and natural rapport that had always been denied me. The night ended with my doppel-gänger punching me twice in the stomach, like the older brother I never had—coincidentally, we had argued about the role of family in our lives—and then graciously putting me into a cab, from which I alighted directly onto an innocent Upper East Side hedge outside the former nurses' dormitory where we were housed, and there, amidst the early-November gloom, enjoyed a brief coma, my first real sleep in weeks.

Fall arrived, the Indian summer finally at an end, the damaged city straining to regain lost glory. Along those lines, my employers were to throw a shindig to welcome the visiting members of the Politburo Standing Committee of the Chinese People's Capitalist Party. The event would be held at the Triplex of one of our Staatling board members, and would double, trendily, as a kind of art opening.

Eunice and I woke up late on the day of the party, and she crawled on top of me and pressed her rib cage into my face and started to close the last juncture between us. It had been a while. The past week, I had been too sad even to think of physical love, and our new gray surroundings were too depressing. "Euny," I said. "Baby." I tried to turn her around, to go down on her, because that's what I do best, because I wasn't sure I could deal with seeing her morning face so close to mine, the slight imperfections of sleep around the eyes, the unedited private version, *my* Eunice Park. But she clasped her legs around my swollen torso, and we were instantly together, two lovers on a tiny bed surrounded exclusively by boxes of books, weak light from the square porthole of a window illuminating nothing about us, save for the fact that we were one.

"I can't do this," I remember saying to myself in the mirror a few minutes later, while Eunice fiddled with the lousy shower. She grabbed my hand, took me inside the bath, and soaped up the great twin confluences of my chest and pubic hair. I tried to wash her down too, but she had her own way of doing it, gingerly and with a loofah. Then I did some things wrong with my soap and Cetaphil skin cleanser and she re-did them for me. She put a great mess of conditioner into what's left of my mane and stroked it alive. How vulnerable her body looked under the water; how translucent. "I can't do this," I said once more.

"It's okay, Lenny," she said, looking away from me. She clambered out of the shower. "Breathe," she said. "Breathe for me."

The art opening/Chinese welcoming party was more formal than I had thought. I guess I should have read the invite more carefully and dressed in something hipper than the dress shirt and slacks I've been trotting out since I was a white-collar dork at age twenty. I can't remember the name of the featured artist (John Mamookian? Astro Piddleby?), but I was moved by his work. He had done a series of extreme satellite zoom-ins of the deadly conditions in parts of the middle and the south of our country. The canvases were these rustling silky things, hung like meat off two or three hooks that descended from the hundred-foot-tall ceilings of the Triplex, and the works actually fluttered a tiny bit when people walked by, so that their presence next to you felt like that of a friend with a wisp of a secret.

Dead is dead, we know where to file another person's extinction, but the artist purposely zoomed in on the living, or, to be more accurate, the forced-to-be-living and the soon-to-be-dead. Grainy close-ups of people using people in ways I had never openly considered, not because murder doesn't run through my veins, but because I grew up in an era when the baroque was safely held at bay. An old man from Wichita without eyes, with the eyes physically removed, with one of the eyeholes being forced open by a laughing young man. A woman on a bridge, naked, frizzy-haired, something of our former civilization represented by an ancient NPR tote bag at her feet, a smashed-in nose atop a bleeding mouth, forced to hold her arms up as something trickled from one armpit and a whole crowd of men all wearing these makeshift uniforms (on which one could see the insignia of a former pizza-delivery service) cheering blatantly around her, assault weapons pointed at her nakedness, an almost bohemian joy on their unshaven faces. All the works had these disarming titles, like *St. Cloud, Minnesota, 7:00 a.m.,* which made them even worse, even scarier. There was one called *The Birthday Party, Phoenix,* with five adolescent girls, anyway, I don't want to talk about this anymore, but these works were amazing to see—real art with a documentary purpose.

The Triplex was really one Triplex on top of another on top of another, each twisted at a forty-five-degree angle from the one below, like three carefully stacked bricks—essentially, a minor skyscraper—and then cantilevered over the East River, so that the destroyers of the visiting People's Liberation Army Navy passed by at eye level, and you could almost reach over and touch the surface-to-air missile batteries glistening like tins of mint candy on their raised decks. About half of the Triplex was the living space carved out from the middle of the three Triplexes to form a busy souk-like area beneath the enormous skylight. It was roughly the size of the main hall in Grand Central Station, I was told. The space had been entirely cleared of furniture (or maybe this is how it always was), except for those frightening artworks shimmering at shoulder level and these little transparent cubes, which once you sat upon them filled with a red or yellow radiance, in deference to the Chinese flag and our guests. The place was so flooded with natural light that the distinction between indoors and outdoors no longer mattered, and at times I felt I was standing in a glass cathedral with the roof blown off.

I wanted to congratulate the artist on his work, that's how strongly I felt about it, and to recommend a trip out to my parents' Westbury so that he could see a different, more hopeful take on post-Rupture America. But they had this gimmicky thing going on, where, any time someone approached the artist whom he didn't know or didn't like the looks of, these spikes shot up from the floor all around him and you had to back away. He was actually a nice-looking guy, kind of square-jawed but with something milky, almost Midwestern, in his eyes, and he was wearing this cougar-print shirt and an old-school pinstriped Armani jacket which was festooned with random numbers made out of masking tape. He was busy talking to a wildly emotive post-American doyenne dressed in a cheongsam covered with dragons and phoenixes. The moment I approached them, the spikes shot out from the floor around him, and some of the serving girls in Onionskins who were standing next to the artist just gave me the old familiar look that denoted I was not a human being. *Oh well,* I thought. At least the art was great.

A lot of young Media people were hanging around one another protectively, clusters of boys and sometimes girls in proper suits and dresses, trying to impress their betters but clearly lost in the immensity of the place. Anyway, they were just so happy to be there, to be fed, to drink their rum and Tsingtaos, to be a part of society, and to avoid the five-jiao lines. I wondered if they had ever heard of Noah or knew how he had died. Like all the Media people left in the city, they were wearing blue badges handed out by Staatling-Wapachung that read "We Do Our Part."

The Staatling-Wapachung bigwigs were dressed like young kids, a lot of vintage Zoo York Basic Cracker hoodies from the 2000s, and tons of dechronification, making me think they were actually their own children, but my äppärät informed me that most of them were in their fifties, sixties, or seventies. Sometimes I saw someone who I thought had been one of my Intakes, and I tried to say hi, but they could not really comprehend me in this glamorous context.

I noticed that none of our clients or our directors wore äppäräti, only the servants and Media folk. Howard Shu had told me that more than once: The truly powerful don't need to be ranked. It made me feel conscious of the shiny, warbling pebble around my neck. I passed by some Media twentysomethings streaming at one another and overheard the little tidbits of verballing that always depressed me. "Did you know November is bike week?" "There's nothing wrong with her except she's completely fucked up." "When they say '12 *p.m.*' does that mean noon or midnight?"

Next to a cluster of StatoilHydro execs, ruddy elongated Norwegians and upper-caste Indians as tall as Norwegians, I spotted Eunice and her sister, Sally, talking to Joshie. As I began to make my way over to them, I passed one of the pieces showing a dead man perched upon the family couch in Omaha, a guy about my age, part Native American by the looks of him, with his face creeping slightly off his skull and the eyes eerily silenced, as if they had just been erased ("an interesting narrative strategy," someone was saying). The picture was no less harrowing than anything else around me, the guy was mercifully *dead,* but for some reason I became agitated just looking at it, and my tongue went dry, sticking painfully to the roof of my mouth. I did what everyone eventually did: looked away.

I want to talk about their clothes. This seems important to me. Joshie was wearing a cashmere sport coat, wool tie, and cotton dress shirt, all JuicyPussy4Men—a slightly more formal approximation of the same clothes Eunice had chosen for me. She was wearing a French-blue two-piece Chanel bouclé suit with a faux-pearl center and knee-high leather boots, so that all of her was concealed except for the tiny glow of her sharp kneecaps. She looked less like a woman than a gift. Sally was also overdressed for the occasion, a pinstriped suit and the pinprick of a golden cross around the soft pad of her neck. I noticed the beginnings of two hard-won laugh lines, and a chin dominated by a single disarming dimple. When I approached them, both sisters stopped talking to Joshie and put their hands to their mouths. And then, apropos of nothing, I realized what was bothering me about the picture of the dead guy on the couch in Omaha. At the corner of the work, beyond a scattering of youthful personal effects heavy on string instruments and obsolete laptops, a bitch lay dead, a German shepherd shot point-blank, a lightning bolt of blood spilling across the warped living-room floor. A puppy of negligible weeks, maybe days, had staked its front paws on the dead animal's exposed stomach, astride her still-swollen teats. You couldn't see the puppy's face, but you could tell its ears were alert and its tail was tucked under its rear, from either sadness or fear. Why, of all things, did this worry me so?

I blanked for a second, catching snatches of what Joshie was saying. "I met him through the skater scene. . . ." "I come from a different budgeting culture. . . ." "When you think about it, the capitalist system is more entrenched in America than anywhere else in the world. . . ."

And then his arm was around me and we were walking away from the girls. I cannot recall our exact surroundings when he gave me his speech. We were lost in negative space, his closeness the only thing I could still cling to. He spoke of the seventy years in which he had not known love. How unfair that had been. How much love he had to give; how I had, in some ways, been a recipient of that love. But now he needed something different: intimacy, closeness, youth. When Eunice first walked into his apartment, he *knew*. He picked up my äppärät and produced a study on how May-December relationships lifted the lifespan ceilings for both partners. He spoke of practical things, my parents in Westbury. He could move them to a safer, peripheral region, like Astoria, Queens. He spoke of how we needed to spend some time apart, but how eventually the three of us could reconcile. "We could be like a family someday," he said, but when he mentioned family, I could think only of my father, my *real* father, the Long Island janitor with the impenetrable accent and true-to-life smells. My mind turned away from what Joshie was saying, and I pondered my father's humiliation. The humiliation of growing up a Jew in the Soviet Union, of cleaning piss-stained bathrooms in the States, of worshiping a country that would collapse as simply and inelegantly as the one he had abandoned.

I lost track of where I was, until Joshie brought me back to Eunice and Sally, who were holding hands and staring up into the blue portal of the skylight, as if awaiting deliverance. "Maybe you and Lenny should be alone right now," he said to Eunice. But she wouldn't let go of her sister and she would not look into my eyes. They stood together, silent, with their little chests thrust out ahead of them, their eyes quiet and blank, the seemingly endless continuation of their lives stretched out before them into the three dimensions of the Triplex.

Words broke out of me. Stupid words. The worst final words I could have chosen, but words nonetheless. "Silly goose," I said to Eunice. "You shouldn't have worn such a warm suit. It's still autumn. Aren't you hot? Aren't you hot, Eunice?"

There was high-pitched yelling from the direction of the vestibule, not far from where we were, and Howard Shu was sprinting ahead like a gorgeous greyhound, shouting things at many people.

The Chinese delegation had arrived. Two giant banners floated into the air, held aloft by an invisible force, as the opening bars of Alphaville's "Forever Young" ("Let's dance in style, let's dance for a while") blared in the background.

Welcome to America 2.0: A GLOBAL Partnership

THIS Is New York: Lifestyle Hub, Trophy City

A series of loud pops exploded in the air, reminding me of tracer fire during the Rupture. Firecrackers were being launched from the center of the souk-like space and through the enormous skylight above us. As the first batch went off, I saw Sally cringe and raise her arm protectively. Then there was a push to get to the front to see the Chinese. I let the bodies wash over me, the young octogenarians, wearing ironic John Deere T-shirts and trucker's caps that barely contained their masses of silky new hair. Separated from the people I loved, pushed out of the glass house, I found myself in the winter-cold air, by a phalanx of limousines bearing the insignia of the People's Capitalist Party, by a row of Triplexes cantilevered over the

FDR Drive and the East River. There had once been housing projects here and a street called Avenue D. Media people ran past me as if there was a fire somewhere, as if tall buildings were burning. I was looking south. I should have been thinking about Eunice, mourning Eunice, but it wasn't happening at the moment.

I wanted to go home. I wanted to go home to the 740 square feet that used to be mine. I wanted to go home to what used to be New York City. I wanted to feel the presence of the mighty Hudson and the angry, besieged East River and the great bay that stretched out from the pediment of Wall Street and made us a part of the world beyond.

I went back to our rooms in the nurses' dormitory. I sat down on the hard bed and clutched the bedspread, then pressed my pillow into the equivalent softness of my stomach. The central air conditioning was still on, for some reason. The room was freezing. Cold sweat trickled down my chin, and my books felt cold to the touch. The wetness confused me, and I touched my eyes to make sure I wasn't crying. I thought of the firecrackers going off. I heard their harsh, unnecessary noise. I saw Sally's arm raised against the phantom punch about to be landed. The look on her face was pleading, but still loving, still believing that it could be different, that at the last moment something would give way, that the fist would fall by his side, and they would be a family.

In the bathroom, Eunice's allergy medications and tampons and expensive lotions were already gone—Joshie must have sent someone down to take them—but a bottle of Cetaphil Gentle Skin Cleanser remained in the corner of the tub. I turned on the shower, climbed in, and poured the Cetaphil over myself. I rubbed it into my shoulders, my chest, my arms, and my face. And I stood there in the water's painful heat, my skin at last as gentle and clean as the bottle promised.

WELCOME BACK, PA'DNER
NOTES ON THE NEW "PEOPLE'S LITERATURE PUBLISHING HOUSE" (北京)
EDITION OF THE LENNY ABRAMOV DIARIES

LARRY ABRAHAM
Donnini, Tuscan Free State

1.

When I was young, I loved my parents so much it could have qualified as child abuse. My eyes watered each time my mother coughed from the "American chemicals in the atmosphere" or my father clutched at his beleaguered liver. If they died, I died. And their deaths always seemed both imminent and a matter of fact. Whenever I tried to picture my parents' souls I thought of these perfectly white Russian snowbanks I saw in history books on the Second World War, all those arrows being drawn into Russia's heart along with the names of German panzer divisions. I was a dark blemish upon these snowbanks. Before I was even born, I had dragged my parents away from Moscow, a city where engineer Papa didn't have to overturn wastebaskets for a living. I had dragged them away just so the fetus inside my mother, that *future-Lenny,* could have a better life. And one day God would punish me for what I had done to them. He would punish me by killing them.

My father drove a typical ninety miles per hour in his boat-like Chevrolet Malibu Classic, swerving from one lane to another as his mood dictated, and eyeing the concrete median with unconcealed glee. He actually flipped over that median on one occasion and thundered into a tree, breaking the bones of his left hand, which kept him from his custodial duties for a month ("Let the Chinamen choke on their garbage!"). One winter day, my father was many hours late in picking up my mother from her secretarial duties, and I was certain he had done the tree maneuver once more. There they were: their faces wide and frozen, their thick Jewish lips an unnatural purple, shards of glass upon their foreheads, dead in some cruel Long Island ditch. Where would they go when they died? I tried to picture this Heavenly place of childhood rumor. It looked, according to the adolescent sages amongst us, like the fairyland castle out of the frustrating wizards-and-swords-and-naked-maidens computer game we all played; it looked, oddly enough, like a copy of the cheap garden-apartment complex where my family lived, only with turrets.

An hour passed. And then another. Weeping and hiccups on my part, my mind journeying to my parents' funeral. Synagogues have no bells, yet bells were tolling, deep and sonorous and thoroughly Russian. A gaggle of faceless, dark-suited Americans had to be conscripted to carry the two caskets down a winding path covered on both sides with that textbook Moscow snow. That was all that was left of my parents, cruel snow on both sides of the funeral path, snow too cold and deep for my spoiled American feet, which knew mostly the warm shag carpet stapled halfheartedly to our living-room floor by a retarded American man named Al.

A key began to turn in the lock. I sprang, gazelle-like, to the door, chanting "Mama! Papa!" But it wasn't them. It was Nettie Fine. A woman too stable, too sweet, too noble to be an Abramov, no matter how hard she tried to pick up our fine Russian phrases—"*Priglashaiu vas za-stol*" ("I invite you to the table")—no matter the rich, silky texture of her homemade borscht, a recipe inherited from her Gomel-born great-great-great-grandmother (how the hell do these native-born Jews keep track of their endless genealogy?).

No, she would not do. The fact was that when she kissed my cheek it didn't hurt afterward, nor did it smell of onions. So *to the devil* with her good intentions, as my parents might say. She was an alien, a trespasser, a woman I couldn't love back. When I saw her at

326 // GARY SHTEYNGART

the door, I threw the first and last punch of my life. It connected with her surprisingly narrow mid-torso, where the last of her three boys had just gestated in fine, cushy comfort. Why did I punch her? Because *she* was alive while my *parents* were dead. Because now she was all I had left.

She did not flinch from my ridiculous assault. She sat down and put me on her lap, held my tiny nine-year-old hands, and let my cry upon the tanned infinity of her scented neck. "I'm sorry, Missus Nettie," I wailed in a Russian accent, for although I was born in the States my parents were my only confidants, and their language was my sacred, frightened one. "I think they die in car!"

"Who died in the car?" Nettie asked. She explained to me that my father had called and asked her to watch me for an hour because my mother was held up at her office. But knowing they were safe would not stop my tears.

"We all die," Nettie told me, after she had fed me a powdered-cocoa-and-fruit concoction she called "the chocolate banana," whose ingredients and manner of preparation I still don't understand. "But someday you'll have children too, Lenny. And when you do you'll stop worrying about your parents' dying so much."

"Why, Missus Nettie?"

"Because your children will become your life." For a moment at least, that made sense. I could feel the presence of another, someone even younger than myself, a kind of prototypical Eunice person, and the fear of parental death was transferred upon her shoulders.

According to the records of the Ospedale San Giovanni in Rome, Nettie Fine died of complications from "pneumonia" only two days after I had seen her at the embassy, after we had talked loudly in the hallway about the future of our country. She was perfectly hale when I saw her, and the records of her treatment were scant enough to appear satirical. I do not know who sent me those GlobalTeens messages from a "secure" address, including the one asking me which ferry Noah had boarded, seconds before it was destroyed. Fabrizia DeSalva died in a supposed *motorino* accident one week before the Rupture. I never had children.

2.

Since the first edition of my diaries and Eunice's messages was published in Beijing and New York two years ago, I have been accused of writing my passages with the hope of eventual publication, while even less kind souls have accused me of slavish emulation of the final generation of American "literary" writers. I would have to disabuse the reader of this notion. When I wrote these diary entries so many decades ago, it never occurred to me that *any* text would *ever* find a new generation of readers. I had no idea that some unknown individual or group of individuals would breach my privacy and Eunice's to pillage our GlobalTeens accounts and put together the text you see on your screen. Not to say that I wrote in a vacuum, entirely. In many ways, my doodlings presage the diaristic flood of contemporary Sino-American writers—for example, Johnny Wei's *Boy, Is My Ass Tired* (Tsinghua-Columbia) and Crystal Weinberg-Cha's *The Children's Zoo Is Closed* (Audacious, HSBC-London)—that appeared after the People's Capitalist Party issued its "Fifty-one Represents" four years ago, the last of which shouted to the masses: "To write text is glorious!"

Despite the abuse heaped upon me in my former homeland, I am heartened by some of the reviews in the People's Republic itself. Writing in the 农民日报 *Farmers' Daily,* the levelheaded Cai Xiangbao anoints my diaries as 对书籍的一种贡献；实际上对文学的一种贡献. That is precisely right. I am not a writer. And yet what I had written was, as Xiangbao put it, "a tribute to literature as it once *was* [emphasis mine]."

But as the Stateside critics have unanimously agreed, the gems in the text are Eunice Park's GlobalTeens entries. They "present a welcome relief from Lenny's relentless navel-gazing," to quote Jeffrey Schott-Liu in *whorefuckrevu.* "She is not a born writer, as befits a generation reared on Images and Retail, but her writing is more interesting and more alive than anything else I have read from that illiterate period. She can be bitchy, to be sure, and there's the patina of upper-middle-class entitlement, but what comes through is a real interest in the world around her—an attempt to negotiate her way through the precarious legacy of her family and to form her own opinions about love and physical attraction and commerce and friendship, all set in a world whose cruelties gradually begin to mirror those of her own childhood." I would add that, whatever one may say about my former love, and whatever terrible things she has written about me, unlike her friends, unlike Joshie, unlike myself, unlike so many Americans at the time of our country's collapse, Eunice Park did not possess the false idea that she was special.

3.

After I left New York, I lived in Toronto, Stability-Canada, for the better part of a decade, where I changed my worthless American passport to a Canadian one and my name from Lenny Abramov to Larry Abraham, which seemed to me very North American, a touch of leisure suit, a touch of Old Testament. In any case, following my parents' death, I could not stomach the idea of bearing the name they had given me and the surname that had followed them across the ocean. But eventually I crossed that ocean myself. I cashed in my remaining Staatling preferred stock, gathered all the yuan I had, and moved to a small farmhouse in the Valdarno Valley of the Tuscan Free State. I wanted to be in a place with less data, less youth, and where old people like myself were not despised simply for being old, where an older man, for example, could be considered beautiful.

A few years after my final immigration, I heard that Joshie Goldmann was coming to the fractured Italian peninsula. Some jerk from Bologna had made a documentary about the heyday of Post-Human Services, and the medical school of the university had flown in whatever was left of Joshie.

"We're all going to die," Grace Kim once said to me, echoing Nettie Fine. "You, me, Vishnu, Eunice, your boss, your clients, everyone." If any part of my diaries yields anything resembling the truth, it is Grace's lament. (Or perhaps it is no lament at all.)

Onstage, my ersatz papa's face, initially contorted into a serious academic expression, quickly fell apart, and he began to twitch from the recently discovered Kapasian Tremors associated with the reversal of dechronification. Drooling magnificently over his interpreter, he told us, without preamble or apology: "We were wrong. The antioxidants were a dead end. There was no way to innovate new technology in time to prevent complications arising from the application of the old.

"Our genocidal war on free radicals proved more damaging than helpful, hurting cellular metabolism, robbing the body of control. In the end, nature simply would not yield."

And, like an idiot, I started to feel sorry for him. When the clients began to die, when the tremors started and the organs failed, the Staatling-Wapachung board of directors fired Joshie. Howard Shu took over Post-Human Services and made of it what he'd always imagined, an enormous lifestyle boutique doling out spa appointments and lip-enhancement surgery. Eunice left Joshie even before the decline began. I know little about the young man she left him for, but what information I have points to a person of perfectly decent temperament and controlled ambition, a Scotsman. For a time, at least, I know they made a home together outside of Aberdeen, a city in the northern reaches of HSBC-London. Their relationship was the only product of the one semester she had spent at Goldsmiths College in London proper, where she had attempted to study art or finance with Joshie's encouragement.

After Joshie had finished his warbling, I ran out of the auditorium. I didn't want to ask him what it was like to know that he was about to die. Even at this late date, even after he had betrayed me, the foundation myth between us precluded that question.

4.

Last winter, I visited my Roman friends Giovanna and Paolo at their country home, a fourteenth-century stone barn in the direction of Orvieto. I spent the first night beneath the wide-beamed timber ceiling of the redesigned living room, drinking my allotted Sagrantino di Montefalco, marveling at the recently built alcoves and wooden shelves, which with their rough-edged simplicity complemented the barn's age, and also surveying, with a kindly glare, my pretty younger friends and their gorgeous five-year-old kid, a Russian adoptee already an expert at Mandarin *and* Cantonese, whose wispy blond hair rebuked his parents' dark physiognomies. Wood smoke filled the room, bathing us all in a sweet olfactory glow. We were talking, placidly despite the wine intake, about global warming and the end of human life on earth. The Italians were describing our role on the planet as that of bothersome horseflies, and the planet's self-regulating ecosystems as a kind of gigantic fly-swatter. I could not understand how, as parents, my friends could even begin to imagine the extinguishing of their son's world, and, perhaps sensing that this topic was depressing me, and knowing that I probably had but a decade or two to live myself, the master and mistress of the house promptly got up to deliver an antibiotic shot to a sick prized goat.

As the evening wore on, my friends received still more visitors, two young Cinecittà actresses just arrived from Rome. They had no idea who I was, but we soon learned that one of these glamorous young personages had just been charged with playing Eunice Park in a new Cinecittà video spray of my diaries. The hacks at Hengdian World Studios in Zhejiang had already clocked in one artistic disaster with their *Lenny ♥ Euny Super Sad True Love* series, and now the Italians were having a go at it.

"I have to do *this* with my face!" the actress playing Eunice said, pulling at her eyelids and then sticking out her upper front teeth. She then launched into a fairly accurate rendition of a spoiled pre-Rupture California girl while her friend hastened to appropriate the luckless Abramov. "My tuna-brain! My jerk-face! My nerd-face!" the first actress belted out, as her colleague, in the role of Abramov, fell prostrate on the ground at her feet, weeping hysterically. This prompted my friends' five-year-old son to jump up and down around them, trying to mimic the funny English words.

My friends smiled warily at me and tried to signal the actresses to end their performance. Nonetheless, I presented a subdued mien. I set my mouth into its own version of Eunice's dead smile and let the laughter come out of me like the first coughs of water from a frozen pipe. I had been mechanically laughing for some time when I realized that the Cinecittà actress playing Eunice was using her performance as a springboard for a long-winded critique of America, reaching as far back as the Reagan era, to a time when even her *parents* were not yet born.

Oh, give it up, I thought. *America's gone.* All these years, and still a visceral hatred for a country that had destructed so suddenly, spectacularly, irreversibly. When would it end already? How long would we be forced to attend this malevolent wake? And then, before I could stop myself, I realized what was happening to me. I had begun to grieve. For all of us. For Joshie and Eunice and her parents and sister and Grillbitch a.k.a. Jenny Kang, and for the land that still shudders between Manhattan and Hermosa Beach.

There was only one way to stop the young actress's diatribe. "They're dead," I lied.

"*Cosa?*"

"They didn't survive." And I laid out a scenario for the final days of Lenny Abramov and Eunice Park more gruesome than any of the grisly infernos splashed on the walls of the neighboring cathedral. The young Italians grew annoyed by this sudden end to their levity. They stared at me, at each other, and then at the beautifully laid wooden floors leading out to the pergola, beyond which a tableau of olive trees and grain fields, arrested by winter, dreamed of a new life. For a while at least, no one said anything, and I was blessed with what I needed the most. Their silence, black and complete.

ACKNOWLEDGMENTS

Writing a book is real hard and lonely, let me tell you. I am so grateful that I have a generous group of readers who lift up their red pens and challenge me to do better.

David Ebershoff's editing of the many drafts of this book was truly heroic. Here is that rare find, an editor who is also a brilliant author, brimming with emotional intelligence and real love for our old dear friend, the sentence. Denise Shannon has been a great agent and terrific reader for over a decade, through tales of immigrant angst, fat gangster sons, and now this. Sara Holloway of *Granta* offered thoughtful advice carrier-pigeoned across the Atlantic. And any Random House author who has Jynne Martin on their case is lucky indeed.

I want to thank my research assistant, Alex Gilvarry, for helping me understand how science works. (Apparently we're all made up of many cells.) He has helped me burrow into the works of two thinkers who have influenced this volume: Ray Kurzweil, author of, among many books, *The Singularity Is Near: When Humans Transcend Biology* and *Fantastic Voyage: Live Long Enough to Live Forever,* and Aubrey de Grey, author of *Ending Aging: The Rejuvenation Breakthrough That Could Reverse Human Aging in Our Lifetime.*

The American Academy in Berlin, the Civitella Ranieri Center in Umbria, Italy, and the Corporation of Yaddo have all given me splendid shelter and mouthwatering fare.

There are so many dear people who have gone through the numerous drafts of this book. I know I'm leaving out at least a half-dozen of them, but that's only because my memory has taken a beating over the years. For everyone who has helped me with this book, please accept my love and gratitude. Among them: Elisa Albert, Doug Choi, Adrienne Day, Joshua Ferris, Rebecca Godfrey, David Grand, Cathy Park Hong, Gabe Hudson, Christine Suewon Lee, Paul LeFarge, Jynne Martin, Daniel Menaker, Alana Newhouse, Ed Park, Shilpa Prasad, Akhil Sharma, and John Wray.

ABOUT THE AUTHOR

GARY SHTEYNGART was born in Leningrad in 1972 and came to the United States seven years later. His debut novel, *The Russian Debutante's Handbook,* won the Stephen Crane Award for First Fiction and the National Jewish Book Award for Fiction. His second novel, *Absurdistan,* was named one of the 10 Best Books of the Year by *The New York Times Book Review,* as well as a best book of the year by *Time, The Washington Post Book World,* the *San Francisco Chronicle,* the *Chicago Tribune,* and many other publications. He has been selected as one of *Granta*'s Best Young American Novelists. His work has appeared in *The New Yorker, Esquire, GQ,* and *Travel + Leisure* and his books have been translated into more than twenty languages. He lives in New York City.

ABOUT THE TYPE

This book was set in Sabon, a typeface designed by the well-known German typographer Jan Tschichold (1902–74). Sabon's design is based upon the original letter forms of Claude Garamond and was created specifically to be used for three sources: foundry type for hand composition, Linotype, and Monotype. Tschichold named his typeface for the famous Frankfurt typefounder Jacques Sabon, who died in 1580.